Praise for Rebecca Chance's debut novel *DIVAS*

'A bright new star in blockbusters, Rebecca Chance's
Divas sizzles with glamour, romance and revenge.
Unputdownable. A glittering page-turner, this debut
had me hooked from the first page'
LOUISE BAGSHAWE

'I laughed, I cried, I very nearly choked.
Just brilliant! This has to be the holiday read of the year.
Rebecca Chance's debut will bring colour to your cheeks
even if the credit crunch means you're reading it in
Bognor rather than the Balearics'
OLIVIA DARLING

Bad Girls

Rebecca Chance

POCKET
BOOKS

LONDON • SYDNEY • NEW YORK • TORONTO

First published in Great Britain by Pocket Books, 2010
An imprint of Simon & Schuster UK Ltd
A CBS COMPANY

5 7 9 10 8 6

Simon & Schuster UK Ltd
1st Floor
222 Gray's Inn Road
London WC1X 8HB

www.simonandschuster.co.uk

Simon & Schuster Australia
Sydney

A CIP catalogue record for this book is available
from the British Library.

ISBN: 978-1-84739-396-8

Typeset by M Rules
Printed by CPI Cox & Wyman, Reading, Berkshire RG1 8EX

To my gorgeous Greg, who's been forced to accompany me to a series of luxury destinations for settings in this book. Thanks so much for sacrificing so many weekends to my research, darling.

Acknowledgements

My agent Anthony Goff has been an absolute tower of strength as always and I'm really lucky to have him and his whole team behind me. Maxine Hitchcock and Libby Yevtushenko – your editing skills, constant encouragement and wholehearted enthusiasm for this book have been a joy, and I feel just as lucky to have you as my publishers! It's been a total pleasure working with you, ladies. Rob Cox and Emma Harrow have been working so hard and creatively to make sure my books reach as many readers as possible – huge thanks for that.

Katharine Walsh, blonde bombshell and PR extraordinaire – thanks so much for introducing me to the Intercontinental Park Lane, the St James Hotel, and the utterly fabulous Bovey Castle: the books sparkle because of your glittering five-star touch! Kirsten Ferguson, you were a star for answering all my questions about the Intercontinental and for organizing the Spa Boudoir experience. And everyone at the Ca' Maria Adele hotel gave us one of the most exquisite visits to Venice that we could possibly imagine.

Prologue

*A*mber was swimming in a sea of vodka with Vicodin islands floating in it, big white oval pills like inflatable boats. The pills looked lovely from a distance, but when she got close they were hard and slippery; her hands kept sliding off them when she tried to clamber aboard. Her mouth tasted metallic and dry, like lead. She was wearing a silk nightdress, which was plastered to her body by the vodka. Maybe she was doing an underwater photoshoot? Amber loved underwater shoots; the feeling of weightlessness, her hair streaming behind her, the serenity of being completely submerged. She never wanted to come up.

But right now, she didn't feel serene at all.

She started to thrash around in panic, trying to swim up to the surface, to breathe. The vodka was thick and viscous, weighing her down. Amber was pushing it away with her hands, a clumsy, ugly breaststroke that would have had her sacked from an underwater shoot immediately. Desperately she tried to open her eyes; her lids were as heavy as if she was wearing ten pairs of fake eyelashes. She turned her head, shaking off the vodka, managing to lift her face a little, to peel open her eyelids, even though her lashes felt glued together.

Light. Daylight. No water. Soft around her. Silk on her body: her peach La Perla nightdress. Silk pillowcase; she always slept on silk pillowcases to avoid wrinkles. And a quilt on top of her. More than just one. Quilts, blankets, enough layers for an Alaskan winter. Or not blankets – books, maybe. Solid things with corners, heavy.

Books? What were a lot of books doing strewn all over her legs?

She heaved herself back on her pillows, eyelids fluttering, her hair matted around her face. Her skin was clammy with sweat. The quilt on top of her smelled of vodka; she managed to get one hand out from under the layers and push back the quilt, shocked by how damp it was. A bottle rolled across the bed and dropped onto the floor beside her with a crash.

And someone laughed. A woman, standing close to her, laughed.

Amber's head was stuffed full of cotton wool. Cotton wool soaked in vodka. She flailed around with her hand, grabbing anything she could reach, frantically searching for clues to what was happening to her. The glossy pages of a magazine crumpled into her palm and she dragged it towards her, craning to see what it was.

Herself. Herself in Interview, wearing a Hervé Léger bandage dress and Galliano ankle-wrap shoes.

She closed her hand on the corner of a book and pulled it into view. A Helmut Newton retrospective, open to a double-page spread of her at sixteen, standing with her legs apart, shot from below so she looked ten feet tall, a beautiful Amazon in a one-piece black belted swimsuit, her expression sulky to conceal the terror she'd felt all the way through the shoot.

The next thing her fingers touched was a vial of Vicodin, transparent yellow with a white plastic lid. That was when Amber really started to panic – when she realized the vial was empty. And what was Vicodin doing anywhere near her? She'd cleaned up! She hadn't had any pills for over a month now!

Twisting, flailing like a fish in a net, weighed down by piles of fabric and paper, she writhed upright enough to get an overview of her bed. It was covered in photographs of herself. Tearsheets from magazines. Her model cards. Polaroids from shoots. Victoria's Secret catalogues – lots and lots of VS catalogues. Huge hard-backed coffee-table books; no wonder she was weighed down. Magazines from her glory days, some almost as heavy as the books: Vogues and Harper's and Vanity Fairs *from all over the world, advertising and editorials. Amber's beautiful face, Amber's statuesque body, selling watches and diamonds and shoes and perfume and handbags and lingerie.*

And then something across the room caught her attention, something incongruous, something that shouldn't be there: she had to look up. Though her head felt as if it weighed fifty pounds and her vision was so blurry white spots danced across her retinas, she managed to tip her skull back and stare, horrified, at the white wall opposite, on which was scrawled, in what looked like dark brown lipstick: 'I'M NOT BEAUTIFUL ANY MORE'.

The woman standing next to her reached out one hand and pushed Amber back down to a prone position.

'Go back to sleep,' she said, holding Amber down with the press of her fingers on Amber's forehead. 'Don't try to move. Just go back to sleep.'

Amber's lips moved, but no sound came out.

'Help me,' she mouthed desperately. 'Please, help me . . .'

Because if she did as the woman said, and passed out, she knew she would never wake up again.

Part One

Amber

Amber Peters was used to being the most beautiful woman in the room. Even if there were other stunning models present – if she were sunbathing on the deck of a yacht moored off Capri, for instance, or at a cocktail party for the Paris collections – Amber would still be the one everyone's eyes returned to, full of envy or desire. Her beauty wasn't currently fashionable: she'd never be booked for French *Vogue*, which preferred editorial models with pale skinny limbs, big bug-eyes and jutting collarbones, girls who hunched their backs awkwardly to look like broken-down dolls. Though she was half English, half Slovak by birth, Amber's beauty was the American dream; in her photos, she was either laughing, showing her perfect teeth, or pouting, sultry-eyed, at the camera over a glossy, suntanned shoulder. With her slanted green eyes, endless legs, and mane of tawny hair, Amber was the girl that every woman wanted to be, and every man wanted to be with.

Since she was fourteen, Amber had made her living from being the incarnation of sexiness. Grooming had been drummed into her till it was as automatic to her as breathing. Currently, as always, she was flawless: her teeth were perfect and pearly, her skin smooth, glowing and lightly tanned, her eyes framed by thick tinted lashes, and her hair cascaded down her back in layers of gently styled curls.

And this was only breakfast time.

'No one here can take their eyes off you, honey,' gloated Tony, smiling at her proudly. 'You look stunning.'

Sure enough, every head in the lavish breakfast room of Bovey Castle Hotel snapped away as soon as Amber glanced around, the unmistakable indication that the other guests had all been staring at her; she was so used to it by now that she took it for granted. The waitress, setting down Amber's cappuccino, blushed and averted her gaze, overwhelmed.

'I don't fit in here,' Amber said, embarrassed.

The clientele were dressed in cords and sweaters, suitable wear for the English countryside; not a jet-setter among them.

'I know! But hey, I don't fit in here either!' Tony said cheerfully. 'This is old-school English, baby. Isn't it cool?' His brow furrowed. 'Don't you like it?' He leaned across the table and took her hand. 'I know it's not the usual kind of place I take you to, but you've got the spa, don't you? And the swimming pool?'

'Yes! I'm fine!' Amber said, smiling back at him. 'I just feel too glitzy.'

She glanced down at her skinny cream jeans, tucked into knee-length suede boots, the silk T-shirt, and the aquamarine silk and cashmere cardigan knotted at her waist. Form-fitting, showing off her long, slim body, her high, round breasts. Perfect for LA or Monaco, but not for a sporting estate in the heart of Devonshire.

'We *are* glitzy, babe,' Tony pointed out. 'I'm from Houston, Texas. We like things big and shiny there. And you're an international supermodel – that's the definition of glitz!' He grinned widely, his teeth a superb example of American dentistry.

Amber was about to respond, but instead she squealed in shock as an enormous bird landed on the sill of the leaded window next to her chair. It was the size of a small dog, its eyes huge and yellow, staring directly at her through the glass.

'Oh my God!' Amber panicked.

'It's the giant owl! Cool!' Tony said happily. 'Remember, from the hallway?'

Amber stared at him blankly.

'Honey, you need more coffee,' he said, beckoning the waitress. 'Remember, in the hallway just now we walked past the guy with the giant owl on a stand? With the black Lab lying at his feet? He's taking me out this morning to do some hawking?'

I walked past a giant owl just now, Amber thought, baffled, and I don't remember?

The owl was still staring at her. She was more thankful than she could say that the leaded panes were between them. It hopped from one huge clawed foot to another, squeaking urgently. Tony reached out and tapped on the glass, and, surprised, it opened its wings, the span at least four feet, and flapped away.

'You scared it,' Amber said sadly, but Tony was already jumping up, throwing his linen napkin on the table.

'Oh boy, that means the falconry's started. I'm gonna go outside to watch, and then I'll head off to go hawking!' he chuckled happily. 'And then I've got fly-fishing on the lake. Jeez, I can't wait to catch us some dinner!' He bent down to kiss her. 'You have a great time in the spa, babe. Be back in the room by four, will ya? I'll be raring to go by then.'

Amber nodded as he dashed out of the breakfast room, almost a head taller than most of the Englishmen there, and much healthier-looking. Square-jawed, with a nice thick head of hair, Tony had the typical, neutral good looks of the American man. He wasn't handsome, but he could pass for it in England because he was so big and healthy from the high-protein diet of milk, beef and eggs that all good ol' Texan boys were raised on.

Reaching into her bag, the Vuitton to which she was almost surgically attached because of its precious contents, Amber extracted her pill dispenser.

'Goodness, that's a lot of pills!' the waitress blurted out, setting down Amber's single poached egg on rye bread, and her second cappuccino.

'Vitamins,' Amber said, smiling at her, as she hooked a French-manicured nail under a big white oval and popped it out.

This should help, she thought.

And whether it was the 'vitamin', or the Fruit Active Glow facial in the Elemis spa, followed by the really superb Aroma Stone massage and mani-pedi, Amber felt wonderful as she lay in the sunken whirlpool bath of her treatment room a few hours later, staring dreamily at the sky. For her, this meant that she was actually feeling very little, utterly suspended in a hazy cloud of bliss that wrapped around her and insulated her from the outside world, just like the bubbles of the whirlpool bath.

Underwater lights cast an eerie, otherworldly glow around her; they had been red when the bath was turned on, but Amber had asked for blue instead, and the beauticians had been only too happy to oblige. Red was much too stimulating. Red was the colour of passion and fire; it stirred you up; while blue was cold and clear, the colour of the sky and the sea. Blue cleansed and purified you.

The swimming pool turned out to be blue as well, cobalt mosaic tiles with gleaming pewter accents. There was a Jacuzzi at the far end, where she sat in another cloud of bubbles and gazed at the Devon moors beyond, the gentle rise of the hills, pale green and grey. Clouds moved slowly across the gunmetal sky. It was hypnotic. She pulled herself out of the water eventually, catching sight of her reflection in the mirrors, her white crochet Shoshanna bikini pale against her lightly tanned skin. The room was lined with large diamonds of Art Deco glass, and at the far end was a sunburst of mirrors, faceted silver; if she tilted in the right direction, she could make herself disappear completely between the diamonds of cut glass.

She wrapped herself in a big, soft white towel, sinking down onto one of the loungers arranged in a semicircle in the glassed-in pool area, staring out over the grounds of Bovey Castle, the stone terraces that led down to the lawns and golf course beyond. It was the perfect English country home. By now she was floating on her own invisible bubbles, and the covert glances everyone else cast her, their whispered speculation about who she was – actress?

model? socialite? all three? – were lost in the pale blue haze that surrounded her.

Outside the curving glass walls was a gravel path on which people strolled past, pausing by the little pond with its pale grey stone fountain of a nymph and fairy, water trickling gently from the nymph's hands. But then they looked through the glass and saw Amber, sun-glazed, her long, perfect limbs the colour of pale biscuit, the white towel turban wrapped around her head emphasizing her slanted green eyes and impossibly high cheekbones, and they double-took in shock, staring at her avidly before they remembered their manners and reluctantly turned away. Amber was much too exotic a creature to be anything but a rarity and a wonder in the English countryside.

Eventually, Amber got dressed and made her way back through the grounds to the stone lodge that she and Tony were occupying for the weekend. Made of local granite and oak, it had three ensuite bedrooms, a kitchen and a living room with a central fireplace and a vaulted oak ceiling, three storeys high. It was much bigger than they needed, and stunningly luxurious. Amber lit the fire, opened the glass, living-room doors, popped some more vitamins, and curled up on the wooden lounger on the deck, smoking a cigarette and gazing down the slope of the hill, through the trees to the lake below. Daffodils and crocuses bloomed in the woodland, pale yellow and white and purple.

Eventually, she roused herself and went upstairs, to the lush, red-carpeted master bedroom. It was three o'clock, and she had completely forgotten to eat any lunch; but then, that was one of the useful side effects of her 'vitamins'. She plugged in her hairdryer and styling tongs, sat down at the mirrored Deco dressing table, and spent forty minutes sculpting her hair into lush, cascading waves, and twenty more making up her face, curling her eyelashes, glossing her lips, dusting glossy highlighter along her cheekbones, turning up the wattage on her beauty. She stroked Lancôme's Star Bronzer all over her body, working it in until her skin glowed pale gold, and slipped on a delicate pale blue silk bra and panty set, drawing matching hold-up stockings up her thighs and smoothing out the ribbed velvet-covered elastic.

She wandered into the bathroom, set under the eaves. When they'd checked in last night, Tony had sighed in ecstasy over its gigantic bath, big enough even for a Texan to stretch out in, and its equally huge power shower. The walls were papered in zebra print, the far one hung with a full-length mirror in which Amber now surveyed herself.

This was one of the moments that gave her the most pleasure of all. Dressed up in exquisite underwear, made up to perfection; she threw some poses in front of the mirror, flicking back her hair, smiling to herself. It was something men didn't understand, the satisfaction that a woman received when all her hard work paid off, the dieting, the exercise, the grooming, the money spent on beauty treatments, the painstaking, detailed construction of the absolutely best image of herself that she could present to the world.

'Babe! I'm back!' Tony yodelled, slamming into the lodge with a burst of energy that made her jump. She walked out of the bathroom to meet him; he was running up the staircase, colour in his cheeks from the sunshine, eyes shining with excitement.

'We bagged a rabbit, plus two trout!' he said triumphantly. 'I've booked a private chef from the hotel to come in tonight and cook dinner for us here, in the lodge! Romantic, huh? And eating what I caught for us, how cool is that! *Wow.*' He reached the top of the stairs, taking in her appearance. 'You look *unbelievable*. I'm getting a massive hard-on just looking at you!'

Amber smiled happily, sitting down on the big, luxurious bed with its red coverlet and matching suede pillows.

'I need to wash before I can even touch you!' Tony apologized. 'I must stink of fish. Lemme go shower and I'll be right with you . . .'

He bounded into the huge bathroom, cursing as his head cracked against the beamed ceiling, and turned on the power shower. Amber listened to the water pounding down, the happy noise of Tony humming to himself as he soaped thoroughly, and his bare feet padding across the floor as he emerged again, naked, his cock rising at the sight of her, a large, shit-eating grin spreading over his face.

'Boy, oh boy,' he said happily, 'what a weekend I'm having . . . Where's the DVD player?'

'Oh, I completely forgot,' Amber said guiltily, looking around.

'No worries, babe.'

He pulled it out of his travel case and set it up on the mirrored dressing table, clicking open the screen, inserting the DVD, lining everything up so he had a good view. Then he pressed Play, and the DVD whirred on, sultry music issuing from the speakers.

'Here you are!' Tony said proudly.

Amber turned her head to see the screen. It was a DVD that *Sports Illustrated* had filmed while they were shooting her for their famous yearly swimsuit issue, the one that could make the career of unknown models and give the ultimate seal of approval to established ones. You had to be healthy, curvy and sexy to appear in *Sports Illustrated*; no skinny high-fashion types allowed. And as Amber appeared on the screen, her hourglass figure emphasized by a cutaway pale pink swimsuit, lifting both hands to flip her hair, walking across a sandy beach, a setting sun glowing behind her, Tony moaned aloud in excitement.

'Come here,' he said, pulling her onto his lap, kissing her thoroughly, his hands running through her curls, his cock stiffening even more against her thigh. 'God, you're so hot . . .'

He eased the silk bra strap off her shoulders, kissing down the gilded skin, his mouth hot and wet, his hands all over her, caressing her breasts, kissing her nipples, easing her back till she lay on the bed, raising her hips so he could slide off her silk knickers. His mouth dived between her legs, making her moan back at him, and he slid his tongue into her, licking her, getting her wetter and wetter until she was gasping for breath, grinding into him, his big hands on her hips pulling her against his mouth.

'You're so *fucking beautiful*!' Tony gasped back, climbing on top of her, reaching for a condom, positioning his dick, guiding it into her, her legs wrapping around him. 'Oh Jesus – this is *so fucking hot* . . .'

Amber's head fell back as he drove into her, her hair streaming over the end of the bed. If she tilted her head back even further she could just see what he was watching so avidly: herself. Lying on a sand dune, back arching, sand rippling beneath her. Walking into the sea, twisting back to look at the camera, smiling seductively over her shoulder, arching to make her waist look even slimmer, her bottom thrust out even more sexily. It was a turn-on for her as well, though she'd never have realized it before Tony proposed the idea. Her entire life revolved around her looking perfect, sexy, desirable, and here was the ultimate proof of that; a man who loved her beauty so much that he wanted multiple versions of it simultaneously. If he could have surrounded them with TV screens all showing Amber on the beach in her swimsuit, he would have done.

I shouldn't suggest that to him, she thought, smiling despite herself. He's crazy enough to do it . . .

She looked up at Tony as he fucked her, his hands running up and down her stocking-clad legs, but his eyes staring greedily at the image of her on the screen. She knew that he was imagining all the other men who'd watched the video and reached down to pull on their stiffening dicks, pretending that they were just behind the camera, about to step forward, see Amber smile at them and pull the swimsuit straps off her shoulders and lay down in the sand so they could have sex with her. Pretending they were the man she wanted, the man she was tossing her hair back and blowing kisses to.

She knew that the thought of how many other men wanted her was the single most powerful reason that Tony got so turned on by her, and she understood why. That was what she was selling, after all. Desire. The DVD wasn't just a way of Tony seeing multiple images of Amber. It was to reinforce the hot rush of knowing that Tony was where every other man, and not a few women, wanted to be. It was his ultimate fantasy.

'I'm fucking you . . .' he moaned. 'I'm making you come . . .'

Actually, he wasn't; but Amber slid her hand between her legs to take care of herself, bucking as her fingers stroked her clit, turned on enough by Tony rearing inside her, ramming her hard, for her to reach climax almost immediately; a scream escaped her lips as she came, rubbing herself against him.

'Oh, yeah – look at you coming, you're so goddamn beautiful . . .' Tony groaned.

There were three Ambers in the room. The Amber on the screen, walking out of the sea now, salt water dripping from her perfect skin, her smooth stomach, smiling at him seductively. The Amber reflected in the mirrored dressing table, her hair spilling down the red coverlet, her legs in their pale blue translucent stockings wrapped around his waist. And the Amber below him, her body jerking as she came, her pink-glossed lips open, panting, her eyes closed, lost in her own orgasm. He wound his fingers in her hair, pulling her head up so he saw her face as clearly as he saw her on the screen, unable to hold out any longer.

'This is the best fuck *ever*!' Tony yelled as he spasmed hard inside her.

Amber felt him come, and tensed immediately, but Tony was always careful, and he barely got his breath back before he was easing out of her, holding the condom as he slipped it off. No one wanted her to get pregnant. He dumped it on the bedside table and collapsed on top of her, mumbling into her hair: 'Babe, you are one hot fuck.'

'I try,' she said sleepily, already in a doze.

'Ever since I saw that DVD –' Tony raised his head for a moment, just to take a final gloating look at the screen image of the woman he'd just had sex with – 'I knew I had to get with you. Remember when I asked you if you'd mind me playing it? I was a bundle of nerves. I couldn't believe it when you said it was OK.'

Amber shrugged beneath him, drifting away on a cool blue sea. 'It's still me,' she mumbled.

'It sure is!'

He rested his head between her breasts. 'Nap time,' he said contentedly. 'And then we'll head up to the bar – I gotta show you off all dressed up – and you can have another one of those crazy purple cocktails you liked last night.'

'Parma Violet,' she said drowsily.

'And then we'll come back and have dinner in front of the fire. Jeez, this is the best weekend *ever*!'

Petal

'*D*on't you know who I *am*?' Petal demanded imperiously.

The doorman looked down at her, rifling through pages of names on the VIP list, waiting for her to announce who she was; but Petal just stood there, blue-fingernailed hands on hips, fringe hanging into her face, ruffled top falling off her shoulder, her dangling resin earrings trembling in the night wind. He needed to work out who she was; she wasn't going to help him along.

'It's Petal Gold!' the PR hissed at him.

'So that's under G, is it?' The doorman rifled back through the list.

'It's *Petal Gold*! She doesn't even need to be on the list! Just let her in!'

As the doorman rushed to unclip the red velvet rope, the PR mouthed, 'Sorry,' at Petal and her entourage.

Petal smiled graciously at her as they sailed on through, Petal's best friend, Tasmeen, snapping at the doorman: 'You need to read *Heat* magazine, man! You're *ignorant*!'

'What is she, a singer or something?' the doorman asked the PR as they went past.

'She's got a handbag line or something – she writes a column for *Downtown* – she's *Gold's daughter*, you idiot!' the PR snapped back.

'Oh fuck! Sorry,' he said guiltily, looking after Petal, trying to see a resemblance between her and her extremely famous father. With her pale skin and thick, unevenly cut bob of red-tinted hair, her eyes heavy with dark blue eyeliner and her lips matte with pink lipstick, Petal looked like plenty of other skinny and sulky London girls in the Camden set. The look was striped T-shirts, bright layers – as if they'd just pulled on some random clothes from their bedroom floor – slouchy boots and artfully disarranged hair.

But the reason Petal looked like all the other girls was because they copied her frenziedly; Petal only had to be photographed in *Grazia* or *Heat* wearing anything to have a ton of teenage girls storming their local shopping parades, looking for a cheap version of her top or her jeans or her bag.

'I've seen her in the papers, come to think of it,' the doorman admitted. 'But her hair's different—'

'You're sacked,' the PR said flatly.

'God, can you *believe* that guy!' Tasmeen said to Petal.

'I *know*. *Total* ignorance. I mean, what's he doing on a door? He should be, I dunno, working for London Transport or something . . .'

The girls broke into giggles as they made their way to the VIP area, where luckily the bouncer was considerably more *au fait* with the latest hip young London girls about town.

'All right, Petal,' he said, waving her and her entourage – Tasmeen, her hairdresser, JC, and JC's boyfriend, Rudy – up the steps into the crammed, slightly smelly, but much-prized corner of the club designated for VIPs.

'I hate my name,' Petal sighed.

'You're kidding!' Rudy exclaimed. 'You're so *lucky* to have a one-word name! You're like Cher! Or Britney! Or *Liza*!'

'You are *so gay*,' his boyfriend muttered.

'Her full name's Petal Serenity Dream Gold,' Tasmeen blurted out.

'*Tas!*' Petal elbowed Tasmeen furiously, utterly embarrassed.

'Serenity Dream?' Rudy was already saying. 'That's *wild*. Your parents weren't even hippies, were they?'

'I need a drink,' Petal said, changing the subject. 'JC?' She fished some cash out of the little clutch bag hanging from her wrist. 'Get them in, will you?'

'God, this place is a bit of a dump, isn't it? And smelly!' Rudy complained, wrinkling his pretty nose.

'It's very exclusive,' Tasmeen reprimanded him.

Rudy looked around him, adjusting his neon-bright T-shirt over his skinny ripped jeans. They were closer to the ceiling on the raised area, which meant less air circulation than down below, and the jammed-full little club in Hoxton, with its painted black walls and ripped plastic upholstery smelled of sweat and perfume and hair products, and the occasional sneaky cigarette. But mostly, it smelled of sweat. The walls were beaded with it.

'Honestly,' he said dismissively, 'you can make *anything* exclusive these days, can't you?'

'Whatever,' Petal shrugged at him. 'KillBuzz are playing. It's a secret gig. That makes this the coolest place in London.'

'Sorry,' he said placatingly as JC returned, narrow green bottles of beer dangling from his hands. 'I *love* your hair, by the way.'

Petal softened. 'JC did it.' She reached up a hand to ruffle her fringe. 'It's really cool. The messier it gets, the better it looks.'

'Wash and wear, darling,' JC said, handing her a Stella. 'Listen, I want to take you blonde next week. The press'll go crazy. Really yellow-blonde, like neon.'

'Really?' Petal said doubtfully. 'I like the red . . .'

'You have to keep changing your look!' JC insisted. 'That's the only way they'll keep wanting to take your photo!' He grinned at Rudy. 'She's my muse,' he said. 'All that lovely thick white skin, you can take her any colour you want. She's like this amazing canvas.'

'Eww! Thick skin! What the fuck, JC?' Petal complained, taking a pull at her beer. 'Also, don't muses, like, *do* something?'

'I meant thick like cream,' JC said quickly. 'Heavy cream.'

'Mmm, delicious!' said Rudy, picking up his cue. 'So lickable!'

Tasmeen shot Petal a do-you-*believe*-this-guy? glance. Petal grinned, swallowing her beer. Tas was endlessly critical. She had a bad temper and a non-stop, twenty-four-seven fuck-you attitude. It was one of the things Petal liked best about Tas: she always said what was on her mind, she never sucked up to Petal because Petal's dad was rock royalty, so famous he was known only by his last name.

Petal had grown up with film stars and rock legends and real royalty, and though her father had gone all Zen in recent years, she remembered the wild parties in her early teens all too well. She'd seen too many world-famous people trashed and behaving badly to have much respect for anyone any more. When you were ten, watching wide-eyed from your window as a gorgeous female singer, famous for her perfect marriage to a film star and her super-healthy macrobiotic diet, had got drunk on tequila, stripped off her clothes, jumped into the pool naked, hit on a member of a girl group, and then thrown up over herself, it sort of did your head in about believing anything anyone ever told you. She'd heard 'do as I say, not as I do' so many times in her childhood it was like her dad's mantra.

Until he got Zen Buddhism and a mantra for real, of course.

'You're a bit of a twat, aren't you?' Tas was saying to Rudy, who bridled.

'Don't let her get to you, Rudy,' JC said, wrapping his arm round his boyfriend's narrow waist. They were both fashionably thin, their skinny jeans dropping off their narrow hips. JC, as befitted an up-and-coming hairstylist, had bleached his hair, dipped the ends in pale green, and razored it in a style that, if hanging just right, gave his round friendly face an angularity that it lacked naturally. Mascara and a hit of lip gloss added to the edgy look that he was desperate to cultivate; he would have given anything to have a sullen, bony face rather than the chubby cheeks he couldn't lose, no matter how much he dieted.

'She's *mean*,' Rudy sniffed, drinking his beer. Rudy looked like all the other boys JC had dated over the years: super-elegant, with smooth beige skin and big dark eyes with ridiculously thick lashes. He pouted prettily with resentment.

'Oh, she's a total key merchant,' JC said. 'Likes to wind everyone up.'

'I just say what I think,' Tas said, shrugging.

She never apologizes, Petal thought. I love that about her.

Also, Petal loved that Tas was definitely on the curvy side, and it didn't seem to bother her at all. Petal was so obsessed, so driven to be thin – not *too* skinny, of course, or the tabloids would say you had an eating disorder. But if you were too skinny, they'd still photograph you; while if you were too fat, you'd get one photo in a 'Who Ate All The Pies?' section of a gossip mag, and then they wouldn't bother with you again. You needed to be able to get into sample sizes for fashion shoots, wear up-and-coming designers' tiny clothes out partying, so that next day you'd be 'Petal Gold, rocking Christopher Kane's stretch neon mini at the launch party for Chanel's new range of mobile phone charms!'

It was all about the press coverage. That was the one thing she'd truly learned from her mum and dad. If you didn't get the column inches, you might as well be dead.

'They're on!' Tas yelled, barrelling her way over to the balcony, which gave an uninterrupted view of the little stage.

This was a secret gig, of course, like all the best ones, with an invite list of London's youngest, trendiest opinion-formers: DJs, models, music journos and celebrities like Petal, famous solely for dressing up and partying hard and being photographed at the launch of the hottest thing that week. KillBuzz, the band playing tonight, were a new discovery from Newcastle, four cool boys whose songs about going out on the lash and trying to pull were, if their record label was to be believed, anthems for the new generation of club kids.

'He's all right!' Tas shouted to Petal over the roar of feedback as the boys, heads ducked, hair falling into their eyes, launched into their first single, 'Sod Off If You Can't Take a Joke'.

Petal looked where Tas was pointing and rolled her eyes. 'Not *another* drummer, Tas!'

'It's OK for you,' Tas yelled. 'You can have anyone you want! I've got to know my limitations!'

Petal couldn't deny the truth of what, with her usual brutal honesty, Tas was saying. In the normal, civilian world, normal boys mostly liked girls who looked, well, normal, with a bit more meat on their bones than Petal. Girls with boobs and bums, girls with sexy curves, girls who ordered dessert when you took them out to dinner.

But in Celeb World, the rules were all flipped on their head. The thinner you were, the better it was. Because the thinner you were, generally, the better you photographed. You had to lose at least the ten pounds the camera put on, and then some more. Tas was brave to hang out in Petal's circles, where her size fourteen figure made her a comparative elephant. She was very striking, with her strong features, thick black hair and rich red-brown skin, but she had to put up with a lot of sarkiness from girls with legs the size of pipe-cleaners and collarbones so prominent you could have hung earrings from them.

'He's hot,' Petal admitted, glancing at the drummer, with his Afro and tattoos. 'But I like *that* one.'

She pointed at the bassist, a sulky-looking boy with full lips, wide cheekbones, and heavy-lidded grey eyes that gave him a look of debauchery. Slanting a glance sideways at Tas, Petal cracked a smile of complete and extreme naughtiness. She didn't smile much as a rule; it wasn't cool, and it wasn't how people wanted to see you. They wanted you bored, petulant, resentful, their image of how teenagers should look and behave. Petal was twenty now, her teens behind her. Still, the shots of her sullenly posing outside nightclubs, fag in one hand, spokesgirl for modern youth, were the ones that the paps wanted.

But when Petal did smile, she came to life, going from pretty to completely bewitching. Twin dimples curved on each side of her mouth, like tiny extra smiles; Petal hated them, but they were entrancing. Her eyes sparkled, her even white teeth gleamed (nothing but the best cosmetic dentists for Gold's only daughter). Her entire face lit up. She looked mischievous and naughty and completely charming.

'I'm having him,' she yelled in Tas's ear. 'Him, me, back of a black cab. Tonight.'

'Fab. And I'll have the drummer boy. Pact?'

'Pact.'

They spat on their hands and shook, their code.

'This is *so* on,' Petal said, leaning far over the balcony rail, whistling loud enough so that, the first song winding down, the lead singer looked up, head drawn by the piercing sound. 'Not you!' Petal shouted cheekily. '*You!*' And she pointed to the bassist.

'I'm Petal,' she said forty minutes later, plopping herself down on the lap of her chosen target. 'And you're fucking sexy.'

He went bright red.

'Um, hi,' he said awkwardly. 'I'm Dan Drummond. Do I know you? You look sort of familiar . . .'

'I do a lot of stuff,' Petal said, shrugging, hating to have to give her surname and watch people's eyes flicker in recognition of her famous dad. 'I caught your show tonight. You were brilliant.'

'Yeah? Cool! We've barely gigged in London at all. I was shitting bricks beforehand. We all were.'

'Well, it didn't show.'

He mimed wiping his forehead in relief. 'It's a lot of pressure, y'know? We're just a bunch of Geordie lads. We've not done much of anything yet, just wrote some songs and got snapped up by this A&R guy who saw a gig we did back home. And now we're hanging out with all this high and mighty lot. It's a bit much sometimes.'

Petal perched back on his knee, letting him get a good look at her. She could tell that, though he was trying to play it cool, he wasn't at all used to girls like her sitting down on his lap and telling him they fancied him; those bone-sharp cheekbones were still pink, and he was babbling away in a mixture of embarrassment and excitement.

'Maybe you need someone to hold your hand a bit,' she purred, looking up at him from under her heavy fringe. 'Guide you through the mad crazy world of London nightlife.'

'That's very nice of you to offer, Petal,' he said, still looking a bit taken aback.

'I *am* nice,' Petal agreed. 'Dan, right?'

He nodded. She could smell his sweat, fresh from throwing himself round the stage like a whirling dervish, his hair still damp with it. His T-shirt clung to his torso, and although he was a typically lean twenty-something boy, his arms had nice definition, whipcord veins standing out along his biceps.

'You smell good,' she said.

'Oh hell – I'm all sweaty.' He pushed his hair back. 'You're so pretty, look at your little top and everything. You shouldn't be this close to me, you'll get all messed up.'

He actually meant it. It was really sweet.

'I like it.' Petal moved towards him till her mouth was nearly touching his. 'I told you, I think you're sexy.' She kissed him, just a brief touch of her pink-lipsticked mouth to his. 'Remember, Dan, you're a rock star now. You're *supposed* to be sweaty when you come off stage. It's sexy.' She kissed him again. 'It makes all the girls fancy you.' A final kiss, still light as a feather.

Dan Drummond's eyes were wide, his mouth open in shock and awe.

'Don't worry,' Petal purred naughtily. 'I won't slap your face if you try to kiss me back.'

'You are *something*,' he said, finally finding his voice.

'I am that!' She jumped up just as he leaned towards her for a kiss, confusing him thoroughly, exactly as she'd planned; then she reached for his hand and pulled him to his feet too. 'Wanna come to the toilet with me?'

'I've never had an invitation I fancied more,' he said devoutly, following her out of the band's crammed dressing room as the rest of KillBuzz whooped encouragement at him.

Tas had already pinned the drummer against the wall with her lavish bosom, and was holding him there, riveted, as he did his best not to stare too openly down her cleavage. Tas always wore low-cut tops to show off her breasts, and tonight the fuchsia lace of her bra showed brightly against her dark skin, the contrast stunning; she was giggling at him while doing her best to shove her bosom up like a shelf.

Hearing the whoops, she glanced over her shoulder, saw that Petal had snagged her target, and shot her a sneaky wink before turning back to her own.

'So, um, what are we going to do in the loo?' Dan asked as they walked down the corridor. 'Are you going to give me a blow job or something?'

'You *what?*' She let go of his hand and planted hers on her hips, furious. 'Do you think I'm a fucking *groupie?*'

'No – sorry – I didn't mean . . .' He hung his head in misery. 'I just haven't done this much, you know? I mean, we were nothing a few weeks ago, just some lads gigging in local pubs. This is all way out of me league, pet. I'm really sorry!'

She softened, because he was genuinely apologetic, and because close-up he was even more gorgeous than he was onstage. But she still stood there, making him suffer.

'Petal! I'm sorry, right!' He dropped to the ground and pretended to kiss the toes of her beaten-up vintage cowboy boots. 'Forgive me, won't you? Pity a poor country boy who doesn't know big-city ways!'

She was laughing now.

'Get up, you idiot!' she said, hauling him to his feet again. 'So – you a friend of Charlie's, Dan?'

'You what?' he said, momentarily baffled. 'Oh, right! Can't afford it usually,' he admitted. 'We're into the whiz up our way. Cheaper, y'know.'

'You'll be able to afford it now,' Petal assured him, pushing back the door of the unisex loo. 'Now that you're a rock star.'

'Keep saying that, babe,' Dan said happily. 'It's really turning me on.'

JC and Rudy were in the loos already, chopping up their own gear on the chipped old sink surround. Petal joined them, pulling her own supply, stashed in a silver cigarette case, from her Gucci bag. JC and Rudy had a bottle of Absolut Pear vodka, and they all took long pulls at it after they'd done nice fat lines, Rudy snapping some photos on his camera phone that sent them into hysterics. It was a grotty backstage loo, the black paint on the walls chipped and peeling, the red stall doors heavily graffitied, the Formica floor sticky with beer and God knew what: the perfect place for an up-and-coming rock star and an urban girl about town to make out.

Coke always made Petal horny. More people came in and out, more lines were snorted, and after half an hour of vodka and charlie, she was more than ready to be alone with Dan. Grabbing his arm, she pulled him into a stall and slammed the door shut as JC and Rudy and the singer of KillBuzz yelled approvingly after them. Dan was a quick learner, or maybe coke had just the same effect on him; he had his tongue down her throat the moment the door closed, kissing her hard and deep, grinding his long skinny body against hers, making her moan into his mouth with excitement and lust.

She reached down and grabbed his arse, pulling his crotch into hers, the stacked heels of her cowboy boots getting her just high enough to wriggle herself where she wanted to be, feeling his instant erection through his tight jeans.

'God, this is good,' she mumbled against him. 'You're a great kisser.'

'And you're wild,' Dan said, biting her neck. 'Are you, like, the fastest girl in London? You're like a fucking lightning bolt.'

'If I'm not –' Petal ran her hands under his T-shirt, grabbing his belt buckle, pulling him in even closer – 'I don't know *who* is.'

'Fuck, you're driving me crazy!' he groaned, sliding his hands up under her skirt. 'You even *wearing* knickers? What do wild girls wear on their bums?'

'That's for me to know . . .'

'. . . And me to find out!'

He hooked his thumbs under the waistband of her tights. She was wet already, totally turned on by him, by the smell of his sweat – no aftershave for an indie kid from Newcastle, nothing but him, the sharp scent of his excitement mingling with her own – by his hands on her, the way he'd really got into it, followed her lead and gone nuclear. Boys were all the same: they'd hang around, nervous of rejection, waiting for the signals that it was OK with you for them to go for it, but when you gave them the green light they couldn't get your knickers off fast enough.

'You can't fuck me here in the loos,' she said, running her hands around his waist, making him moan. 'Not with everyone right outside.'

'Nah,' he said, his grey eyes bright, his grin wide. 'I'm going to eat you out. Seems the least I can do by way of apology for treating you like a groupie. I'm going to get down on me knees and give you a good old seeing to. How's that sound?'

Petal was practically dripping with anticipation.

'Fantastic,' she drawled. 'If you're really good at it, maybe I'll give you that blow job after all.'

'*Fuck*,' Dan Drummond said devoutly, dropping to his knees and pulling her tights and knickers down as he went. 'This is *definitely* the best fucking night of me life!'

Joe

Joe Jeffreys was on top of the world. His world: Hollywood. Which, if he'd wanted to, he could have ruled like a despotic emperor. He was one of the biggest movie stars in the world, he made tens of millions of dollars per picture, and if he threw his weight around, the reverberations would have been heard all round the planet.

But that wasn't Joe's style. Never had been, never would be. Everything had always come easily to him; he didn't need to throw his weight around to get what he wanted, because what he wanted had always dropped into his lap before he'd even figured out what it might be. By seventeen, he'd already been drop-dead gorgeous, and he'd only improved with age. At six foot two, with linebacker shoulders, he was that rare breed of movie star, the kind who is even more physically imposing in person than he is onscreen. Not since Clint Eastwood had Hollywood seen such a hunk of a man. Blond and blue-eyed, tanned to a perfect even bronze, his corn-fed Midwestern handsomeness was dazzling.

Meeting Joe for the first time was as blinding as a visitation from a sun god: you blinked hard, overwhelmed, and fell instantly under the spell cast by his looks and his charm. It had been like that for the model scout who'd spotted him on Joe's first-ever trip out of state – a family vacation to Disneyland – snapped a Polaroid of him, and signed him up then and there. It had been like that for the agent who'd seen him in a Gap ad on TV, flown him out to LA and got him a walk-on role in a movie as a hot bartender. And it had been like that for the casting director who'd cast him in an action movie as a tough young cop, his breakout role, the one that had precipitated him on his swift upward climb to his current status as the king of the blockbusters.

Joe had never taken an acting class in his life. He was a natural. Besides, Joe would be the first one to acknowledge that he wasn't an actor: he was a movie star. That was his job. He was damn good at it. And he loved it and pretty much everything that came with it.

Joe was also damn good at being happy, a talent very few people are lucky enough to possess. Most of the time, he felt like the luckiest guy ever, and right then, having just hiked up LA's spectacular Runyon Canyon, he couldn't see a cloud in the sky. Literally or metaphorically. He stood at the top, hands on hips, surveying the dramatic, sun-kissed landscape, breathing in the smog with a happy smile on his face, his two Great Danes, Hengist and Horsa, bumping at his legs.

Below, at the bottom of the long steep hill, the bright sunlight gleamed off the lenses of the waiting paparazzi, eager for photographs of the godlike Joe Jeffreys, hot and sweaty from a bracing run. Even though Joe knew they couldn't see him, not from the distance, he raised his hand and waved at them, a good-old-boy, friendly wave. Joe'd never had a beef with the paparazzi; they were just doing their job. Everyone had to make a living, after all.

Joe took off his baseball cap, ran one hand through his thick fair hair, and jammed the cap back on again. Much as he liked to feel the sun on his face, it was definitely ageing. Plus you had to worry about skin cancer now, and he hated when his dermatologist yelled at him. He took a long pull at his water bottle and squirted some into the open mouths of each of the Great Danes, who had sat down expectantly as soon as he untapped the bottle. They knew the routine; they got a drink when Joe did.

'Right, guys,' he said, hooking the bottle back onto his belt, 'let's sprint back down, drive home, crack a beer and watch the game, OK? Sound like a plan to you?'

Great Danes were hunting dogs; they could spend all day running with horses, tracking down wolves or wild boar. Even though Joe was at the peak of physical fitness, there was no way that the pace he set back down the canyon path was a challenge to them. But they lolloped along beside him, tongues lolling out happily, always happy to run with their human, the leader of their pack. The paparazzi had been briefed on the names of the dogs, and called them out as Joe approached, the lenses clicking frantically as they fought to get the best action shot of him, the damp white T-shirt clinging to his firm round pecs, gold hairs glinting on his tanned arms, his strong thighs pounding a steady rhythm down the hill.

'Joe! How's Jennifer doing?'

'Hengist! Horsa! Over here! Over here!'

'Joe! How's it feel to be engaged?'

'Joe, could you lose the baseball cap?'

Joe flashed them all a wide smile, keeping up a steady pace as he jogged to his Lexus Hybrid 4 × 4 and unlocked it, throwing the back open for the dogs to leap in. The paps all knew what to expect by now: he never uttered a word, never reacted apart from giving them the big Joe Jeffreys photogenic grin. There was no point provoking him by yelling insults or foul language, as they did with other celebrities who might rise to the bait; but they'd get what they came for, a great shot of a sweaty, sexy Joe out with his dogs. A good morning's work.

'Joe! Did you have a good time in Vancouver?' yelled one guy just as Joe was pulling his door shut.

Weird question, Joe thought as he drove home. I mean, you go to film in Vancouver cause it's a hell of a lot cheaper, you shoot a movie, you come back to LA. Who asks if you had a good time in Vancouver? Must be a newbie.

It wasn't much of a drive from Runyon Canyon to Joe's compound in the Hollywood Hills. As the electronic gates swung open, Joe was already picturing the rest of the day laid out before him, a whole series of his favourite things, one after the other. A long steamy hydro-massage shower, the body jets turned up to the max, pounding out his tight muscles from the run. A couple of cold beers, put in the freezer by Estrelita, the housekeeper, when he drove out, so they'd be ideally chilled for his return, moisture beading on the green glass of the bottle. Chips, celery, and plenty of blue cheese dip; he'd just wrapped a movie, so for a couple of weeks he could eat whatever the hell he wanted.

And the game, fired up in his private screening room, so vivid you'd think you were right on the baseball diamond with the Royals. They'd done nothing for twenty-five years, the last time they made it to the World Series, but who else could a Kansas boy support but the Royals? Sure, it'd be easier to transfer allegiance to the LA Dodgers, but where was the integrity in that?

Plus, of course, a couple of bongs of British Columbia's best hydroponic bud, just enough to get him all loose and happy. Soak in the pool for a while, catch some rays when the sun was past its peak. And then, who knew? Call up a couple of girls he knew, see if they wanted to come over and party. Or just chill out at home, enjoying the peace and quiet after a long hard shooting schedule – rifle through his extensive porn collection and show himself a good time.

Decisions, decisions. Joe sighed, a long happy near-groan of pure anticipation. The dogs, hearing their master's voice, flopped their tails heavily in response.

Then the Lexus rounded the corner of the long white mansion, turning onto the gravelled parking area, and Joe said, 'Ah, *fuck*,' so explosively that one of the dogs whined in empathy.

It wasn't the sight of his fiancée Jennifer's red Prius parked next to the staff's cars that bothered him. Jennifer lived in an entirely separate area of the compound, in a self-contained house with her own private pool; they could happily go for days on end without seeing each other, unless they had some red carpet to walk hand in hand.

No, Jennifer wasn't the problem. What had rattled Joe was the vehicle parked next to hers, the gas-guzzling, very much non-environmentally friendly SUV belonging to their publicist, the much-feared Carmen Delgado. Joe and Jennifer had to drive hybrids, because otherwise they'd have been slated by the press. But Carmen made the news, she didn't appear in it. Therefore, Carmen could drive whatever the hell she wanted.

There was only one reason for Carmen to be making an unscheduled visit during the day: some sort of crisis. And even if it were a crisis about some shit Jen had pulled, there was no way in hell Joe wasn't going to be sucked into it too. *Damn.* If he'd known the Bitch Queen was dropping by, he'd have made sure to have a couple of beers beforehand. In Joe's long experience of dealing with Carmen, it was never a good idea to go into it totally sober.

They were waiting for him in the main living room, Carmen pacing up and down, a tigress strapped into Louboutin spike heels, which clicked up and down the slate floor, sounding like a whip-fast game of speed chess. She was dressed to the nines, as always, in a red tailored Roland Mouret dress that flamed gloriously against her dark golden Latina skin. Her blue-black hair was curled into loose ringlets down her back, and her makeup was impeccable; she carried a professional Smashbox case in her Range Rover at all times for touch-ups. If you didn't know that Carmen was one of the top three publicists in this town, that she ruled it with an iron fist in a clanking iron glove, you would have realized it as soon as you met her.

But you certainly wouldn't have identified the tiny, almost frail girl curled up on the huge white suede sofa as one of the most successful movie actresses of the moment. Jennifer Downs had just come off the set of her latest film, a thriller in which she played an LAPD detective who, while investigating a serial killer who preyed on prostitutes, was conducting torrid affairs with two separate men, both of whom were suspects in the case. In order to lend Jennifer's fragile build and doe-eyed features a tougher edge, which would make casting her as a hard-bitten detective remotely plausible, her light brown hair had been given a short, shaggy crop. Her skin was bare, without a scrap of makeup, and she was wearing soft, fleecy sweats and flip-flops which were specially engineered to prevent cellulite. She looked ten years younger than her true age, which was twenty-five. This was partly because she was underweight, which made her eyes look as huge as headlights in her small heart-shaped face.

'Hey, ladies!' Joe said easily as he strolled into the living room. Estrelita had met him at the door with a cold Bud, and he tilted it to his lips, relishing the clean sharp taste of the chilled lager, the bubbles popping on his tongue.

He was hoping against hope that this wasn't a biggie. And then he noticed the magazine on the huge glass coffee table, and his heart sank right down to the floor.

Oh boy, I'm in trouble now, he thought ruefully.

'You're an idiot!' Jennifer said furiously, glaring at him. 'A stupid fucking idiot *dickhead* who can't keep it in his pants for more than two fucking seconds at a time!'

'Careful, honey,' Joe said, drinking some more Bud. 'Your personality is showing.'

Jennifer would have burned holes in him with her stare if she could.

Carmen swung to a halt, swivelled, and pointed one red-tipped, perfectly manicured finger at him.

'She's on the money,' Carmen hissed. 'You *are* a fucking idiot.'

'Wow, you're taking her side. No surprises there,' Joe commented ironically.

He walked over to the built-in wet bar, where Estrelita had set out his snack, beautifully arranged in a huge bone china dish: in the centre was blue cheese dressing, dusted with freshly ground white pepper. Sticks of celery and carrot rested on one side, and a stack of his favourite Doritos on the other.

'Yay! Cool Ranch Doritos! Estrelita's the best!' Joe said, dunking a chip into the whipped dressing. 'Ladies? Chip and dip?'

As he'd known they would, both Carmen and Jennifer recoiled as if he'd offered them arsenic laced with weedkiller.

'Oh, yeah, sorry, Jen. Forgot you don't eat solid food on week-days,' he said cheerfully.

'God, I hate you sometimes,' Jennifer said, turning away so she didn't have to watch him eat. She looked to the left, not because she wanted to examine the Roy Lichtenstein painting of the cartoon woman firing a ray gun, the words 'BANG! ZAP! KAPOW!' explod-ing above her head, for which Joe's designer had paid tens of millions of dollars; no, Jennifer always automatically turned to the left, because she knew how perfect her profile was from that side.

'Is that *cheese?*' Carmen asked, horrified.

'Sure is,' Joe confirmed.

'He's *so* freaking lucky not to be lactose intolerant,' Jennifer sighed.

'He should be *allergic* to *strippers!*' Carmen yelled, getting right back to the point, batting aside Joe's attempt to distract her. 'Look at that fucking magazine cover!'

Fortified now with beer and Doritos, Joe strolled over to the coffee table. It was one huge slab of glass, six feet long and two feet high, with artfully rough edges, stacked with two perfect piles of the latest sports and cigar magazines. And tossed right in the centre was the latest issue of the *National Investigator*, a blurred picture on its cover of a woman sitting on the lap of a man, another woman lying beside them, her legs draped elegantly up a pole. Over the photo, in bright yellow, deliberately obscuring much of it so that readers would have to buy the issue to look inside, blared the head-line: 'JOE CHEATS ON JEN WITH STRIPPER!'

'Hey, I wonder how much time they put into thinking that head-line up,' Joe said, uncapping a second beer. 'You think they worked all night to come up with something that catchy?'

Carmen froze him with a glare colder than his bottle of Bud. 'Cut the crap, Joe,' she snapped.

Joe sighed. 'OK, I'm holding my hands up,' he said, suiting the action to the words. 'I fucked up. I'm really sorry. Can you fix this,

Carmen? Stage me apologizing to Jen, or something? Say it was my early bachelor party?'

'You *agreed* to this whole deal, Joe,' Carmen said, flicking a cigarette out of the pack of Merits that lay on the table, and lighting up. 'We went over and over it, remember? You needed an image makeover. There were too many George Clooney-type stories about you being an eternal bachelor. People speculating all over the Internet that you were gay.'

Joe couldn't help smirking at that one.

'Hey, being a pussy-hound who can't stay away from cheap whores is almost as bad as being a faggot for the movie-going public!' Carmen hissed, firing smoke out of both her nostrils like a glamorous dragon.

Jennifer nodded vigorously, reaching for the Merits herself.

'It looks *terrible*,' she chimed in. 'You *know* how important the women's magazines are. I mean, if you were serial dating, that's one thing. But *strip clubs* . . .'

'You're thirty-five, Joe,' Carmen said coldly. 'You can't keep playing the playboy card.'

Hell, I know she's right, Joe thought gloomily, snagging a piece of celery and dragging it through the dip. That's why we cooked up this whole engagement crap in the first place. Jennifer and I, we both needed to get married. Shoot a romantic comedy together, say we fell in love on set, sell the hell out of the movie, get married on a Malibu clifftop, stay together for a few years, see how it goes . . .

That's why the rendezvous with the paparazzi had been set up by Carmen's assistant today; candid shots of him with his dogs, to publicize the movie he and Jen were starring in, which was due to be released in a couple of months' time. It was an adaptation of a best-selling memoir called *Me, Him and Mr Paws*, about feuding neighbours who have to put aside their differences to look after a cute chow puppy that gets dumped on their doorstep. Jennifer played the uptight career woman, Joe the laid-back commitment-phobe, drawn to each other despite themselves. It was going to make everyone involved a shitload of money.

Joe being photographed taking his dogs for a run was perfect pre-release publicity. Or it had been, until that damn gossip rag had screwed up all their carefully laid plans.

'This is going to need really serious damage control,' Carmen pronounced, staring hard at Joe, her black eyes shiny and hard as rifle casings.

'Stage a really big apology?' Joe offered weakly, finishing his second beer. 'I mean, I just wrapped a movie, I was celebrating with a couple of consenting adults . . . Could I sweep Jen off to Venice for the weekend or something? Make some huge romantic gesture? Buy her some of Liz Taylor's diamonds?'

Carmen laughed hollowly. Jen, sitting up straight on the sofa, feet curled under her, shook her head.

'Joe, they've got a lot of photos,' Carmen informed him. 'There's a whole series of one of the girls going down on you.'

Joe pulled an agonized face. 'That's not good,' he said feebly.

Hengist and Horsa, who had padded off into the kitchen to drink some water, re-emerged and flopped down in the marble-tiled hall-way, which didn't get the sun and therefore was the coolest place in the entire house. Their heavy tails pounded a few times before they settled down for a nice long nap, breathing heavily and sighing to each other.

'You're addicted,' Jennifer said.

'Say what?' Joe spun round to look at her.

'You're *addicted*,' she said, eyes wide, her photogenic face composed into the precise expression of utter conviction that had appeared on all the posters for her movie last year, *Saving Susan*, in which she'd played a nun battling to prevent her drug-addicted sister from being convicted of killing her abusive husband.

'You're a sex addict,' Carmen confirmed. 'You just can't stay away from strippers. It's a disease. Which means it's not your fault. Neat, huh! I've set it all up. You make a huge apology to Jen, then you go into Cascabel for a few weeks for a residential stay. Work through the programme, Jen meets you when you get discharged, you have a reunion, she falls into your arms, you promise to be good, the movie premieres, you two lovebirds get married. The End.'

'Cascabel? That's a *rehab clinic*!' Joe protested. He really wanted another beer, but three in a row, this fast . . . Even if he'd just finished a movie, that wasn't such a good idea. He tried the yoga breathing that one of his trainers swore by; pulling right up from his gut, in through the nose, out down his shoulder blades. It just made him feel dizzy.

'It's very plush,' Carmen assured him. 'You can have a private room. There's a pool, the food's great . . . think of it as a country club.'

'Or a health spa,' Jennifer chimed in, shooting a pointed look at the empty bottles of beer and the chip-and-dip plate on the wet bar. 'You might even shed a few pounds.'

'Look, you little bitch!' Joe said angrily, taking a couple of steps towards her. 'You need this goddamn wedding more than I do! So I like to party with strippers every now and then – what man doesn't? And maybe some of the women who see those pictures will turn their noses up, but I tell you, the guys are thinking, Good for Joe!'

'Endorsements,' Carmen chanted. 'Commercials in Japan.'

'Yeah, yeah, Carmen, I *know*, OK? I know I need to watch my rep! That's why, when you pitched it to me, I agreed to marry your *girlfriend*, OK?' Joe stormed over to the bar, slammed open the Sub-Zero and grabbed himself another cold one. 'So don't make it like I need you more than you need me! Jodie Foster, Portia de Rossi – the celebrity rug-munchers aren't exactly racking up the nominations or the big bucks, are they? You thought it was too dangerous to set Jennifer up with a gay guy, 'cause if that blows up in your face, everyone looks bad! Oh no, you wanted *me*! I'm the big score, 'cause everyone knows damn well that I'm as straight as Sean mother-fucking Penn!'

'Ew, that *animal*,' Jennifer muttered.

'So don't play this like I'm the total fuckup here!' Joe looked at the beer, swore in fury, and slammed it down, unopened, on the granite surface of the bar. 'I can't believe I'm pounding the beers like this! *Man*, you got me all wound up!'

'You should switch to low-carb,' Jennifer offered.

'Tastes like shit,' Joe said gloomily, sinking down in one of the big leather recliners and kicking out the footrest. He rubbed his eyes with his knuckles. 'I'm fucked, aren't I? These pictures, coming out before *Mr Paws* . . . ugh, I'm sorry, Jen.' He looked directly at his fiancée, the whites of his eyes a little red now, but their bright candid blue as clear and charming as ever. 'And I'm sorry I called you two rug-munchers,' he added to placate a fuming Carmen. 'It's not like I don't like a pussy appetizer myself.'

'*Please.*' Jen rolled her huge, beautiful eyes. 'Like I care what you do in bed.'

Carmen stalked across the room, round the back of the sofa, to lean down and wrap her arms around Jennifer's neck. Jennifer turned to kiss her lover's cheek lightly.

'You know how this looks, Joe,' Carmen said, calming down as Jennifer reached up to stroke one of her ringlets. 'Like Jennifer's a total patsy for staying with you. This wasn't just getting drunk in a bar, letting off steam by flirting with some girls. This was getting blown by a stripper.'

'She was a nice chick,' Joe muttered. 'We all had a good time.'

'I can stage all the apologies I want, but this is the worst time possible. Your movie's coming out . . . it could tank Jen's career if she doesn't dump you. She's supposed to be a strong modern role model! Strong modern role models don't stick with guys who cheat on them!'

'Ah, *fuck*,' Joe said, once again, the weight of what Carmen was saying slowly sinking in. 'I've got no choice, do I?'

The two women shook their heads in unison.

'I've booked you into Cascabel from tomorrow,' Carmen said. 'And I'm putting out a press statement from the both of you. I've got the first draft for you to look at.'

With increasing misery, Joe began to realize what was in store for him over the coming month, which he had planned to spend chilling out, catching up on his TV shows – there was a boxed set of *The Wire* he'd been dying to get to – having his stuntmen buddies round to shoot some pool, calling up some girls to come over and party. Relaxing his rigid diet and exercise schedule, just enough to make him feel like a man, not a performing animal on a treadmill. Hanging out with Hengist and Horsa, throwing Frisbees for them on the lawn, taking them for runs; their company was the best tonic he knew. Just now, one of them was snoring lightly, which normally would have made him chuckle with amusement.

'God *damn it*,' Joe said with such deep feeling that both dogs woke, looking up to see what was wrong with their beloved human. Hengist clambered to his feet and lumbered over to Joe, shoving his damp nose into Joe's hand for comfort.

'If those slobbery things come anywhere near me, so help me God . . .' Jennifer muttered to Carmen.

'I can't take the dogs with me, can I?' Joe asked Carmen, the hopelessness in his voice indicating that he knew the answer perfectly well already.

'To rehab?' Carmen's perfectly threaded black eyebrows shot up. 'Don't you think that might just tell people you're not taking this whole thing seriously?'

'Ah, fuck,' Joe said for the last time, rubbing Hengist's huge head for comfort. 'Do you know what shit I'm going to take for this? The rest of my life, they're going to talk about the sex addiction every time my goddamn name comes up.'

He leaned down and hugged Hengist round his neck. Hengist was drooling on his hand. Yeah, Great Danes were slobbery, but who cared? Women were always bitching about the dogs, but they didn't realize that Joe would choose over them a stinky big dog that couldn't quit dribbling any day of the week. At least you knew where you stood with a dog.

He sighed deeply, thinking of the month he'd been planning for himself, and the one that was actually coming down the pike. Trapped in a rehab centre with a bunch of drunks and junkies whining about their miserable lives. Without even a beer now and then to take the edge off.

And then another thought struck him, such an awful one that he involuntarily tightened his arms too hard round Hengist's neck, making the poor dog squeal and scrabble back in panic.

'Oh, *no*,' he groaned. 'Clooney and Pitt are going to rip me a new one when they hear about this!'

Skye

*I*f Tinkerbell were completely naked, and if she worked as an exotic dancer in a Manhattan strip club called the Midnight Lounge, she would look exactly like Skye Simmons did that Saturday night. Skye gleamed like she'd been brushed with gold. Her blonde hair was pinned back at the crown, falling down her back in an arrangement of carefully arranged curls. Her big blue eyes looked huge, thanks to her battery-operated eyelash curlers and three coats of lash-building mascara. Her lips were glossed, her cheekbones highlighted with a dewy gel stick. She smelled of peony and chypre, and if someone had licked her, they would have tasted strawberries.

Skye examined her nude body in the mirror as she affixed a pair of gold pasties to her nipples. Yup, she looked good enough to eat. It was the umpteenth confirmation of what Skye had known ever since she got her first training bra; her pretty angel face, combined with her tight, curvaceous body, had meant that she'd had guys chasing her ever since she could remember. At school it hadn't been just the boys; teachers had hit on her too. She couldn't walk down the street without hearing hoots and catcalls or, if she was in a Hispanic area, hisses of appreciation from between their teeth at every involuntary swing of her hips.

Skye'd grown up in Trenton, New Jersey, an ugly manufacturing town where more people were laid off than had jobs, and the prospects were only getting bleaker: huge clusters of concrete buildings, the factories that were still open spewing filthy smoke, tens of thousands of people crammed too close together. Always guys hanging around, like nobody ever went to work, or at least had the kind of job where the IRS took a cut of your paycheque. Men on every street corner, every doorway, every alley, whistling and yelling and hissing at Skye.

Not that it wasn't good to know you were sexy. Whenever Skye had complained about it to her mom, all she'd heard was, 'Honey, when the guys stop whistling, that's when you should worry.' Living a hardscrabble existence with five kids by two different guys, neither of whom had stuck around to help her raise them, had taken its toll on Leanne, and she had no sympathy to spare for a daughter whose problem was being so pretty and sexy she practically had to fight men off with a stick.

Well, Skye had learned that lesson. No point in getting mad, no point in asking for help. So she figured out how to roll with it instead. Guys were still staring at Skye – more than ever – but now they had to pay for it. She put on a damn good show, she worked it with everything she had, and all those years of hassles and catcalls and filthy propositions were turned on their head. It was Skye who had the power now. And she loved to use it.

She picked up the giant can of Elnett and misted her hair with it, the chemical tang of hairspray adding to all the other odours in the dressing room: nail-varnish remover, sweat, body spray, perfume, and traces of cigarette and dope smoke – it was illegal to smoke in here, but sometimes the girls just couldn't wait to run down the back stairs to the side door to the alley. While the hairspray was still fresh, Skye scooped a handful of gold glitter out of her jar, held her fist as high as she could over her head, and opened it, turning on her toes at the same time so the gold dust landed evenly on her hair, sticking to the hairspray: the final touch.

'You *love* your glitter dust, baby doll,' Maria, the house mom, said from her cosy nest in her battered old armchair. 'How much do you blow on that stuff every week?'

'Hey, better on my hair than up my nose!' Skye retorted, which caused Jada, pulling on a leather bra at the other side of the dressing room, to crack up with laughter.

'*Right*,' she commented. 'Like it's one or the other.'

Skye grinned at Maria over her shoulder. Hired by the management to run the dressing room and keep a lid on trouble, Maria was always there, refereeing conflicts, pouring oil on the waters, eternally ready with a needle and thread for rips in costumes. Often house moms in strip clubs were ex-dancers themselves, but tiny, wizened Maria had never been that glamorous. She'd been a costume maker for years, till her eyes got too strained. Now she sat, every day from noon until closing, in her big armchair, a piece of knitting on her lap, and a big mug of coffee, laced with something stronger, on a table at her side, and though her eyesight wasn't up to sewing on sequins for hours on end, she never missed a thing that went on in her dressing room.

'It's gonna be a good night,' Jada said, lifting her surgically enhanced breasts one after the other and settling them into the bra cups. 'There's a real buzz out there. I can smell it.'

'All you can smell right now is hairspray, honey,' Maria cackled, as Skye pulled on a gold G-string and wriggled into two shiny gold stretch tubes, one barely covering her breasts, the other doing the same for her bottom. 'Skye, honey, you wanna coffee before you start work?'

'Sure,' Skye said, taking a polystyrene cup from the wobbly stack on the table.

Maria reached for a Thermos and poured Skye a cup.

'You wanna top-up?' she asked, winking.

This was a special favour, and you couldn't say no. Maria was already pulling a bottle from its hiding place down by the side of her chair. Skye perched on a battered chair, too ripped up to be used in the club any longer, as Maria laced the coffee with Kahlúa.

'Hits the spot, huh?' Maria said, as Skye took her first sip.

How many times had Skye heard Maria say that? Thousands, probably. How many nights had she sat here, drinking coffee, coming up or coming down, listening to the girls chatter and bitch and fight?

'Hit me too, Maria,' Jada said, a six-foot Amazon with pale mocha skin in her black leather bra and panties, and black spike heels, coming over with a cup of her own.

'Girl, you look like a porn warrior,' Skye giggled.

Jada threw her hip sideways and clenched a fist, posing hard. 'I will lap dance the *fuck* out of you!' she said menacingly.

Skye finished her coffee and stood up, whooping to get herself into the zone.

'OK!' she said, throwing her cup into the trash. 'Let's go and take those suckers out there for everything they've got!'

'From your mouth to God's ear,' Jada said devoutly.

They looked at themselves for a moment in the mirror.

'We are *so* going for different markets,' Jada giggled, towering over her friend.

Skye was the archetypal American blonde, with rounded cheeks and a pouty pink mouth; she had the full, lush features of a teenager, or the baby doll for which Maria had nicknamed her. But her figure was pure Barbie, with implausible breasts and a butter-wouldn't-melt-in-my-mouth, wide-eyed, innocent stare that had patrons of the club reaching for their wallets in reflex.

Jada was the opposite to Skye in every way: breathtaking, tall and imposing, with narrow hips and swimmer's shoulders. Her cheek-bones were a sculptural miracle, and her mouth was so wide and full she didn't like to smile too much; she called it the grin that ate her face.

'Better that way,' Maria said drily. 'You got a shot at staying friends.'

Skye grinned, acknowledging the truth of this.

'Come on, girlfriend!' she said, grabbing Jada's hand, winking at Maria over her shoulder. 'Time to empty out some wallets!'

The main floor of the Midnight Lounge was already half full at six in the evening. In a couple of hours, it would be packed. And Skye and Jada, striding in through the double doors at the back of the club, the bouncer stationed there nodding at them as they made their entrance, were the queens of the club. Even though there were girls gyrating on the poles, writhing on the lit-up stage, all the men's heads turned at the sight of the dark Amazon and her blonde little baby-doll friend.

Skye wiggled up to the bar in her four-inch-high Lucite heels and flashed a smile at the bartender.

'Set us up, honey,' she said. And, turning to the guy on the stool beside her, who was goggling at the sight of her: 'What's *your* name, sexy?'

After a lot of throat-clearing, he managed to get out: 'Marvin,' his eyes flickering between her boobs and her face as if he didn't know which he wanted to focus on.

'Well, Marvin honey, ever heard of buying two beautiful girls a drink or three?' she said.

Marvin was already fumbling for his wallet. He looked like most guys who came into the Midnight Lounge: white, forty-something, in a suit, with an office drone haircut. Faceless, instantly forgettable.

'You want some Kamikazes too?' the bartender asked him, and although he was working on a beer, Marvin nodded enthusiastically, only too keen to join the girls.

Men, Skye thought, rolling her eyes. If I said, 'Jump,' he wouldn't even wait to ask, 'How high?' He'd just do it first and ask questions later. It's like shooting fish in a barrel.

Skye shot a quick, practised glance round the club. Plenty of fish here. And plenty of them were staring in her direction, at her small round arse covered, barely, in a narrow strip of gold stretch Lycra. She'd make thousands tonight. She could smell the money in the air. The Saturday night shift, six p.m. to four a.m.: ten hours' work at maybe a grand an hour, if she worked everyone just right. God knew why men wanted to blow their paycheque on her when they could get laid for a fraction of the notes they so eagerly stuffed in her bra, but she certainly wasn't complaining.

The Kamikazes were set up now: tequila, triple sec and lime, with a champagne float from a freshly opened bottle, the Midnight Lounge version of an old-school classic. The champagne, of course, made them way more expensive. And that was exactly the point.

'One in each hand,' Skye told Marvin, 'you ready?'

He nodded, wide-eyed, unable to talk – unable, almost, to breathe with excitement.

This is why they spend the big bucks, Skye thought. They tell themselves we're actually hanging out with them because we *want* to. Finally, the cheerleaders who snubbed them in high school are listening to their jokes and laughing like they're funny. Right now, all over Manhattan, guys are buying girls twenty-dollar drinks and kidding themselves the girls are hanging out with them for their conversation, when the girls are in it for the free Cosmos and hitting on the bartender behind their date's back. At least here we're honest about it.

She smiled at the thought, a chipmunk-cute, cheek-dimpling, white-teeth-flashing smile that was so dazzling it nearly made Marvin drop his shot glasses.

'One!' Jada said, and they all sunk their first. 'Two!' she called, and the second set of empty glasses clinked down on the bar.

'Whoo!' Skye wiped her mouth. 'Now, we have a glass of champagne.' She looked seductively at Marvin. 'And *then*, you and me go have some fun, what do you say? You up for that, Marvin? You man enough to have some fun with me?'

She picked up his tie and ran her fingers up and down it, slowly, mimicking what he'd like her to be doing to a part of his anatomy, her glossy mouth slightly open, her pink tongue sliding out to touch her upper lip briefly.

Just briefly. If he came in his pants right now, that would turn off the money tap, which was the last thing she wanted.

Marvin's eyes were bugging out like a cartoon character's.

'You want a lap dance, don't you, honey?' she whispered to him.

He was so paralysed with excitement he could barely nod in assent.

Jada handed Skye two glasses of house champagne, and Marvin took one, staring, hypnotized, at Skye. He wore a wedding ring, natch. Pretty much every client at the Midnight Lounge was married. They came here to spend a fortune that they probably needed for the mortgage on their nice house in the suburbs on some fantasy girl with gold dust in her hair.

Sorry, Mrs Marvin, Skye thought ruefully. Bet he's got a photo of you in that wallet. But hey, maybe this works for you. Maybe this way he doesn't bother you so much for stuff you don't want to do.

The bartender was swiping Marvin's card for the drinks. Now, Skye, still caressing his tie, gave it a flirtatious little pull, enough to have him jumping off the bar stool and following her.

'I think we want the private room, don't we, Marvin honey?' she cooed. 'You've got a big –' she winked – '*wallet* you're just dying to show me, haven't you?'

Fish in a barrel. Really.

Jada had already attracted a little guy whose eyes were on a level with her tits, one of her regulars, who was staring up at her as worshipfully as if she were a dominatrix. She glanced at Skye over his head and shrugged. Skye knew exactly what Jada was saying. You had to know your market. Jada would be lap dancing Mini-Mes all evening. Her signature move was slapping their faces when they were all worked up. They begged for it sometimes, Jada had told her.

Skye weaved her way across the club floor, glass of champagne in one hand, Marvin's tie in the other. She picked a route between the tables, showing herself off to maximum effect. One of the Midnight Lounge's top pole dancers, Oksana, was wreathing herself round the central pole, and as Skye passed half the guys at least turned away from Oksana's contortions to watch Skye's cute little ass wiggle its way past them. Skye cast coy, eyes-up-under-lashes glances at as many as she could. Partly because she was touting for business, partly just to get Oksana pissy: there was no love lost between them.

The look Oksana shot Skye dripped poison. *Which is rich, considering the shit she's tried to pull on me in her time!* Skye thought crossly.

Hair bleached so blonde it was like straw, skin tanned satsuma orange, everything about Oksana was fake, from her stick-on nails to her pencilled-in brows to her coloured lenses. She'd tread over her mother's dead body to beat another girl to a fifty-buck note.

Screw her. By the time Skye had navigated between the smoked-glass tables, every man who gawked at her wished devoutly that they were in Marvin's shoes. Skye practically never liked the guys she danced for, but it was still a major turn-on to know that she was desired so much that men would gasp and groan as she walked by.

Like you said, Mom. I'll worry when they stop *leching after me.*

'Private dance, DeVaughan,' she cooed at the big bouncer, who was posted at the door to the back room.

'No probs, babe,' he said, holding open the door and looking significantly at Marvin, who was so overcome by excitement that it took him much longer than it should have done to slide a twenty into DeVaughan's huge hand.

Skye took her hand off Marvin's tie and touched her fingernails to her palm so quickly that he didn't even notice. It was a signal to DeVaughan, who acknowledged it with an equally swift nod.

Five minutes, is what the hand signal meant. Five fingers, snapping open and closed. *This one's not going to take any time at all.*

Skye had been bang on. As it were. She exited the room barely five minutes later, back into the pounding music and pulsating stage lights of the main club, her smile at DeVaughan positively demure.

'Give him a few seconds,' she said, and DeVaughan nodded in absolute understanding.

Skye wasn't a hooker. Her bits didn't touch the men's bits without layers of clothing between them. That was her rule, though some skanks, she was sure, did more, even at the Midnight Lounge, which was pretty damn upscale. Those Russian girls, with their cold, dead eyes, would do anything for money. But Skye had her standards. She'd dance for the guys, she'd turn them on, she'd grind as much as they wanted, and they could touch themselves, sure: but they weren't allowed to get their things out. That would be crossing the line Skye had set for herself years ago, when she started in this business.

'Cause that's not really what they're after, she told herself.

It had seemed weird, at first, and sometimes it still did; her clients could get laid for a great deal less than they paid for Skye's services.

It's the fantasy of picking up a hot chick in a club and getting a little alone time with her. That's what they're paying for. She shrugged. *Whatever floats their boats.*

'Skye! Baby!'

The man calling her name was loud enough to be heard even over the pumping bass line of Def Leppard's 'Pour Some Sugar on Me', one of the most tired anthems of exotic dancers all over the world. Skye flicked her eyes to the stage: yup, Oksana was up there, wiggling her skinny arse.

I know you're a huge attention-whore, but you better get down off that pole and onto some laps if you want to make any money tonight, Skye thought nastily as she crossed to the table where Lew James, the guy who'd just called her name, was sitting.

Lew was an old client: he never paid her much himself, but he often brought in guys who spent like it was going out of style, and he always hooked her up with them. Lew was a journalist, if you could call it that, on one of the main gossip weeklies, the *National Investigator*. He went through trash cans and tapped phone lines and pulled all kinds of sordid crap so that Skye and millions like her could read about the secrets stars were desperate to keep hidden.

Lew liked showing that he was on first-name terms with the prettiest blonde in the whole of the Midnight Lounge. And if Lew got the Lounge name-checked in the *Investigator*, he drank on the house the next time he was in. Judging by the two bottles of champagne on Lew's table and his air of smugness, Paulie, the manager, was comping Lew tonight.

Skye sat down next to him, despite the fact that he was patting his lap invitingly. You had to make guys work for it.

'Hey, honey,' she cooed. 'Pour me a glass, won't you? And introduce me to your sexy friend!' She smiled at the other man at the table. 'I'm Skye. Pleasure to meet you. Sorry about Lew, he lost his manners dumpster-diving.'

'I told you she was a firecracker!' Lew crowed, quite unoffended. A small, ferret-faced man, Lew was too rattily dressed to have made it past the Lounge's door staff if he hadn't worked for the *Investigator*. His friend, though, was in the classic chinos-and-polo shirt combo worn by every off-duty businessman in America.

'I'm Kevin Sanders,' he said, reaching across the table to shake her hand. 'And the pleasure's all mine.' He was much bigger than Lew, and much fitter, with a shaved head, wire-framed glasses, and the kind of tan you didn't get naturally in New York in the springtime. 'I work with Lew. I'm the LA bureau chief of the *Investigator*.'

Skye widened her eyes in fake fascination.

'So *that's* where you got that great tan! LA!' she said, leaning forward to run one manicured fingernail along his forearm. 'Is it all over?'

He choked on his drink – vodka and tonic it looked like. Smart guy, Skye thought. This champagne's pretty crappy. I mean, I like it, but what do I know? She'd noticed that the classy clients ordered the champagne for the girls and something else for themselves.

'Cute,' Kevin Sanders observed, without answering her question. 'Tell me a bit about yourself, Skye.'

Oh crap, Skye thought. I hate when they pull the 'I want to get to know you' routine. It's so lame.

'College dropout, no idea what I wanted to do, but I make a hell of a lot more here than working in an office,' she said, sipping some more champagne. 'I can dance a bit, but not good enough for Broadway. Can't carry a tune and I'm not tall enough to be a Rockette. So here I am! I'll do it for a few more years while I figure out what I want to do next. But I'm having a ball. It's like a party every night!'

She flashed her best smile again, having trotted out the practised spiel she used for all the guys who asked her that kind of dumb question. *He's got five minutes more,* she calculated. *Ten, tops. Then, if he doesn't want a dance, I move on.*

'And what were you majoring in at college?' Kevin Sanders asked.

It was Skye's turn to gulp on her champagne. *Is this guy for real?* She shot a glance at Lew, but he nodded at her, telling her to answer the question.

'Acting and creative writing,' she admitted. 'I thought I'd maybe be the next Jennifer Aniston or Sophie Kinsella. But college wasn't for me.'

She was embarrassed now, pissed off with this guy for pointing out the distance between her dreams and her reality. *And no way is he spending any money on me.* Skye's instincts were very well honed by now. *He's not gay, but I'm not his type, either. Clock's ticking . . .* Finishing off the champagne, she jumped up, still smiling. Being an exotic dancer was kind of like being a pageant contestant – you had to keep flashing your pearly whites.

'I'm gonna hit the stage now, guys,' she said. 'Pleasure talking to you, Kevin! Lew, honey . . .' She blew him a kiss.

Skye hadn't been fishing for compliments before. She knew she was no great shakes as a dancer. She took a few classes, sure, but those were as much about staying in shape as honing her craft. Oksana and the Russian girls who'd been gymnasts back home were stunning on the pole, much as Skye hated to admit it; they could pull all kinds of crazy stunts. But Skye's talent didn't lie in her gymnastic ability. It lay in her innate ability to be breathtakingly, fabulously sexy.

Britney Spears' 'Gimme More' was playing, and much as the song bored Skye, it was great for this kind of dancing, perfect for bumps and grinds, perfect for swaying round a pole, dropping down till her bottom grazed her heels, switching it back and forth, popping up again; flipping round with her back to the pole, running it between her buttocks, arching her back so her breasts looked even higher and fuller, sliding up and down the pole, working it with everything she had.

When Oksana was on the pole, it was a gymnastic prop, like a balance beam or parallel bars. When Skye was working the pole, it was exactly what every guy in the Midnight Lounge imagined it to be: a stand-in for the part of their anatomy they were most interested in introducing to her, but bigger, harder and shinier than theirs would ever be.

As she flipped her blonde hair back, and wiggled her luscious little bottom and hooked the pole between her gold-glittering bare knees, arching back, it was with the wide-eyed wonder of a girl who had never seen anything this big before, and was overwhelmed by it. The whoops and cheers from the men pressing up to the stage were much louder than they'd been for the previous dancers, even though those girls had shown an awful lot more than Skye did, writhing round on the stage, spreading their legs.

Head tilted back, Skye surveyed the faces closest around the stage, and smiled to herself; they were sweaty, pleading, mouths hanging open in hopeless lust. Time to start working them, now she'd got them all wound up, time to sashay round the footlights and let them work their sweaty twenties and fifties into her tiny gold outfit.

And just then, the whoops rose into a roar of excitement.

Jeez, feeding time at the zoo! Skye thought, grinning as she swivelled to see Jada striding onto the stage behind her, over six foot in her spike heels. They had a little routine for the changeover on the pole that all the regulars eagerly awaited; Skye clasped the pole with both hands, undulating her hips, flirting with Jada over her shoulder as Jada mimed a forehand and backhanded slap to Skye's arse.

'Yeah! Give it to her!' one guy yelled.

'Spank her good, baby!' another chipped in.

Jada grabbed the pole above Skye and ground herself against her friend. Skye smelled Jada's light sweat, musky under her Paloma Picasso perfume, and the new leather of her little bra-and-hotpants outfit, felt Jada's pubic bone tapping against her buttocks, caught the rhythm and went with it, the girls dancing now, grinding against each other, the pole between Skye's breasts as she parted her lips and raised one hand to her mouth in faux-shock, winking at the spectators, doing a fifties pin-up face that had them screaming appreciation.

We are gonna *rake* it in tonight! she reflected happily. Queens of the club!

Off by the bar, she spotted Oksana, picking her out by the dark orange tan and the hair so bleached it looked as white as bone. She was sucking on a straw, her mouth twisted as bitterly as if it were a lemon.

Skye shoved back against Jada, listening to the hoots and catcalls of the guys, every yell a promise of money to come. It was literally like music to her ears.

Amber

The helicopter was landing at Bovey Castle at noon; before-hand, Tony had dragged Amber out to the terrace to watch the daily falconry display. Because she was nervous at having the big birds fly close to her, she had taken a Klonopin, and now, leaning back against Tony, she watched the enormous owl, which turned out to be called Merlin, hopping around on the grass from one huge, clawed foot to another, squawking imperiously for food.

'He follows the guy round like he's a dog,' Tony muttered to her. 'The guy actually had to teach him how to fly. Funny, huh?'

Amber nodded as the falconer called Merlin up to his arm and carried him over to the big black box in which he was transported. Two harris hawks came out of the boxes next, brown with white tails, and Tony squeezed her arm excitedly.

'That's what I hunted with yesterday!' he said. 'The Lab flushes out the rabbits and then the birds pick them off – one bird actually jumped on the Lab's head, it was crazy! The best bit's coming next – he's got a gyrfalcon, they go from nought to sixty as fast as a Ferrari. He'll take it down to the lawn. Very cool.'

Amber sighed, holding onto his arm to balance in the heels of her suede Jimmy Choo boots on the gravel path. Even though Tony had hired a golf cart to drive them back and forth from the lodge to the hotel – a bare five-minute walk, but the stone steps were ankle-threatening in the Balenciaga spikes she'd been wearing the night before – you still had to navigate some gravel and grass, both of which were murder on expensive shoes.

The falconer was bringing out a large whitish bird, which took off over the velvety green lawns below the terrace as if it had been fired out of a gun. The bird soared up, disappeared behind the castle, and circled it, darting down out of the trees to swing back in a pale blur as it swooped down on the lure the falconer was swinging.

An hour later, as Amber and Tony's helicopter rose from the helipad, she looked down at the castle and had a momentary sense of what the falcon and the hawks must see, how free they must feel for that short time they were unhooded, free to fly. The noise of the whirring blades drowned out everything else: she loved helicopters for exactly that reason. Settling back into the hand-stitched leather seat, she stroked the walnut panelling on the door with her finger. It was a Bentley.

Only the best for Tony. A Bentley four-seater helicopter, a five-star luxury hotel with its own falconer and fishing lake. And so that her luggage would be the best, too, he'd bought her a matched set of Vuitton suitcases, some of which were stacked in the seat next to her: the weekender, the garment bag and the vanity case, an adorable, hard-sided oval with padded leather straps inside to hold all her creams and lotions and perfumes standing up. Amber gazed at it lovingly.

Fifty minutes later, the Bentley set down at the Battersea heliport, the pilot jumping down to hand out Amber and carry her luggage to the limo parked a short distance away. Tony kissed her goodbye.

'I'm heading straight off, babe,' he said. 'Hopping over to Stansted to catch a ride back to the States with some oil guys on their Gulfstream. The car'll take you home, or wherever you want to go. And, hey –' he reached into his pocket and pulled out an envelope, which he pressed into her hand – 'I know Jared takes care of bookings for you, but I wanted to give you an extra present.

You deserve it, OK? Pick yourself up something really nice.' He grinned at her. 'My fantasy girl. I'll see you soon, babe.'

He stroked her cheek wistfully, sighed, and swung round, striding back to the helicopter, raising a hand to her in farewell. Amber climbed into the limo without looking back. The weekend was over.

'Green Street,' she said to the driver, and slid open the minibar as the car smoothly pulled out onto the road. Selecting a gold shiny bottle of Pommery Pop, she pulled off the foil and untwisted the wire, popping the cork, pouring the champagne into an equally chilled glass. She washed a couple of Xanax down with the fizz before she slid a manicured nail under the flap of the envelope and prised it open.

She always needed a little Dutch courage for this moment. Reaching for her glass, she took another long sip.

Fifty-pound notes. Probably three grand worth. And that was just the tip; Tony had paid her modelling agent much more than that for her company this weekend.

By the time the limo took a right off Park Lane, in Mayfair, onto Green Street, Amber had finished the Pommery and was feeling much better. The limo driver carried her bags through the marble-tiled hall and into the lift. The apartment she currently rented was the top two floors of this Georgian house, and it was exquisitely decorated, with pale yellow walls and polished wood floors. The lower floor was a huge living room overlooking Green Street, with a luxurious kitchen and dining room at the back. Upstairs were two bedrooms with Turkish travertine ensuite bathrooms, and a roof terrace above with a patio heater and trellised gazebo covered in trailing wisteria. The estate agent had described it as superb for entertaining, which was ironic, as Amber hadn't had anyone visit the entire two years she had lived here.

'*Matka!* I'm home!' she called, wheeling in her cases.

'Amber? I didn't expect you this early!' her mother exclaimed.

Slava was, as always, ensconced in front of the TV in the kitchen. The living room was furnished with a set of brocade sofas and armchairs around an elaborately carved coffee table. The apartment had been rented furnished, and the decorators had added the final touches: arrangements of dried flowers and blown-glass spheres in the fireplace and in waist-high vases in the corners of the room. Huge matching brocade curtains draped the floor-to-ceiling windows that led out onto the wrought-iron balcony. It was a stunning room, a real showpiece, and Slava only ever entered it to keep it polished and dusted and to water the flowers in pots on the balcony. She said it was too smart for her.

Slava didn't like to go out. She spent ninety per cent of her waking hours in the kitchen, in her comfy old armchair, knitting and doing embroidery, watching daytime TV. It was no surprise to Amber to find her mother in her usual place, a circular wooden tapestry frame on her lap, a wooden sewing box by her side, its lid open to show skeins of silk arranged by colour.

'Tony had to get back to the States by tonight,' Amber said, coming into the kitchen, kissing her mother on her forehead. 'He had a lift with some oil guys in their jet.'

'So glamorous,' Slava sighed approvingly. 'But you always come back to your old mother in the end. Did you have fun, *láska*?'

Slovakian by birth, Slava prided herself on her good English, but still larded it with endearments and emphases from her mother tongue, which meant that she and Amber often slipped between English and Slovak without realizing it.

'Yes, *Matka*,' Amber said, responding automatically with the Slovak word for 'mother'.

Amber took a glass tumbler from the drainer and slid it into the dispensers in the front of the Sub-Zero refrigerator, filling it with crescent-shaped pieces of ice, then filtered water.

'Give me some Lucozade,' Slava said. 'I'm thirsty. My throat is always dry.'

'It's the pills, Mum,' Amber said, reaching into the fridge for the open bottle of Lucozade, which was one of the few items it contained. 'They're dehydrating.'

'Well, at least I don't smoke,' Slava said as Amber brought over her glass. 'Do you want to watch a film? They have new ones to buy on the film channels.'

'In a couple of hours,' Amber said. 'I should unpack now.'

'Oh, yes!' Slava looked animated, her green eyes sparkling. 'Your beautiful clothes, you must take care of them!'

She shook out two Vicodins from the prescription container on her side table and swallowed them with the Lucozade. Her fingers were heavy with rings; Slava was inordinately proud of her jewellery, and the first thing she did every morning was to reach out to her bedside table and slide on the rings, with their crusted gold and diamond settings and bezel-cut stones.

'My back is bad again,' she said.

'You should go for a walk,' Amber responded. 'It's a lovely day. You could walk round Grosvenor Square. Even go to Green Park.'

'Maybe later,' Slava said, turning back to the television.

Amber knew this meant 'never'. She leaned against the door jamb, finishing her water, looking at her mother's profile. Slava was as elegant as ever, dressed up so smartly that any observer would think that she was about to go out to tea with girlfriends at the Ritz: slim shantung trousers, a beige silk twinset, a big necklace of cultured pearls to hide the wrinkles on her neck that she was very sensitive about, her ash-pale hair, as thick as Amber's, piled on top of her head. Slava's hair was carefully dyed by one of the most expensive colourists in London, streaked in delicate shades of grey-blonde that looked as natural as possible. Her eyebrows were pencilled in, and her cheeks were dusted with light pink blush.

Slava had been a good-looking young woman, but she couldn't hold a candle to Amber. Amber had the same slanting green eyes as her mother, but Slava's eyelids were hooded and heavy-lidded; her jaw was a little square, her nose a little too wide for beauty, while Amber had a prettily rounded chin and a long, straight, perfect nose. Slava had always been slender as a wand, but Amber, though slim, had the curves that made people's palms sweat: firm, high breasts, gently rounded hips, and a tiny waist. Slava's eyebrows had been faint, before they'd faded almost completely; Amber's were two perfect straight lines, rising fractionally at the outer corners, slanting upwards in parallel with the slant of her thick-lashed green eyes.

'Just you and me,' Slava said comfortably. 'That's all we need in the end. Just you and me, so cosy together.'

It was a regular incantation, what Slava always said when Amber returned from a shoot away, or a weekend date, and Amber responded as she always did: 'Just you and me, *Matka.*'

Slava nodded happily. 'You're still here?' she asked, her eyes on the television. 'Why are you still here, silly girl? You said you need to unpack your pretty clothes.' Slava waved her hand. 'Don't look at me. It's not worth looking at me,' she added. 'Go and look at yourself in the mirror. God was only practising when he made me. With you, he got it right.'

Amber was still smiling as she went into the hall and carried her luggage upstairs to her bedroom. She looked at it for a moment, then pulled her Cartier gold and enamel cigarette case out of her pocket and unlocked the door to the roof terrace. There was a light breeze blowing, and she settled onto the wooden bench in the little trellised gazebo.

I've got so much to thank *Matka* for, she thought, pulling out a Silk Cut and lighting it up. I wouldn't have any of this if it weren't for her. And what other mother would say 'God was only practising when he made me,' and actually mean it?

This was a favourite expression of Slava's, and, crucially, it never contained a shred of self-pity or fishing for a compliment. Slava was brutally realistic. Amber's father had walked out when Amber was only a baby, but Slava had coped bravely, despite being a penniless immigrant with a limited command of English. Not once had his name been mentioned between them that Amber could remember. Slava had moved out of London for a fresh start, to Margate, a flea-bitten seaside town in Kent, once a lively resort, now run down and dispirited. With no real skills, Slava had taken jobs cleaning offices at night to support her and her daughter, living in a hostel at first, and then a series of one-room rented flats above newsagents and bookies and fast-food places. Always noisy, always poor, always grimy and often mouse-infested, no matter how much Slava cleaned.

Amber's memory of those years was of her mother watching over her like a hawk during the day, walking her to school, picking her up, then locking her in every night when Slava went out to her cleaning job. Slava had alluded darkly to all the bad things that could happen to unattended girls, things she saw on the night streets as she went back and forth to work. She was determined to keep Amber safe. No teenage pregnancies or drug habits for her daughter; Amber wasn't going to turn out like most of her classmates, knocked up at sixteen, trying to get a flat off the council, planning to live off benefits for the rest of her life. Slava saw the big picture, always. Her ex-husband had been a very handsome man. Slava herself wasn't so bad. Maybe the daughter they had made would inherit their good looks; maybe Amber would be her passport out of poverty.

But when it came, it was much earlier and much faster and infinitely more life-changing than Slava could ever have anticipated. At fourteen, Amber hit puberty, and everything changed. The gangly, awkward, skinny teenager, ignored by all her classmates, suddenly sprouted, almost overnight, into a pin-up girl. The high cheekbones, the full lips, the long legs, all the features that had got her nicknamed 'Duck-Mouth' and 'Skeletor' now turned her into an object of such desire that Slava was quick to pull her out of school. The boys weren't the problem so much as the girls. Amber was already getting threats from jealous prima donnas who'd been the centre of attention before Amber blossomed into a sex object. Amber's face was clearly going to be her fortune, and Slava didn't want it sliced up with a box cutter by some envious rival.

She did her research, took Amber up to London, and walked her round what was planned to be a circuit of the top model agencies. But the second one snapped her up, and after that Amber's life changed so completely that Margate was just a distant memory to her by now. The girls at school, shoving their acne-spotted faces at her, hissing threats at her to stay away from Daz and Kevin and

Matt; the last flat above a Chinese takeaway, stinking of old frying oil; the nights waking up as Slava came back in at five in the morning, but pretending to be asleep, because Slava would be cross if she knew she was awake . . . all that might have happened to another girl.

They had travelled all over the world: they'd lived in Paris, Milan, New York, Slava always by Amber's side, chaperoning her, keeping the predators who circled around young models well away from her. Amber had some tutors assigned to her by her model agency, as she was legally required to keep studying until she was sixteen. But it was mostly for show, and Amber was kept too busy to bother much with textbooks. Fourteen was young then, but as soon as they put makeup on Amber, as soon as they curled her hair into big heavy waves, she looked more than old enough to be a model.

And *Matka* kept me safe, Amber reflected with gratitude. Even when I started wanting a bit more freedom, even when I started going out with guys, she was always watchful. And she made sure I didn't get into any of the bad stuff. When I got nervous doing catwalk, or lingerie shoots, all the other girls would tell me to drink, or do some lines. But *Matka* made sure I had legal stuff instead, pills to help with the anxiety. Stuff I could travel with safely, because I had prescriptions for it. I never had to worry about getting busted at airports, or scoring, or taking something that was cut with crap and getting sick. *Matka* took care of me . . .

Her phone buzzed, and she pulled it out of her pocket, glancing at the screen to see who it was.

Jared, her agent. She snapped it open.

'Hey, babycakes!' came Jared's three-pack-a-day croak. 'Just checking in to see how your weekend went!'

'Really nice,' Amber said, lighting a second cigarette from the butt of her first. You'd think that the sound of Jared's ruined vocal cords would put her off smoking, but it never worked that way.

'Did he give you a present?'

'Yes,' Amber said, thinking of the envelope stuffed in her handbag.

'Double excellent! So everyone's happy. Now, more good news: you've got a catalogue shoot on Tuesday. Very high-end. Swimsuits and cruise wear. You're in swimsuit shape, aren't you, sweetie? We don't need to panic?'

'No, I'm fine,' Amber reassured him.

'Weight?'

'One twenty, like always.'

'Good girl! OK, I'll email you the details. And Amber, sweetie? It's been a while since a modelling gig came up for you.' He coughed, a long, hacking rasp. 'Give it everything you have, sweetie.'

The jasmine growing over the pergola was coming into flower, its scent delicate, its flowers small and white. The pale smoke of Amber's Silk Cut blended with it, the tobacco somehow picking out the floral notes of the jasmine. Amber loved to sit up here; she'd bring out cushions and pile them on the bench and sit there, flicking through fashion magazines, London's most beautiful hidden gardens and elegant architecture laid out below her, the rich grass spread of Green Park just at the end of the street.

I need to earn enough to buy this place, she thought. I need security for me and *Matka*. I'm making way more from the dates I go on than the modelling jobs, but *Matka* mustn't ever realize that. She must never find out about Tony and the other guys. She must never know that they rang my agency and asked how much it would cost to take me out, and that Jared sets my rate for that just like he does for magazine and catalogue and advertising work.

She's so proud of me. It would kill her if she ever knew.

Skye

'You walk in front of my act,' Oksana hissed menacingly as soon as Skye stepped down off the stage, leaving Jada to work the pole on her own.

'Oksana, it's not an *act*,' Skye sighed, trying to move past her. 'You're not on *Broadway*. We're just shaking our asses for money, and I've got a bunch of guys waiting. Let's finish this – oh, I dunno, *never*, OK?'

'You *never* walk in front of my act again, American whore!' Oksana insisted.

'Or what?' Skye snapped. 'You'll claw my eyes out with those tacky acrylics of yours?'

Oksana's head snapped back in shock. Insulting another dancer's nails was almost the worst thing you could do. (The absolutely worst thing, of course, was calling someone fat or diseased; those were grounds for open warfare, which was frowned on by the management.)

Oksana couldn't help a quick glance down at her nails; they were so elaborately coated with swirls and appliqués that the effect was almost 3-D. That was enough distraction for Skye to slip past her and wiggle sexily over to a guy she'd spotted as a prime prospect while dancing. His bold eye contact told her that he was ready for business, and his very expensive suit and haircut that he could afford whatever she wanted to charge him.

He was waving at her now; Skye flicked her glance to his wrist and saw that his watch was top quality. He was actually quite handsome in a preppy-banker way, with slicked-back fair hair and pink full lips, and he radiated the confidence that comes directly from having a wallet stuffed with cash. Shimmying up to him, she sank down on his lap with a sexy little wiggle of her hips, her gold-dusted curls dripping enticingly down her bare back.

'So, you want a private dance tonight, baby?' she murmured in his ear, noticing his high-priced aftershave. This guy was looking better and better.

'Do I ever!' he groaned. 'Lead the way, gorgeous. I've got a whole stack of hundreds burning a whole in my pocket. And not just hundreds, y'know?'

He sneaked a pinch at her ass, which wasn't allowed – touching the girls was strictly forbidden, in the public areas of the Lounge, at least – but Skye let it pass. No one had seen. And now she was rising off his lap, leading him by his tie through the rest of the johns. It was corny, the tie thing, but they all loved it; it made them feel somehow as if the girl actually wanted them, couldn't wait to be alone with them; not for their money, but for themselves.

They were total fucking morons, the clients. Every man was a moron who let his dick make decisions for him.

Behind her, Skye knew that Oksana was still shooting her daggers with her eyes. Well, let her. Oksana was an idiot to waste her time on being jealous of Skye instead of working her clients.

They reached the door to the private room, and, unlike poor hapless Marvin, this guy knew the drill. He was already flipping a twenty out of his money clip and slapping it into DeVaughan's hand.

The room was small, lit by a few recessed spots. Black walls, black carpet, an old curved banquette standing in the centre. Mirrors ran around it, cheap, rough-edged, rectangular panels in which almost every angle of the room was reflected, and it smelled of sweat and semen.

It was in the back room that Skye missed the smoking ban most. She'd ground herself on many clients puffing on big Montecristos or Davidoffs and even though the rich pungent smoke had made her choke and cough, it was still better than this stink, the mouldy smell of spilled dry come. But you couldn't read any of that on her smiling, sexy face. She knew, because she was keeping an eye on herself in the mirrors.

Skye tossed her hair back and widened her blue eyes enticingly. R&B pumped through the built-in speakers in an endless loop, bass line thumping, singers moaning horny lyrics, their voices husky, crooning sex words till humping was all you could think about.

'What's your name, baby?' she cooed, pushing him gently down onto the banquette and straddling him, working her four-inch Perspex-and-diamanté heels into position under her so she didn't break an ankle when she got going.

'You can call me Gary,' he said, grinning, so she knew that wasn't what it said on his driver's licence.

Crap. For some reason, it always went easier when they told you their real name.

'Well, Gary baby,' she purred. 'You ready to sit back and enjoy the ride?'

He nodded eagerly.

'You know the rules, don't you?' Skye ran one long nail down the side of his face, lightly, sliding her tongue round her lips, giving him a little push of her crotch into his to really get him going, make him agree to everything she asked. 'I'll give you the ride of your life, but no touching me while I'm doing it.' She smiled temptingly. 'Still, ask for what you want and we'll see what we can do. It's going to be $500 straight up.'

'I'll give you a grand if you blow me,' he said immediately.

Skye shook her head. 'Sorry, baby, I'm no hooker.'

'Two grand?'

She shook her head again, marvelling at someone who was

willing to shell out two grand for something he could buy on the street for a twenty.

'Tell you what,' he said, grinning up at her. 'You take off your G-string when you give me that ride, and I'll up it to a grand. How's that sound?'

'I'm not supposed to get naked . . .' She slid the finger into her own mouth and sucked on it, hoping to get him to up his offer.

His pupils dilated, and she could feel his cock move under her. But he wouldn't budge on the price.

'A grand. Come on! I'm not paying more than that unless you get my dick out and get working on it.'

Charming, Skye thought. This one's a prince.

'OK, baby, you got yourself a deal,' she said, rising so she could slip off her tiny golden mini and her matching G-string.

He groaned at the sight of her naked lower body, shaved and smooth.

'Oh, baby, yeah,' he said, licking his lips. 'That's what I'm talking about! Come here and rub that dirty-girl pussy all over me!'

Ugh. This guy is *not* rocking my world. I'm going to make this fast and furious, Skye decided, as she flipped one leg over his lap to straddle him again.

'Put the money in my bra, Gary baby,' she said, licking his ear as she ground down on him.

He fumbled for his money clip, dragging out a fold of greenbacks that he fed into her bra, getting a good feel at the same time. That way she got the money in advance, but gave them a little thrill. Gary actually squeezed her left tit hard enough to hurt before dropping his hand. Jesus, this one just didn't give up.

She started work now in earnest, running her hands up and down his shirt, twisting and shifting cunningly, working her naked crotch against his trousered one, feeling the size and angle of his cock – small, right-hanging, tangled up a bit in his boxers. She was really good by now at feeling out the tip through a pair of trousers, working herself against it, putting maximum pressure precisely where the guy wanted it, sliding herself up and down the shaft.

Making him feel like he was getting the closest he could get to fucking her with his clothes on.

'Hey, hey,' Gary started to chant, his head thrown back, his eyes closing.

What? Skye thought, pausing momentarily, wondering if he was trying to tell her something.

'Don't stop, baby, don't stop . . .' he panted, and she realized that it was just what he said when he was getting close.

Some men really are fucking freaks, Skye sighed. I mean, who says 'Hey, hey' when they're getting laid?

'Hey, hey, hey, hey . . .' Gary chanted, as if it was a mantra or something. 'Hey, *hey*, *hey*, HEY—'

His eyes snapped open, wild and staring. He bit his lips, thrusting his bottom up, trying to get as much contact as possible between her naked crotch and his small cock.

No wonder he's such an asshole, Skye thought almost sympathetically, with a tiny little pencil between his legs. Poor bastard.

'Oh, *yeah*! You dirty little – ugh – dirty little *slut* – hey, hey, *hey*—' Gary spluttered.

Skye had her hands twined up in her hair, arching her back to make her boobs look bigger, humping him frantically, desperate to get this over with. From the frenzied jerkings of his hips, she was sure he was about to come, and it couldn't happen fast enough for her. She had a bad feeling about him.

And just then, she felt something scrape painfully up inside her. She screamed, and jumped away, but awkwardly, because of her high platform heels. Everything happened in a rush. She looked down in horror between her legs and saw that this dickhead had sneaked his hand between their bodies while she was working away at him. He had managed to get a finger up inside her.

He had done it deliberately. He'd shoved his finger up her, hooked it, and scratched her deliberately.

'Fuck!' she screamed. 'That fucking *hurt*!'

But Gary, or whatever he was called, was oblivious to her protest, because he had started to come in his trousers.

'Dirty little, filthy little *whore* . . .' he was moaning.

His arms flailed around, grabbing for her, and she slapped at him as she scrambled uncomfortably off him. Unbelievably, after what the fucker had pulled on her already, he was still going for her crotch. She lurched back from his clawing fingers, tripped, and fell on her ass.

Gary was still convulsing on the banquette when DeVaughan shoved open the door and stomped in, six foot six of solid muscle in a suit as dark as he was.

'Heard you scream, Skye. Everything cool?' he barked.

Then he took in the scene: Skye on the carpet, legs in the air, flashing her naked crotch; Gary collapsed on the banquette, a stain spreading over the front of his suit trousers.

DeVaughan's eyes widened. 'Jeez, girl, you OK?'

He reached down one huge hand and pulled Skye to her feet.

'The fucker *hurt* me,' Skye said furiously, bending over to grab her G-string and miniskirt. It was incredibly hard to get back into the flimsy G-string with her platform heels on, and she had to grip DeVaughan's jacket sleeve for balance. Gary watched her with a sly smile as she teetered and swore, her heel catching in the elastic.

'Hey, asshole, you push the lady so she fell over like that?' DeVaughan said to Gary.

'*Lady?*' Gary grinned smugly. 'Little whore, more like.'

'No need for that, man,' DeVaughan said, folding his arms across his chest. 'You making a bad situation worse, know what I'm saying?'

'No,' Gary said, throwing his arms wide on the back of the banquette and giving DeVaughan a big, cocky, I'm-a-rich-banker-and-you're-just-a-bouncer smile. 'I've got no idea. What *are* you saying, man?'

'I'm saying that you gotta pay up, dude,' DeVaughan said firmly. 'You got one of our top girls fallen on the floor. You lucky she's OK. If she'd turned an ankle or something and couldn't dance for a while, you'd be in deep shit for sure. Manager'd have a fit if I told him what happened.'

That was a hundred per cent true. The manager didn't care about the dancers' welfare, but he got very steamed up if any of them were off work for any reason.

Gary sighed and pulled out his wallet. 'OK, let's make this all go away, shall we?' he said. 'Five hundred for the little whore and a hundred for her big black pimp.'

'*Man*—' DeVaughan started towards him.

Skye grabbed his arm, as much of it as she could; DeVaughan's forearm was bigger than one of her thighs. 'Five hundred for him too,' she said levelly to Gary. 'Since you got personal with him.'

'Ah, fuck it.' Gary got up, throwing some money on the banquette. 'There's another grand. You fight it out between you.' He winked salaciously at DeVaughan. 'Spend it on getting her to go for a ride with you, man. She made me come like a geyser. And hey, baby?' He looked at Skye. 'Nice tight pussy. Congratulations. Might even buy a piece of that next time. Glad I got myself a sample, eh?'

Now it was Skye who took a furious step towards him, and DeVaughan who threw out one enormous arm to hold her back. Gary sauntered out, and Skye looked over at the money on the banquette.

'We'll split it,' she said.

DeVaughan picked up the hundreds and dealt off five for Skye. 'Go have a drink,' he said. 'Put it on the club tab.'

Skye nodded, winding all the bills up into one tight curl, tucking them safely just above the wire of her sparkly bra.

Out in the club again, the noise and brightness, the faces turned to her, the men pressing her for lap dances, were as overwhelming as a slap in the face. She crossed to the bar and ordered a double shot of vodka.

I'll feel better when I've got some liquor in me, she said to herself. DeVaughan's right.

But she didn't: she felt worse. Instead of warming her, it was as if the neat vodka sank promptly to the pit of her stomach, a cold, solid mass. She could feel that bastard's finger up inside her, and she wanted to douche herself with bleach to burn his touch away. Clients were always trying, of course. But usually, once you'd nego-tiated a deal with them, they kept it: they didn't want DeVaughan throwing them out, didn't want to be barred from the Lounge. The problem came from men like Gary: rich cocky ones, who thought they could buy anything.

She couldn't feel his fingernail inside her any longer. The vodka might be helping with that, she supposed. The truth was, it hadn't been a bad scratch, nothing even to draw blood: she'd checked. But she felt invaded. It was a shitty, shitty feeling. You spent so much time telling yourself you were an exotic dancer, not a stripper, and certainly not the whore that Oksana had called her.

But then a man did something like that to you, showed you that, in his eyes, you *were* a whore, and it made you question everything. Because if the johns saw you like that, then maybe, just maybe, that's what you really were.

'Hey, honey!' A man reared up next to her, big and sweaty, his eyes eager. 'I saw your act – wow! Come give me a lap dance, OK?'

'Hey,' boomed a deep voice behind her, and the would-be client instantly backed off, looking so terrified that, without even recog-nizing the voice, Skye would have known it was DeVaughan looming over them both.

She swivelled to look at him. He jerked his head, indicating she should follow him, and strode off through the crowd.

'Hold that thought, baby. I'll be right back,' Skye said to the man, and slipped down off her barstool.

In his cramped little backroom, the door locked behind them, DeVaughan pulled out a Baggie of white powder from his trouser pocket.

'Took this off some asshole earlier who was so loaded he was trying to do lines on the table, can you believe it?' DeVaughan said, tipping some of the coke out onto his desk top. 'I was like, man, you think you're still in the nineties? We can't even *smoke inside* no more, and you're doing blow out in the open? Come *on*.'

He cut two fat lines with a card as Skye extracted a hundred from her bra – the one curled up inside the others, so it wasn't too damp – and rolled it up into a neat little tube.

'Thanks, DeVaughan,' she said gratefully, bending over the desk top and inhaling one of the lines.

'No problem.' DeVaughan took the hundred from her; it looked tiny in his huge hand, like toy money from a Monopoly game. 'I figured you could do with a boost.'

She sniffed deeply, tilting back her head, feeling the sharp chemical rush of the cocaine flooding her bloodstream, fizzing her up, instantly wiping out the resentment and anger she'd been feeling a bare minute ago.

'Whooh!' she said, grinning at him. 'Good call! I'm ready to go back and work the hell out of that room!'

'That's how we like it,' DeVaughan said drily.

Skye bounced out of the back room as if she had springs under her platform heels.

'Girl, you are buzzing!' Jada said, gliding up next to her, smelling intoxicatingly of her own fresh sweat from dancing, mingled with the heavy Paloma Picasso perfume she doused herself in every evening, a rich musk.

Skye pulled a guilty little-girl face. 'I know we said we weren't going to for a while,' she confessed, 'but—'

'Oh, no, you *didn't*!' Jada, recognizing the brightness in Skye's eyes, was way ahead of her. 'You holding?'

Skye shook her head. 'DeVaughan. He boosted some off a john.'

'I'm gonna have a word with him right now!'

Jada's place was instantly taken by the guy from the bar, his eyes bulging, his face red with excitement.

'You said five minutes, babe, and it's been, like, *ten*!' he complained.

'Oh, *no*,' Skye said, smiling up at him as he leered down at her diminutive, glittering golden body. 'That's so *naughty* of me! What could I possibly do to make it up to you?'

And she took hold of his tie, leading him off to the private room, as if her last encounter there had never happened at all.

Petal

*T*he publicist who'd booked KillBuzz into the InterContinental
Park Lane was definitely going to get the sack. Not for her choice
of hotel – the InterContinental was stunning, with its amazing location on Hyde Park Corner, its luxurious lobby with its specially
made glass chandeliers, and floral arrangements provided every day
by Moyses Stevens, the florist who also supplied Buckingham
Palace.

No, she was going to get the sack because, as well as booking the
band members into individual suites of their own, she had had the
bright idea to hire the hotel's superb Spa Boudoir for them all to
party in. Even Petal, who had a great deal of experience with five-
star hotels, was impressed by the Spa Boudoir, which was a luxury
suite, plus a private spa treatment room off a state-of-the-art bathroom with wetroom and Jacuzzi. The décor was rich and luxurious;
expensive wenge wood, chaise longues piled high with silk cushions,
Bang and Olufsen plasma screens with Bose sound systems in every
room, even the spa.

It would have been the perfect venue for a romantic weekend,
or an exclusive hen night, if you wanted to be cocooned together
in a private world, where you'd be visited only by room service,
your Elemis-trained masseuse, or your private butler. It was

definitely, however, *not* the perfect venue for a budding rock group of coked-up, drunken, and generally over-stimulated musicians and their entourage, fresh from the high of a riotously successful gig.

The InterContinental staff had prepared the suite to the last detail. Every table was covered with white linen cloths and arranged with plates of hot and cold canapés and exquisite bowls of spring flowers. Ice buckets filled with miniature blue and silver bottles of Pommery Pop were scattered on every ledge. In the spa treatment room, tealight candles had been lit all along narrow glass shelves, flickering gently in the soft lighting. Elemis products were arranged between the candles, their tiny flames glinting off the elegant silver packaging. A low white leather chair on silver rockers with a matching footstool was placed by the window, the curtains drawn back to display the marble arch of Hyde Park Corner and the glittering lights of the traffic flowing round it.

And through it, KillBuzz and their hangers-on rampaged like bulls in a china shop. In the space of half an hour, the Spa Boudoir suite was unrecognizable.

'God, these people are *animals*,' Petal drawled as she sprawled back on the white leather rocking chair in the spa room, a glass of champagne in her hand. The plasma TV was playing videos, but she was watching two girls in tight skirts as they climbed onto the silk-upholstered corner bench seat, teetering in their stack heels, pulling down the boxes of Elemis creams with acquisitive squeals.

'Oh, fuck, there's nothing inside!' screamed one of them petulantly, throwing the box across the room.

'Cheap bastards, putting empty boxes up there!' the other one chimed in.

'I checked those out as soon as I came in,' Tas, perched on the table, muttered to Petal. 'How stupid *are* those twats?'

'Trust you to look for freebies, Tas,' Petal grinned.

'I don't have a fucking trust fund, do I?' Tas said, quite unabashed. 'I'll take all the goodie bags I can get!'

'Hey, pet, fancy a bath?'

Petal turned her head to see Dan Drummond, a bottle of champagne in his hand. He'd already stripped off his sweaty T-shirt, and his chest was bare above the tight black jeans that clung to his narrow hips. If there was an ounce of fat on his entire body, Petal couldn't see it. Just how she liked her boys: lean and hungry.

'I've got the Jacuzzi going,' he said happily. 'It's *ace.*'

He stretched out the hand that wasn't holding the bottle. His hair flopped over his handsome face, with those full sexy lips and cheekbones that could cut glass. His torso was almost perfectly smooth, white skin that looked as if it had never seen the sun; there were just a few hairs curling over the waistband of his jeans, slightly darker brown than the hair on his head. Petal licked her lips. A gorgeous about-to-be rock star, already half-naked, gagging to get her into the bath with him. Life didn't get much better than this.

'And we got 'em to send up a ton more booze,' he added triumphantly. 'I wasn't bloody drinking out of those little girlie bottles.'

'Well, it sounds like you've got it all planned out!' Petal said, sliding off the treatment table and taking his hand.

The whirlpool bath looked like it had been carved out of a huge single piece of smooth white stone. Free-standing, with nowhere on its narrow rim to put so much as a piece of soap, it would have been insanity anywhere but a five-star hotel suite, where its design-over-function aesthetic merely added to the over-the-top level of pampering. It was churning like a cauldron, with red velvety rose petals – scattered there earlier by the private butler – caught in the swirls of water, bringing an 'aah' of appreciation to Petal's lips.

'You can't say I don't know how to show a girl a good time!' Dan laughed, putting the champagne bottle down on the Brazilian marble surround of the double sinks. But the incredulity in his eyes betrayed how unused he was to this level of glamour and pampering; he was talking a good game, but his inability to stop grinning was a dead giveaway.

'Here,' he said, reaching for her glass and refilling it. 'And aren't you wearing too many clothes? I took me top off already.'

Standing there, his chest bare, the jeans as snug as a second skin, Dan already looked more than half-naked.

But instead of stripping her own top off with as much eagerness as he was showing, Petal just stood there like a lemon.

I hate this part! she thought, panicking, trying to cover her racing nerves by drinking more champagne. Why didn't I think to run in here first and take all my clothes off and jump in the bath really quickly?

It seemed ridiculous even to her, this bashfulness about getting naked in front of a guy who'd already pulled her tights and knickers down to her ankles and gone down on her. But for all Petal's wild-child ways, she had her body insecurities. Petal's Achilles heel was her breasts. Or rather, the lack of them. You didn't get to be thin enough to wear designer sample sizes and simultaneously have breasts bigger than bee-stings – not naturally, anyway.

She was terrified Dan would be disappointed by them.

'Come on!' Dan had his hands at the waistband of his jeans.

Just do it quickly, Petal told herself, reaching down to unbuckle the belt slung around her hips. The trouble with projecting your image as incredibly sophisticated and confident was that, once you'd established your cool credentials and ensured that everyone was in awe of your poise, you couldn't really let down your force-field of assurance . . . Petal's belt dropped to the floor, its buckle clanging as it landed on the granite slab. Dan whooped and unbuckled his own belt.

Just do it quickly. Petal grabbed the hem of her ruffled top and dragged it up and over her head, shaking her hair as she threw the top aside so that her bob would fall back into its smooth shape again.

She wasn't wearing a bra. God knew, she didn't need to. And though she wouldn't want to be as big all over as Tas, Petal did flash back for a moment on the fuchsia lace of Tas's bra, so clearly on display, and had a rush of envy for how good her friend's 36DD boobs had looked.

Warily, she met Dan's eyes. She wasn't an idiot; she knew he wasn't expecting C cups to magically pop out from nowhere. Still, she was bracing herself against any disappointment, any expression that said, You're joking! Is that it?

But as she looked into his grey eyes, her heart stopped for a brief moment. His mouth was open, his gaze was misty. His Adam's apple bobbed as he swallowed hard.

'You're so *beautiful*,' he breathed.

Petal felt her entire body grow warm under his stare of admiration. It was so blatant, so unabashedly appreciative, that she blossomed, the remnants of insecurity about her flat chest falling away like dried-up husks, with herself fresh and smooth and pretty at the centre, and a really cute boy staring at her as if he wanted to eat her up with a spoon.

'Tell me something I *don't* know,' she said saucily, grabbing the waistbands of her mini, tights and knickers and pulling them all down in one fell swoop, kicking off her cowboy boots, wadding her discarded clothes up into a ball and punting them across the bathroom, onto the granite floor between the two glass screens of the wetroom area. 'Well?' she taunted, hands on her bare hips. 'What are you waiting for?'

Then she screamed as Dan picked her up by the waist, swung her in the air, and dumped her into the swirling bath water. He stripped down in a few seconds, his boots dragged off, the buttons of his jeans fly hitting metallically against the bidet as he discarded them in a frantic rush of excitement.

'Aww,' Petal cooed as he vaulted into the bath. She reached between his legs, gripping his penis, making him groan with pleasure. 'You got me a present! That's so sweet of you!'

'Sit on my lap and I can give it to you properly,' he said eagerly, grabbing her round the waist, trying to pull her onto his cock.

'No, I want to suck you off,' Petal said, resisting. 'I said I was going to, didn't I?'

'No, I want you to fuck me! Come on, pet, sit on me cock. I've been busting to fuck you for hours and hours now. I swear I'll pull out in time . . .'

He looked so handsome that Petal wrapped her arms around his neck and slid her tongue into his mouth, wriggling around, feeling the tip of his cock bobbing eagerly under her. Dan seized his opportunity; he grabbed her waist, lifting her a little, sliding one hand to his penis and directing it just where he wanted it, gasping with excitement, moaning: 'Oh, fuck, *yeah*, that's it, that's fucking *it*!' as his hard cock edged its way inside her, moving gently, nervous of going too far, too fast.

'I'll suck you off later, OK?' Petal said, pulling back a little.

They were both wet from head to toe now, the splashing water jets drenching them as they writhed around.

'Yeah, thanks, that'd be great,' Dan mumbled, so overwhelmed with sensation he was barely able to get a word out.

'I give *really* good blow jobs,' Petal assured him, grabbing hold of the edges of the tub, using the leverage to twist and wriggle herself further down on top of him, taking more of him inside her, feeling his hips jerking frantically as he responded to her encouragement.

He reached out and stroked her nipples, making her sigh with pleasure; her nipples were very sensitive, maybe because her breasts were so small.

'Your tits are so pretty,' Dan said, picking up handfuls of bubbles and rubbing them over her breasts. 'They're so pretty and perfect, like two little mouthfuls . . .'

He pulled her towards him, his lips closing over one of them as she writhed on top of him, so flooded with delight and so flattered by his compliments that she broke a usually iron-clad rule about her having to come first, and offered generously: 'Go on, you can come. You got me off already, and I know you want to.'

'*Really?*' he got out.

Petal smiled. 'Yeah, go on then,' she said nobly, feeling him already bucking beneath her, his thighs pumping, barely able to maintain the last remnants of his self-control.

Dan was beyond words. He threw his head back, gasping, his eyes closing, as Petal pulled up off him, wriggling her knees up the sides of the bath to get enough purchase, reaching forward to take hold of him just as he started to come, his arms draped over the sides of the bath, his hips thrusting upwards. The water was so warm that Petal, her hands wrapped around the tip of his penis, couldn't actually sense his rush of heat as he exploded between her fingers. But she could feel his spasms, hear him groaning, as the bath bubbled all around them and his come mingled with the bubbles pumping up to the surface.

Dan's eyelids fluttered open again, and he stared dazedly at Petal.

'You're *amazing*,' he mumbled blissfully.

You're amazing, Petal thought, remembering him kissing her breasts. I just really, *really* hope you don't know who my dad is. I really hope no one told you by now. I want to think you like me just for myself, flat chest and all . . .

Skye

Skye raised her head, slowly and cautiously, and squinted her eyes open a crack. It hurt as badly as if someone were squirting bleach through the chinks. Trying not to moan aloud with pain, she wriggled up into a sitting position. As she opened her eyes fully, the sunlight, flooding in because she hadn't drawn the drapes the night before, scorched her retinas.

We did it again. We fucking went and did it again. After we promised each other we wouldn't.

The display on her bedside clock, bright red numbers flashing mockingly at her, told her that it was just past noon. Swinging her legs over the side of the bed, Skye sat for a while, head down, fighting the waves of nausea that were threatening to rise dangerously up to her throat. The sunlight didn't help. The apartment was on the fifth floor, high up enough in this low-rise part of Hell's Kitchen so it got excellent morning light. It wasn't ideal for a girl who worked night shifts: she'd had to buy blackout drapes.

And now my head hurts too much for me to even reach out and draw them. Fuck it.

Anyway, her priority was to get to the bathroom. Eventually, she pushed herself unsteadily to her feet.

I'm still drunk. Tequila shots till dawn, for fuck's sake? What was I thinking? Oh, that's right! I was letting the blow do my thinking for me! And it always makes such good decisions!

The apartment was trashed. Skye didn't even dare to glance sideways into the kitchen as she passed down the corridor. She could tell from the sour odour in the bathroom that someone had upchucked in the toilet, but at least they'd flushed it. Skye rinsed out a discarded glass, took two Advils and washed them down with two glassfuls of water from the tap. A good five minutes later, just as she was beginning to think she was OK, which meant she wasn't going to puke her guts up, she heard someone stagger down the corridor and push open the door that Skye hadn't bothered to latch.

'Why didn't you *stop* me?' Jada moaned.

Jada looked like hell. She was wearing the jacket of her favourite Victoria's Secret flannel pyjamas, lime green printed with pink strawberries, and her long shapely legs, emerging from the short jacket hem, were as stunning as ever. At the neck, it was a different story: the bright green, which usually suited her rich dark skin, was a scary contrast with the ashy grey tint of her face. The whites of her eyes were red and inflamed, and the bags under her eyes were puffed out like a frog's.

She slumped against the chipped paint of the door jamb, staring reproachfully at Skye.

'Why didn't *you* stop *me*?' Skye retorted.

'At least you don't have to see yours again!' Jada complained. 'I just keep pulling the same old shit, over and over. It's like a dog going back to its own vomit.'

Skye's stomach churned ominously. 'Could you *please* not use that word?' she begged, pressing both her hands to her stomach as if that would somehow keep her from puking.

'I need to pee,' Jada said. 'You're going to have to move.'

Staggering to the side of the bath as Jada sat on the toilet, Skye began to replay the events of the night before. She and Jada had got through plenty of blow at the Midnight Lounge – of course they had, that was the trouble with blow. They'd partied and danced till four a.m., closing time, and then, naturally, they'd been all ramped up and no way ready to crash, so they'd had a few more drinks and lines at the Lounge with DeVaughan, and then they'd—

'Oh, *no*.'

Skye had just realized what Jada was talking about. Not the blow, though they'd said they were cutting back on that too. No, Jada meant DeVaughan. He'd come back to their apartment, picking up a bottle of tequila on the way, and that only meant one thing. Well, two, if you counted the tequila shots with champagne floats. But basically, it meant that Jada and DeVaughan had hooked up again.

'You did DeVaughan?'

Jada nodded gloomily. 'It's not going anywhere, so what the hell am I doing?' she sighed. 'The man's a damn *bouncer*! That's never going to get me out of this dump!'

It *was* a dump, no question about it. The irony was, a lot of people would have killed for their midtown apartment. It was rent-stabilized, which meant the landlord couldn't raise the rent more than four per cent a year, and it was a proper two-bedroom, which meant that both Skye and Jada had their own rooms with doors that closed – neither of them had to sleep in a walk-through corridor in a railroad-style apartment.

But it was still a dump. Because the whole building was rent-stabilized, the landlord, resentful at not making a market rent off his tenants, did the bare minimum of repairs. The plaster ceilings were crumbling so badly that sometimes chunks would fall on them while they were sleeping. They had to throw bottlefuls of Liquid-Plumr down the bath and sink every week to get them to drain. The Formica of the kitchen worktops was patterned with mould. Jada and Skye's bedrooms were barely large enough for a bed and a cupboard, and they'd only managed to turn the kitchen into a sitting room by disconnecting the cooker and putting a piece of plywood over it to use it as a table instead. They lived off takeout food, which they reheated in the microwave.

The kicker was, they paid eight hundred dollars a month each for the privilege of living there, and they could have sublet it instantly for double that sum. Girls at the Lounge commuted in from Bay Ridge, Forest Hills, Harlem, and Bushwick: Jada and Skye were envied by everyone for having had the luck to snag this place a few years ago through a friend of Skye's mom, who knew the building super.

And sometimes, they'd get drunk and do blow to stay out as long as possible, just to avoid having to come back to it.

'I need a sugar daddy,' Jada continued, 'not some guy who makes less than I do!' She flushed the toilet, stood up, and stared at herself in the mirror. 'Ugh, I should have shares in Visine, the amount I go through,' she said, reaching for her eyedrops.

'Is DeVaughan still here?' Skye looked down at the slip she'd pulled on; it was barely long enough to cover her ass. It wasn't like he hadn't seen her prancing round the Midnight Lounge with even less on, but she'd at least like to put on some panties if there was a guy in the apartment.

'DeVaughan isn't. But your guy is,' Jada said, tilting back her head and squirting half a bottle of Visine into each eyeball.

'*My* guy?' Skye's stomach turned over again.

'Oh, come *on*. You don't remember? Go check out the kitchen couch!'

There was nothing in life Skye wanted to do less. She'd have given a great deal to go back to her bedroom, pull on some sweats, and sneak out for coffee. But it was like the horror movies they loved: when you knew some really gruesome murder was coming, no way you didn't peek at the screen to see the gory details. Even though she knew she'd regret it, she just *had* to see what was on the damn couch.

At first sight, it could have been worse. Even sprawled there, snoring lightly, his mouth sagging open, he was pretty cute. He was white, with short, spiky hair, and the sunlight, pouring in through the grimy windows, glinted off his multiple piercings. Early twenties, tops, with a flat belly and muscled bare thighs, he was in really good shape. Layered T-shirts had ridden up his torso, but thank God he had dragged on his boxers. No one wanted to see a strange man's junk first thing in the morning. And, in a heap on the floor next to him, instead of jeans or combat pants, were black leggings that looked almost like tights . . .

Oh *God*. They weren't leggings. They were cycle tights.

He was a bike messenger.

And that was the last piece of information Skye needed to open the lock and have all the sordid, stupid, self-destructive, *dumb-ass shit* she'd got up to last night, or rather, this morning, come flooding back in one horrible rush of memory.

Stumbling down 46th Street, DeVaughan in the middle, she and Jada hanging off his enormous arms, a bottle of tequila dangling from one of his hands, champagne in the other; emptying the plastic Baggie of coke onto a mirror placed flat on the kitchen 'table', and moaning aloud at how little there was left; DeVaughan, seeing his chance to get with Jada evaporating, calling up a dealer he knew to get a delivery made; Skye, buzzing in the delivery guy, pulling money out of her bra to pay for the blow, and flirting with him, automatically, to try to get the price down . . .

Well, she'd gone a little further with *that* than she'd intended.

She remembered pushing him onto one of the kitchen chairs, sitting on his lap; his hands on her ass, his eyes wide with excitement and shock, unable to believe he'd stumbled into a stripper party, trying to turn his head so he could watch Jada and DeVaughan taking it in turns to do body shots off each other on the couch . . .

Jesus. She hadn't actually fucked him. Or had she? Jada and DeVaughan had eventually headed off to Jada's room, and Skye had turned up the stereo to drown them out. Ugh. Mrs Chen from downstairs would be on the warpath today, all the noise they'd made. She and Bike Boy had fooled around, yeah, but surely he'd be in bed with her if they'd fucked? And surely he wouldn't still have his clothes on?

'We in trouble?' she called to Jada over her shoulder. ''Cause of him not getting back to blow headquarters last night with the money?'

'Nah.' Jada shuffled down the corridor, having slipped on the big green fluffy slippers that matched her PJs. 'DeVaughan rang the guy before we crashed. Said we'd send him back this morning. DeVaughan said the guy thought it was pretty funny, actually. He was laughing his ass off. Said every guy deserves one free night with a drunken stripper.' She yawned, long and deep.

Skye stood there, staring down at the guy on the couch. The bright sunlight had ceased to bother her, and that was only partially because the Advil had kicked in. She had something much bigger to worry about. Not the guy in front of her, his lip ring wobbling slightly every time he blew air out of his mouth; he was just a symptom, not the problem itself.

This is my life. Getting toasted with my best friend, doing bouncers and delivery boys. This is so not where I want to be.

But the real shitter is, I've got no idea where I do want to be. Or how to get there.

Her phone rang. She was in no mood to talk to anyone, so she didn't answer it, just stood and watched her bag vibrate wildly with the ringing of her phone. It stopped, and after a few seconds she expected the beep that said a message had been left on her voice-mail: but no. It just started ringing again. Muttering curses under her breath, Skye cracked and lunged for her bag. The number wasn't showing up on Caller ID, but that meant nothing.

'Yeah?' she said crossly.

'Skye? Skye, baby, this is Lew. From the *National Investigator*.'

Skye's eyebrows rose to the ceiling. 'How did you get hold of my number?'

He chuckled. 'Straight to the chase. I like that. Well, I talked Paulie into giving it to me.'

Skye had thought her eyebrows couldn't go any higher. She'd been wrong. It was unheard of for Paulie, the manager of the Midnight Lounge, to give a dancer's number out to a client. Literally unheard of. It was the first thing they taught you at strip-club-manager school, class 101: *you do not give a dancer's number to anyone*.

'You're *kidding*,' she said dubiously.

'*And* untrusting! Better and better!' Lew sounded happy as Larry; Skye couldn't imagine why. 'You wouldn't believe what I had to promise him. I need to talk to you, babe. I got an offer for you I think you're going to like.'

Skye opened her mouth, but Lew was way ahead of her.

'Don't worry. You don't gotta do me, and you don't gotta do Kevin. You don't gotta do *anyone* you don't wanna.' He chortled to himself, in what was clearly some private joke he found very amusing. 'All you gotta do is let me and Kevin take you out for a drink this evening, OK? You name the place and time, we'll bring our credit cards.'

'And Paulie knows I'm meeting you?' Skye was wary. 'I'm not supposed to see clients out of the Lounge. I could get the sack for that.'

'Don't worry, babe. You call Paulie and check it out. It's all legit. Why don't we set a time and place now?'

Skye thought quickly. He probably assumed she'd pick the kind of expensive, flashy place that a stripper would be expected to go for, something in the Meatpacking District: the Buddha Bar, Lotus, a bar where the bridge and tunnellers would go because it cost a ton of money and they thought that meant quality. Well, she wasn't going to fall into that kind of trap.

'The Cellar Bar at the Bryant Park Hotel,' she said instead, naming somewhere she'd seen mentioned on page six of the *New York Post* – some hip young movie director had been hanging out there with his equally trendy singer girlfriend. 'Seven tonight.'

Lew whistled down the phone. 'Classy choice!' he said. 'It's going to be a pleasure doing business with you.'

'What was that?' Jada asked, unselfconsciously lifting up her pyjama jacket to scratch her muscled stomach.

The springs of the old couch groaned as Skye's love interest of the night before stirred, groaning as he sat up, rubbing the sleep out of his eyes. The first thing he saw was Jada, her PJ jacket pulled up just below her breasts, her entire stomach above her hipster panties bare, and his eyes bugged out as he fixated on the sight.

'What're *you* looking at?' she said amiably enough, still scratching her stomach as if he weren't even in the room. 'Come on, lover boy, the party's over. Time to get back on your bike.'

'You better tell us how much we owe you,' Skye said.

Not fully awake yet, he blinked, madly trying to work out what she meant.

'Yeah, you were so good in bed we wanna pay you for it,' Jada added, deadpan, and then the two girls burst out laughing at the expression of incredulity on his face.

'Oh boy, that was *totally worth* making my head hurt all over again!' Skye giggled, clutching her skull.

But this still sucks, her headache told her. *You still just spent a ton of money on blow last night and fooled around with the bike messenger, for fuck's sake. You live in a dump and you get wasted most nights and wake up with me pounding nails into your brain. You're not saving a cent, you've got no health plan, and last night some guy put his finger up you and scratched you for kicks.*

Your life is shit, Skye. You better fix it soon.

One of the big plusses to being an exotic dancer was that your costumes didn't take up any room at all in your handbag. The pale blue sequined Lycra hotpants and halter top that Skye was planning to wear that night folded up so small that she could easily fit them in her best bag, an oversized Dolce and Gabbana clutch on which she'd blown way too much money just a couple of weeks ago. Still, its shiny black patent was totally current, the gold D&G clasp was nice and big, so you could see even across the room who the bag was by, and it felt really expensive. After all, if you were going to spend thousands of bucks on a bag (Skye shivered briefly at the memory of exactly how much she'd paid) it should damn well look and feel as if you had.

Skye was assuming that Lew wanted to pick her brains about gossip on the celebrities who came into the Midnight Lounge. That was more than OK with her. Exotic dancers didn't exactly have a culture of kissing and not telling. The *National Investigator* would have had trouble filling its pages without all its stories about guys making out with strippers: Kiefer Sutherland, Ben Affleck, Joe Jeffreys . . .

So, although it was weird that Paulie had given her number to Lew, Skye didn't waste any time on speculating about other reasons he and Kevin might want to have a drink with her. What she *had* been determined to do was to dress as classily as possible. She knew exactly what everyone's image was of an off-duty exotic dancer, and she had to admit, when people pictured a girl caked in makeup, dyed hair scraped back into a tight ponytail, wearing Juicy Couture sweatpants and a T-shirt straining over her artificially inflated breasts, ninety-nine per cent of the time they'd be right on the money.

She'd noticed the way Kevin-from-the-LA-office looked at her last night; not dismissively, but as if he'd met girls like her a million times before and knew exactly what to expect. Well, if there was one thing Skye hated, it was being taken for granted. When she emerged from her bedroom, ready to go out, Jada whistled, long and slow.

'Honey,' she said admiringly, 'it ain't you, but it looks damn fine.'

Maybe it *is* me, though, Skye thought, catching a glimpse of herself in the mirrored lobby of the Bryant Park Hotel. Just a different me. Someone who looks like she belongs in a place like this – here in her own right, not just visiting to party with some rock star.

New York girls – classy Manhattan girls – were all about the subtle approach. They wore as much makeup as a stripper did, and spent the same amount of time applying it, but their aim was to look, not shiny and plastic, but invisibly, exquisitely groomed. It was a hell of a lot of work. Skye had spent half the time just blending stuff in. No bright colours at all: if Bobbi Brown didn't make it, Skye didn't have it on her face. Mocha, peach, caramel, dark brown mascara. Her hair was coiled into a chignon at the back of her head, just a couple of loose blonde strands artfully working their way free, so it looked as if she'd just twisted it up and pinned it in a couple of minutes, rather than spent half an hour with a ceramic straightener and a box of hairgrips. She was dressed all in black, of course, purchased at the boutiques on West Broadway that were her major stamping ground.

Lovely pieces, all of them. She had just never put them together before. The shantung Alice + Olivia cigarette pants were usually worn with a tight T-shirt, and the fine silk knit sweater, caught elegantly round her slim hips with a wide laser-cut suede belt, was normally thrown over a sky-high mini. Her only jewellery was a silver Tiffany chain necklace, the classic Paloma Picasso design with a big central clasp. Her butter-soft suede wedges, from Otto Tootsi Plohound, were a mere three inches high – definitely not the spikes you'd expect an exotic dancer to flaunt.

Skye might not have a savings account or health insurance, but she had some *really* sharp investment dressing.

As she passed through the lobby and down to the bar, male heads turned, as always. But their glances were completely different from the way they'd have looked at her in her itsy-bitsy blue hot-pants outfit in the Midnight Lounge. Now, the way they checked her out was downright respectful. Appreciative, sure, but it was the appreciation a man gave to a woman he saw as girlfriend, even wife, material. Skye dressed in her hooker gear was arm candy, a toy to play with. Skye dressed up in her chic black and her Tiffany was nothing short of trophy-wife potential.

Kevin didn't even recognize her as she rounded one of the uplit vaulted pillars of the cellar bar and approached the high table where he and Lew were sitting. It was Lew who jumped up and pulled out the padded bar stool for her, a gentlemanly courtesy he would never have paid to exotic dancer Skye.

'Baby, you clean up *really* nice,' he said, grinning a wide-as-watermelon smile. 'Kevin? See? Was I right about this one, or was I right?'

Kevin's eyebrows had practically disappeared into his hairline.

'Boy, oh boy,' he said, as Skye hopped up on the stool, crossing her legs demurely, and flashed him her best smile. 'Now this is what I call versatile.'

'Skye, honey, why don't you order yourself a drink?' Lew gestured to a waiter, who glided forward smoothly.

'I'll have a mojito,' Skye said. Mojitos were always safe; they were above fashion. She knew better than to pick something like a Cosmo or an apple martini. Only out-of-towners went for those now.

'So I'm going to let Kevin do the talking,' Lew said, grinning, as the waiter disappeared. 'This is his baby. He's come up with an idea so sleazy even *I* was shocked by it.' Lew's eyes gleamed behind the thick lenses of his glasses. 'He looks all clean cut and Boy Scoutish, but I tell you, he's got a mind as dirty as a fucking tar pit.'

'Skye,' Kevin began, leaning forward, 'I *was* going to start by asking you if you really see yourself as an exotic dancer, longer term, but I can see already that I don't need to go there. Look at you.' He gestured at her. 'The way you're dressed, the way you're presenting yourself. Picking this bar as a rendezvous. You've answered the question already.'

Skye gave him her best smile and waited for him to continue.

'I have an undercover investigation I'm setting up,' Kevin continued. 'And I need a very . . . *specific* kind of operative to help me with it. And it has to be a female. We've got women journalists on the *Investigator*, of course, but none of them –' he exchanged a smile with Lew – 'none of them exactly have the attributes we're looking for.'

He wasn't looking at her breasts when he said that: Skye gave him points. She actually wished she hadn't had any work done on them at all. She'd gone up from a B to a D cup, and though there weren't any scars – the surgeon had gone in through her bellybutton – you heard so many horror stories at a strip club about implants going wrong that she really just wanted to take them out now and have done with it. Right now she was wearing a minimizer bra, which she always needed when she wanted to look classy. It was nuts. She should just have bought some padded bras for work and saved the plastic surgery fee.

'You mean they're not blondes with boob jobs?' she asked sweetly, as the waiter returned with her mojito.

She'd wanted to see if she could embarrass Kevin, who seemed so poised, but he was made of much tougher stuff than her usual Midnight Lounge client.

He just smiled, as if he saw exactly what she was trying to do, and responded: 'I mean there's no way they could pass for an exotic dancer.' His expression grew completely serious. 'This is something we've never tried before. I need a girl with your kind of beauty and brains. And believe me, that's much harder to find than you'd think. Lew said you were sharp as a whip, and I think he might just be right.'

'And the boob job doesn't hurt,' Lew said cheerfully, winking at Skye. 'So? How about it? You wanna hear the rest?'

'Can't wait,' she said, smiling back.

Petal

Petal was on a collision course with something, something big and scary with a lot of pointed edges. She could feel it in the dark, waiting for her, ready to cut her into pieces when she made the last in a series of very wrong moves and smashed right into it.

But she couldn't stop for the life of her. She was going way too fast, and her brakes had broken. In retrospect, they had broken the night she picked up Dan Drummond, the night she'd realized she'd met a boy who she actually really liked, one who seemed to like her back. Dan had everything: a cool career, drop-dead-gorgeous looks, and a total enthusiasm for her that was unlike anything she'd met before.

She'd watched him like a hawk when she threw out casually the revelation that her dad was Gold, the world-famous rock star, and though his eyes had widened in awe, all he had said was: 'Well, no wonder you walk around like you own the world, eh, pet?'

Which, although it had annoyed the fuck out of her initially, had actually, when she thought about it, been a huge relief. A boy who was teasing her about having a sense of entitlement as big as the Grand Canyon wasn't simultaneously going to suck up to her madly for the chance to play on Gold's new album or write a song for him, like so many of his would-be predecessors had done.

If anything, Dan seemed a bit intimidated by her status as rock-star royalty, second generation. They were photographed together endlessly, the media falling over themselves to anoint them as a couple. In and out of nightclubs; at secret gigs; partying with real royalty at the posh clubs in Kensington, for a laugh, where braying rich brats with titles wearing rugby shirts were way more impressed with them than any cool club kid in Hoxton. They leaned against each other, thin as rails, pouting sulkily, as if bored with the world.

'He's such a *sweetie*,' JC drawled, as he was dying Petal's hair the daffodil yellow he'd promised. 'And so *gorgeous*! Honestly, are you *sure* he's not even a little bit gay?'

'Well, he fancies me,' Petal said, pulling a face, eternally obsessed about her lack of tits. 'I mean, I'm not exactly a porn star . . .'

'Turn you over, you're almost like the real thing!' JC giggled. 'I was going out with a posh boy once, he'd been to university at Cambridge and everything, and he said there was a tutor there who was a raging queen and that's what he'd say about the skinny girls. "Turn her over, she's almost like the real thing!" Can you *imagine*?' He sighed. 'I had to dump him in the end. He was totally fucked up. All the posh boys are, really. I blame public school.'

He finished wrapping Petal's head in silver foil.

'Right, that's forty minutes,' he said, setting the timer he'd brought. 'And then you'll be all fresh and new. Is Tas coming round to do your makeup?'

Petal started to nod, then stopped, nervous of shifting the paste and foil on her head.

'She said she wanted to work out a new look for me now you've done this whole freaky blonde thing,' she told JC.

'Oh, fantastic.' He beamed. '*Tons* of press tonight. You'll get into all the daily freebies, plus *Heat*, *Grazia*, all the celeb websites . . .'

JC and Tas did Petal's hair, makeup and styling for free, but the perks for them were huge. The sheer volume of free stuff that was sent to Petal – hoping she would wear the clothes or the bags or the jewellery or the shoes, mention the perfumes, travel to the luxury resorts – was gigantic, and JC and Tas got to plunder the goodie pile at will.

But the main benefit to them was that Petal was their canvas, their walking advertisement of their creativity to the world. If Petal's new haircut and colour was deemed a success, JC would book advertising campaigns, be tapped by haircare companies to advise on new products, be seen as a celebrity hairstylist who had his finger firmly on the pulse of what the youth of today wanted.

And it was the same for Tas, who was desperate to be a stylist in her own right and break free of assistant jobs. With Petal, Tas could show the world that she could dress an It girl to perfection, find the latest trendy designers before anyone else had heard of them, prove her credentials in photos that would be on the web for everyone to see.

'Ooh, look! A houseboat! You have the *coolest* place!'

JC was on the balcony, staring down at a boat chugging by on the Regent's Canal below. Petal's father had bought her a two-bedroom flat in Camden when she passed her A levels; Camden incarnated scruffy chic. The flat, in a building that jutted out to the side of the canal like the prow of a boat, had a wraparound balcony that ran its full length, culminating in a terrace at the tip where Petal loved to gather her inner circle to sit and drink before heading out for the evening.

JC swung round to face her, resting his arms along the balcony, his green-tipped asymmetric fringe of hair swinging over his face and coming to rest along the right side, just as he'd styled it to do.

'I'm dumping Rudy,' he announced gloomily, in one of the sudden mood swings with which Petal was all too familiar.

'Really? Why?' Petal didn't really care about JC's latest fling; they never lasted longer than a few months.

'He's a little starfucker,' JC informed her. 'It wasn't about me, it was all the famous people he might meet. You know?' He sighed gustily. 'I'm not saying we had to stay in every night and watch TV like boring *marrieds*. But he *barely* wanted to be alone with me. Apart from fucking, of course. The rest of the time he was doing his makeup and asking what new hot club we were going to tonight and who was going to be there? I mean, I picked him up at *Starbucks*. This was all the biggest thrill of his life. But he shouldn't have made it so clear he was only with me for the celebs, you know?'

Petal pulled as much of a face as she could. 'I'm sorry, JC,' she said.

'Yeah.' He sighed again. 'I know. It's tricky, isn't it? I mean, at least you and Dan, he's got his own thing too. If KillBuzz keep going like this, they're going to be *huge*. You're so lucky. I mean, he's not just in it because of your daddy or your famous friends.'

Petal winced.

'Sometimes I'm scared it's the other way round,' she admitted frankly. 'That I'm sort of tagging onto him, you know? I mean, what do I actually *do*?'

JC's carefully lined eyes widened in shock and horror. He pushed off the balcony and came back into the huge open-plan living space where Petal was sitting at the kitchen counter, the foil on her head matching the entire chrome-and-steel décor of the room so perfectly it might have been a fashion shot.

'Petal! You have a column in *Downtown*! You did that Secret Agent campaign last year! Accessorize wants you to do a limited-edition handbag line for them . . . and didn't Rimmel want to name a lipstick after you?'

'I keep missing the appointments,' Petal confessed. The foil rustled as she ducked her head in shame. 'I was talking to this agent woman who wanted to take me on, but I've been caning it so much lately I just wake up feeling like shit and take something to make me go back to sleep, and then it's five or something and I've missed going in to see the Accessorize and the Rimmel people, and I get too embarrassed to ring them up and schedule a new appointment—'

'*Petal!*' JC was horrified. 'This isn't all fun and games, you know! Your dad may be famous, but if you don't do stuff on your own, people will burn out on you after a while!'

It was more truth than Petal could handle. She bridled angrily.

Luckily for JC, the entryphone buzzed just then, and he hurried to cross the wide expanse of shiny wooden floor to admit Tas from the little vestibule.

As soon as he was out of sight, Petal jumped up, went to the fridge and pulled a bottle of Absolut Pear out of the freezer, pouring herself a long slug in a heavy tumbler. JC would lecture her about starting to drink this early if he realized; it was only five. With any luck, he'd think this was a glass of water. She drank some down, a warm hazy rush flooding through her immediately at the perfumed taste of the spirit; it was like an alcoholic version of Appletiser. Immediately, her anxiety about the missed Accessorize and Rimmel appointments, her insecurity about whether she really had enough to keep Dan interested in her, ebbed away.

I'm Petal Gold, she told herself. Everyone knows my name and my face. I can get into any club I want. My spare bedroom's piled with freebies I haven't even opened yet, I'm going out with one of the coolest guys in London, and, unlike JC and Tas, I don't have to work for a living, 'cause I've got a ginormous trust fund and this amazing flat . . .

'Hey, Tas!' she said brightly, taking another drink of her vodka as her friend stormed into the room, her big makeup box slung under one arm.

'What's all this about not going to your Accessorize appointment?' Tas said bluntly. 'You've got to do that stuff, man! It's for all of us, you know, not just you! It's to make us all famous, yeah? That's the fucking *point*!'

Petal set her glass down, empty, and pushed it discreetly to the side of the chrome bar. Alcohol lent her tongue wings. She said smoothly: 'Chill, Tas. I was just waiting till I got this new hair colour. I'm going to walk in there with my yellow hair and my fab clothes and they'll be totally blown away and give me my own campaign. And they'll hire you to do a limited edition set of colours, and L'Oréal will get JC to do their latest look-book, and we'll all be rolling in it!'

'Whee!' JC said, clapping his hands happily. 'I can't *wait*! Let's rinse your hair, sweetie!'

'Do you think Dan'll like it?' Petal stopped momentarily, suddenly nervous again.

'Of course he will,' Tas said, rolling her eyes.

'Who cares if he doesn't?' JC said, pulling up a kitchen chair in front of the sink for her to sit on. 'Straight boys! What do they know?'

I really want Dan to like it, Petal thought, crossing her fingers tightly so that neither of her friends could see. I'm always nervous he'll realize how many other girls are prettier than me. After all, if KillBuzz get really big, he could have anyone he wants. What if he wakes up and realizes that I'm just Gold's skinny little daughter with bright yellow hair, not pretty enough or talented enough to be famous on my own? All I can do is get dressed up and act outrageously so the paps'll take pictures of me . . .

JC tipped her head back and started pouring jugfuls of water on her scalp, cooing to himself at how well the colour had come out.

Now I've talked myself into a total confidence downer. I'm going to have to get *so* tanked up to cope with tonight, Petal thought gloomily. She reached her hand down to her hip, where a wrap of coke – three grams – sat plumply in that little extra jeans pocket which she'd never known what to do with until she'd developed a drug habit.

We'll get through that tonight, no probs. Thank fuck for coke. At least it always makes me feel cool . . .

Amber

'It's bad, Amber,' Jared said in his hoarse smoker's croak. 'I'm not going to piss around here. It's bad.'

'What do you mean?'

'Bad! Bad!' Jared said impatiently. 'What about the word "bad" do you not understand? How many sodding pills did you pop this morning?'

'I . . .' Amber stuttered.

'You need to come into the office,' Jared ordered.

'What, *now*?'

Amber had been watching TV with her mother when Jared rang. They were cosily ensconced in the kitchen, silently sipping diet Lucozade, Slava crocheting lace, happily settled in for the day. Amber had been planning to go for a walk later; she always tried to do a constitutional in Hyde Park for about an hour, stroll around the Serpentine and over the bridges.

'Yeah, now! There's something you need to see!' Jared said impatiently. 'Don't piss around like you usually do, OK? Now means *now*, not three hours' time!'

But that was impossible for Amber, trained since birth by Slava never to leave the house without looking her best. Especially for a meeting with her agent. Her hair had to be straightened, her foundation flawlessly blended, her eyes accented with a careful mix of no fewer than three different pencils in shades of brown, copper and jade, her lips invisibly lined and shined, her body dusted with subtle golden powder. Though she was dressed in the off-duty model's uniform of T-shirt and jeans, there was a polished, European-sexy gloss to her that the British girls didn't have; Slava's old-fashioned, glamorous ideas of what a woman should look like were clearly in evidence. The jeans clung to Amber like stretch leggings, and her T-bar Louboutins were four inches high.

'No point telling you to dress down,' Jared sighed as she entered his office. 'But hey, that's why you're such a success on your dates, I suppose. More on that later.'

At fifty, Jared had had so much plastic surgery that his mother would probably not have recognized him. He certainly didn't look fifty; his skin was as shiny as a stripper's pole, his eyes were unnaturally large due to a series of eyelid tucks, and an implant in his jaw gave it a masculine squareness that contrasted oddly with the rest of his soft, pudgy face.

'Sit,' he said, gesturing to the chair on the other side of his desk. 'And look at this.'

He swivelled the monitor of his computer, a state-of-the-art Apple sitting on the equally white surface of his marble desk. On the screen was an image of Amber from the shoot she had done last week for the swimsuit catalogue. She was wearing a tiny suede bikini and high gold stilettos.

'Your body's perfect,' Jared said. 'And no one cares. Because look at your damn face.'

Reluctantly, Amber's gaze turned to the screen. And despite the cocktail of prescription medicines that kept her calm, she flinched, the leather of the spring-loaded chair creaking as she did so.

Her eyes were dead. There was no denying it, no blaming bad lighting or an incompetent photographer.

Numbly, she heard Jared say: 'Like a fish on a slab with ice packed round it! I had red snapper for lunch today at J Sheekey's that had more life in it than you do!'

Her perfect lips parted, but no words came out. Jared tapped on his mouse and another image of her popped up, this one of her in a snakeskin swimsuit with cut-outs, her head thrown back, curls cascading, hands on her hips. Everything was flawless: her skin, her hair, her features. She had found the light and turned towards it, and on first glance, she looked superb. Until you looked into her eyes – because you always, always looked into a model's eyes – and saw nothing there at all. Just two green voids, blank and empty, as glassy as if she were a reanimated corpse.

'Same again! Look! You look like you're in a coma and they propped you up and took your picture!' Jared said mercilessly. 'How many pills did you pop before the shoot? The only decent photo's in profile, so you can't see your eyes, and you can't make a living being shot only in profile, can you? Did someone tell you it was a Rohypnol chic shoot for *Vogue Italia*?'

He tapped again, closing the image of Amber.

'They're scrapping the whole thing,' he said. 'Booking the whole shoot again. You have any idea how much that costs? It'd've been better if you had cellulite. Or spots. You can't retouch someone not sodding *being there mentally*.' He rested his elbows on the desk, staring hard at Amber. 'They're not paying you, of course. Which means they're not paying me. Which means that you've not only wasted the client's time, but you've wasted mine too.'

'I'm sorry—' Amber began, but Jared waved a small, plump hand, cutting her off.

'Not interested. Not interested in what models have to say at the best of times, definitely not interested in "sorry" when it's too sodding late, OK?'

Amber crossed her legs nervously.

'So now you think I'm going to drop you, right?' Jared predicted. He looked at her almost pityingly. 'Your pictures have been borderline for a while, Amber, you know that. If you were younger I'd say, let's send you off to the Priory and try to sort you out, but that costs a ton, and it's not like you've got a career waiting for you at the end of it to pay off the investment, is it? What are you, twenty-seven?'

Amber nodded wordlessly.

'So forget modelling,' he said frankly. 'That's a dead end for you now. Word gets around, and this is a biggie. No one's going to book you any more. Not for shoots, anyway. But hey, there's still plenty of money to be made. Much more than whatever you could get from modelling at twenty-seven, which, let's face it, is practically *geriatric.*'

He clicked once more, and the screen filled up with an image of Amber, a still from the famous *Sports Illustrated* shoot the DVD of which Tony loved so much. Light in her eyes, a genuine smile on her lips, everything the swimsuit shoot should have been. Years ago, on that Californian beach, Amber had been fully connected with the camera, and it showed.

'*This*,' Jared said complacently, 'is *gold*. I send this to anyone, they're going to want to get with that girl. You still look fantastic, you make yourself up and do your hair like you're in Miss Universe. I got no problems telling anyone that sure, when you turn up, they're going to get the girl in this photo.' He jabbed at the screen for emphasis. 'And you have a great time on your dates, don't you? They take you to the best places, they treat you like a princess?'

Thinking of her recent stay at Bovey Castle, of the matched luggage set Tony had given her, of the compliments he paid her and the care he took to make her happy, Amber nodded again.

'So wouldn't you like more of that?' Jared asked, as if he already knew the answer. 'More trips? More presents? More money?'

'I definitely need to make money,' Amber agreed, thinking of what her and Slava's futures would be like without the kind of income to which they were accustomed. Rent, shopping for clothes, the doctors' bills – Slava did all the bookkeeping, she always had done, but Amber knew their lifestyle couldn't continue without the kind of money a top model could bring in.

'Exactly!' Jared said triumphantly. 'So here's what I'm going to suggest. You go off to Dubai for a week with some other of my girls. All expenses paid, of course. Major, major luxury. You just have to lift a finger and say what you want and they bring it to you on a solid gold tray. And forget what you've been making on your weekend trips. This is the big time. We're talking a good five-figure sum for a girl with your kind of pedigree. Maybe as much as fifty grand. They pay hundreds of thousands for ex-*Baywatch* actresses over there, you know that?'

Amber shook her head, and Jared named a couple of famous names that made her eyes widen.

'So what do you say?' Jared said, fizzing with enthusiasm now. He rubbed his hands together. 'You make money, I make money, you get to lie around a pool in Dubai and work on your tan. Sounds great all round, doesn't it?'

'I suppose so,' Amber said.

But there was enough doubt in her voice to make Jared reach for his BlackBerry, scroll down swiftly and announce: 'There's a model party, tonight, at the St James's hotel behind the Ritz. Penthouse suite, drinks on the terrace from seven. Mara's going – you know Mara, right? She works these things with everything she's got. Drink some champagne, talk to her. She does most of the Dubai trips and she has a great time. Making a fortune, too. I know you're a homebody, but this one you have to go to, OK?'

'OK.' Amber did know Mara, a curvy blonde with enviable energy and *joie de vivre*; she'd feel more confident going to a party if Mara were there to take her under her wing.

'I'd tell you to dress up, but you never need to be told that, do you?' Jared was positively jovial as he stood up to usher Amber out of his office. He looked taller than usual, she noticed. He must have had new lifts made for his shoes.

'And talk to Slava, too,' he said, patting her arm. 'That mother of yours is a sensible woman. She's always had her feet on the ground. She'll know this is best for you both. The logical next step in your career.' He smiled at her, his teeth a marvel of modern dentistry. 'I've got a few girls going out to Dubai in a fortnight. Jumeirah, private beach, business-class flights with Emirates, nothing but the best. Mara's ticket's booked already. You'll have a blast.'

Jared tilted his head back, looking up at her, his eyes focused on her tawny mane of hair.

'And, Amber? Next time you're at Nicky Clarke's, get more of those blonde streaks done, why don't you? You could lighten up the whole head too, while you're about it,' he said thoughtfully. 'Middle Eastern clients, they can't get enough of the blondes . . .'

From the penthouse terrace of the St James's Hotel and Club, tucked away in an elegant Mayfair cul-de-sac just behind the Ritz, most of London's major landmarks could be seen: the London Eye, the dome of St Paul's, even the black glittering Gherkin building. There was a well-stocked bar set up on the terrace, and a series of bar tables on which exquisitely dressed, reed-slender models and men in very expensive suits were propping their champagne flutes. Amber, who had just emerged from the plush, grey-suede-uphol-stered suite inside, stopped on the narrow walkway to the terrace, taking in the scene. She scanned the guests, looking for Mara; Amber didn't have the confidence to walk into a party where she didn't know at least one person.

'Foie gras foam, miss?'

A waiter brushed past Amber as she stood there, proffering a tray on which stood several narrow shot glasses, each filled with dark pink purée beneath a white bubbly cloud of foam. Slender silver spoons stood in each glass. It looked so pretty that Amber was actually tempted, before she remembered that she never ate at parties, for fear of messing up her makeup. Slava had trained her well; Amber put grooming at much higher a priority than her appetite.

She shook her head reluctantly to the waiter, who moved past her onto the terrace. As a group of people at a bar table turned to survey what he was offering, Amber caught sight of Mara with great relief. It took her a few seconds to realize why she hadn't immediately recognized Mara: Mara had always been a curvy blonde girl, but now those two adjectives were all you would ever need to describe her. She was no longer a sample size; she must be an

English ten, at least. It was a girlfriend body, rather than a model one. Her light-blonde hair was now a bright gold which would be considered too shiny for anything but an Italian TV presenter. It was as if Mara had turned up the volume on her appearance to make sure that no one could fail to notice her. And her dress – a leopard-skin-and-cappuccino print chiffon Uli Herzner dress whose layers fluttered wildly in the breeze – was the perfect final touch, a daring split up the side seeming to risk exposure of an entire long, tanned leg at any moment.

Sensing someone looking at her, Mara turned, spotted Amber and waved.

'Amber! Hi!'

And at once, all the attention was on Mara, who had skilfully positioned herself by the edge of the balcony, knowing exactly how her dress would blow and cling to her figure to show it off seductively. Amber pegged her chin to the perfect angle, covering the short distance down the walkway to Mara with such catwalk poise that a couple of men sighed 'Wow' in unison.

Amber's dress was Dolce and Gabbana. It nipped in her waist, gathered over her hips, and lifted her breasts onto a cupped-out balcony, a little shelf presenting them to viewers. It was natural for Amber to be dressed-up, natural for her to be looked at; she felt totally confident with her appearance, and it showed.

Mara exclaimed happily: 'Sweetie, you look fabulous!' Expertly, Mara had turned away from the group of men she was talking to, leaning one arm along the balcony, posing so everyone could see her and Amber, watch how the breeze lifted their hair, but not hear their conversation. '*So*,' she continued excitedly, 'I hear you're coming on the party plane to Dubai! We're going to have a brilliant time!'

'Really?' Amber's spirits rose at Mara's enthusiasm.

'God, yeah!' Mara's baby-blue eyes widened. She'd always been a very pretty girl, too pretty for full-on high-fashion modelling, which needed a stronger bone structure than Mara's rounded features. But it meant that she looked much younger than twenty-nine, her real age; she could easily pass for twenty-four or -five. Which, in their industry, was a huge benefit.

'Jared said you wanted to know what it was like,' Mara continued. 'Well, it's fantastic over there. Like a big tap just pouring out champagne and diamonds all over you. Everything's the best of the best. Private beaches, waterfalls at the villa, massages and beauty treatment whenever you want. *And* you get fabulous pressies to bring home with you that Jared doesn't take a cut of.' She winked. 'I can help you sell anything on afterwards. I know a great dealer who'll give you a good price. I mean, it's lovely to get sapphires the exact colour of your eyes, but I'd rather have the cash value to invest, wouldn't you?'

She read a certain blankness in Amber's expression, and interpreted it correctly.

'*And* I'll put you in touch with a good investment advisor, OK?' she added helpfully. 'Looks like you need one!'

'I'm not very good at being businesslike,' Amber confessed.

'Oh, I'm not that great either,' Mara said, patting Amber's arm. 'But I take good advice, that's the trick. We'll hang out in Dubai and I'll spill my whole bag of tricks, shall I? I mean, let's face it, we've only got a few years left – I want a nice portfolio and some good buy-to-let investments by the time no one wants to fly me around the world to party with them, don't you?'

She flashed Amber a big smile, and Amber found herself smiling back with equal warmth. There was something very endearing about Mara; Amber had always liked her when they'd found themselves on the same ad shoots together, but Amber had never been that good at making friends: she had no experience of childhood friendships to take into adult life. And Slava had never encouraged her daughter to work at befriending other girls, feeling that they would interfere with her closeness with Amber.

'I'm looking forward to it,' Amber said. She blushed a little, a faint pink tinting her perfect cheekbones. 'Having a bit of a holiday with you, I mean. I don't get away with other girls at all, really. It's usually just me and my mother, and she's not that keen on travelling any more.'

Mara's smile ebbed for a moment. Amber hoped she hadn't sounded too needy.

'Hey, enough girl talk!' called one of the guys from Mara's table. 'We've got a bottle of Dom here that needs drinking, ladies . . .'

'Hedge-funders,' Mara said out of the corner of her mouth to Amber, 'and a guy who's big in SunSeeker yachts. *Fabulous* party, isn't it?'

Swept up on the wave of Mara's enthusiasm, Amber threw herself into the party with what, for her, was gusto. She drank several glasses of champagne, till she was floating pleasantly on a fuzzy cloud of happiness; she felt as if she were a few feet off the ground, buoyed up on bubbles. The waiters brought some sushi in little china spoons, which she was able to eat without smudging her lipstick – practically calorie-free yellowtail, so fresh it must have been caught that morning, touched with jalapeno pepper and lime. And the male attention was always fun, especially as she was always surrounded by at least two or three men at any one time.

Every time one man would try to isolate Amber from the group, however, she would smile and slide through his fingers, never letting him succeed; she didn't like that kind of solo attention, didn't know what to do with it. Inevitably, he would ask her more personal questions, want to get to know her, or at least pretend to, and she was never comfortable with a conversation that became more intimate.

Though Amber hadn't quite admitted it to herself, the 'dates' Jared arranged for her with Tony, and the other couple of guys she saw when they were in town, were a perfect set-up for her. For them she was an exquisite doll, a toy they could take out of her silk-lined box and play with reverently. Amber had been treated as a doll ever since she entered the world of modelling, at fourteen, but photographers, editors, fashion designers, were very hard on their toys. Amber had been pinched, prodded, and told in merciless detail about all her defects for the last ten years; she'd had men make it clear that they wanted her sexual services in return for being booked on prestigious jobs, and, very conscious of being the only breadwinner in the family, she'd pretty much always gone along with what they wanted.

Compared with her treatment at the hands of the model industry, Tony's concern for her made him a prince among men. Besides, he never expected anything from her that she didn't know how to give. With Tony and the others, it was a clear contract. She knew where the sides of the box were, and she liked that.

So, a couple of hours later, as a hedge-funder called Jeremy took a plate of pink champagne truffles from a waiter so that he could offer it to her with a flirtatious wink, using it to drive a physical wedge between her and the other men at the table, she smiled and shook her head and, adjusting the wrist strap of her eelskin Hayden-Harnett clutch, slipped away to the toilet, saying she'd be back in a minute, and not meaning a word of it.

Inside the penthouse suite, a glossy group of jet-setters were lounging on the grey suede wraparound sofas, watching music videos on the huge plasma TV, lightly toasted on champagne, giggling as one hot young body crawled provocatively over another, half-naked and oiled up, singing about love and sex and magic. Amber moved past them with her usual veiled half-smile, not quite meeting anyone's eyes, walking into the bedroom, looking for the bathroom beyond. On the bed, talking on her mobile phone, was Mara, chattering away animatedly; she looked up and flashed her fingertips at Amber, giving her a big smile.

'*Ciao, ciao!*' she said to the phone, snapping it closed.

It must have been the champagne on top of the pills she'd taken that day, sending a rush of real human feeling to flood her ribcage with warmth and affection, but Amber found herself sitting down next to Mara on the bed, reaching over, and giving her a hug that was not just a fashion-world brush of clothes, but a genuine embrace.

'I *do* look forward to going away with you,' Amber said, surprising herself with how fervent she sounded. 'We'll have lots of fun getting to know each other, I hope.'

Mara's shoulders moved against her, and Amber thought Mara

was reaching up to hug her back. And then, to her horror, she realized that Mara was sobbing.

'Mara?' she said, pulling back, scared that she'd made an idiot of herself. 'Did I say something wrong?'

Mara's hands were up, covering her face. She was crying hard, and her display of emotion frightened Amber, who had no idea what to do. Amber looked around nervously; all she could think of was to get up and close the bedroom door, to give Mara some privacy. Not wanting to leave her, she went back and sat down next to Mara, perching carefully on the edge of the bed, not daring to reach out to touch Mara in case this upset her still further.

'You're being so nice!' Mara sobbed from behind her hands. 'I can't do this if you're going to be this nice!'

'Do what?' Amber asked, puzzled.

'Tell you all that crap about how great it is in Dubai!' Mara lowered her hands, revealing a face smeared with makeup. Her eyes were a wet mess, the liner and mascara that had defined her light blue irises so successfully now blending with her tears to drip brown tears down her smooth round cheeks. 'You *do* make a ton of money, and you *do* get fantastic presents if one of the guys likes you – that's all true. I didn't actually lie to you. But, Amber, it's a whole different level from going on a weekend away somewhere safe, in Europe, with people around.'

She choked up, swallowing hard, and flailed around her, grabbing a silver box of tissues from the bedside table.

'If anything goes wrong, you're on your own,' she said, blowing her nose. 'Do you know what I mean? The other girls can't help you. There's no one to talk to who cares if something bad happens.' She gulped. 'Not that anything *really* bad's going to happen. I mean, they're paying a lot of money, a *lot*. They don't just want high-quality girls, they want ones they've seen in magazines, ones they can boast about being with. They're not going to mess up their connections to the model agencies. They're not going to *hurt* you, or make you stay there longer, or – you know, really bad stuff.'

Amber waited. She was good at that; a working model's life was all about hurry up and wait. Mara looked up from her tissue, met Amber's gaze, and started crying again.

'You need to get tested,' she said faintly. 'You know what I mean? If they don't want to wear condoms, you can't make them. And if you don't like party scenes, or getting friendly with other girls, they're really not happy about it. You can't start saying "no" to things – you just have to go along with whatever they want. And you have to not mind them looking straight through you as soon as they've finished.'

Amber stared at Mara in horror as the words sank in.

'It's worse than I thought it would be,' Mara said plaintively, 'but it pays so well! I keep saying I won't go back, but then I think how much I'll make, and I tell myself it's just a week . . .' She grabbed another tissue, her nails perfect pale pink varnished shells. 'There's one guy I actually really like, I look forward to seeing him, I just always worry he won't pick me the next time and I'll get someone really gross – oh God, I'm making it sound so awful, and it's really not *that* bad! I mean, ninety per cent of the time it's the most fabulous place to be . . .'

Amber had so little experience of taking care of a crying girl who was sharing her secrets that she didn't know what to do. With every fibre of her being, though, she wanted to help Mara feel better. So she did the only thing she could think of: she unzipped her clutch and pulled out two orange plastic vials of pills, Xanax and Klonopin. Silently, she proffered them to Mara, who was wiping her eyes now, gulping deep breaths of air.

'Do you want to take something?' Amber asked.

Mara looked at what Amber was holding out, and gasped in laughter. 'Oh God, no, that's the last thing I need!' she said, standing up. 'Downers, the way I feel right now? I'm going to do a couple of big fat lines and put my face back on!'

She went through into the bathroom, calling over her shoulder: 'Do you have any makeup on you?'

Of course Amber did. Her clutch bag was packed carefully with a whole armoury of travel-size touch-ups. She followed Mara into the bathroom and helped her make up her face to perfection once more, a final dusting of the violet-scented pastel beads of Guerlain's Les Meteorites giving Mara's pale peach skin a delicate, healthy glow. Then Mara flicked open a silver cardholder, pulled out a wrap of coke and cut herself a pick-me-up on the glass shelf beneath the mirror.

'Models, coke and toilets,' she said drily, throwing back her head and inhaling hard to make sure all the cocaine had been sniffed down her nasal cavities. She flashed herself a quick look in the mirror, licking her finger and running it round her nostrils to remove any faint white stains. 'It's like the ultimate combination.'

Amber nodded: how many times had she seen this scene play out in front of her? She flicked out a Klonopin and swallowed it with a swig of water.

Seeing this, Mara smiled wryly. 'I like to go up, you like to go down. We'd never be best drug buddies, would we?'

'Thank you for telling me about Dubai,' Amber said seriously.

'Look, I got a bit hysterical. I'm sorry,' Mara said, grimacing. 'Champagne always makes me a bit morbid. Forget what I said before. You should definitely come. The money really is amazing. And we could look out for each other.' She arranged her blonde curls around her face, tilting her head to get the styling just right. 'Well! Time to go back to the party! I *really* need another drink. Or three.'

'Come home with me,' Amber blurted out as they walked back into the bedroom, so unexpectedly that she took herself by surprise.

'*What?*' Mara's eyes dilated in shock. 'Amber? I didn't think you went that way . . .'

'No,' Amber said. 'I meant – don't go back to the party. Come back to mine instead. My mum's there, we could just watch some TV, have a quiet evening . . . We've got vodka and wine at home, if you want some . . .'

Mara took a deep breath, leaned forward and hugged Amber as tightly as Amber had previously hugged her.

'You're a really nice girl,' she said into Amber's hair. 'I appreciate the offer, OK? Don't think I don't. But out there –' she gestured to the window of the bedroom, through which they could see the party on the terrace, now bathed in the soft golden light of sunset, laughter and the sound of glasses clinking audible through the open window – 'might just be my future husband! Or at least the man who'll take me away from all this! I was really hitting it off with that guy from SunSeeker – he's divorcing a Russian girl right now – I mean, who knows if he's ready for a rebound?'

She dropped a quick kiss on Amber's cheek, light enough not to smudge either of the girls' makeup, but still full of affection.

'You're a really nice girl, Amber,' she said again. 'I wish I'd got to know you years ago. We'll have a great time in Dubai together, OK?'

And then, in a swirl of Valentino Rock'n Rose perfume and leopard-print chiffon, Mara opened the bedroom door and threw herself into the swing of the party without looking back.

Skye

'*B*abe!' Maria croaked two hours later, looking Skye up and down as she walked into the changing room at the Lounge. 'What the hell! You moved to Park Avenue all of a sudden?'

'Don't worry,' Skye said wryly, pulling her baby-blue hotpant outfit from her clutch and waving it at Maria. 'I got my scanties right here.'

'Well, *that's* a relief!' Maria chortled, sipping coffee. 'I thought you were going off to work in some fancy art gallery!'

'Yeah, making a couple of hundred bucks a day if she's lucky,' Jada said, smoothing down her flyaways with heavy-duty hair cream.

But Skye barely heard them. She was staring down at the tiny wisps of fabric in her hand, shiny sequined Lycra that looked even more cheap and tacky than ever in contrast with the classy, expensive sweater and pants she was wearing.

Weird. I don't want to put these on, she thought in surprise. The admiring glances from the men in the Bryant Park Cellar Bar, from guys on the street as she hailed a cab to take her across town to the Lounge, must have had more of an effect on her than she realized. She'd spent the early evening looking like a Manhattan career girl, sleek and groomed, the kind of woman you'd want on your arm.

Now she was about to take off almost all her clothes, and turn herself into the kind of woman you'd pay to sit on your lap. The idea was growing less and less attractive.

'What happened with that journalist guy?' Jada asked, turning away from the mirror, her cornrows now perfectly defined.

'I can't tell you,' Skye said absently, still looking down at her handful of pale blue Lycra.

'Oh my God – it was *that* freaky?' Jada's eyebrows shot up practically to her hairline. It was really hard to imagine any proposal that could shock an exotic dancer so badly she couldn't even talk about it.

Skye laughed drily. 'In a way. But I mean I literally can't talk about it. They paid me to sign a confidentiality agreement.'

'You're *kidding*,' Jada breathed, enthralled now.

Skye shook her head. She felt strangely detached: her body was here in the dilapidated, sweat-and-smoke-stinky dressing room, but her mind was still back at the table in the Cellar Bar two hours ago, her eyes wide with amazement as she exclaimed: 'A grand just for *listening* to you?'

'And for signing this.' Kevin Sanders had extracted a piece of paper from his briefcase and slid it across the table, where it joined the discreet white envelope containing a grand in twenties that Lew had just placed in front of Skye. Lew James wasn't an experienced *National Investigator* journalist for nothing; he knew there was no better way to focus a subject's mind than showing them the cash up front.

'Take your time, honey,' Lew said amiably. 'Read it through. All it says is you can't talk to anyone about what we're going to propose to you, OK? It ain't exactly that enforceable, but the legal department loves this shit.'

Kevin flinched.

'Hey, she's a smart girl, and we want her on our side, Kev,' Lew said, as Skye scanned through the document, nodded, and reached for the pen that Kevin was holding out to her. She signed at the bottom. Then she took the envelope, opened her D&G clutch and wedged the cash firmly inside, snapping the clasp. Whatever they proceeded to suggest to her, she was damn well holding onto that grand.

Lew snorted a laugh of approval as Kevin said: 'Skye, you ever had Joe Jeffreys in your club?'

She shook her head. 'I wish.'

'That's good,' Kevin observed, looking at Lew. 'She'd be fresh meat.'

'Excuse me?' Skye said sharply.

'Sorry, no offence meant,' Kevin said, adjusting his wire-framed glasses and leaning forward. 'You read the *Investigator*? You read that Joe likes the strip clubs, big-time? Watches the ladies dancing, drops big bucks, gets his liquor on, parties hard. And you know who he always picks to get up close and personal with? Pretty blondes like you. The all-American type, if we can say that any more.'

'Nah,' Lew muttered. 'You can't.'

'Everyone's got a type,' Skye said, sipping her mojito, waiting to see where this was going. Joe Jeffreys' name definitely had her full attention. Not only was he a huge movie star – A+ list, no question – but he was super-hot. Skye had straightforward tastes in guys. No skinny Williamsburg hipsters or short, spectacled intellectuals need apply. She liked her men muscly and well built: square-jawed, with handsome faces. All-American guys, like Joe Jeffreys – or Bike Boy. She bit her lip in self-reproval at the memory of what she'd done last night.

'Joe Jeffreys is engaged to Jennifer Downs, which probably isn't news to you either,' Kevin continued. 'They're America's sweethearts. Big movie about to open, huge publicity push being planned. Only problem is—'

'He can't keep it in his pants,' Lew finished. 'We've got photos of him in a strip club, getting it on with a young lady who's pretty much a dead ringer for you.'

'And you want me to pretend to be the girl in the photos?' Skye said, baffled. 'Because she won't come forward or something?'

'Uh-uh,' Kevin said, shaking his head. 'That's all sewn up. We got her story, done and dusted. Nah, we're after the next scoop. Joe's people are making him go into rehab for sex addiction. Cascabel, in California. Only way to spin this. He'll be in there for a few weeks, they'll say he's cured, and he'll have to swear off the strip clubs from now on.'

'But just *imagine*,' Lew said, hunching his elbows on the table to put his face closer to Skye's, 'if while Joe was in rehab for sex addiction, he met a chick who's *exactly* his type, and got it on with her? And there were photos? Or even a *video*? I mean, how hot would *that* be? We'd all make fucking fortunes!'

Skye had just taken another ladylike sip of her mojito when the significance of Lew's words made her snort it up her sinuses in shock. Managing to find the tabletop with her glass, if only barely, she said, 'You want me to go *into rehab*?'

'Sure! We'll pay for everything, of course!' Lew beamed. 'You can pick your addiction – drugs, booze, sex – whatever you like. We'll set you up with a spycam in your bag; Kevin already found some orderly there who'll smuggle it in for you. Then you get to work on Joe. You do him, you get it on film, we give you a big old bonus, everyone's happy.'

'Get to work on him? *Do* him?' Skye pushed her chair back from the table furiously. 'I'm not a *whore*!' she said, her voice rising. 'How dare you? Just because I work in a strip club – I don't even get *naked*!'

And then she remembered herself, just last night, taking off her G-string because that Wall Street creep had paid her a thousand bucks extra, and she felt a red angry flush flooding her face as she jumped to her feet. She stalked out of the bar, her head high, her demeanour so completely that of a respectable young woman who has just been deeply offended by an indecent proposal that heads turned, shocked, to stare in her wake at the two men at her table who had clearly suggested something absolutely filthy to her.

Now, looking down at her handful of costume, Skye felt like the biggest hypocrite in the world. Who was she kidding? She stripped for money all the time. She'd done naked dances in the private room, of course she had. She'd come pretty close, on occasion, to being a whore. Or at least, she'd walked a line so fine that it would be almost invisible to the naked eye.

'Baby girl, you just went somewhere else,' Jada said, laughing. 'That must have been one hell of a conversation you had.'

'You better get changed, Skye,' Maria said warningly. 'Your shift's starting, and you know what Paulie's like about timekeeping. Here.' She poured Skye a mug of coffee and tipped in some Kahlúa. 'That'll get you going.'

Slowly, automatically, Skye dropped the tiny top and hotpants on the bench in front of her locker, undid her Tiffany necklace, and started to pull the sweater over her head. She was standing there in her black minimizer bra and cigarette pants when she heard a sound that made her heart sink to the soles of her suede ankle boots.

Dog nails, clicking on the painted concrete floor. Clicking heavily, because the body above them was so overweight that the nails were carrying much too much pressure. And a painful wheezing sound, rasping, panting for breath. Skye closed her eyes for a moment, hoping that when she opened them she wouldn't see what she was expecting to see.

But the sight before her was exactly what she knew it would be. It was a small pug, the beige of dirty cream, and so fat its rolls of flesh were stacked one against the other like doughnuts lined up on their sides. Skye could barely see its feet; they were hidden under the mass of its flesh.

'Lev just *loves* Auntie Maria!' cooed a harsh, familiar voice. 'Lev couldn't *wait* to get to Auntie Maria, could you, Levski?'

'Oksana . . .' Maria started, as Lev came to a halt in front of Maria's chair and squatted down in front of her, jaw open, tongue lolling, whining for a pat. Reluctantly, Maria leaned down to drop a couple of taps on the dog's head. 'He shouldn't be here, you know, Oksana. Paulie don't like you bringing him in,' she said.

'Oh, Lev can sleep under Aunt Maria's chair, can't he?' Oksana insisted. 'Lev *loves* it under Aunt Maria's chair!'

'Oksana, you gotta get that fucking dog out of here,' Jada said firmly. 'It gave Sugar a damn asthma attack last time you brought it in.'

'Lev is a he! My little lion! He is not an it!' Oksana squealed.

'He, she, it – I don't care if the dog's a fucking hermaphrodite! He can't be here, OK?' Jada snapped.

'You don't talk to me like that!'

Oksana bristled with menace. As usual, she was wearing so much foundation that her face looked like an orange mask. Her fur gilet, which bulked up her skinny frame, was the same colour as her white-blonde bleached hair and the tight white jeans tucked into cowboy boots. Huge diamanté hoops glittered in her ears. Oksana believed in dressing up for any occasion; she probably put on full makeup before she went to the toilet in the middle of the night. She was pointing a finger at Jada, its terrifyingly pointed acrylic nail shining with fake diamonds.

'Hey,' Skye said, feeling that she needed to wade in on this one. 'Jada's got a point here. You can't make another girl sick—'

'Sugar isn't working tonight, I check it out,' Oksana interrupted. 'So Lev can be here! He gets lonely at home,' she added, as Lev collapsed to the ground with a loud groan and started making stertorous noises.

'He can't be here at all – it's the hair and the dander,' Skye said, sighing. 'You *know* that, Oksana.'

'You shut the fuck up!' Oksana hissed. 'You two! Coke whores, both of you! I know you both fuck that bouncer for drugs! Why should I care what you say?'

'Why, you nasty little—' Jada strode across the room towards Oksana, over six feet of fury. Skye had to give Oksana credit; despite being much smaller than Jada, the Russian girl didn't flinch. Instead, she clamped her hands on her hips and faced Jada down.

'You hit me, you get sack!' she said triumphantly. 'You put one finger on me, you get sack! Go on!'

'Jada, leave her alone,' Skye cut in, seeing Jada's hands clench into fists. 'I mean, you can't get mad at someone who can't even speak the freaking language properly.'

As Skye had known it would, this snapped Oksana's head round. Oksana was very sensitive about her command of English and her heavy Russian accent; it was her Achilles heel.

'Fuck you, you stupid American whore!' she yelled. 'You don't talk bad to me! All you think about is drugs and fucking!' Looking around her frenziedly, she snatched up the brimming cup of coffee Maria had poured for Skye and threw the contents directly at Skye.

Maria screamed. Good reflexes meant Skye managed to jump partially out of the way, avoiding a mugful of hot coffee in the face, but enough of it landed on her bare torso and trousered legs to make her curse and wipe herself down frantically with both hands. Jada grabbed a bottle of water, uncapped it and threw it over Skye, cold after hot, making Skye yelp.

'Trying to cool your skin down,' Jada explained, 'so you don't get burned.'

'What are you, *crazy*?' Skye yelled at Oksana.

Her trousers were drenched, her boots – the lovely new suede ankle boots she'd barely worn – were ruined. Lev, who had been sniffing round Maria's big handbag, suddenly reacted to his mistress's anger and broke into a series of shrill, angry yaps. Coffee dripped down the wall, and the polystyrene cup rolled across the uneven floor, chased by a hysterical Lev.

'I'm going to Paulie!' Jada said in fury. 'You'll get canned for this!'

'No!' Oksana's shrill voice rose above Jada's. '*I* go to Paulie! I tell him you are fucking the bouncer for drugs, and he sacks *you*!'

Oksana turned on her heel and pushed at the dressing-room door so hard that it slammed against the opposite wall, her stilettos tapping furiously on the concrete as she stormed out.

'Just for that,' Skye said furiously to Maria, 'I'm not stopping her little mutt from getting drunk and buzzed.' She nodded to Lev, busy lapping up a pool of Kahlúa-laced coffee.

Maria flapped her hand. 'Let him drink, honey. He'll run round for a while and then pass out. Believe me, he's much less trouble asleep than awake. And now he's here, he's staying the night. No way she's gonna take him home.'

'She could have really hurt you!' Jada exclaimed to Skye. 'You could have got your face burned! Should I go after her? Tell Paulie?'

Both girls looked at Maria, who had decades of experiences of stripper fights and rivalries, for advice.

She put her lips together and blew out her breath noisily. 'Nah, honey, leave her. Paulie'll let her run her mouth off, but he won't do nothing. You're his top girls, you three. He won't want to lose any of you. You work the room hard tonight and he won't say a word to you. Just keep it under wraps with DeVaughan, OK?'

'God, I *hate* that bitch,' Jada fumed.

Maria shrugged. 'Oksana's good, you know? She works the guys. You know how it is, Skye. You're good too. You get extra slack cut you if you know how to work the guys, right?' She topped up her coffee with more Kahlúa. 'Those Russian girls, you gotta respect them. They know men. They got cash machines for hearts, but they know men. Paulie ain't gonna sack her. Not unless she cuts someone.'

Maria wasn't speaking anything less than the truth. Skye knew that. No one in the Lounge was looking out for your welfare; no one cared about anything but the bottom line. She'd known that coming in. And yet a cold, hard ball of anger and resentment was forming inside her as she stood there, liquid dripping off her trouser hems and into the once-beautiful ankle boots for which she had paid hundreds of bucks not a fortnight ago, the shock of thinking she was about to get badly burned not yet dissipated from her body.

'That's it,' she heard herself say.

'What?' Maria looked at her.

'That's it,' Skye said, louder now.

She'd been so offended when the *National Investigator* guys thought they could pay her to seduce Joe Jeffreys. Well, she'd been an idiot. What did she do all her working hours but seduce guys who weren't half as sexy as one of the world's most famous movie stars? Hadn't some dickhead put his finger up her last night and scratched her deliberately? Hadn't she done something she couldn't even remember with a *coke delivery boy* just last night?

What Skye knew most clearly at this moment was that she wasn't going to stay around the Lounge to work with Oksana every day, to hear that bitch call her a coke whore, and feel, in her heart, that the words weren't that far off the truth.

Lew had already left two messages on her cell in the time it had taken her to find a cab and make the cross-town drive. He wanted her to reconsider. He'd promised her a lot of money – some upfront, but plenty on the back end if she managed to catch Joe Jeffreys with his pants down, on film. Plus, of course, all travel expenses and the huge rehab fees.

I've never been to California, she thought. Lew says Cascabel's got a great pool and better food than a five-star hotel. It'll be like a spa holiday, he says. With one of the hottest movie stars on the planet.

She grabbed her sweater and pulled it on. Her feet squelched in the damp suede boots as she bent down to grab her clutch, but she didn't care any more that they were ruined. Who needed boots in California?

'I quit,' she announced, seeing Maria's jaw drop in shock, Jada's eyes bug out. 'And you can tell Paulie it's all that slut Oksana's fault, OK? Maybe *that*'ll get her the goddamn sack!'

Petal

*P*etal had been asked to leave three schools. Not actually expelled, because her father was too famous for the schools to do that; but asked to leave, in interviews with various head-mistresses attended by various nannies. She had always hated school and everything about it, but most of all she loathed the regimentation. You kept having to do what other people told you to do, not what you wanted. Lesson now; lunch now; assembly now, each new hell announced by a series of loud, incredibly annoying bells. On and on, the bells, ringing and ringing, not letting up until they made her do what they wanted her to do, like someone standing over her, ringing a huge hand-held bell, its clapper clanging against the metal, louder and louder and louder—

Not an alarm clock. Petal didn't even own one. It was her phone, she realized gradually, blaring through her dreams, forcing her to wake up. Ugh. Her mouth was as dry and rough as a wooden board, and her eyelids were stuck together with something thick and gluey. She reached out, scrabbling with her hand, to find her phone and make it stop, trying not to open her eyes, as she knew from bitter experience that any more light would just make her head hurt even worse.

The rings were making some sort of pattern: five, stop, five, stop. Someone was calling her, hanging up whenever the phone went to voicemail, and promptly hitting Redial.

Petal's hand was sweeping in big circles, but not finding anything. No phone, no nothing. Her face was pressed into something soft and fluffy, which she slowly began to realize was the Flokati rug beside her bed. Painfully, cursing, she levered herself up to her hands and knees, discovering that she was fully dressed. She lifted her head, squinting at the bedside table, but couldn't see her phone. And she would definitely have seen it, because it was customized with hundreds of Swarovski gems, the whole point being that it was so shiny you could spot it anywhere.

'What the *fuck* is that *fucking noise?*' Dan mumbled, his voice muffled.

Turning her head, gulping in pain at the movement, Petal saw Dan, clad in his boxers and T-shirt from the night before, sprawled on her bed, the duvet kicked away at his feet, but every single one of her four pillows piled up on top of his head.

'Make it *stop*,' he moaned feebly as Petal clambered up on the bed to lie beside him, the sound of the phone seeming to follow her. She bumped one hip on the bedframe and screamed in agony, her protruding bone colliding with the wood so sharply that it felt like it was grating through her skin.

No, wait. How could it be *grating*? She slid a hand down to the area and hissed in triumph as she felt her phone, shoved into her jeans pocket, its crystals digging into her fingers as she extracted it and turned off the call.

'Yesss!' she muttered as she managed it.

'Who the fuck keeps ringing this early?' Dan groaned, reaching out one arm to pull Petal close to him, his T-shirt reeking of sweat and smoke. 'You got the debt collectors after you, or what?'

'*Oh*,' Petal said in a tiny voice as she checked the phone screen to see who'd been calling her.

'Come to bed, pet,' he mumbled, reaching for the duvet.

'I can't,' Petal said, her voice still infinitesimal. 'It's my dad.'

'Your *dad*?' Dan shot up to a sitting position as if he'd been galvanized, pillows flying off to all sides.

'Yes,' Petal said, still staring at the phone, which was ringing again, but silently now. 'And he never rings me. But now, he is. At nine thirty in the morning. That's *not* good.'

Dan opened his mouth, saw the expression on her face, and shut it again. They looked at each other like two scared children caught out doing something very naughty indeed.

'You'd better answer it, pet,' he said finally, nodding at the phone, swallowing nervously at the mere thought of Gold. 'He's been ringing for ages. It'll just get worse the longer you wait.'

Petal silently thumbed the Answer button, nicking on the speakerphone too so that Dan could hear; at least she didn't have to face this alone.

'Hello?' she said faintly.

'Petal! At last!' a woman responded sharply: Jinhee, Gold's girlfriend. 'Hold on. Your father wants to talk to you.'

Dan's hand wrapped around Petal's, squeezing it hard, his eyes widening as he heard one of the world's most famous voices, the husky tenor drawl of Gold. Many journalists had tried to describe it; Petal knew the ones her father liked the most were warm honey over river rocks (*Rolling Stone*) and brown sugar and Jack Daniel's (the *New York Times*). Gold's voice could seduce and enchant, break and mend hearts, croon a lullaby, bring tears to your eyes, raise the hairs on the back of your neck; his song 'Now Is the Time' had been played at more weddings in the last decade than any other.

'Petal,' her father said softly, and every muscle in his daughter's body tensed. 'I've seen the papers this morning. Get over here right now.'

The line clicked off.

'Fuck,' Dan whispered. 'I never knew he could sound that scary.'

But Petal was already jumping off the bed and racing to the bathroom for the Solpadeine.

*

Gold had bought Petal the canal-side flat in Camden Town not just because it was a fashionable area, perfect for a young trendy girl about town, and therefore a good investment: Gold's canniness about finances was one of the reasons he had become a megastar. No, the clinching reason for choosing Petal's location was that it shared the same postcode as his own.

Gold had scarcely been what even the most generous person would call a hands-on parent. After Linda, Petal's mother, left for LA in an attempt to become an actress, Petal was brought up by a series of nannies in the basement flat below the house where Gold lived with a series of girlfriends; she'd seen her father only by appointment when she was younger. From about fourteen onwards, she slipped into the house whenever a party was going on, which was pretty much all the time; what she experienced there was a much more comprehensive education than she received at any of the smart schools that, one by one, had asked her to leave.

But, despite his lack of oversight of his daughter's formative years, Gold still liked to be able to summon her swiftly if he needed to. One phone call, a sharp tug on the strings, and Petal was frantically brushing dry shampoo through her hair, pulling on a fresh T-shirt, spraying herself with deodorant and half a bottle of Boss Orange, running down filthy, bustling Camden Road. Across the five-pronged intersection at the tube station, where bikes and mopeds darted across illegal turns, and aged drunks – already, at ten in the morning – propped on the metal safety railings, drinking Tennent's Super and swearing at passers-by.

Past Camden High Street's boot shops and mobile phone shacks, and into Parkway, signs of gentrification immediately obvious, like a trail that led to the richer and richer areas beyond, a golden fountain of money that had welled up from the centre of Primrose Hill, and washed down as far as here, where pubs that had once been scrappy local boozers with stained red carpets and tatty upholstery had now gone gastro, painted charcoal-black, with stripped floorboards and rocket salads. Past the organic delicatessen and the shiny new estate agents, past the marble tile shop with its chic subtle palette of beiges and chocolates and greys and creams.

Onto Regent's Park Road, her heart pounding now, palms of her hands clammy. Into a part of NW1 that was a whole world away from the grime and chaos of Camden: Primrose Hill, where a house cost in the millions, where heads of advertising agencies, film stars and celebrity chefs bumped into each other buying lattes at the pavement cafés, and where Gold, years ago, not content with his own house overlooking the park, had bought the one next door and knocked the two together into a mansion that was referred to by local estate agents as reverently as priests talking about the Sistine Chapel.

Up the main steps, lined with pewter pots of exquisitely culti-vated topiary. The door swinging open, a tiny dark-skinned woman in white shirt and black trousers bobbing her head in acknowledge-ment of Petal's identity and gesturing with swift, imperative flicks of her hand across the light-flooded atrium, paved in Siberian rose malachite, to the living room beyond.

Sri Lankan, Petal thought as she went past the maid. I remember Jinhee saying she was staffing all their houses with Sri Lankans because they're cheap and work hard and don't take up much room.

Walking across the wide hall, past the huge painting of Gold's villa in Tuscany, its vineyards and olive groves stretching away in perfect pale green lines to either side of the sprawling stone build-ing. Into the white, white living room: white leather-tiled floor, white velvet wraparound sofas, white lilies in five-foot-high glass vases, a six-fold Japanese screen depicting a snowscape hung on the wall overlooking the garden beyond.

The sliding glass doors of the living room were wide open, and Petal could see her father in the garden beyond. As always at this time of day, he was ducked over, a small rake in hand, wearing a short natural linen robe and loose trousers, sculpting the gravel of his Zen garden into perfect waves to represent the ocean swirling around the rocks and moss that symbolized islands and forests. After meeting Jinhee and deciding to give up his hard-partying life, Gold had studied with the monks at a Kyoto temple for over a month to learn the art of *Karesansui* – raking sand and gravel into even and balanced ridges.

Of course, Gold had summoned her imperiously, and she'd had to rush over straight away. And of course, Petal had to wait another twenty minutes until he had set down his rake, taken up his shears and clipped near-invisible adjustments to the bonsai trees, and turned to survey the rest of the garden – the covered swimming pool surrounded by climbing roses (white, naturally, on black trellises), the dark granite water features blending beautifully into the ivy-covered walls – before coming back inside.

One of the many reasons Jinhee had survived this long as Gold's official girlfriend was her ability to anticipate his needs. Almost at the moment Gold stepped over the threshold of the living room, Jinhee appeared from the atrium. Small, her hips square, her chest flat, wearing black crepe trousers and a long-sleeved black T-shirt, Jinhee was carrying a black-lacquered tray laden with a stone teapot and three handleless cups. She crossed the room, soundless in her soft black suede slippers, and set the tray down on a table that was a solid cube of glass, motioning Petal to sit down on another cube – white suede – while she and Gold took the sofa opposite.

Typical, Petal thought sourly, as she obeyed. I hate these pouffe things. Now I'll be wriggling around the whole time and Gold'll be cross with me. Jinhee always manages to put me in the wrong.

Petal had never got on that well with any of Gold's previous girls. But they'd been like her mother Linda: fluffy glamourpusses with more boobs than brains. Jinhee was their polar opposite, smart and manipulative, and it seemed to Petal that she took pleasure in outmanoeuvring Petal and making her look silly.

'So, Petal,' Gold said quietly. 'We have things to talk about.'

He reached down with his left hand into the chrome magazine rack next to the sofa, and pulled out a stack of newspapers, which he fanned out on the glass coffee table. It was one smooth gesture,

theatrical and completely unnecessary, done with the showman-
ship that had made Gold the star he was. But what was incredibly
effective when staging a six-month-long world tour was vastly
annoying when done by your own father.

Petal met Gold's eyes for the first time that morning. It was like
an electrical shock, even for her. Gold's charisma was a finely honed
rapier, a weapon that after nearly fifty years he knew exactly how
to wield. His face, though not handsome, was very striking, his
intensely blue eyes bright and clear against his lightly tanned skin.
Decades of performing, first as the lead singer of his band, then as
a solo artist, had given him the ability to draw all the attention
towards him, and his daily yoga sessions reinforced his physical
confidence.

He held Petal's gaze for a few seconds, long enough to establish
control. Then he nodded downwards, leading her eyes towards the
covers of the tabloid newspapers.

A faint gasp emerged from Petal's lips. She'd thought it would be
just the usual: that she'd been drunk last night, tumbling out of a
black cab with Dan, her skirt riding up to her crotch – *no*. She
glanced down for a split second. *I'm still in the jeans I put on yesterday evening.*

And the photos in front of her hadn't been taken last night, but
ten days ago, more or less. Petal recognized them straight away: the
black walls, the bottle of Absolut Pear on the chipped sink, JC
reflected in the mirror, laughing, as Petal, in the foreground, bent
over the lines chopped out on the edge of the sink, holding a rolled-
up note to her nostrils. A white smudge blurred part of the frame:
the camera flash, bounced back off the mirror, concealing the person
who was holding it.

Rudy. Rudy was taking pictures on his phone.

*JC dumped Rudy last night. And Rudy turned right round and sold
the photos of me and JC taking coke to the tabloids.*

Bastard.

And then she thought frantically: Oh, *no* . . . Dan was there that
night . . .

She grabbed at the papers, fanning them out further. As she feared, the next one had her and Dan together, Dan with the bottle of vodka upended to his mouth, Petal reaching for it, a small white lump clearly visible in her nose as she looked up at him, laughing.

'I was set up,' Petal said quickly. 'The guy who took the photos, he was a boyfriend of a friend of mine, he must have planned this all out—'

But her father was already raising one silver-ringed hand to stop her. His linen shirt fell back, revealing the Sanskrit tattoo around his wrist.

'There's no way you can explain this away, Petal,' Gold said, 'so please don't insult my intelligence.'

'Do you know how bad this makes your father look?' Jinhee asked, reaching forward to pour out the tea. 'His latest album is a reworking of Gregorian chants! We have a Channel 4 documentary coming out next month where he visits monasteries and leads guided meditation sessions. This is *not* a good time for you to be acting out some childish rebellion with deliberately provocative behaviour.'

Gold nodded sombrely as Jinhee handed him the cup. Petal narrowed her eyes in anger at Jinhee; ever since Jinhee had come into his life, Petal had realized that the model/actress wannabes he'd dated previously were infinitely preferable to this one. The other girlfriends might have been so petrifyingly beautiful that they took your breath away, but at least they hadn't lectured Petal while her father nodded in agreement.

I was such an idiot, Petal thought. I thought that she wouldn't last two seconds with Gold, because she wasn't pretty enough for him.

It was the mistake that Gold's Russian supermodel girlfriend, Ekaterina, had made a few years ago, when she booked them a series of tantric sex lessons, thinking it would bring them closer than Gold had ever been to another woman. Instead, Jinhee, the tantric sex guru, had cut Ekaterina out of Gold's life in a mere couple of months, effortlessly moving in on her target. In that time, she had managed to install herself in the Primrose Hill mansion, making it clear to Gold's party animal friends that they were no longer welcome, while cleverly establishing herself with Gold's manager and publicists as exactly what he needed to revamp his image; no longer was he dating a stream of girls half his age, but settling down with a woman whose austere appearance and stabilizing influence was the perfect way to consolidate him as the serious musician he aspired to be.

She's cleverer than all the others; Jinhee doesn't want to be his queen. She's worked out that the real power is behind the throne, Petal thought sourly.

Jinhee continued: 'If you had done this deliberately, to mess up your father's latest project, you couldn't have managed better! Luckily for you, however, we have discussed this and decided that we see this as a subconscious acting out of your aggressive urges rather than a direct attack on your father.'

Petal knew she should bite her tongue and take her medicine. But every time she saw Gold – always, now, with Jinhee – it got worse and worse. More lectures, more pop-psychology nonsense from a woman who barely knew her. It was unbearable.

'You're having a laugh, right? All I did was what I learned in this house!' Petal snapped back at Jinhee, irritated beyond endurance. 'I know I shouldn't have let anyone take photos, OK? But when I was growing up, there were *bowls* of coke lying round the place! *Much* more partying than I've ever done! Like, *orgies*, all sorts of things!' She looked passionately at her father. 'Gold, you know it's true! It's *totally* not fair to sit here and have her lecture me, like a shrink! I'm not doing *anything* I haven't seen you do!'

Gold nodded gravely, his left hand coming up to trace a symbolic gesture over his chest which Petal didn't recognize.

'It's certainly true that I lived a rock-star life for years,' he agreed. 'But remember, Petal, all that time, I was producing art. Making albums. Doing tours.'

'*Award-winning* albums,' Jinhee chimed in. '*Sell-out* tours.'

Petal tensed, sensing what was coming. To fend it off, she said quickly, 'Well, I have a whole range of stuff I'm designing coming out with Accessorize! *And* there's my column, and Rimmel are going to name a lipstick after me . . .'

Right . . . she thought sadly. Even if that was all true, Accessorize and Rimmel won't want anything to do with me as soon as their PRs see these photos. No big company's going to want to be associated with a druggie. I just messed up every single pathetic little career prospect I have.

'I don't see any moral seriousness in that,' Jinhee observed, looking at Gold. 'Do you?'

It was clearly a rhetorical question. He shook his head.

'Not like *your* work, Gold. Which, as I've pointed out many times, *always* had a fundamental core of moral seriousness,' she informed him.

Gold lit up with pleasure, his eyes sparkling aquamarine, his shoulders drawing back to sit up even straighter.

Wow, Petal thought. She knows exactly the right thing to say to him. All the right buttons to press.

'You're clearly on the wrong track, Petal,' Gold said piously. 'I feel it's my obligation to step in at this point and redirect you to a better course. Tough love, it's called. I've neglected you over the years. I admit that. But with the course of meditation Jinhee and I have been doing, I've realized I need to work on that. We've talked it over –' he glanced at Jinhee – 'and we've decided that it's time I put my foot down.'

It was more than Petal could bear. She jumped to her feet, knocking against the glass cube in front of her, the white suede pouffe sliding back on the leather tiles, catching, and tipping over with the force of her surge.

'*We*? I can't *believe* this!' she exclaimed passionately. 'You've only been with her a few years – you're not even *married*!'

This was a direct hit on Jinhee, whose eyes narrowed menacingly. Jinhee was wise enough not to look over at Gold, but her whole body tightened with resentment.

'And, Gold, when you were my age I bet you were doing much, much worse stuff than just some lines of coke with friends!' Petal insisted. 'This is *so* hypocritical! And how dare she sit there and tell me I'm not being "morally serious" enough, when she practically has sex with people for money—'

'That is *not* what tantric sex is about at *all*,' Jinhee snapped angrily.

'I mean, that's how you two *met*! I'm not going to stand here and be lectured by you about how I'm behaving!' Petal said to her father furiously. 'Just because it's trendy now to be all yoga-macrobiotic-meditation! I know *you* weren't like that when you were twenty – or thirty, or forty, for fuck's sake!'

Direct hit on Gold now, who flinched; at nearly fifty, he liked to think he could pass for at least ten years younger, and hated any reference to his age.

'Your father wants to stop you making the same mistakes he made,' Jinhee said icily. 'That's what good parents do.'

'And I was earning my own money when I was twenty, unlike you!' Gold snapped at his daughter, real feeling breaking through his poised façade for the first time that morning. 'I was already world-famous! It was my own bloody money I was throwing away! I'd like to know how much you're pulling in from one sodding Accessorize contract! You're pissing away your opportunities because you're too out of it to see what's in front of your face! Two of Mick's kids have modelling gigs – Ozzy's kids have their own TV shows – you could be doing all sorts of telly work if you got your act together! I could be proud of that! I worked hard for everything I have!' He pounded his fist on the sofa. 'And I don't want my daughter to be so spoiled she can't do an honest day's work! You're just fucking some wannabe rock star and getting in the papers for all the wrong reasons!'

Direct hit on Petal. She froze, her heart sinking: her father had just articulated exactly what the voice inside her head told her maliciously at five in the morning, when the drink and the drugs from the night before woke her up to preach at her, nagging away inside her skull, forcing her to pull herself painfully to her feet and rummage in the bathroom cabinets for a Zimovane and fall back into bed, an eye mask donned to block out the eventual daylight.

She knew she wasn't making the most of all the opportunities her surname gave her. Though she wasn't tall enough to model seriously, she was actually prettier and more photogenic than any of Mick Jagger's daughters, and she was deeply jealous of Jack and Kelly Osbourne, who had parlayed their stint on a reality show with their parents into successful TV-presenter careers of their own.

'Gold's getting carried away,' Jinhee said, frowning at her boyfriend, who raised his hands in apology for his language. 'But it's because he cares about you. He wants to see you making something of yourself, not just leeching off him. And we feel there's only one way for you to achieve that.'

Gold raised both his hands to his chest, touched the fingertips and then parted them again, sketching a half-circle in the air as his hands lowered to join in his lap, breathing in and out deeply through his nose as he executed this calming ritual.

'Ozzy's kids,' Gold said, his voice controlled once again. 'That's a very good example. Both of them with big drug problems, both had stays in rehab, both are doing really well now. I've discussed this with Jinhee and we want to catch this problem of yours right now, Petal. Nip it in the bud.'

'I don't have a problem!' Petal protested quickly. She had a sudden idea of where this was going, and she didn't like it one little bit.

'Oh, *Petal*,' Jinhee said sorrowfully, and Petal saw the trap: if she admitted she might not be quite as on top of her drug use as she declared, then she was in trouble; and if she denied it, well, then, she was in denial, which was even worse . . .

'You're booked into Cascabel rehab clinic,' Gold informed her. 'Jinhee's made all the arrangements. You fly out to LA tomorrow morning.'

'*LA!*' Petal exclaimed in horror. 'But that's so far away! It's the other side of the *world*!'

'We hear it's the best,' Jinhee said. 'And it won't hurt to get you away from the bad influences around you in London.'

'No! I don't *need* rehab!' Petal said frantically. 'I'm just young and having fun! I'm only twenty! I promise I won't get into any more trouble – you won't see me in any more papers unless it's something really positive. And Dan – my boyfriend – he's lovely . . .'

Jinhee reached out and tapped the photo of Dan in the paper, drinking vodka from the bottle.

'He doesn't look like the best influence, does he?' Gold commented. 'Musicians . . .' He sighed. 'I'm afraid I know exactly what they're like.'

'What – you're sending me to rehab because I'm not going out with an *accountant*?' Petal protested. 'This is so *unfair*!'

'You don't sound very mature, Petal,' Jinhee said. 'I'm afraid you're just reinforcing our decision.'

'*Your*—' Petal couldn't bear it any more. She looked desperately at her father, but to no avail.

'You have a choice, Petal,' he said. 'We always have a choice. But I'm not prepared to support you financially any longer unless you go to Cascabel.'

'Ohh!' Petal screamed. More than a direct hit, this was the killing blow below the ribs, the sword sliding into her weakest spot. No way could she survive without her father's accountants depositing a juicy sum into her bank every month, and taking care of all her bills.

But who knows how long they'll keep me in rehab? Sometimes people stay there for months! And if I'm not in London, how quickly will another girl move in on Dan?

'You're ruining my life!' she yelled, and she reached down, upended the tray and sent the teacups and pot flying across the room to crash against the marble fireplace. *In for a penny, in for a hundred fucking pounds.* 'I *hate* you! I wish I'd never been *born*! You're such a fucking *hypocrite*!'

Panting with anger, her eyes flashing, she put her hands on her hips and confronted Jinhee and Gold. To her horror, she saw a small smile curving Jinhee's pale lips. The tea trickled slowly down the wall, the sound of the drops falling on the floor the only noise in the room for a good thirty seconds, as it sank into Petal's mind how fully she had acted out the stereotype of a spoiled rich girl who badly needed a wake-up call.

'You're booked on the 11.15 a.m. Virgin flight from Heathrow to LA tomorrow,' Jinhee said quietly. 'First class, of course. The chauffeur will be at your apartment at 8.15 tomorrow morning. As your father says, it's your choice. But I suggest, for your own good, that you're on that plane. Someone from Cascabel will meet you at LAX.'

Tears were forming in Petal's eyes. Exile from London, for an indefinite period of time. Exile from Tas, from JC, and above all from Dan. Banishment to a treatment centre with a bunch of druggies whining about their sad lives, and therapists doing everything they could to break her into little pieces. She looked imploringly at her father, all fight drained out from her as surely as the tea from the pot, dripping onto the leather tiles of the floor. There was no way out of this, no way but to get on the plane.

And she was gradually working out why Gold was coming down on her so hard for what was, by his standards, a comparatively minor infraction: that bloody Gregorian chant album. Gold was due on a publicity tour to promote it that would touch down in four out of the five continents. When he was asked the inevitable questions about Petal, he would be able to respond, sadly but wisely, that he had done the right paternal thing by shipping her straight off to rehab. Petal on the loose in London, generating bad publicity for Gold and his reformed-sinner image, was the last thing he needed.

'*Dad?*' she said in a tiny voice, something she hadn't called her father since she was ten, when she'd been told she was too old for that name now, and besides, it wasn't cool; from then on, she'd had to call him Gold, like everyone else.

Her father's eyes met hers; they were the same light blue as hers, but his were as calm as hers were wild.

'Please call me Gold, Petal. And keep in mind – this is for your own good. It's part of my job as your parent to stop you making the mistakes I did. You'll thank me for this in years to come,' he said.

This was so unbelievably annoying that, if she hadn't already thrown the tea tray, she'd have picked it up then and there and chucked it right in his holier-than-thou face.

Amber

'So, she's a nice girl, this Mara,' Slava said comfortably, pouring boiling water into the teapot. Slava always waited up on the rare occasions that Amber was out at a work party, to make her camomile tea when she came home. She was bundled up in her dressing gown and slippers, her makeup removed, but her big chunky gold and pearl jewellery still on ears and neck and wrists and fingers; she only took it off to sleep.

'Very nice,' Amber said, kicking off her shoes. 'But, *Matka*—'

'You sit down, you have your tea,' Slava said. 'And you can tell me all about this Mara.'

Amber unzipped her Dolce dress and pulled it off, folding it carefully over the back of a chair. Slava had put out a robe ready for her, and Amber slipped it on, belting it round her slim waist. It was so nice to be comfortable. Dressing up in tight, constricting clothes was part of her job; even off-duty, Slava insisted Amber be groomed to the nines whenever she left the house. When she pulled on a soft dressing gown and slid her feet into fur-lined slippers, it was one of her favourite moments of the day.

She sank into one of the two kitchen armchairs. Slava had muted the TV when Amber came in, and some old black-and-white film was showing, a woman in a toque and raincoat climbing onto a train in a cloud of steam.

'I'm scared, *Matka*,' Amber blurted as Slava put the tea down on the table at her elbow.

It came out louder than she had meant; she surprised herself with the strength of it. The champagne she had drunk at the party must have won out over the pills, giving her Dutch courage.

'Scared?' Slava's slanting eyes opened in shock. 'What is to be scared of? You need some fun! You don't go out enough, I say that all the time! You go have nice holiday with other girls!'

Amber stared at her mother, amazed. In all her life, she couldn't remember Slava ever saying that Amber didn't go out enough, that she needed fun: Slava's line had always been that she and Amber were enough for each other.

'The men pay to have pretty girls at parties, that's normal.' She settled into the other armchair, next to Amber, putting up her calves on the pouffe in front of her with a grunt of relief. She suffered badly from swollen ankles. 'And you – American and Russian *Vogue*, on the covers, no less! Of course they give you money to come to their parties! You never know, you might meet some rich man there who wants to marry you!'

'I thought it was "just you and me, that's all we need"?' Amber blurted out, utterly confused by her mother's change in attitude. 'You never talked before about me getting married!'

Slava shrugged. 'Things change, *láska*,' she said, reaching for the glass at her elbow. Clear liquid, which meant vodka and Sprite. The mixer was always Sprite or Lucozade, and the spirit was always vodka. Slava's tastes in drink were those of the old-fashioned Eastern European she was, and she could hold her liquor better than anyone Amber had ever met; no matter how much vodka Slava put away, Amber had never seen her mother affected by it.

'You've been working for thirteen years now,' Slava continued. 'And they want models younger and younger. All these little Russian girls they find in Nizhny Novgorod at fourteen, like you were. Little skinny peasants they can dress up how they want to. You're twenty-seven, and all you can do is look pretty. You should get married. So, you go to parties, you meet a rich man, he marries you, he buys you a big house near Harrods with a flat for me.' She sighed. 'I thought we would save money. I thought I would buy property and we would own something by now. I don't know where it all went.'

Pills, Amber thought. Clothes and jewellery and vodka and renting flats in Mayfair. And lots and lots of pills from private doctors in Harley Street, who charge hundreds of pounds just to write prescriptions.

She closed her eyes. Somehow, if she weren't looking at her mother, it was easier for her to say, in a small, frightened voice: '*Matka*, this trip to Dubai – it isn't just going there for a few smart parties.'

'Maybe thirty thousand pounds, you said! For a week!' Slava said dreamily. 'More than even the biggest advertising money you've made! And now for the advertisements they don't want models, not so much. They want actresses. Or daughters of famous people.' She pulled a face. 'Ugly, some of them. Not models at all. You see that daughter of Mick Jagger, with the teeth like a rabbit? With a gap between each one, like her father is so poor he can't take her to a dentist?' She clicked her tongue and reached for her glass again. 'They take work away from you. The world is changing. But thank the heavens, someone will pay you thirty thousand pounds for a week! I was so worried, but now we're safe again!'

'*Matka!*' Amber said desperately. 'Please, you're not listening! This trip away . . .'

She got to her feet in a fluid gesture and started pacing the kitchen, her slippers soft on the Tuscan tiles, unable to face her mother. If she thought about what she was going to say she would never have the courage to get it out, but her fear of what Mara had told her was overriding everything else, and the champagne was still bubbling in her bloodstream, helping her on.

'It's like the dates I've been on, in the last year,' she continued swiftly. 'With Tony, and Stephan, and Hans. I didn't meet them at parties, like I told you. Jared set them up for me.'

'Very nice of him,' Slava said, nodding in approval.

'*No!*' Amber exclaimed in frustration. 'No, *Matka*! These men *ordered* me – they took me away and pretended that I was their girlfriend for the weekend, and they paid Jared for it, and they paid me extra. They *paid a fee*. Do you see what I mean? They paid so they could be sure of having sex with me. And now, in Dubai, it's the same thing. Only there it isn't just one guy, and it isn't in a big hotel, where there are people around if something goes wrong. It's groups of men, and it's in their own private compound, and it's for a whole week – and they're *definitely* not pretending that I'm their girlfriend!'

She ran out of breath. Her circuit of the kitchen had taken her in a loop past the Sub-Zero fridge, past the Smeg twin ovens and hobs (pristinely shining, because they were never used by Amber or Slava) and back to her mother's cosy nest in front of the TV. Leaning with both hands on the back of her armchair, blushing with embarrassment as she told her mother the truth at last, Amber met Slava's eyes, mutely pleading for her mother not to be disgusted at what she'd done for money.

'They were very nice,' she said in a tiny voice. 'All the men. It was like it was real. They treated me so well. When Jared told me Tony was in town, I would even look forward to it. He was nice and handsome and he wanted to make sure I was happy . . .'

'You're lucky,' Slava said, her voice so harsh that Amber started in shock.

'*Matka?*' she asked, daring now to meet her mother's green eyes, so similar to her own.

Slava was glaring up at her daughter, her mouth pursed in a tight line. Amber might have expected this fury from her mother at hearing that Amber had been paid to be a high-end escort, but not the words that had just emerged. Her brain raced, trying to make sense of her mother's reaction.

'Sit,' Slava said grimly, pointing at Amber's armchair, her fingers tipped with the bright red nail polish she always wore; it lasted for ever, as Slava's household tasks didn't involve any cooking, washing up or cleaning.

'Sit,' she repeated, speaking Slovak now. That meant that this was a hundred per cent serious. Amber dropped obediently into the chair as Slava got up and shuffled over to the fridge. She poured Smirnoff, neat, into a tumbler and brought it back to Amber, who took it dutifully, wide eyes focused on her mother.

'You need to listen now,' Slava said, settling back into her own chair, reaching for her own drink. 'Listen carefully to what I am going to tell you. It's easy for you. You are so beautiful, *láska*. The men who take you out, they have millions of pounds. They take you to five-star hotels and they treat you like a queen, and you're nice to them, to show you like them and the presents they give you. That's what all women do. And almost every woman wants your life, to have these rich men ask to take you away for the weekend and buy you Louis Vuitton suitcases because you smile at them and lie down for them.'

She reached over and clinked glasses with Amber, who was staring at her mother in disbelief.

'Drink,' Slava said, nodding at the vodka she had poured Amber. 'It's good to drink vodka when you hear hard things. Because you will hear hard things, now, *láska*. What you do with those men you go away with, I have done myself. But not nice and easy, in smart hotels, on silk sheets with people to clean them for me afterwards. I have done it for years, standing on the street with other whores like me, waiting for men to come by, doing it in dirty corners or in their dirty cars.'

Amber's jaw dropped open. Numbly, she fumbled the glass to her lips and drank some of the cheap vodka; it burned going down, but Slava was right. It did help.

'You thought I was cleaning offices when I went out at night and locked you in,' Slava's harsh voice continued relentlessly, the guttural consonants of her native language adding emphasis to her message. 'But no; I needed to make more money than a poor immigrant could do on my hands and knees scrubbing floors and emptying rubbish for two pounds an hour. I needed to make money to buy nice clothes for us, to save, so that when we went to London to try to make you a model they didn't laugh at us. I needed to make money to put in the bank in case they didn't want you as a model, because if that was the case, we still needed to go to London, but to find a rich man who would want to meet you because you are so beautiful. You had to have the right clothes, your hair done at the best places, the right things. And there isn't much time for girls. Maybe ten years, not much more. I was a fool. I married your father when I was young and pretty. I wasted myself on a bad man, a drunk. But I wasn't a beauty like you. I wasn't a prize like you. You're worth a fortune.'

She indicated her daughter with that red-tipped hand. 'You were my fortune. I could tell that, even when you were young. So I made myself a prostitute for you. Yes, I did that, so that we could get away from *Margate*.' Slava never said the name of the town Amber had grown up in without making a ritualistic spitting gesture over her shoulder, and she did it now. 'So that we could go away and never go back. What I did there, I've left behind me. I'll never see those men again, and it is nothing to me. They were dirt, and what they wanted was dirt. But now that's all over.'

She took another long sip of her drink, and motioned impatiently at Amber to do the same. Mutely, Amber obeyed, finishing her vodka, her head cold and hot at the same time. Slava's every word had the unmistakable ring of truth. Flashes of memory were swirling through Amber's champagne-and-vodka-soaked brain: Slava putting on makeup to go out to work in the evening, snapping at Amber if she told her mother she looked pretty; the fact that Slava never seemed to have a fixed schedule for her cleaning jobs, but would come home in the early hours, almost always at different times, so that Amber could never be sure when to expect her; and the long, stiff drink Slava always poured herself when she came in, kicking off her shoes, swearing to herself in Slovak, crawling into bed next to Amber smelling hot and rank and musky, smelling, Amber realized now, of odours that were not her own.

She was crying. Tears were pouring down her face, dropping into her lap, into the empty glass she held there.

'I'm so sorry, *Matka*,' she whispered. 'I'm so sorry you had to do that for me . . .'

'It's over now,' Slava said impatiently. 'Don't cry for what is over, *láska*. It's too late for that. But we haven't been careful, either of us. We haven't saved like I did then in Margate.' Another spit. 'I was foolish too. When the money started to come in, I thought it would go on for ever. But nothing goes on for ever. We need to buy this flat. I like it here. And maybe other flats too. An income. Or we'll find you a rich husband. It's not too late, but now we must plan.'

She reached out to her side table, unpopped a vial of Vicodin and poured out a handful for her daughter, handing her own glass of vodka and Sprite for Amber to swallow them down with.

'Be calm, *láska*. Much worse things have happened in the world,' she said, as Amber took the pills from her. 'This trip to Dubai – bad things won't happen to you there, not like they did with me. These men won't say they'll pay you, and then cheat you and laugh at you. They won't call you bad names. Every time I got in a car with a man, every time I walked down an alley with him, I would think: will he kill me? Will my Amber be left all alone, locked inside our flat, thinking her mother will come back, waiting for me, as I lie dead on the ground?'

She shook her head. 'But you – no dirty cars or dirty streets for you. You'll fly business class, you'll stay in paradise. You'll have this girl Mara with you, to make sure you're happy. A friend! You look like a queen and they'll treat you like a queen, that's how it is in this world. They'll give you wonderful presents, these men. And soon we will have this flat, and then maybe more.'

Amber was crying even harder now, but if someone had asked her why, she would have had trouble telling them; the Vicodin was knocking her out, making her brain so woozy that she could barely focus on her mother's face. The aftertaste of Sprite was sticky in her mouth. She couldn't help the tears, and she could do nothing but sit there as they poured out; she felt completely helpless, overwhelmed by her mother's revelations. Slava, observing this, shrugged and got up, standing behind her daughter, stroking the thick mane of chestnut hair.

'So cry,' she said philosophically. 'Cry and then sleep. It's good to cry and sleep. Tomorrow you'll see that I am right, *láska*.' She bent to drop a kiss on top of her daughter's head. 'All this was for you. To make you safe and happy. You know that, don't you?'

Amber had never felt such intense pain. The revelation of what her mother had done for her – the terrible guilt Amber felt as a consequence, and the guilt she felt now at being so reluctant to go to Dubai – Mara's words in the bedroom at the St James's Hotel, the knowledge of what lay in wait for Amber in Dubai if she agreed to go – and her mother, pushing her to take the money, to agree, effectively, to become a prostitute . . .

But I should do it, Amber thought frantically, shouldn't I? If Matka did it for me, I should do it for her, to keep her safe now as she kept me safe when I was little. There's no way out.

Amber thought her head would burst from the agony of this dilemma. She was under so much pressure, and there was nowhere to run, no safe place to fall.

Reaching out, she grabbed the vial of Vicodin and palmed some more pills, washing them down with Slava's vodka.

Oblivion, she thought. That's all I want right now. Oblivion.

And all the time, Slava was smoothing back Amber's hair from her tear-streaked face, stroking her forehead gently, crooning to her daughter: 'Everything I have done was for you, *láska*. Everything has only ever been for you . . .'

Interlude

*A*mber was fighting unconsciousness with everything she had. Ironic: she'd spent more than half of her life partially sedated, in a haze of Percocet and Vicodin, wrapped in a big fluffy cloud she'd never wanted to shed.

And now she had to push that cloud away with every fibre of willpower she had. If she wanted to stay alive.

She tried to sit up, but she could barely raise her back an inch. Still, if she couldn't sit up, there had to be another way to get off this bed. Because the bed was a big part of the problem: it was so comfy, so soft, so yielding. She'd never manage to stay awake if she stayed here.

Heaving one elbow into the mattress, she used the leverage to twist her body up and over in an awkward roll, impeded by the weight of the coverlet and all the books and magazines and photographs strewn on top of it. Impatiently, she kicked out, and heard some books fall to the floor.

One whole turn. She was on her back again, further away from the woman standing over her, closer to the side of the bed. Another roll over, this one easier; she'd almost got the hang of it. Then she tried to slide her legs off the bed and everything went horribly wrong. Her silk nightdress slid too easily along the sheet below her; she'd meant to feel for the ground with her feet, but before she knew it she was slipping. She threw *out her arms, desperately trying to catch hold of something to slow her down. Instead, she hit the bedside table, whacking one forearm on its sharp corner; she heard herself whimper aloud in pain as she collapsed to the floor, her legs crumpling under her.*

The pain in her left arm was cutting through the haze of drugs and vodka like a knife. She'd sliced herself open on that table; there was a wet trail of blood dripping down her arm.

Good. It was waking her up. Amber hauled her legs back, one at a time, getting to her knees, bracing herself on hands and knees. Hands flat to the carpet, pulling herself along, knees shuffling after; round the corner of the bed. The blood drops on her arm were tickling, and she rubbed it impatiently against the carpet, which hurt still more; even better.

Amber had been avoiding pain all her life, and now she was actually seeking it out. The realization actually made her lips twist into a sort of smile.

She was at the door now, pushing back with her hands, forcing herself to sit up high enough to reach for the door handle. She had to get her balance before she could loosen her grip and manage to turn the knob, pull it, crack the door open . . .

In her debilitated state, it was like having a torch shone directly in her eyes. The windows in the bedroom had their curtains drawn; she'd assumed it was evening. But the sunlight in the hallway was clear and bright and dazzling. Amber blinked, overwhelmed. She was still hanging on to the doorknob, and she tried to pull on it to help her to her feet; but her legs were like lead. No way was she going to manage that.

Gritting her teeth, Amber dropped to all fours like an animal, and started to crawl through the open door.

'No, no,' said the woman, crossing the room with swift steps, catching the edge of the door and slamming it shut, catching Amber's fingers as it went.

Amber yelped in pain. The woman leaned down, put her hand on Amber's back and pushed her over, onto the carpet. Amber was much weaker than she'd realized; she went over like a toy toppled easily by a child's hand.

'You can stay there,' the woman said coldly. 'It looks even better – you realized you took too much and tried to get help. Just a sad, sad accident.'

No! *Amber thought frantically.* No!

But the burst of energy that had carried her across the room had been a bubble that popped as soon as the daylight vanished, as soon as she'd been tipped back over onto the carpet. The waves of Vicodin and vodka-induced sleep were rolling over her, pulling her under. And despite every effort she could make to prevent it, Amber's eyelids slowly sank closed.

Part Two

Skye

*U*p until the moment she clapped eyes on Joe Jeffreys in the flesh, Skye had been having *serious* second thoughts about this whole crazy rehab setup.

Sure, California was unbelievable. It really was the way it seemed in the movies and TV shows: the palm trees, the low white Spanish Colonial houses, the blue, blue skies, everything bathed in sunlight, everyone acting easy and friendly like they were always bathed in sunlight too. Tans and smiles and wide generous streets, nothing like New Yorkers, with their grim expressions and grey faces. No twenty-foot-high canyons of buildings, dark and menacing. After years in the Big Apple, trying not to get eaten by the worms hiding in its rotten core, Skye realized, as she stepped out of Burbank Airport and drew in a long happy breath of warm damp golden air, that she was more than ready for a change of pace.

She remembered her tearful farewell to Jada early that morning; Jada had hugged Skye so hard she'd picked her right up off the ground, made her promise to keep in touch with tons of calls and texts, sobbing that Skye was going but excited for her too.

'You're never coming back!' Jada had wailed, her chin resting on Skye's head. 'I can feel it in my bones!'

Skye had told her not to be so silly, that LA and Joe Jeffreys and this crazy assignment were just a temporary thing. But, dragging her cases through their crappy apartment, bumping them down five flights of mildewed-lino-covered stairs and out onto garbage-strewn 37th Street, Skye had realized that Jada might know her better than she did herself. Skye was ready for a change, for a new adventure. And she was ready to leave her New York life far behind her.

Jada's the only thing I'll miss out of that whole stinking city, Skye thought. Look how gorgeous this place is!

New Yorkers were always snotty about LA: well, that was clearly because it was so much nicer on the West Coast, and they were eaten up with jealousy. The warmth, the sunshine, the positivity; the flowering shrubs, the palm trees, the greenery everywhere were a world away from grey old NYC. Even the wide generous roads had birds-of-paradise flowering gorgeously in the centre dividers. And she was being paid to be here – all expenses, plus twenty grand just for taking the assignment, and a promised bonus of up to eighty grand more if she got the goods on Joe.

Eighty grand, just for having sex with one of the hottest men alive, Skye marvelled. This is insane. Of course, I do have to go through rehab. And that's not going to be a bundle of laughs.

Rehab was the downside to this setup. Rehab meant that she had been met off her JetBlue flight not by a chauffeur-driven limo, but a guy called Ramon driving a white minivan. And that she'd been taken, not to the Roosevelt Hotel or the Chateau Marmont, but to the Cascabel Recovery Center. Though Cascabel almost looked like a hotel from the outside, with its long white ranch-style buildings, its wide path leading up to the big sliding glass doors, surrounded by palm trees and oleander bushes, its gardens landscaped with plantain lilies, their leaves a riot of colour, from chartreuse to a verdant, almost bluish-green. Tiny white flowers were spiking up from the foliage. It was beautiful and welcoming.

And then the glass doors slid open, and Skye came down to earth with a bang. So much for Kevin selling this as a luxury spa. No hotel reception, no chic designer lighting and smiling greeters holding the door open. The only reason Ramon was pulling her bag from the back of the van was so he could hand it over to a guy in a white uniform, flashing him a significant look.

'Skye?' said a slim woman, coming forward.

She was dressed in jeans and a white shirt, no makeup; her brown skin was great, smooth and shiny, but drawn tightly over her bones. And her eyes were . . . Skye hesitated for a moment, wanting for some reason to find exactly the right word to describe the expression in the woman's hazel eyes. She looked as if she had seen everything there was to see, and yet there was no disillusionment or cynicism there. A little weariness, maybe, but that might just be that she'd been up since dawn dealing with other people's problems.

Experienced, Skye thought suddenly. She looks experienced. It wasn't a word Skye had ever thought of applying to someone as a compliment before, but in a weird way, now it was.

'I'm Daniyel,' the woman said, reaching out to shake Skye's hand, her own warm and very dry. 'That's D-A-N-I-Y-E-L.'

Daniyel smiled at Skye, and Skye recognized something else in Daniyel's gaze; an absolute boundary. Skye was used to that kind of thing in the Midnight Lounge, a look that another girl would give you on first meeting that told you not to mess with her, to back the fuck off and stay there. But this was different. Daniyel's look – *oh, Skye had it now*. She was like a teacher in reform school. A teacher who'd be fair and do her best by you, but one who let you know upfront, without a word being said, that she wouldn't stand any nonsense either.

Fair enough, Skye thought. But she knew damn well that there was no bribing this one. If Daniyel found the camera in Skye's bag, Skye'd be out on her ass before she could say 'whoops'.

'I'm the head tech around here. We're like the doctors' assistants,' Daniyel said. 'Me and the other techs are the people you'll see most of on a day-to-day basis.'

She led Skye through a set of swing doors, past a seating area decorated in middle-price-range IKEA, and down a corridor hung with paintings done in egg-yolk yellows and oranges: meant, Skye assumed, to cheer up residents going through withdrawal. When

Daniyel stopped, pushed open another door and gestured Skye to walk through, Skye found herself in a bedroom so bright with the same colours that she blinked hard.

'I guess we're not supposed to relax in here too much,' she observed drily.

Daniyel smiled, but there was watchfulness behind it; nothing Skye did or said would escape her scrutiny.

I'm being observed all the time, Skye realized. I've got to play the part twenty-four seven.

Accordingly, she slumped onto the closest bed, heaving a sigh. Then she did a genuine double-take.

'I'm *sharing*?' she exclaimed in horror, looking over at the other bed. 'I don't even share in *New York*, and our apartment's *tiny*!'

'Hopefully your roommate and you will build a supportive relationship,' Daniyel said cheerfully. 'That's the point of shared rooms. She's coming in tomorrow.'

'You're *kidding*,' Skye said in utter gloom.

Luxury spa my ass, she thought furiously. Kevin's in such shit when I get out of here, I swear to God. No one said *anything* about having to share a room!

A tap on the door heralded the arrival of Skye's bag, carried by the burly guy in white to whom Ramon had handed it in the entrance lobby.

'Dave's going to unpack your bag and check it for anything on our banned list while I go through the house rules with you,' Daniyel said, sitting down on the small orange armchair as Dave put Skye's suitcase down on the other bed and started to rifle through its contents. 'I understand you're a stripper, Skye.'

'Exotic dancer,' Skye said automatically.

'Did you bring any toys with you? Sex toys?'

Skye shook her head.

'Any prescription drugs? Sleeping pills?'

'I've got some Xanax,' Skye said, just as Dave pulled it out of her toiletry bag and brandished it in the air.

'We'll have to confiscate that, I'm afraid,' Daniyel said.

Skye threw herself back on the bed, sulking. It wasn't completely faked. And the sulks intensified when she felt the cheap mattress and pillows. Everything in this place was goddamn IKEA.

'How am I going to get to sleep?' she whined.

'We've got a wide selection of herbal teas,' Daniyel said calmly. 'And I suggest you avoid smoking before bed. Most clients here are smokers and I tell them all the same thing – nicotine's a stimulant.' Her voice softened a little. 'We do have meds if you really need them,' she assured Skye. 'But I think you'll find you'll be so exhausted by the work you're doing here that getting to sleep will be a non-issue.'

She glanced over at Dave. 'Anything else?'

'Clean,' he grunted.

'You didn't have to throw everything around like that,' Skye complained, looking over at her suitcase, which looked like the contents had exploded; she shouldn't seem too relaxed at having a strange guy go through her stuff.

'He's just doing his job,' Daniyel said pacifyingly as Dave popped open Skye's handbag and pawed inside.

She held her breath, watching him; had she misread that look between him and Ramon? What if Dave had decided to take the *Investigator*'s money and turn her in all the same?

Though honestly, she thought, weeks here without a drink or a Xanax, sleeping in a fucking single bed in a shared fucking *dorm room*, having to do *therapy* – maybe if Dave announces he's found the camera, it won't be the worst thing ever to happen to me in the world.

'Just some more Xanax,' Dave announced, tossing Daniyel another vial.

'I'm a nervous flyer,' Skye said.

'Believe me,' Daniyel said wryly, 'no need to explain. No one's come in this clean in years.'

'Found an eight-ball on a guy last week,' Dave grunted. 'Wouldn't't've been such a biggie, but he'd flown in from Hong Kong with it in his jeans pocket. Can you believe it?'

'Thanks, Dave,' Daniyel said as Dave nodded and lumbered out of the room. 'So, Skye, the rules of Cascabel: no one of the opposite sex in your room at any time. No overtly provocative clothes or behaviour. No asking people their last names. No touching other members of the group without asking their permission first. Smoking only outside. You have to be present for all group meetings, which start at eight a.m.'

'*Eight in the morning?*'

But Daniyel must have been used to this objection, because she rolled straight over it and continued: 'You must stay on the grounds, unless you're on a supervised excursion. If you're found with any forbidden substances on you, you will be asked to leave immediately. And obviously, there's no sexual contact at any time. Even –' she cleared her throat – 'with yourself.'

Skye sat up and stared at Daniyel, speechless with shock.

'You're here for sex addiction, right?' Daniyel asked, frowning, her gaze cool and assessing as she focused on Skye's reaction.

Skye nodded. 'And, uh, I do too much coke,' she managed to get out. 'Plus I overuse the Xanax, after I've binged on coke. You know?'

'Cross-addiction is really common,' Daniyel assured her. 'That's why our groups always have a variety of addicts.'

She uncrossed her slender legs and stood up. 'Well, I'll leave you to unpack and settle in. We have dinner at six and then a meditation session afterwards before bed.'

'I'm really jonesing for a cigarette,' Skye confessed. 'Can I go smoke now?'

Daniyel's frown decreased; Skye had clearly said something right.

'I *thought* you seemed too OK with us taking your Xanax!' Daniyel said. 'I've never seen an addict who didn't put up a fight to keep their sleeping pills before.'

'It's all a front,' Skye said quickly. 'Inside I'm screaming.'

'Well, this is a safe place to scream,' Daniyel said, but she didn't look completely convinced.

I've got to look more addicted, Skye told herself firmly, as Daniyel led her out of the room. I've got to watch the others and act more like them. Daniyel's as smart as a whip, as my mom used to say. And if I'm not fooling Daniyel, I sure as hell won't fool the shrinks.

'The garden area is through there,' Daniyel was saying, pointing down the corridor. 'Please use the ashtrays provided, OK? I'll come to collect you for your intake interview. And welcome to Cascabel, Skye. We hope you find what you're looking for here.'

That was weirdly prescient. Because what Skye was looking for happened to be in the garden, lying on a long stone slab that bordered a pool into which was trickling a tall, elegant bamboo water feature. His head thrown back to the sky, he seemed completely absorbed in an attempt to blow a perfect series of smoke rings. Hearing her step out onto the paving stones, he tilted his head sideways to see who had just arrived; and, on spotting Skye's blonde hair and curvy figure, he sat up enthusiastically.

'Well, hey!' he said, looking her up and down. 'Just joined us at the Cascabel five-star spa retreat?'

Skye thought she giggled, but she couldn't be sure. It was as if she had lost control of her entire body the moment her eyes made contact with his. Of course she'd met celebrities before: the Lounge had hosted plenty of them: TV actors and presenters, sports stars, politicians. But never celebrity with this sheer wattage: never a major movie star at the height of his fame and glamour.

Joe Jeffreys was the sexiest man Skye had ever met. Actors were almost always a disappointment, height-wise; an action hero might look over six foot onscreen but in the flesh would turn out to be five foot six. Joe Jeffreys had to be six foot two, wide-shouldered and big-muscled; he towered over her. And he had so much natural charisma that it actually radiated from him like a wave of heat. It was what hit her first, even before she realized how handsome he was: his sheer personal magnetism. She found herself walking towards him without even being aware of what she was doing, as if he'd lassoed her and pulled her in like the big gorgeous suntanned cowboy he could easily have been.

Golden hair, bright denim-blue eyes, dark-gold skin; he was like sunshine come to life. She could have held out her hands and warmed them in his force-field.

Skye goggled at him as he said, looking at her with a more-than-appreciative grin, his deep sexy drawl infinitely familiar to her already from all the movies of his she'd seen: 'I'm Joe.'

'I'm Skye,' she managed, amazed she could even get her lips to move, let alone form coherent words.

'I'd give you a hug to say hi, but they've got these no-touching rules here,' Joe said, rolling his eyes, 'and I've got busted a coupla times already.'

The mere thought of being hugged by him sent waves of heat up and down Skye's body.

Thank God I touched up my makeup when we were taxiing to the stand at Burbank, she thought with huge relief. Her big blue eyes were outlined with mascara, her cheeks were lightly touched with blusher, her lips were pale pink and shiny with L'Oréal plumping gloss. She'd applied fresh DKNY perfume; she was wearing snug jeans and a T-shirt that clung to her without being so low-cut that Daniyel would make her change it. And she'd brushed her hair into a glossy, high ponytail. There wasn't a man in the States who didn't like a ponytail. It reminded them of cheerleaders.

'Yeah, I just got the rules breakdown from Daniyel,' Skye said, pulling her cigarettes out of her pocket. Joe was there with a lighter before she'd even put the Merit to her lips.

'Thanks,' she said, inhaling, raising her gaze so he got the full, upward-tilted flirty look through her long lashes. 'Oh, and you're not supposed to ask me my last name either.' She flashed him her best sexy stare; the nicotine, plus the familiar routine of dragging on her cigarette, were helping her get her confidence back. 'Though you probably recognized me as soon as you saw me, right? 'Cause I'm a really famous movie star.'

Joe frowned automatically, aware that couldn't be true, because he would have known her if it were. It took a beat, no more, before he realized she was finding a cute way to refer to his near-godlike status without sucking up to him.

His grin widened into a big, appreciative smile.

'Pretty *and* funny,' he said happily. 'Well, I got lucky, didn't I? Come over here, Miss Skye, and tell me all about yourself.'

Not half as lucky as you're going to get, Skye thought happily, following Joe Jeffreys over to the fountain. The back view was nearly as breathtaking as the front. The muscles of his back and arms were clearly defined, even through his T-shirt; his ass, in faded blue jeans, was as firm and round as a speed skater's, and he walked like an athlete. Skye remembered photos she'd seen of him in *People* magazine, a high-school quarterback at eighteen, holding his helmet and grinning at the camera, before he'd been spotted by a model scout and whisked away from the Iowa corn-fields for ever.

Joe lowered himself on the stone slab again. It was warm from the sun, and as she curled up opposite him, she felt like a cat settling itself down, purring with pleasure.

All I need is Joe stroking my fur, she thought naughtily.

She looked at him, and was more than happy to see that his gaze was openly directed to her figure, checking her out, lingering on her thighs, her narrow waist, and the swell of her breasts, before rising again to her face. She met it with a glint of acknowledgement in her eyes, a dimpling smile, that told him she knew exactly what he'd been looking at and she didn't have the least objection in the world.

'I should tell you straight up, Joe, what I do for a living,' she said, going in for the kill. 'I'm an exotic dancer.'

She widened her eyes and gave him her most innocent stare, knowing that her big blue eyes, her pretty, girlish features, were a perfect contrast to the admission she was making. Reaching round, she took hold of her ponytail with one hand and played with it, tilt-ing her head to the side as she continued: 'Well, a stripper, if I'm being completely honest.'

'Joe might be at Cascabel under false pretences, but he's got to think you're completely legit,' Kevin had warned her. 'Don't be fooled by that country-boy act he pulls. He's pretty smart. If he thinks for a moment you're a plant, you're fucked.'

'You're not going to look down on me 'cause of my job, are you?' Skye finished, giving him a pleading, seductive look.

Have I gone too far? she wondered for a second. Was that too obvious?

And then Joe's ridiculously handsome face broke into a shit-eating grin, as he threw his head back and burst out laughing.

'Look down on you? Baby, I'm more likely to . . .' He winked at her. 'Well, let's just say I'd goddamn *love* to look down on you, if you catch my drift! Jesus . . .' He shifted on the stone, and Skye's gaze was drawn down to his crotch. His jeans were old and worn, but not so loose that she couldn't see the effect her body and her admission had had on him.

Oh, thank *God* – he's built to scale, she noted with huge relief. He was smiling at her ruefully, acknowledging his erection, giving a slight shrug of his shoulders that said, Hey, what can I do? You're a gorgeous chick and now you've got me picturing you in a thong on a pole!

All her flirtatious artifice forgotten, Skye broke into a big, happy smile, as natural as his. This was how things were supposed to be: easy, fun, both of you laughing from the get-go, knowing perfectly well you were going to end up naked and giving each other the ride of a lifetime.

'Boy oh boy,' Joe said, shaking his head, his eyes glinting, and reaching for his pack of Camels. 'Trapped in sex rehab with the girl of my dreams, and banned from laying a finger on her.'

He lit up and blew a big, round smoke ring straight at her. Skye puckered her lips into a kiss and blew it back at him; for a moment, before it dissolved, they watched it hang in the air between them. Shifting again, pulling at his jeans to ease off the pressure on his crotch, Joe let out a long sigh of infinite frustration.

'I tell you, babe,' he said frankly, 'this is going to be the longest goddamn month of my entire life.'

Petal

'*T*his is *crap*! This is *total*, *fucking crap*! I shouldn't even *be* here!'
Petal wailed. 'This is a *shitheap*!'

She kicked the bed furiously, then wailed as she stubbed her toe.

'And *you* – get out of my *bag*, for fuck's sake!'

Stumbling, she lunged towards Dave, who was unbuckling the straps of her beloved Balenciaga bag and reaching in one wide, meaty hand.

'That's *my* stuff! It's *personal*!'

'We have to go through everything, Petal,' said Daniyel from behind her. 'It's Cascabel policy.'

Petal swung round on her, hands on her hips, her small form radiating fury, like a kitten having a tantrum.

'You get off on this, don't you?' she snapped furiously. 'You get off on the power!'

Infuriatingly, Daniyel refused to be drawn. Instead, she replied sympathetically: 'I understand it's unpleasant to see someone going through your things. But we can't let you keep items that are banned here. If you're carrying drugs, you could risk an overdose, for instance—'

'I just flew in from London! How the fuck do you think I'd manage to score between the airport and here!' Petal screamed.

'Codeine,' Dave said flatly, dropping onto the coverlet the two big red packets of Solpadeine Petal had picked up at Heathrow.

'That's *headache pills*!' Petal wailed. 'What if I get a *headache*?'

'Codeine's a narcotic,' Daniyel pointed out, as Dave unzipped Petal's gold leather Tarte vanity bag and dumped out the contents. 'We can give you medication for headaches, if you have any withdrawal symptoms.'

'Ritalin, Xanax . . .' Dave said, pawing through the plastic strips of pills and containers. 'Uppers, downers. The usual suspects.'

'Oh my *God*, you're taking *those*?' Petal's jaw dropped. 'I thought I was just here about doing coke!'

She watched in horror as Dave pulled a flimsy plastic bag out of his pocket and scooped all her pills into it, handing it over to Daniyel. Desperately, she lunged towards the bag, trying to rip it away from them; but somehow Dave's bulk interposed itself between her and Daniyel, and his sheer size blocked her completely. He had to weigh over twenty stone; her hands, beating briefly on his torso, looked so tiny and futile they fell to her sides almost immediately in defeat.

'You *can't* . . .' she wailed, but she already knew it was a lost battle. Gulping, throwing herself on the bed, she grabbed her handbag and rifled through it, going for the snug inside pocket that contained her Swarovski-studded mobile phone. Frantically, she hit a familiar key sequence and started texting; but the next thing she knew, Daniyel's slim hand reached down over her shoulder and slid the phone out of her grasp so efficiently that Petal didn't even have time to tighten her grip.

'That's *mine*!' she yelled.

'Cellphones are banned,' Daniyel said gently, slipping Petal's into her pocket, 'though we may allow you to have yours back for controlled periods if you're responding well to treatment. We do have a phone here that you're allowed to use, out in the hall.'

'Oh my *God*!'

Petal burst into hysterical floods of tears. She was jet-lagged, mildly hungover – she'd been hitting the free champagne heavily on her Virgin flight over, knowing it would be the last alcohol she'd get for weeks – and in huge withdrawal from Dan, who she was already missing terribly. She'd practically crawled home from her meeting with Gold and Jinhee and spent the rest of the day, and her last night, wrapped in his arms, crying and cursing her fate.

Tas and JC had come round, of course. And they'd all come in the limo with her to Heathrow, drinking fizz like it was going out of fashion in a vain attempt to cheer her up. Tas, the only practical one in the bunch, had done her best to spin Petal's stay at Cascabel as a positive outcome.

'You *were* caning it,' she'd said with her normal brutal frankness. 'You know you were, man.'

'Tas—' JC started, but Tas wouldn't be cut off.

'No, come on!' she'd said, looking around her. 'We all know Petal was caning it! She missed every single appointment we got for her. We're a team, yeah? All for one and one for all. But we can't make it without Petal doing her bit.'

Petal had slumped back against Dan, hanging her head.

'Accessorize . . . Rimmel . . . they won't look at me now,' she'd muttered guiltily.

'No, but what about when you come back all cleaned up?' Tas had said encouragingly. 'They'll be all over you! Everyone goes to rehab nowadays, it's cool! You do some big interviews . . .'

'"My Drug Hell",' JC muttered.

'– and everyone'll be queuing up to get your face on their ads!' Tas had finished cheerfully.

'Bit of scandal never hurt anyone in the long run,' Dan had agreed, stroking her hair. 'And we're going into the recording studio next week, pet. I'll be in there all hours. You'd barely have seen me anyway.'

'You'll all ring me, won't you?' Petal had pleaded miserably. 'Every day? I'm going to be so lonely . . .'

They'd all promised faithfully that they would; but she'd assumed, of course, that she'd be able to keep her mobile with her.

Now, looking around her nasty shared room at Cascabel, Petal could see that there was no TV – worse, no computer. And her phone was tucked into Daniyel's pocket.

'I wouldn't have *come*!' Petal collapsed on the bed, grabbing a pillow to hug for comfort. 'I wouldn't have *come* to this fucking place if I'd known I wasn't even going to be allowed to *text* my *boyfriend* . . . *God!*'

I'll be gone for a whole month, she thought frantically. Anything could happen in a month! There'll be tons of girls after him – he's so gorgeous, and now we've been photographed together all the time, everyone'll be chasing him to try to get where I've been. How is he ever going to resist all those girls throwing themselves at him if I can't even get in touch with him?

'We can schedule calls for you and your boyfriend,' Daniyel said kindly, but that just made Petal sob even harder.

'He's in a *band*! He's practically a *rock star*!' she yelled through the pillow. 'You don't schedule calls with *rock stars*, for fuck's sake! He doesn't work in a bloody *bank*!'

'I'm going to give you half an hour to feel your feelings,' Daniyel said, as Dave left the room with Petal's stash of pills. 'Then I'll come and collect you for your intake interview. Would you like me to bring you a cup of tea? Maybe camomile? It's very calming.'

'Go away!' Petal screeched, her voice rising high enough that it could easily have been heard by any bats in the Los Angeles area. 'Go *away*, go *away*, go *away*!'

The pillow was already drenched with tears. She grabbed the other one, and the duvet too, bundling them all up over and around her, packing herself in under layers of padding, insulating herself as best she could from the outside world and the horrible, brutal reality of this place she'd been dumped in. Her nose was clogged up with snot, her head was throbbing; she'd been craving a text from Dan, or at least the ability to read through the lovely ones he'd sent her since they'd been dating.

When Daniyel returned, carrying a big glass of water, Petal was almost passed out in a sodden, tear-stained mess of sheets and duvets. Daniyel eased them off her, handed her the water and went into the ensuite bathroom to dampen a hand towel for Petal's face. Petal was so exhausted by her emotional meltdown that she didn't have a drop of energy left to resist: like a zombie, she sat up, washed her face with the towel that was handed to her, drank the water and got to her feet as she was told, following Daniyel out of the room and down the corridor.

Daniyel had paused and was about to tap on a door when it swung open, and a stunning girl emerged. Even in Petal's debilitated state, she could tell what a bombshell the girl was: blonde, slim, but with curves in all the right places, and a baby-sweet face with big blue eyes, smooth skin and a shiny pink pout.

And also, Petal noticed, the girl seemed shell-shocked. She barely acknowledged Petal and Daniyel, moving slowly past them and down the corridor in a sort of trance, her blonde ponytail, its end curled prettily into one big ringlet, bouncing behind her as she walked.

'Dr Raf?' Daniyel was saying as she entered the room, Petal on her heels. 'I have Petal Gold here. Do you want to take five, or shall I bring her in now?'

It was a doctor's office, lined with bookshelves, an examination table on one side with a curtain on a rail half drawn around it. A man was rising from behind a desk, coming round it to greet them, and as soon as Petal caught sight of him, she realized why the girl who'd just left had had that stunned expression.

God, he's fucking *gorgeous*, Petal thought inelegantly. He looks like an actor playing a doctor on a TV show. Or one of those American soaps – *General Hospital* or something.

'Hi, Petal, and welcome to Cascabel,' he was saying, smiling at her, taking her hand and enfolding it briefly in both of his, which were dry and warm and strong. 'I'm Dr Rafael Green, one of the consulting psychiatrists here at the clinic. Call me Dr Raf, everyone else does. Please, take a seat. Thank you, Daniyel,' he added over Petal's shoulder.

'Just beep me when you're finished here, and I'll come back and give Petal a tour of the facility,' Daniyel said, and Petal could hear how even tough, focused Daniyel softened her voice when she spoke to Dr Raf.

Daniyel closed the door, and Dr Raf took the seat opposite Petal, in front of the desk; they were face to face, and Petal almost found herself wishing that he was sitting behind the desk instead, in a more formal setup. Having him this close was disconcerting. Although he was pretty old by Petal's standards – he had to be mid-thirties, at least, and when guys that age hit on Petal in clubs, she was merciless in mocking their aspirations – he was so handsome that it was hard to feel natural around him.

'How are you feeling, Petal?' he asked gently, his dark eyes intent and empathetic. 'You must be pretty jet-lagged, right?'

Even though he wore glasses, his eyes were amazing, so dark brown they were almost black. His hair was the same colour, thick and so curly it was almost in ringlets; a couple of curls fell over his forehead as he leaned forward to hear Petal's response. His features were strong, dominated by a Roman nose and a very defined jaw-line, and his skin was pale olive. He looked like his family came from the Mediterranean. Italian or Jewish, maybe.

Awkward, feeling she was gawking at Dr Raf's chiselled features, Petal lowered her gaze, but that didn't help much. He was wearing a white shirt, the sleeves rolled up to below the elbows, showing lean, strong forearms. Petal's ideal was a guy built like Dan: definitely muscled, but skinny enough to fit into toothpick-sized jeans. Dr Raf would *not* fit into Dan's jeans, that was definite. His flat-fronted black trousers showed off slim hips, but the way his trousers pulled a little over his thighs, the way the cotton of his shirt stretched over his chest and shoulders, it was clear that he was no stranger to the weights room at the gym.

'Petal?' he repeated. 'Can you tell me how you're holding up?'

Petal snapped her attention back to his questions. To be honest, she'd been focusing on his looks to avoid answering; she was exhausted and woozy, she had a screaming headache, and the last thing she felt like doing was running through a list of her woes. She just wanted to be left alone and, preferably, pass out.

'I'm really tired,' she muttered.

He nodded sympathetically.

'Maybe we scheduled this talk a little early,' he said. 'Here's a suggestion: why don't you go back to your room and catch up on some sleep? Not too much, because we want to get you onto LA time. But you could have a nap, maybe shower and freshen up, and then I could see you back here in a couple of hours? How does that sound?'

His voice was a light tenor: cappuccino, rather than dark black coffee. It was soft and soothing and so easy to listen to that the effect was almost hypnotic, like sliding into a warm bath. Petal met his brown eyes again, and what she saw in them was an empathetic concern for her wellbeing. He was frowning slightly as he attempted to work out what would be best for her.

And that was all it took. She hadn't realized how alone she was feeling till right at that moment, cut off from everyone she cared about. Tas, JC, Dan were all left behind in London; they'd waved goodbye to her at the departure gates, and then they'd all got to go back together, while Petal had had to set off on her own. She lived in a bubble of activity, a posse always around her, and since she'd got together with Dan, they'd been pretty much attached at the hip. This was the first time she'd been without her boyfriend or her entourage, and she absolutely hated it.

Suddenly, it all came pouring out. Dr Raf, without taking his eyes off Petal, reached for a box of tissues on his desk and slid it over so it was right next to her, and Petal grabbed a whole wodge with one hand as the words and the tears streamed out of her.

The frustration of growing up with a father who was world-famous even before you were born; people's ridiculous expectations for you, how you could never achieve them, so it felt stupid even to try. Her mum, Linda, pretty much just dumping her on Gold and fucking off to the States to try to become an actress, which was totally doomed, because her mum wasn't remotely talented at anything but taking most of her clothes off and smiling brightly. Her mum going on at her – whenever she bothered to get in touch, which was practically never – because Gold wasn't doing enough to help Linda get cast in things.

How she'd grown up, bounced from one nanny to another, practically never seeing her dad. Being taught to call him Gold, not Daddy, practically from the beginning. The parties and bad behaviour and revolving door of models and starlets she'd seen at Gold's mansion, because honestly, all of the nannies had a huge crush on Gold and though they were told to keep Petal away, they mostly didn't, because they had fantasies that Gold would see what a fantastic mother they were being to his little girl and fall madly in love with them, so instead of keeping Petal away from the action, they'd let her run straight into it so they could hang out too. They'd always got the sack, but in the process Petal had seen way more than a kid her age should have done.

'Which makes it so bloody *unfair*,' she sobbed, knuckling her eyes, which were red and sore by now. 'He's such a fucking *hypocrite*! I mean, all I did was a bit of charlie! Gold's done *everything*! It's a miracle he's still alive! It's all very well to clean up when you've had your fun and got all your bad behaviour out of the way, yeah, but I'm, like, just *twenty*! I'm *supposed* to be going to parties and getting a bit pissed and acting like an idiot. It's what people my age do!'

She ran out of breath, blowing her nose and staring at Dr Raf defiantly, daring him to disagree with a word she'd said.

'Is it?' Dr Raf asked mildly.

'You what?' Petal said, confused.

'*Is* it what people of your age do, generally?' he clarified, his gaze just as friendly and open as ever.

'Well, yeah!' Petal said defensively. 'I mean, all my mates – we're always going out on the lash! And it's not like we're the only ones.'

'This is probably going to make me sound like I'm a hundred

years old,' Dr Raf said, with such a sweet, open, self-deprecating smile that Petal found herself smiling back at him, 'but with all the partying you're describing, isn't it very hard to get up in the morning and go to work? Or get any studying done?'

Petal flinched. He'd managed to find her weakest spot.

'We're more alternative than that,' she said. 'I mean, we don't have the kind of nine-to-five jobs that mean you have to get up at the crack of dawn.'

'Lucky you!'

'Well, yeah, obviously. I mean, Tas is a stylist, so she *does* work really hard, it's just freelance, and JC – my hairdresser – he's freelance too, but he's getting booked a lot for shoots and stuff because all the photos of me in the papers are really good publicity for him . . .' Petal fingered her lemon-coloured bob. 'And Dan, that's my boyfriend –' Tears welled up again, and she grabbed for more tissues – 'his band's really taking off now, so he's doing tons of press and they're booking a tour of the States, they're supporting the Arctic Monkeys, so that's, like, *huge* . . .'

'And you?' Dr Raf's expression was as friendly and interested as ever. 'Are you as busy as all of them?'

'I've got a column,' Petal said defiantly, though a voice in her head was saying loudly: *You don't actually write that, though. They just ring you up once a week and ask what you think about other celebs, or bubble skirts, or what's on the TV, and then they edit it all together and put it in the magazine.*

There was a long pause. Petal was scrabbling for something else, anything, that she could come up with as an achievement, or source of income. She found herself desperately needing Dr Raf to think well of her, not just dismiss her as a spoiled rich kid. There was something about him, something so understanding and non-judgemental, that made her want to put her best foot forward with him, hear his soft voice approving of the way she was living her life. Dr Raf sat back, crossing one black-trousered leg over the other, looking as if he was happy for Petal to take all the time she needed.

The tap on the door, followed almost immediately by the turn of the handle as it was opened, took them both by surprise.

'Lucy!' Dr Raf turned to face the intruder. 'I'm in session.'

'Oh!'

Petal, swivelling too, saw a very slender woman in a white knee-length lab coat, hanging open at the front, which pronounced her a doctor as clearly as if she had a stethoscope around her neck. Her hair was dark and pulled back into a sleek chignon, and her white shirt and slim dark trousers were so well fitted they were clearly very expensive. A tall, striking figure, she was still standing in the open doorway, which seemed a bit odd to Petal; shouldn't she have excused herself as soon as she saw Dr Raf had a patient?

'It's just,' the Lucy woman said, 'I thought we had a meeting now – it's in my BlackBerry.'

Dr Raf, grimacing, raised his shoulders and let them fall again.

'Can you check that with Daniyel?' he said, his voice tight, as if he were trying not to show irritation.

'Um, sure! Sorry!'

The woman called Lucy hadn't even looked at Petal during this interchange; Petal was bristling with annoyance.

It's bloody rude just to barge in and not say sorry to me! she thought furiously. I mean, it's *my* session – my dad's *paying* for this.

'I'm dying for a fag, anyway,' she said loudly, standing up to make the point to this rude Lucy that she existed. 'I'll let you two have your meeting.'

'Petal, please feel free to stay,' Dr Raf said quickly. 'I'm so sorry about this. Lucy can come back later – this is Dr Lucy Tennant, she's part of our consulting team.'

'No, it's ruined now.' Petal knew she was sounding spoiled, but she didn't care. 'And you should say sorry to *me*, not *him*,' she added to the Lucy woman, tossing her head. 'It was you who interrupted when I was talking about really personal stuff. If you're a doctor, you should totally know better than that.'

Lucy's jaw dropped, Petal was pleased to see.

And she's actually not that good-looking, Petal thought, getting a closer look at her. Her eyes are too close together, and her lips are really thin.

'You can smoke in the garden, Petal,' Dr Raf said, smiling apologetically at her. 'I'm sorry our session was interrupted, but you did some very good work. I look forward to seeing you in group tomorrow morning.'

It was stupid, but Petal was ridiculously boosted by Dr Raf's words of approval. Not to mention having put that Lucy bitch in her place. But the high lasted only until, snatching the Balenciaga bag with her fags and lighter from her room, she caught sight of herself in the mirror and blanched. All her mascara was long gone, sobbed away on her pillowcases. Her eyes were red and swollen and her skin was blotchy. The lemon-yellow hair colour only worked when she had makeup on; without it, she looked as drained as if DynoRod had just done a job on her.

For a moment Petal considered trying to patch up the damage, and then shrugged miserably; what was the point? She didn't give a shit about anyone here. She just had to keep her head down, make sure she didn't get kicked out, and serve her month's sentence. By that time Dan would be out of the recording studio. Maybe he could fly out here for a holiday. And in the meantime, who gave a fuck if a bunch of junkies thought she looked like death warmed up?

The garden was stunning. Her bedroom might look like something from a Howard Johnson motel, but the garden was top-notch serious designer stuff. Petal had grown up with the best, and she recognized it immediately. The sound of running water greeted her as soon as she stepped out of the air-conditioned hallway into the soft, slightly moist, California spring air. Tall palms shaded a patio eating area equipped with a long pine-and-steel table, surrounded by a set of matching chairs. Beyond was a fountain, water streaming gently from a series of high bamboo poles into a wide shallow pool in which water lilies floated. The enclosing walls were rich with bougainvillaea, and to the left, loungers were dotted on a lawn whose grass was clustered with tiny white daisies.

Sunshine flooded onto Petal as she grabbed an ashtray from the table and walked onto the lawn, intending to collapse on a lounger and have a couple of cigarettes back to back to compensate her for everything she'd been through that day. But as she crossed the grass, she heard a high, flirty laugh, saw the sun catching and glinting on a flash of blonde hair; a second later, she realized that she had walked in on a very cosy twosome.

Lying on the grass, arms spread out in the sunshine, was the blonde who Petal had seen exiting Dr Raf's office. One leg was bent, her bare sole on the grass; it was a sexy, camera-ready pose the girl would never have affected without an audience.

There was only one spectator, stretched on a lounger, eyeing the girl on the grass with blatant appreciation, but he was famous enough to be worth a whole theatreful of nonentities. Most people would have done a double-take at realizing they were in the presence of Joe Jeffreys, voted *People*'s Sexiest Man Alive this year, earner of $25 million a picture, action star supreme. But Petal wasn't most people. She'd grown up in Gold's house, seeing Jude Law flirt with her nannies.

She had to admit, though, that Joe Jeffreys was pretty fucking amazing in the flesh. Jude Law was a bit of a potato-head in real life. But Joe Jeffreys – well, apart from being hot in that beefy American way, he had that whole charisma thing going on.

Still, Petal wasn't going to let Joe Jeffreys and some bleach-blonde wannabe deter her from lying out in the sunshine. Marching up to the lounger she'd picked out, she dropped onto it, throwing out: 'Hi, I'm Petal,' curtly as she did so.

'Hey, I'm Skye,' said the girl on the grass.

She had nerve, Petal had to admit; she hadn't been the slightest bit taken aback at the sudden intrusion of a stranger into her cosy little setup. Most girls would have jumped or something, Petal thought, lighting up a Silk Cut. This one hasn't moved an inch. She's tough.

Joe Jeffreys grinned at Petal. 'And I'm Joe,' he drawled.

'Yeah, I know,' she said, barely favouring him with a glance.

As she'd known it would from her long experience, this piqued his interest.

'I know you from somewhere?' he asked.

'My dad's Gold,' she said bluntly. Always better to get it out of the way first, she'd found.

'Cool,' said the blonde girl, Skye. 'I love his music.'

'I met him at a fundraiser for Darfur last year,' Joe Jeffreys said. 'Nice guy.'

'You must be thinking of someone else,' Petal said coldly.

There was a pause, and then Skye giggled; Joe Jeffreys let out a burst of laughter. 'Jesus,' he said. 'I'm so glad I don't have kids.'

'But you're *engaged*,' said Skye, rolling over onto her flat stomach so her pert bottom poked up in the air, picking a piece of grass and running it slowly over her full pink mouth so Joe Jeffreys' attention was completely riveted on her again. 'You're going to get married to America's sweetheart and have lots of beautiful blond, blue-eyed rugrats just like the nation wants, right?'

'Whatever you say, darlin',' Joe drawled, his eyes nailed to Skye's parted lips, her white teeth biting down on the blade of grass.

'What are you guys here for?' Petal asked.

There was another pause. Then Skye said lightly: 'I'm a sex addict. Just can't live without it.'

'Me too,' Joe Jeffreys said in a heartfelt tone. 'Me too, babe.'

'What about you, Petal?' Skye looked over at the other girl, seeing her properly for the first time. 'What are you here for? Oh my God, you're like, a baby! Don't tell me *you're* a sex addict!'

'I'm twenty,' Petal blurted out crossly, wishing she'd done her makeup after all. 'And no, I'm not a sex addict, OK? Gold dumped me in here 'cause I got in the British papers doing a bit of coke. *Total* fucking overreaction.'

Joe Jeffreys stretched his big, muscled arms over his head; the wood of the lounger creaked as he moved, and neither girl could help her eyes being drawn to him. He was like a big golden lion, basking in the sun.

'At least he cares about you, honey,' he said kindly. 'That's more than a lot of people I know in this town do. They just let their kids run wild.'

'Oh, for *fuck's sake*!' Petal jumped up, grabbing her bag. 'You don't know *anything* about my life – you know *nothing* about me or Gold or what a shitty dad he's been.'

She stormed off across the grass, seething with frustration. That was all she needed – some film star taking a moment out of perving at some blonde bimbo to lecture her about her dad.

Joe a sex addict? Bollocks. No one's that relaxed in rehab, Petal thought furiously. He's probably just here for some publicity bullshit. That's how their world works. That's why I'm here – with Gold's new CD coming out, he's dumped me in rehab 'cause he needs to look like he's doing something about me.

Petal had reached the patio. The sight of the fountain – water pouring from the bamboo poles, filling the pool, flowing over the lip of the stone rim – was so mesmerizing that she stopped in her tracks, realizing that she had flounced off without any destination in mind. Her room wasn't exactly a refuge, with its single bed and cheap sheets. There wasn't even a tub in the bathroom – probably because the miserable inmates couldn't be trusted not to drown themselves. She was frantic to get out of here, but her father's threat to cut off her finances was huge; it kept her in Cascabel as securely as if there were iron bars on every door.

There's nowhere to go, she thought desperately.

She stood, looking at the fountain, the water flowing down, so beautiful, so hypnotizing.

Maybe I should have a shower. I'm all jet-lagged and my head hurts. Or maybe . . .

Petal threw her bag on the pine table, kicked off her trainers, unzipped her hoodie and tossed it on one of the chairs, and, hopping as she pulled off her socks, crossed the flagstones of the patio, climbed up on the stone lip of the fountain, and jumped into the pool. The water was wonderfully cool. She sat down, gasping at the shock of it, and put her head directly under the bamboo poles.

Water flooded over her face, her hair, in a constant stream. She was sitting among white and mauve water lilies, her T-shirt and jeans clinging to her skin, her arms floating on the surface, blinking to keep her eyes clear, sunshine dappling the surface of the pond.

It felt absolutely brilliant.

Amber

*A*mber had barely any memory of anything that happened between her sinking what must have been almost a litre of vodka and God knew how many Vicodins and Percocets in her bedroom on Green Street, and waking up, dazed, in a narrow bed in a darkened room whose topography she could not recognize at all. Totally confused, head still heavy and feeling like it was stuffed with cotton wool, she managed to pull herself back and up till she was half sitting, propped on a pillow, and let her eyes adjust to the murky lighting.

This can't be a hotel – not with a bed this small. Am I in someone's house?

Next to her was a small side table, with a lamp on it, and a pile of magazines. Fumbling for the light switch, she ran her fingers up the base of the lamp to see if it was under the shade. When it didn't seem to be there, she tried to locate the cord instead, in case the switch was on it; but she must have pulled the cord too hard, because as she tugged, there came a crash as the magazines thunked heavily to the floor in a cascade of solid glossy paper, slipping off each other in a series of thuds.

Oh, no . . .

'Hey!' The door opened, and a shaft of light sliced into the darkened room as a girl put her head round it. 'You're awake! How are you?'

'Where am I?' Amber asked feebly.

'You're in rehab, honey,' the girl said drily. 'I'm going to get the nurse, OK? They said to call them when you woke up.'

She disappeared, leaving the door ajar.

In rehab? Amber wriggled up a bit further till her back was fully against the headboard. *And that girl sounded American . . .*

Oh my God.

The American accent had triggered flashes of memory. She'd been on a plane, hadn't she? With Slava? Slava hated to travel – hated, really, to leave the flat; if Amber remembered being on a plane with her mother, it must have been really recently, because it would be the only time it had ever happened. And the accent – she'd been pushed in a wheelchair, with someone talking over her shoulder, handing her passport to a man in a uniform sitting behind a glass screen, who had to crane over to look down at her . . . He'd asked her questions, but she didn't understand, or couldn't make her lips move to answer him, and the guy pushing her had had to ask her mother to respond to him instead . . .

Why am I in America, for God's sake? What happened *to me?*

'Amber! You're awake!' said a woman's voice from the doorway, and the overhead light was turned on, flooding the room.

Amber blinked, raising a hand to shelter her eyes.

'Where am I?' she asked again.

'You're at the Cascabel rehab clinic. You came in this morning.'

Neatly pleating up her grey tailored trousers above her knees, the woman sat down on the bed next to Amber's, leaning forward to scrutinize Amber's face.

'I'm Daniyel. How are you doing?' she asked.

'I don't know!' Amber shook her head in an attempt to clear it. 'I don't know where I am or how I got here!'

Daniyel nodded understandingly. She was slender, dressed in a grey jacket that matched her trousers, with taut, light brown skin and dark circles under her eyes.

'You were still under some sort of sedation when you came in,' she said. 'We ran checks on you and you seemed in a stable condition, so the doctor decided you should be left to sleep it off. We've been monitoring you, of course, but your breathing's been fine. I'm not surprised you don't remember your arrival.'

'But how did I even . . .?' Amber could barely get the words out, there were so many questions to ask. 'Where *is* Cascabel?'

'We're in California, just outside Los Angeles. Your boyfriend wanted you to come here when you had your overdose.'

'My *boyfriend*?'

Amber's voice had risen dangerously, and Daniyel was beginning to look worried.

'You don't remember a whole lot, do you, sweetie?' she said, frowning.

'Where's my mother?' Amber demanded. 'She was on the plane with me, wasn't she? And I remember her going through security – where is she? Is she here?'

'She's in LA, yes. She checked you in and then left. But the doctor will be coming in soon – he just needs to finish up a consultation and then he'll be right here. He can answer all your questions in more detail.'

'No, I want to talk to my mother!' Amber was almost wailing now. 'I need to find out what's been going on! I thought I was going to *Dubai*,' she added more feebly. 'I thought, when I was on the plane . . .' This was coming back to her now, panicked moments coming to consciousness on the airplane, when she'd believed she was heading to Dubai with Mara.

I freaked out, she remembered. I totally freaked out. I started crying and saying I didn't want to go to Dubai – and then I saw *Matka*, and I thought she was coming with me to make sure I went to Dubai after all, and I panicked, and she got me to take some pills to calm me down. No wonder I was zonked when they checked me in here. *Matka* must have given me a whole handful . . .

'Dubai?' Daniyel was looking really worried now. 'Look, I have a

number for where your mom's staying, OK? If you'd like to call
her –'

Amber was nodding frantically now.

'– I'll bring a phone straight in.' Daniyel was standing up, heading for the door. 'But you have to stay calm, OK?'

She was back almost immediately with an old-fashioned phone,
its handset connected by a cord. Bending down, she plugged it into
a socket behind the side table.

'I'm going to dial the number for you,' she said to Amber. 'And I
have to stay here during your conversation, so I can make sure it's
not making you too agitated . . .'

Amber was barely listening. She practically snatched the receiver
from Daniyel, panicking when the ring tone went on and on, gasping with relief when, finally, it was answered and Slava snapped
abruptly: 'Yes?'

'*Matka*!' Amber gulped in a deep breath. '*Matka*, what's been
happening? They said something about a *boyfriend*. *Matka*, why am
I here? Why are we in *California*?'

Slava sighed. 'You don't remember, *láska*?' she said heavily. 'You
were very sick. I was frightened for you. You would not wake up,
even when I shook you and called your name. I ring Jared, he says to
call the ambulance. They come to take you to the hospital, but first
they put tube into you and empty your stomach.'

'They had to *pump my stomach*?'

'Then they drive you to the hospital. I go with you. The doctor
says you will be OK, but they are not happy. They want to keep you
there one day, but I say no, I will look after you, I am your mother.'

Amber bit her lip. She was remembering now, more bits and
pieces – feeling the tube down her throat, thrashing around, being
held down . . .

'I bring you back home, but you are not well,' Slava was saying.
'I think I will telephone to the doctor you go to when you get the
pills. But then someone comes. This nice man! He rings Jared to see
you, and Jared says you are sick, so he comes with flowers. Tony. I
take him to you and he is very –' she searched for a word – 'sad,' she

finished finally. 'He says he wants to help you. A man he knows has come to the hospital where you are, in America, and he is very well now. Not sick any more. So Tony says you must come here. He pays for *everything*,' she said triumphantly. 'I come with you, he pays for that. Business class, very nice. He has house – his company has house – here in Los Angeles. I stay here while you get well.'

Amber was finding it almost impossible to take in the sheer stream of information pouring out of her mother.

'*Tony* . . .?' she repeated blankly, bewildered by this completely unexpected turn of events.

'He's good man, *láska*!' her mother said happily. 'And the house here, it's very nice too! Don't worry for me, I do very good here.'

A picture of Tony swam into Amber's mind: big, brawny, perpetually smiling Tony, with his tan and his perfect white teeth. Tony, with his childish love of the *Sports Illustrated* video of her, his excitement at seeing her all dressed up. 'My fantasy girl', he'd called her.

Never in a million years would she have thought that Tony would go to this trouble to look after her. But Amber didn't know the first thing about what went on in men's minds. She really only had experience with their bodies.

'Amber?' said a male voice.

Disconcerted, utterly confused by everything her mother was telling her, Amber looked over, past Daniyel sitting on the bed, to the man in the doorway.

And as soon as she laid eyes on him, she fell in love.

It was ridiculous: you couldn't really fall in love at first sight. It was just that she was so stressed and confused and anxious, and her head was pounding, and her body felt sore and heavy whenever she moved, and there was something about the man in the doorway that was so calm and centred and real that looking at him made Amber feel calm and centred and real too, three qualities she had never, ever possessed in her life before.

She took a long breath, just staring at him, as if he were the human version of a relaxing DVD. A burning fire, logs crackling in the golden flames. Or waves lapping gently up and down a white sandy beach. His eyes were so dark and warm; she was completely hypnotized by him.

In the receiver, Slava was prattling away, her voice high and urgent.

'I have to go now, *Matka*,' Amber said absently, and put the phone down, fumbling to place it on its base. Nothing could have made her look away from the man in the doorway, his elegant bone structure, his lean body, his black hair with its unexpected curls, an almost feminine contrast with his strong nose and jawline.

She was so caught up in her intense awareness of him that she had no sense of how long they had been looking at each other.

She had no realization of why Daniyel was twisting now to stare at the man, her brows drawing together as she prompted: 'Dr Raf?' jolting him out of the trance into which he and Amber had fallen.

'Oh!' His pale olive cheekbones flushed with a little colour. 'Yes, thank you, Daniyel.'

He stepped into the room, and all Amber could think was: He's coming closer. Maybe he'll touch me.

Her whole body heated up at the idea. Quickly, she looked down at her hands; her manicure was still in place, thank goodness.

Well, I've practically been in a coma for the last day or so, she thought with humour that was unusually bitter for her. I didn't exactly get the chance to chip them, did I?

'Amber was just talking to her mother,' Daniyel was telling Dr Raf, as she unplugged the phone again. 'She was disoriented and wanted to hear what had happened and why she was here.'

'Very good,' Dr Raf said, nodding approvingly at Daniyel. 'Amber, how are you feeling now? Did it help to speak to your mother?'

Not trusting her voice to work properly if she spoke to him directly, Amber nodded, her eyes wide and fixed on his face.

'I'm sorry, I should introduce myself,' he said, sitting down in the place on the other bed where Daniyel had been. 'I'm Dr Rafael

Green, one of the consultants here at Cascabel. Call me Dr Raf, everyone does.'

He smiled at her, a sweet, open smile that softened the austerely handsome lines of his face and made him look, momentarily, much younger.

'Well, Amber, you came in late last night, as your mother probably told you. And you slept through without any sedation, which is a very good start.'

'What time is it?' Amber managed to ask.

Wow, she thought, again with that bitter humour that was entirely new. Nice, Amber. You've got a crush on this guy the size of Antarctica and the first words you say to him are: 'What time is it?'

Dr Raf turned his arm, glancing down at his watch, and Amber's gaze was drawn like iron to a magnet at the sight of his hand, the extra inch of skin she could see as he popped his shirt cuff. His hand was elegant, long-fingered, the skin smooth and as Mediterranean-olive as his face, but she could see dark hairs at his wrist, one curling around the stainless steel of the wristband. The shirt cuff sliding slightly up his arm felt extraordinarily intimate, erotic, as if he were baring his flesh for Amber's eyes alone. She swallowed hard.

'It's almost noon,' he said, and she immediately looked up at his mouth, watching his full lips move as he spoke, noticing, too, that there was colour in his cheeks again as he realized how intently she was watching him.

I'm embarrassing him, she thought miserably. I have to stop.

But she knew she couldn't.

'You slept for a very long time,' Dr Raf observed, not meeting her eyes now. 'That's excellent.'

'My mother gave me stuff on the plane,' Amber admitted. 'That's probably why.'

'*Really*?' He swung round to Daniyel, who was leaning against the bathroom door, the phone in her hands. 'Did we know that?' he was asking urgently.

'Absolutely not,' Daniyel said, frowning. 'I checked with Mom myself. She said the hospital in London didn't give Amber anything,

and she certainly didn't mention any pills on the plane. As far as we knew, Amber was clean when she came in.'

'Damn.' Dr Raf sighed. 'That's not good news. Amber, do you know what she gave you?'

Amber shook her head. 'My mother probably won't know either,' she admitted. 'She just pulls stuff out of her bag and takes it without looking at the labels. Vicodin, or Xanax, probably. I was really wound up. I thought I was . . . I thought I was going somewhere bad. I was crying and freaking out. Honestly, I was really upset and she just wanted to calm me down,' she added, not wanting them to think badly of Slava.

'Uh-huh,' Dr Raf said, standing up. 'Well, I'd better give her a call right away. Amber, you should eat something. Daniyel will sort something out for you. And unless you feel significantly worse in the next few hours, I'll see you at group this afternoon.'

'Why would I feel worse?' Amber said nervously. 'I feel pretty awful already – my head hurts really badly.'

He nodded. A dark ringlet fell onto his forehead; she wanted to reach up and twist her finger through it, wind herself tightly into his curls.

'We'll get you some meds for the headache. Basically –' he hesitated – 'the bad news is that if your mother gave you what you think she did on the plane, you still have full opiate withdrawal to go through.' He looked grave, his deep brown eyes so serious that the expression melted Amber completely. 'Withdrawal can be quite unpleasant. But we'll be with you all the way, Amber.'

Wordlessly, she reached out a hand to him. He looked completely taken aback.

And then he leaned down and took her hand in his.

It was like joining two live wires. Amber's blood fizzed like sherbet at the shock of it, the warmth flooding into her, the strength of his hand around hers. She stared at their hands, connected, her fingers twining around his the way she wanted her entire body to wrap around him. His nails were smooth, pale pink ovals. Every detail about him was utterly fascinating to her; she could have looked at him for hours, till she had memorized every line on his knuckles, every tiny mole on his skin, every bone in his body.

From miles away across the room, the door swung open, knocking against the wall.

'Oh, sorry! I didn't realize you were still in here.'

It was the blonde girl from before, the girl who'd come in when Amber had knocked the magazines over.

'That's fine, Skye, we were just finishing up,' Dr Raf said hastily, letting go of Amber's hand. 'Amber . . . um, Daniyel will show you round and make sure you have what you need. I'll see both of you in group.'

He nodded to Skye and was gone; Amber's eyes followed him out of the door, not turning back to look at the girl called Skye until he was long gone.

'Amber, this is your roommate, Skye. You remember her from last night at all?' Daniyel said briskly.

Amber shook her head.

'You were pretty dopey,' Skye said, smiling at her.

'Amber, you OK to walk?' Daniyel asked. 'I could take you through to the kitchen if you think you can manage it. Fix you some toast, maybe. Or a bowl of cereal. We should get something in your stomach.'

'I can do that,' Skye said cheerfully.

She's really pretty, Amber thought, and she couldn't help but be jealous: Skye's blonde, blue-eyed good looks were so perfect, so exactly what men generally wanted. Too small to model, too busty for fashion, but the Barbie blueprint of the ideal girlfriend, adorable and dainty-featured. With her wide eyes and slightly up-tilted nose, she resembled a cute Pekinese.

Swinging her legs out of bed, standing up cautiously, Amber, who was nearly five foot ten, towered over her roommate.

'I'm bored out of my mind, honestly,' Skye was assuring Daniyel. 'It'll give me something to do, showing Amber round.'

But Amber had just caught sight of herself in the mirror and let out a little scream. Bird's nest hair, no makeup at all, and a dent in her cheek where she must have lain on a corner of the pillow. Her skin was dull, and there were bags under her eyes.

Oh no – the first time I meet Dr Raf, and that's what I look like. No wonder he was staring at me – he must have been shocked at how awful I looked . . .

'I need to shower first,' she said firmly. 'And blow-dry my hair, and do my makeup. God, I hope my mother packed my straighteners! And my tongs!'

When he sees me again, she told herself, *I'm going to look fantastic. I'm going to look like I just stepped out of that Sports Illustrated shoot. I'm going to smell wonderful and – shit, did Matka pack me any perfume at all?*

She was down on her knees, rummaging through her suitcase frantically. Skye cracked a grin. 'Well, we've definitely got *something* in common!' she said. 'And look, hon, you can always borrow my straighteners, OK? I know how important they are to a girl . . .'

Skye's straighteners weren't the GHD to which Amber was addicted – Slava hadn't thought to pack either those or the tongs that Amber used to flip the ends of her hair. Still, Amber had over a decade's experience of grooming herself to the kind of high-gloss shine expected from a top model, and when you were travelling all round the world, you didn't always have your favourite tools to work with. An hour later, she emerged from the ensuite bathroom so transformed that Skye, lying on her bed reading *InStyle*, gaped when she saw her roommate.

'Wow,' she said. 'You clean up nice.'

'Thanks,' Amber said a little warily. She wasn't used to girls paying her compliments and meaning them; the isolation of her life with Slava, combined with the vicious competitiveness of the modelling world, had made her cautious about trusting anyone. Especially a girl as pretty as Skye.

Still, Skye wasn't lying. Amber surveyed herself in the bedroom mirror. Citizens of Humanity jeans clung to her slender legs, the slight bootcut making them seem impossibly endless. Her fitted tank top was emerald green to match her eyes, while the pale grey, feather-light oversized silk cashmere cardigan hung off her shoulders, its wrap front dangling down elegantly, the translucent fabric part-showing off, part-veiling the curves of her body as she moved.

She was in a cloud of perfume: lilac, white cedar and peony. Thank goodness, Slava had packed her favourite daytime scent, Éclat d'Arpège. Her hair was a silky, tawny mane, her eyebrows perfectly plucked and pencilled, her long lashes mascaraed dark brown, her cheeks and lips stained lightly with the same dark rose. Amber had gone as natural as she dared; instinct told her that Dr Raf preferred women without too much obvious artifice.

'You hungry?' Skye asked, putting down the magazine.

It was a question Amber never knew how to answer truthfully. She was always hungry, but that had been her normal state for so long that she barely noticed it any longer.

'I suppose I should eat something,' she said. 'Cereal sounded nice.'

'Don't worry,' Skye said wryly. 'They've got skim milk here.'

Amber was in a haze the whole time Skye showed her round the clinic. Her near-obsession with Dr Raf made it almost impossible for her to take in anything Skye was telling her; the garden, the kitchen, the gym, the communal lounge area, the people Skye introduced her to, passed in a blur. She spooned up the Cheerios Skye had poured into a bowl for her without tasting them – they might have been made of cardboard for all she knew. All she was aware of was that in a short while, she would see Dr Raf again, hear his voice. It was extraordinary, and unprecedented; she'd had crushes on men before, of course, but never had she felt anything this strong, this all-encompassing.

By the time Skye, checking the time, announced that it was time for afternoon group therapy, Amber's impatience was almost unbearable. Not that you could read any of that on her face. She was so used to presenting a beautiful, impassive mask to the world that all Skye, or anyone, could see was an exquisite, poised model, dressed and made-up so perfectly that she could be ready for a shoot at any moment.

'Don't get too freaked about the group,' Skye said, leading Amber into a large, sun-filled room. 'Everyone's cool. And you just go at your own pace, you know? I mean, you don't have to talk about stuff you really don't want to.'

A semicircle of square, red armchairs was arranged facing another, single, red armchair. Apart from the chair setup, the room was decorated like an ideal living room in a show flat for an upmarket development, from the circular, orange-striped rug on the floor, to the abstract prints on the walls, to the wooden shelves in staggered lines, which held ornamental glass vases in shades of gold and silver. The floor-to-ceiling windows looked out onto the garden, but thick hibiscus shrubs clustering close to the glass provided reassuring privacy.

Amber glanced over at Skye as they sat down in chairs next to each other, her curiosity finally stirred.

'So what are you here for?' she asked.

Normally, Amber would never have asked something that direct. But something about passing out in London and waking up in Los Angeles, in an environment where everything was unfamiliar, away from every reassurance and security she knew, was making her strangely unlike herself.

And Skye didn't seem to mind. Flashing a beautiful smile, she said easily: 'Sex addiction.' She tilted her head to one side. 'I'm an exotic dancer. Or I was. One of my clients got this huge crush on me. Didn't like that I was screwing around – you know how it is.'

Amber found herself nodding in agreement.

'So he's stumped up for me to come here to get cured,' Skye concluded. 'Then I guess he thinks he'll put me on his white horse and ride off into the sunset.' She rolled her big blue eyes.

Great story, huh? Skye thought smugly. And I came up with that all by myself – Kevin didn't help out. I'm turning out to be a pretty good actress.

'Hey, baby,' drawled a man's voice.

Amber turned in her chair, recognizing the voice. And when she saw him, she was sure she'd met him before; it took a good ten seconds for the penny to drop.

Wow, Joe Jeffreys. He's just as handsome in person. And he's really into Skye – look how he's grinning at her.

'Hey back atcha,' Skye was saying, flipping her long blonde hair over one shoulder, arching her back to show off her firm round breasts, smiling bewitchingly at Joe Jeffreys as he took a seat across the semicircle from the two of them, stretching his long, long legs out in front of him, his frame a little too large for the chair, which looked insubstantial by comparison with his big, strongly muscled body.

So he can get a good view of Skye.

'Hey, a newbie!' Joe said, taking in Amber's presence. 'I'm Joe.' He leaned forward, tilting over the axis of his legs, to shake her hand. 'You look kind of familiar. You act, sweetie?'

'I used to model,' Amber said, surprising herself with the past tense.

'Oh, right.' He looked her up and down, his eyes full of appreciation. 'Well, it's a pleasure to meet you.'

Beside her, Amber heard Skye stir in her chair. But just then, a bustle of movement signalled other arrivals: a skinny, unhappy-looking young man with two nose rings, an older guy in chinos and a button-down shirt, and a girl barely out of her teens with a flaming-yellow bob of hair, a lot of dark makeup smeared around her eyes, and a sulky pout to her mouth. She flung herself into the chair closest to the door, scowling furiously as she wrapped herself into a cocoon with the plaid blanket she'd brought with her.

'Hey, Petal,' Joe said to her.

'Fuck off,' the girl called Petal snapped back at him.

'Nice to see you too,' Joe said, not a whit fazed, leaning back and crossing his legs at the ankles. He exchanged a brief, amused look with Skye, who wiggled her eyebrows at him in response.

The door shut.

'Good afternoon, everyone,' said Dr Raf, and Amber's heart leaped into her throat; for a long moment she couldn't breathe.

'I'm just going to pull out a second chair,' he said, 'because Dr Lucy Tennant is joining us today. Some of you have already met Dr Lucy, I know.'

'Hi, everyone,' said Dr Lucy, striding into view around the edge of the semicircle, her jaw pegged at a high angle, her hands in the pockets of the white coat hanging loose over her fitted shirt and flat-fronted beige trousers.

I hate her, Amber thought instantly. She looks like the kind of woman who thinks she's always right and everyone else is always wrong. And why is she wearing that coat? To show us she's a doctor? I mean, Dr Raf doesn't need to wear a white coat to be authoritative . . .

But then Amber realized that Dr Raf's shirtsleeves were rolled up, showing off his forearms, and she completely lost her train of thought as she stared at him, watching him lift the armchair as easily as if it weighed nothing at all, swinging it round and placing it next to his, gesturing courteously at Dr Lucy to sit down before he did.

I can look at him as much as I want, and no one will think it's weird, Amber realized, a tide of excitement surging in her. He's our doctor – we're supposed to be focusing on him, that's the point of these sessions, isn't it?

And just then, as Dr Raf surveyed the group, his steady dark gaze met Amber's. The naked longing in her eyes was impossible to disguise; somehow, in his presence, she felt that she had absolutely no control over her reactions. There was nothing flirtatious about Amber; she'd never learned how to be coquettish. All the cute tricks she'd seen Skye use on Joe were completely alien to her. She just looked at Dr Raf as she had never looked at any man, with her heart and soul in her green eyes.

And she could have sworn that she connected with him com-pletely for that moment. That he saw her, fully, and that it was genuinely hard for him to drag his eyes away from her and turn to the next person in the circle.

'Um, let's start as we always do, OK?' Dr Raf said gruffly, his light tenor voice a little rougher than usual. 'We'll go round the circle and say our names. And if you're feeling up to it, why don't you tell us why you're here?'

He looked encouragingly at the far side of the circle from Amber, at the man dressed like a mid-level executive at a corporate retreat.

Hands on his chino-clad knees, the man muttered, staring at the floor: 'I'm Mitch. Coke addict. Third time round.'

'I'm Brian,' the boy with the piercings contributed. 'Only I fucking hate my name, so I'm changing it when I come up with something better. I'm an addict. Crystal meth, mainly.'

Dr Raf and Dr Lucy were following the progress with their eyes, and now they were both looking at Petal, curled up in her blanket, whose turn it was next.

'Petal?' Dr Lucy prompted finally. 'Will you introduce yourself?'

Ugh, she has a horrible voice, Amber observed. Squeaky and nasal. Amber had met plenty of American women – fashion editors, models – with that voice, and they had all been snobbish and entitled.

'I'm Petal,' the girl mumbled finally, shaking her bright yellow bob over her face. 'Like you all didn't sodding know already. And I'm here 'cause my fucking hypocrite bastard of a dad says I'm doing too much coke. I hate it here, I miss my boyfriend and my mates, and the food here's total *shit*.'

Brian choked back a giggle.

'Thanks, Petal,' Dr Lucy said seriously, as Joe, next in line, said with great good humour, running one big tanned hand through his blond hair: 'Hey, you guys. I'm Joe and I'm a sex addict, but I'm here to get *cured*!'

'Praise the Lord!' Skye added irrepressibly, as Joe flashed her a huge grin that was so sexy even Amber blinked at the sheer energy he could project just by smiling at a girl.

'*Skye*,' Dr Lucy reproved. '*Please*.' Her dark, perfectly threaded brows pulled together, but her smooth pale forehead didn't move at all.

Botox, Amber recognized instantly, contemptuously; she was proud of never having had any surgical interventions.

'Sorry.' Skye ducked her pretty head, flashing a swift blue conspiratorial glance at Joe under her eyelashes. 'I'm Skye, and I'm a sex addict. Oh, and I've totally hit the coke too heavily from time to time.'

It was Amber's turn. She sat there, suddenly paralysed, her heart pounding: she hated having to speak in front of people, let alone confess personal stuff to them. One of the reasons she'd been such a success as a model was, paradoxically, her shyness. She would infinitely rather have her body communicate for her. Her facial expressions, her poses, were all the more eloquent because her body told stories her lips could not.

Dr Lucy started to speak, but Dr Raf raised his hand slightly, heading her off.

'Amber?' he said very gently. 'Do you feel up to saying anything?'

Amber looked straight at him, and the rest of the people present, the entire surroundings, faded away like an effect in a film, the focus so tight on Dr Raf that everything else was blurred and meaningless. All she could see was Dr Raf, vivid and clear: so clear that she could see the faint five o'clock shadow on his jawline, the slight part of his lips, his white teeth. She almost thought she could hear him breathing.

'I'm Amber,' she heard herself say clearly. 'And I'm addicted to painkillers. Muscle relaxants, downers . . .' she remembered how Dr Raf had described them, '. . . opiates. Since I was in my teens. I took too many and had an overdose. I didn't mean to. Or –' she couldn't lie when she was looking at Dr Raf, '– I don't *think* I did. All I really wanted was the pain to stop.'

There was a long pause, during which Amber and Dr Raf's eyes never left one another.

It was broken only by Dr Lucy saying eventually in clear, sharp tones: 'Very good, Amber! Excellent sharing!'

As Amber's concentration on Dr Raf was broken, she realized with a shock that her face was wet. Tears were pouring from her eyes; she hadn't even been aware of it. Skye was pushing something at her – a tissue box.

'Skye, I know you're trying to be sympathetic,' Dr Lucy said brightly, 'but what's the rule here about handing people Kleenex?'

'God,' the girl called Petal observed sarcastically, 'sometimes you sound *exactly* like my form teacher at kindergarten.'

Both Joe and Brian, the young man with piercings, snorted with amusement at this sally.

Dr Lucy's head snapped round; even more brightly, she said: 'Petal, could *you* tell us the rule about Kleenex, please?'

Petal rolled her eyes.

'Don't-offer-anyone-else-tissues-'cause-it's-like-you're-telling-them-to-stop-crying,' she recited.

'That's right.' Dr Lucy looked back at Amber. 'We want everyone here to be free to feel their feelings,' Dr Lucy said, smiling compassionately.

'I just thought Skye was being nice,' Amber heard herself saying. 'I mean, my face was all wet.'

'It totally was,' Brian said, leaning forward enthusiastically. 'You know what you just had? Buddha's tears. Daniyel was talking about those in meditation class last week. It's when you don't really feel like you're crying, but, like, this tap gets turned on inside you to cleanse everything out.'

'Thanks, Brian,' Dr Raf said. 'Very empathetic.'

Dr Lucy cleared her throat. 'I was going to do some work this session on body image,' she said, reaching up one perfectly manicured hand and smoothing her already sleek dark hair back along her skull. 'Skye, I wonder if we could talk briefly about your T-shirt? I thought we could use that to open a discussion about how people perceive us.'

Skye looked down at her tight, hot-pink T-shirt. Over her breasts, in wriggly lines, was written: 'My body's not a temple – it's an amusement park'.

'What kind of message do you think that sends out?' Dr Lucy

asked. 'And do you think it's in keeping with the house rules of Cascabel?'

God, does this woman ever ask a question she doesn't know the answer to? Amber thought.

Skye widened her big blue eyes and said in her best little baby-girl voice: 'Oh! You're saying that it's like I'm telling people I'm a *ride*! Whoops!'

Joe guffawed.

'I think I have a positive body image, though,' Skye continued, tightening her pecs so that her breasts jutted forward. 'I mean, if I were a ride, it would be at Disneyland. Like, the best one out there. I wouldn't be, you know, some shitty old Coney Island thing made of wood and falling down every two seconds.'

Even Mitch, who had been completely silent the entire session apart from saying his name, sniggered at this one. Dr Lucy's lips tightened as she stared at Skye, who returned her look with an innocent little smile.

'I think Dr Lucy is saying that your T-shirt isn't appropriate, Skye,' Dr Raf said, stepping in. 'We have a ban on provocative cloth-ing here, for the good of the group.'

No one can resist him, Amber realized wistfully, as even Skye dropped her teasing façade and nodded dutifully at Dr Raf.

'Maybe we could ask for comments on Skye's T-shirt,' Dr Lucy suggested. 'It will help us work on how we deal with issues like this in the outside world.'

'Well, it makes me think about sex,' Joe offered cheerfully. 'So, yeah, I guess it isn't appropriate.' He frowned comically at Skye. 'I mean, me being a sex addict and all.'

'I don't know if the T-shirt makes that much difference,' Brian said, his voice squeaking. 'Uh, I would think about sex when I look at Skye anyway.'

'Oh, thank you, Brian,' Skye said, smiling at him warmly and tossing back her ponytail. 'That's so sweet.'

Dr Lucy jerked forward angrily, but Dr Raf managed to speak first.

'Again, this is useful interaction on how we're going to deal with our problems outside rehab,' he said gently. 'Obviously, everyone's going to think about sex, and especially when it's the subject under discussion. Sex is one of our most powerful triggers. In rehab, we're all here to help each other, so that means not triggering each other into relapse. But I want to stress that no one should feel guilty about their thoughts. It's whether we act on them or not that's the important thing.'

Mitch, the coke addict, nodded vigorously. 'I have all *kinds* of thoughts,' he said gloomily, staring at his kneecaps.

Everyone went quiet for a while, until it became obvious that Mitch had shot his bolt.

'Amber,' Dr Lucy turned to her. 'You were a model for a *long* time, weren't you?'

Nice, Amber thought resentfully. That makes me sound like I'm about a hundred.

'Do you have anything to share with us about your body image?' Dr Lucy prompted. 'This can often be a really hot-button issue for women in the modelling world.'

'I've modelled too,' Petal mumbled competitively.

Amber opened her mouth, but had absolutely no idea how to respond. All she could picture was her last, failed photoshoot: Jared clicking on the images of her in one tiny swimsuit after another, gold dangling from her ears, high heels making her legs seem endless, her hair a thick chestnut mane; but her green eyes empty and unfocused. Nothing there at all.

Nothing but the Xanax.

And then, even more powerfully, she remembered her last weekend away with Tony. The DVD of her on the *Sports Illustrated* shoot. Herself, stepping out of the sea, glossy and gorgeous, laughing into the camera, before the drugs had got such a grip on her that she couldn't even connect with a lens, let alone the person holding it.

Images that had sold her as a commodity to all the men who had 'dated' her.

Amber had thought she'd feel better when the tears stopped

flowing, but her head was spinning even faster now. Everyone was looking at her, and their expressions were so sympathetic that she felt utterly overwhelmed. Even Joe's handsome face was grimacing in sympathy, his eyes soft.

Amber raised her hands to her head, palms pressed to each side, feeling as if her head were about to explode with confusion and stress. I need to lie down, she thought, starting to panic. I need to get to bed before something really bad happens.

She tried to stand up, but though she managed to get her feet underneath her, her knees buckled almost immediately. She swayed, her vision blurring, her lashes fluttering down to her cheeks. The last thing she saw was Joe, lunging forward to try to catch her before she hit the ground.

But it was Dr Raf whose arms she tumbled into. Even with her eyes closed, she recognized him immediately. His shirt was crisp and starched, freshly scented with fabric conditioner, and his skin smelled of green ferns, fresh and clean and rich. He caught her round the waist, and the next thing she knew, he had swung her up against his chest, her head tilting against him, her hair tumbling back over his shoulder.

'I'll take her to her room,' she heard him say, his breath against her head. 'It was too much for her first day. My misjudgement. Please, go on with the session.'

And then he was walking, long steady strides, Amber securely carried in his arms, rocking closer to him with every step, inhaling his scent. As soon as Dr Raf had touched her, a delicious cool had spread through her, calming her down, soothing the panic away. And yet he was so warm, like fresh-baked bread . . .

She turned her head into his chest even more. She couldn't have spoken, and even if she could, she didn't know what she would have said, but her lips moved against his shirt front, pressing into the firm muscles below.

I mustn't make an idiot of myself, she thought dimly. I mustn't kiss him.

When he reached her room and laid her down on the bed, she

could have cried with frustration as his skin pulled away from hers. She wrenched her eyelids open, determined at least to see him; his face was still close to hers as he leaned over her, and colour flooded into his cheeks as he looked down at her, his breath warm on her face.

'I'm going to get Daniyel to come check on you,' he said, his fingers around her wrist, taking her pulse. 'I have a nasty feeling you're going to have a hard time of this withdrawal, Amber.'

Amber's lips moved, but she couldn't manage to say a word.

'Your pulse is racing,' he said seriously. 'Don't worry. We're all here for you. The next forty-eight hours will be tough, but you'll come out the other side.'

The hand holding her wrist loosened its grip; he pulled back. And then she felt his fingers on her forehead, gently pushing back a lock of hair.

'Don't be afraid,' he said softly. 'You're safe now.'

Petal

'*H*ow's she doing?' Joe asked as soon as Skye came out onto the patio. He jumped to his feet, and Petal, curled up on one of the chairs, knew instantly that his eagerness was not due to Skye's presence, but because he was worried about Amber.

Skye pulled a face.

'Puking a lot,' she said frankly. 'Apparently that happens in withdrawal. And she's got the shakes.'

'It's like kicking smack,' Brian volunteered from the far end of the long table, where he was occupying himself by laying out incredibly complicated games of patience, featuring two whole decks of cards.

Joe sighed. 'That poor girl,' he said with real emotion. 'She's like this beautiful fallen angel.'

'Totally,' Brian agreed fervently.

'Like a beautiful fallen angel with broken wings,' Joe said, striding across the patio, restless suddenly at the thought of Amber. 'There's something so damn pure about her, you know what I mean? Like a princess in a castle needing to be rescued. Sleeping Beauty or something.' He burst out laughing at his own words. 'Jesus, she's got me going, right? Hey –' he loped back to the table and reached for his pack of Camels – 'there's a reason I don't write my own dialogue!'

He lit up, coughing. 'Rest cure my ass,' he added, blowing out a smoke ring. 'I may not be boozing but I'm smoking like a damn chimney.'

'Me too,' Skye said, sinking into a chair, stretching her legs out on the table, and kicking off her flip-flops so her pretty feet, with their painted toenails and silver ankle bracelet, were on display. 'And I'm drinking so much Coke I'm buzzed the whole time.'

'I hear you.' Joe winked at her. 'It's because we're going out of our damn minds with boredom.'

'You could play cards with me,' Brian said wistfully.

'Kid, I told you already,' Joe said over his shoulder. 'I don't play cards unless money's involved.'

'So how long till she gets out of doctor lockdown?' Joe asked.

Petal noticed Skye's lips tightening in frustration as Joe brought the conversation back to Amber yet again.

'She'll be back in our room tomorrow,' Skye said shortly. 'They just want to keep her under observation tonight. *And*,' she added, 'they want to make sure I'm not disturbed by her puking her guts up all through the night.'

She stretched her arms behind her head, which drew attention to her breasts; she'd changed her T-shirt since group, but though the one she was wearing was free of sexy slogans, it was as clingy as what it had replaced.

'I'll have a whole night by myself,' she said, shooting Joe a saucy look. 'You'd think I'd be happy about that, but actually, I get pretty lonely . . .'

Nice play, Petal thought, giving Skye some points. First she reminds Joe that Amber's a vomit factory at the moment, and then she gets Joe to think about her in bed by herself. She's working hard, this girl.

Petal hadn't done brilliantly at school, but if they'd had exams covering the various techniques women used to interest men, she'd have aced every single one. Petal had seen a parade of girlfriends, would-be girlfriends, and party girls troop through her father's life, briefly queening it in the Primrose Hill mansion, the Tuscan estate, villas on Capri, private islands in the Caribbean, penthouses in New York: until Jinhee had come along, there had been so many women in Gold's life it had been like non-stop castings for La Perla catalogues.

Legs up to their armpits, hair down to their waist, flashing teeth, glossy skin of every colour available to humanity, perfect breasts, all auditioning for the once-in-a-lifetime opportunity – the role of Gold's wife, or at least live-in-girlfriend-with-palimony-rights. They used their acquaintances to get entrée to Gold, and then they dropped them like hot potatoes. They would have trampled in stiletto heels over their sisters and their mothers if it would have given them the slimmest of chances of being part of Gold's life.

Petal had seen girls deliberately get their friends trashed, or spike their drinks to knock them out. And she'd watched these antics with nothing but fascinated amusement. Often, she'd been their pet, a miniature version of them, dressed up in their clothes, walking precariously in their high heels, her nails painted bright colours, privy to secrets they didn't know they were sharing.

Of course, she shouldn't have been hanging out with girls like that at all. But Petal's nanny situation had been as chaotic as the rest of her upbringing. The responsible ones, shocked by the goings-on, had never lasted longer than a few months, worn out by trying to discipline a spoiled little girl. And the less responsible ones . . . well, they had been just as busy trying to grab and hold Gold's attention as the models and socialites and party girls had been. Robin Williams had married his kids' nanny; Jude Law had had an affair with his. Who was to say that they might not hit the jackpot when Gold saw how caring and sweet and motherly they were with his adorable daughter?

So if Petal, with her experience, admired Skye's technique, that meant that Skye was doing a very good job indeed of seducing Joe.

'The beds are so *narrow*, though,' Skye was complaining. 'Single beds, can you believe it?' She flashed a look at Joe under her eyelashes. 'You must have a California king at home, right? You're *so* big!'

Joe grinned widely in response. 'Baby, I got a double here,' he informed Skye. 'It's no California king, but it's better than a damn single. *And* I don't have to share a room.'

'How'd you swing that?' Skye sat up straighter. 'I'd kill not to have to share!'

'Modesty forbids,' he said smugly.

'It's 'cause of who he is,' Petal informed Skye. She and Joe jumped slightly; they'd been so caught up in their mutual attraction they'd forgotten Petal was even there. 'A roommate could sell their story of sharing with Joe.'

'We could still all do that,' Brian piped up. He went bright red. 'Not that we would! Of course we wouldn't! But all I'm saying is . . .'

'No worries, kid,' Joe said kindly. 'I got a room to myself 'cause my agent insisted. No one wants "I SHARED A ROOM WITH SEX ADDICT JOE" headlines in the *Investigator*. What if some guy says I hit on him?'

He chortled happily at the unlikeliness of this scenario. Skye's chair tipped as she laughed too, and she had to catch onto the table to stop herself falling back.

Joe reached out and caught one slim ankle to balance her as Brian said gloomily: 'I have to share with *Mitch*.'

'What's that like?' Petal asked curiously. 'He's such a weirdo.'

'Totally,' Brian agreed. 'He never says anything. It completely freaks me out. He's sitting in there right now, reading the Narcotics Anonymous Blue Book from cover to cover. That's all he does when he's not in therapy.'

'I've got this woman called Sujata,' Petal said, 'but she's in this work therapy programme. I think she's volunteering at a homeless shelter or something. She never gets back till ten and then she goes straight to bed. And she's up hours before I am, so I hardly see her. That's weird too. I mean, I wake up in the middle of the night with jet lag and there's someone else in there, breathing, but I barely even *know* her.'

'This entire fucking gig is weird,' Brian said, heaving a deep sigh.

'I shouldn't even *be* here,' Petal complained. 'I'm *so* not a drug addict.'

'No offence,' Brian said, twiddling his eyebrow ring, which was his tendency in times of stress, 'but, like, *everyone* says that at first.'

'Amber said she was an addict,' Petal pointed out, duly offended.

'Yeah, but Amber freaking *overdosed*,' Brian said. 'What's she going to say?'

'And Joe and Skye say they're sex addicts,' Petal countered.

Brian looked over at Joe and Skye, who had moved close to each other at the far end of the table. Joe's hand was still on Skye's ankle, wrapped intimately around it; he was pulling her closer to him as she giggled and pretended to resist. Her hair was tied into two bunches with dark blue ribbon, and she twisted one of them between her fingers, playing with the long blonde locks. Her varnished toes were pointed towards Joe, her head tilted away from him; every line of her body was balanced around Joe's anchoring hand.

You can tell she's a dancer, Petal thought. She's really graceful.

'Joe and Skye . . .' Brian's voice was lowered. 'Dude, I don't get this whole sex addict thing at *all*. I mean, they both seem totally cool about it! And look at them. They'd like, totally get it on if they could.'

'And if Skye doesn't mind that Joe thinks Amber's a beautiful fallen angel,' Petal said drily. 'He didn't say anything half that nice about *her*.'

'There's a really good song about fallen angels,' Brian said, starting to hum a tune.

'I know that!' Petal hummed along with him.

'You want to play cards?' Brian said as they came to the end of the chorus.

'You guys, it's thirty minutes to curfew, OK?' said a man's gruff voice from the patio doors.

Petal looked up; it was Dave, the orderly, standing there, hands in his overall pockets, chin down.

'Half-hour warning before lockdown,' he said. 'Then it's everyone in their rooms.'

Skye leaned forward and whispered something to Joe, her fingers slipping in a swift caress over his hand on her ankle before she pulled her leg away and sat back in her chair.

'Dave, my man,' Joe pushed his chair back and stood up, rotating his head like an athlete limbering up. 'I gotta stretch my legs before we turn in. Walk with me, won't you? You're a smoker, right?' He offered his pack to Dave. 'How did the Dodgers do last night? You catch the game?'

Joe threw a big, muscled arm over Dave's meaty shoulders as they strolled off onto the lawn. It should have looked impossibly cheesy, but instead, as with every single gesture Joe made, it seemed the height of easy, confident manliness. Brian stared after him wistfully, Petal noticed: she bet men always looked at Joe like that, with envy and admiration in equal measure. Joe was like the ultimate expression of maleness: a big, ridiculously handsome man who was so utterly confident of who he was that he had nothing to prove to anyone. It was irresistible.

'Guys,' Skye said to Petal and Brian, rolling her eyes. 'It all comes down to sports in the end.'

'Not me,' Brian said. 'I don't give a shit about sports.'

'*Really?*' Skye said teasingly. 'I bet you play games on your computer, don't you? X-box? Nintendo? Go online and compete against other guys? And you're playing cards, aren't you?'

'Yeah, but . . .' Brian blushed, pausing as he separated out the two packs. 'OK, those are games. I suppose it's sort of sporty.'

'Gotcha!' Skye cocked her finger and pretended to shoot him. He wriggled happily at being teased by a girl so pretty that, in the outside world, she wouldn't have given a geek like him the time of day.

And Skye's like Joe, Petal realized; the girl version. She's totally confident about being a woman. She knows just how to talk to men. Joe and Brian are completely different, but she can charm both of them.

Resentment of Skye's self-assurance rose in Petal like bile; she said meanly: 'So what's it like sharing a room with a supermodel, Skye? I bet Amber's one of those girls who looks gorgeous all the time.'

Skye hadn't worked in strip clubs for years to be unaware of when a girl was having a dig at her. Quite unfazed, she responded: 'She probably does, when she's not feeling like shit. And she's going to get worse before she gets better, Dr Raf says.'

'Wow, how about when she fainted and he carried her out of group?' Brian said. 'It was like a movie!'

'Or a romance novel,' Skye said dreamily, lighting another cigarette and tilting back in her chair. 'I *love* romance novels. It was like the cover of one, you know? Her in his arms. He just needed to have his shirt off. And be really ripped,' she added naughtily. 'I bet Dr Raf strips well, but he's more the lean and mean type.'

'You could ask Dr Lucy what he looks like with his shirt off,' Brian suggested, which got both girls' full attention.

'*Dr Lucy?*' Petal exclaimed.

'Nooo,' Skye said simultaneously, eyes sparkling with enjoyment of a good gossip. 'He's not doing Dr Lucy on the side, is he? Honestly!' She sat up straighter. 'Here they are lecturing us about being sex addicts and they're at it like rabbits behind our backs! That's so—'

'They're a couple,' Brian said smugly, knowing what a sensation this would cause. 'Daniyel told me.'

'No shit,' Skye marvelled. 'I mean, I can see it's convenient and all, but I'd've thought he could do better. Dr Raf is a stone fox.'

'Does that mean he's totally hot?' Petal asked.

'*Oh* yeah,' Skye told her, grinning. 'Wow. I bet Dr Lucy wasn't too keen on Dr Raf doing that whole romance-hero thing with Amber today.'

'She's a bitch, Dr Lucy,' Petal said in heartfelt tones. 'Everything she says is *so* mean.'

'Yeah, she really doesn't like me,' Skye agreed.

In a squeaky voice, Brian said bravely: 'Actually, I've been doing one-on-one with her for weeks and she's really cool. She's helped me a lot.'

'Give the devil her due,' Skye said, grimacing.

'No, she's been great,' Brian insisted. 'She just takes a bit of time to warm up.'

'I bet she never warms up to me,' Skye said, shrugging. 'She doesn't much like other women. I know the type.'

'I fucking hate one-on-ones, even with Dr Raf,' Petal said sullenly, kicking the leg of the table. 'He just keeps on nagging me to say I'm addicted to coke, and I'm so not.'

Brian looked at her seriously. 'OK, let's say you don't need to use it every day,' he said, 'but ask yourself this: does it affect your life? Did you ever, like, have sex with someone you didn't really want to because you were high? Do you spend too much on it? Or does it affect your work decisions?'

Petal had been shaking her head vehemently till Brian asked her the last question. Then she froze, thinking of all those meetings she'd blown off, because she had a coke or drink hangover and couldn't get out of bed.

'I mean, to be an addict you don't need to be living on the streets with your mouth wrapped round a crack pipe,' Brian said.

Petal was on her feet. 'I don't need to be lectured by *you*,' she said angrily. 'You nicked a ton of stuff off your mum to blow on meth! You pawned her *jewellery*!'

Brian looked devastated.

'What's said in group stays in group, Petal,' Dave boomed reprovingly, lumbering back onto the patio. 'You should know better.'

'You're all against me!' Petal sobbed. 'I hate it here!'

She fled back into the building, stumbling over the step up to the glass doors in her haste, running back to her room and slamming the door. Throwing herself on her bed, she burst into a sob storm of misery, pounding the pillow with her fists, working out her anger and frustration. She was lost to the world for a long while till her energy ran out, and, her sobs slowing down to the occasional gulp, she lay there, blowing her nose and feeling utterly sorry for herself.

Eventually, footsteps resounded in the corridor, Dave's heavy tread and the rumble of his voice, talking to someone; she was sure she heard her name mentioned. Wanting to hear what was being said about her, she nipped over to the door, easing it open a crack.

Growing up a curious child around a raft of very famous people getting up to all sorts of interesting activities, she had honed her eavesdropping skills to perfection.

'You just gotta rise above,' Dave was saying. 'You can't give other people the power to affect you. That's how you relapse.'

'It was just such a kick in the teeth!' Brian whined miserably.

'Petal acting out is nothing to do with you,' Dave advised.

They were passing Petal's door now, Dave's heavy footsteps making the frame rattle a little as they went by.

'It's about trust,' Brian's voice began to fade now his back was to Petal's room. 'I don't know if I can trust her now . . .'

Oh, that's not fair!

But the next second, as Brian's words settled in, Petal began to feel guilty.

He *can* trust me, she thought defiantly. I didn't mean it. I'll tell him I'm sorry tomorrow.

'Mmm, sounds *great*,' purred Skye's voice, so close that Petal jumped: distracted by her conscience, she hadn't heard Skye and Joe's approach.

'Eleven thirty, OK?' Joe said in an undertone. 'I swung it with Dave.'

'Cool!' Skye's voice was hushed. 'But—'

'Hustle it up, you two!' Dave called from further down the corridor. 'It's past curfew! No more talking!'

The room Skye shared with Amber was next to Petal's. Petal heard her go in and shut the door. The men's rooms were way down the other end of the facility, to make sure it wasn't too easy for the sexes to be tempted to mingle; Skye had giggled yesterday in Dr Lucy's hearing about lesbians and gays getting a free pass for high jinks, which had not amused Dr Lucy one little bit.

Petal speculated wildly – what had Skye and Joe been talking about? It was ten now, a curfew that had seemed impossibly early to her when she arrived at Cascabel. But when you were woken up at seven thirty for an eight o'clock breakfast, followed by meditation and morning group, you found yourself unexpectedly exhausted really early in the evening. By half-past eleven, everyone would be fast asleep. Therapy was really tiring. Even when you were resisting it with everything you had.

No way am I going to miss what happens at eleven thirty, though.

The door swung open, and Petal jumped back just in time. She'd forgotten all about Sujata, her roommate, coming back from her volunteer work.

'Hey,' Sujata said flatly. She looked wiped out; there were dark smudges circling her eye sockets, and her skin had an ashy tinge. 'OK if I use the bathroom?'

She emerged a mere five minutes later in her pyjamas, crossed to her bed and curled up in it, her back to Petal, saying, 'We need to turn the light off soon, OK? I've got a really early start tomorrow.'

And how was *your* day? Petal thought sarcastically, though actually that wasn't really fair. She was totally fine with Sujata not being the chatty type; with her sustainable-bamboo-fibre clothes, sloppy haircut and Birkenstocks, Sujata was clearly a nouveau hippie, and Petal and hippies had about as much in common as she did with – well, with people who volunteered in homeless shelters.

Luckily, Sujata always fell asleep almost immediately. After just a few minutes of clicking off the bedside lamp, Petal could tell from Sujata's heavy, slow exhalations that she was dead to the world. It was surprisingly hard for Petal to lie there in the dark without falling asleep too; the hypnotic rhythm of Sujata's breathing would have lulled even an insomniac into slumber. Petal kept her eyes open as best she could, glancing every so often at the orange digital display on the bedside alarm clock.

Still, drowsiness crept up on her surreptitiously. She was in that pre-sleep haze where everything seems slowed down, when a small sound from outside caught her attention. Blinking, she focused on the clock, which read 11:38.

Shit! Suddenly alert, she slid out from beneath the duvet as quietly as she could, padding across the room in bare feet, turning the handle and pulling the door towards her slowly and carefully. Every tiny noise sounded horrendously loud in the silence of the sleeping building; by the time she'd got the door open enough to risk tentatively poking her head out, she was scared she'd missed all the excitement.

It took all Petal's self-control not to jump back, betraying herself, when she saw Skye. Wrapped in a velvety robe, her hair still in the bunches from earlier, Skye was – luckily for Petal – looking in the other direction, down the corridor towards the branch that led off to the men's bedrooms. She was so close Petal could hear her breathing and smell her perfume, which had clearly been freshly applied. Her blonde hair gleamed against the blue of the robe, which was belted tightly to show off her slender figure. On her feet were little blue backless mules.

All dressed up and sexy for Joe.

'Psst!' came a noise from the direction in which Skye was looking. Petal could barely see that far through the open door jamb, just a sliver; but she still recognized Joe's long jeans-clad leg, his arm, beckoning to Skye, who promptly eased her bedroom door shut and slipped soundlessly along the corridor to meet him.

Betting that they'd be thoroughly distracted now, Petal risked craning her head out further, enough to see Skye flitting up to Joe, her robe flaring out. She looked up and whispered something to him, and his arm came round her, closing possessively around her. His hand was low on her back, just at the base of her spine, his fingers flaring out over the rise of her bottom, and as Petal watched, he applied extra pressure that pulled her along with him as he whisked her off round the corner in the direction of his room.

Oh my God. Petal hadn't been sure until this moment how specific this rendezvous was. *They're totally going back to his room to do it!*

If they get caught, they're in so much trouble!

And then, quite unexpectedly, the thrill of knowing a secret was overlaid with even stronger sensations. Violent envy, and violent frustration.

I want Dan. I want to be sneaking off to have sex with him right now. I want to be out of this fucking dump, in a proper bed, with my fucking boyfriend!

Depression hit her like a tidal wave. She closed the door and slumped back onto her bed, not even bothering to pull the duvet up over herself. She couldn't help picturing everything Joe and Skye were doing to each other at that very moment. It might just be some desperate, stupid hookup between two sex addicts who ought to know better, but she couldn't help feeling hopelessly, horribly jealous of them . . .

Skye

'*I* thought you were coming to me!' Skye hissed at Joe, as his arm closed around her, his hand on her bottom.

'I told you, babe, I have a double bed!' he whispered back, pulling her around the corner, down the corridor.

Not very gentlemanly, though, Skye thought crossly, even as she trotted along next to him. I'm the one that runs the risk of getting caught if I come to you. And then she sighed. Who am I kidding? I'm a stripper who's fucking a movie star for a gossip rag! Why the hell should I expect him to be acting like he's taking me on a date?

It took a couple of seconds for the rest of it to click.

Oh, shit. The camera's back in my room, all set up on the table inside my bag, on night setting, ready to go – but how could I bring my goddamn bag if he wants to do it in his room?

Joe's hand was slipping down her bottom, squeezing her buttocks so sexily that she squirmed with excitement.

Ah, hell. I'll just have to do such a good job that he's desperate to come back for more. And next time, I'll figure out a way to bring the damn bag with me . . .

A door slammed, so close that they both jumped in shock.

'I thought you fixed Dave!' she hissed.

'I did!' Joe looked agonized. '*Fuck!* He said there wouldn't be anyone but him doing the rounds!'

But this was definitely not Dave. On the parquet of the lounge area beyond came the fast tap of high heels, moving swiftly in their direction. The men's bedrooms were on the other side of the lounge; there was no way they could make it to Joe's room, and Skye's was down a long open corridor. If the woman turned onto it, they'd be spotted immediately.

Skye looked frantically from side to side. 'Here!'

She grabbed Joe's arm with one hand. With the other, she swung open the door closest to them, the wheelchair plaque on the door indicating that it was the disabled lavatory. Dragging Joe behind her, she pulled him in. The footsteps were so close now she didn't dare to shut the door completely, in case the noise of the metal latch clicking shut drew attention; holding the door nearly closed, she saw a flash of white coat, and then a dark ponytail, switching back and forward as if it were attached to a bad-tempered horse.

Dr Lucy. Stomping down the corridor towards the main door like she's in a tearing hurry. Or really angry about something . . .

The light in the toilet had come on automatically with the opening of the door. Skye took in their surroundings, and an entire scenario flashed through her brain, perfectly formed, and so much fun that a grin spread across her pretty mouth as she shut the door, flicked the lock shut, and swivelled round to face Joe, hands on her hips.

'Is the coast clear?' he asked.

'No idea,' Skye said sweetly. 'We'll have to hang out here for a while. Sit.'

She pressed on his shoulders, pushing him down till he sank onto the toilet seat. Thank God the lid was down.

'Baby,' he started, 'this isn't exactly where I had in mind—'

Skye put her mouth against his and said, her breath warm on his skin, her lips moving seductively, 'My name's Skye, OK? Use it.'

He groaned at her closeness, his hands reaching for her, kissing her before she backed away, untying the sash of her robe, pulling it out of the loops, letting the robe fall open. Underneath it she was wearing the flimsiest slip she'd thought she could succeed in bringing to rehab: Victoria's Secret's finest, a pale cream, clinging and transparent enough to show her nipples through the lacy bodice.

She let the robe fall to the floor and stepped towards Joe once more. His legs were planted wide, his eyes bright with anticipation; she wiggled in between his legs, reaching for his hands, pulling them up to cover her breasts. Sighing in sheer pleasure, he tugged down the bodice, his hands big and warm on her bare skin, squeezing, caressing her so expertly that Skye's lower body melted towards him.

Wow, he actually knows what he's doing . . .

Good-looking guys, in Skye's experience, just didn't try as hard. They tended to assume that all the foreplay you needed was a flash of their smile and a good look at their six-pack before they stuck it in you and started pumping away. And celebrities – well, the baseball players and politicians and actors Skye had met in the Midnight Lounge had been all about sitting back complacently while she did the work.

But Joe was very much the exception to the rule. He was licking her nipples now, kissing each breast in turn, flicking his tongue around them in a way that made her moan loudly and grind herself against him and forget, temporarily, all about the plan she'd concocted just a few minutes ago . . .

Focus, Skye, for Christ's sake! she snapped impatiently at herself. This has to be a first fuck he'll remember for ever!

She had discarded her robe, but not before she had slid its satin belt out of its loops; it was wadded up in her hand. And now she slipped it round Joe's left wrist, knotting the belt swiftly and passing it through the white rail fixed to the left side of the narrow bathroom wall. As she had anticipated, he was so distracted by her breasts that he didn't take in what she was doing till she had brought the rest of the belt round his back, through the right-hand rail and looped round his right wrist, dragging it tight. Joe suddenly found his arms pulled out to each side, his wrists secured to the bars, which had been installed so that handicapped users could pull themselves up from the toilet.

Skye had to hand it to Joe: he wasn't slow on the uptake. A big, gorgeous grin spread over his face as he looked from side to side, checking out what she'd just done.

'Well, Skye, baby,' he drawled appreciatively, 'you are one *very* resourceful young lady . . .'

Skye hooked her thumbs into her skimpy nightdress, which was now down to her waist, and wiggled out of it in one smooth shimmy, standing completely naked in front of him. The lighting in the bathroom was brutal, a fluorescent strip directly overhead: it would have shown up any flaws immediately. But Skye's body was young and smooth and perfect, and her complacent smile said she knew it. She stood there for a long moment, letting Joe look her up and down like she was cheesecake and he was starving, letting him get a good stare at everything he was about to get; then she turned round in a long, slow spin, hearing him groan again at the sight of her breasts in silhouette, her firm, high ass, her flat stomach.

'You're *killing* me,' he moaned, his voice thick with lust. 'Baby, would you *please* unzip my fly before my dick busts it open? I've got a hard-on the size of Omaha waiting for you here . . .'

He wasn't exaggerating much. Skye had already checked out the shape and size of Joe's cock before, through his jeans; but as she undid his jeans and eased out his swollen dick through the fly of his boxers, she gulped in happy anticipation.

'Wow, baby, you're *packing*,' she said, leaning over to lick its head as his dick strained towards her eagerly.

'I bet you say that to all the boys,' Joe managed, but his voice was jerky now, he was losing control, and as her mouth closed around his head, tight and wet and warm, he let out a long moan of relief, so fervent and heartfelt that Skye knew her tactics were exactly right.

I've gotta keep on teasing him, she planned, nibbling at his cock with soft lips, running her tongue around him in little circles, one hand sinking to its base and pulling on him firmly, fast and slow, hard and soft, her mouth and her hands always contrasting with each other, mixing things up, finding one rhythm only to slip into another, playing him with everything she had, till at last, when she reared back to look up at his face, his eyes were closed and his lips clenched together, the grimace of a man who was blissed-out but determined to hold on as long as possible . . .

Perfect. Skye's lips curved into a little smile of triumph as his eyes opened again.

'Baby! Why'd you stop?' he pleaded.

She lowered her head and nipped him with her teeth, just lightly, but enough for him to get the message.

'*Skye!* Baby! Don't stop!' he begged. 'You're *amazing* . . .'

'You got any condoms?' Skye asked, rising from her knees.

His face contorted in frustration. *Wow, I thought I'd already seen every expression Joe had, up on the big screen. Turns out I haven't. She grinned. I can't wait to see what he looks like when he comes . . .*

'Dave said he'd score some for me,' Joe panted. 'Couldn't get 'em tonight, though.'

'I'll just have to improvise,' Skye said, turning away from him, smiling devilishly at him over her shoulder.

'Oh God. I bet you're damn good at that,' Joe said fervently, as she backed in towards him, lifting her ass, lowering herself onto the tip of his cock, her hands braced on his thighs, feeling her way, getting her balance. 'I bet you're a fricking Olympic-level expert at improvising.'

Skye smiled at him, her blue eyes dancing with enjoyment.

'My favourite position,' she said conversationally, moving her hips in tiny circles around the head of his dick, 'is the reverse cowgirl. You like the reverse cowgirl, Joe?'

He could barely talk now. All he could manage was a long moan of assent.

'But then, I *love* to lap dance,' she continued. 'And, you know, it's really good exercise for me. So this is what I like to think of as a combination of the two.'

Into her bare back, Joe groaned something that sounded like: 'You're fucking *killing me*,' as she finally relented and lowered herself onto him in one deep thrust, his big cock plunging all the way up inside her. She was dripping wet by now, had been dying to fuck him for what felt like hours, but she'd been determined to hold out till he was about to burst with frustration; both of them sighed a long 'Aaaah!' of utter and total satisfaction as their bodies joined, Skye grinding a corkscrew twist of her ass around him before she lifted and drove down on him again, and again, and again.

There was nothing gentle, nothing restrained about what she did to him. They were both going to be sore tomorrow, and they were loving every minute of it. She was fucking his brains out, lifting right up so that the tip of his thick, hard cock was almost out of her, holding it for a split second and then driving back down, riding him, using him to get herself off in a way that was simultaneously totally selfish and something she knew men absolutely loved. Nothing they adored more than thinking you were working their cock like a big juicy dildo, treating them like a total sex object.

And Joe's cock was a miracle of nature. She'd been afraid he'd come almost as soon as she straddled him, shooting off without caring whether she'd joined him or not; but no, he could hold out for a long time, long enough for her to get where she was going. Plus, he fit her like he'd been made for her. There was a slight curve to him that hit right against her G-spot when she lined everything up just right; with every stroke, she ground her clit down on him, getting closer and closer, teasing herself now as well as him, making herself wait and wait until she couldn't hold out any longer, her thighs beginning to tremble, her back arching, her lips clamped together so she didn't scream the place down—

Oh God Jesus God Jesus I'm coming so hard—

Fireworks exploded between her legs. She spasmed around him, and as he felt her coming, his hands wrapped around the rails, giving him purchase; he thrust his hips up, driving his cock even further inside her, sending her into a series of further orgasms that crashed over the first one in such fast succession that she saw stars.

For the next minute or so she almost passed out with pleasure. It was all she could do not to collapse on the floor. She drove her

knuckles into her mouth, biting down on them, to stop her screaming aloud; her entire body was a mass of sensation, shaking with the
aftermath of the most powerful orgasms she had ever had. Joe was
a totally amazing fuck. And the power trip of knowing it was Joe
Jeffreys inside her, Joe Jeffreys going crazy for her, had been unbelievable.

I'm a genius, she thought dizzily, as her brain slowly began to
assimilate the sensations pouring through her body. I mean, who
fucks a world-famous, A-list movie star for the first time and deliberately doesn't even *look* at him? How cool is *that*?

She leaned forward, but her legs were so wobbly they buckled
under her.

'Don't worry, I gotcha,' Joe said into her ear, his voice warm
with amusement, and she realized that his hands were round her
waist, holding her steady. 'Oh, and, baby – *Skye*?' She felt him grin.
'I owe you a new robe, OK? I kinda busted the belt of this one.'

He'd pulled out of her just in time; she could feel his cock deflat-
ing gently against the small of her back, the heady smell of sex all
around them. He rested his head on her shoulder, breathing deeply,
as they reacclimated to a normal level of sensation. They were both
drenched in sweat, his chest hairs rough against her skin.

And yet it was weirdly cosy, which was the last word Skye would
have thought she'd use to describe the aftermath of a hookup in a
disabled toilet.

Don't get sentimental, she told herself swiftly.

'Well, that wasn't much good,' she managed to mumble.

'No, it was pretty crappy,' Joe agreed, his grin deepening. He
kissed her shoulder. 'But, hey, practice makes perfect, right? I figure
if we keep at it, we might get a little better at this.'

'You think?'

'Hey,' Joe licked her earlobe, which sent a whole aftershock of
shivers running through Skye's body, 'it's worth a try, right?'

Amber

*A*mber had never talked so much in her life. Her throat was actually hoarse. Dr Raf handed her a glass of water, and dutifully she took it and drank it down. Putting down the glass on the coffee table, she looked up and met his eyes. They were the colour of deep, dark chocolate; she could have stared into them all day, losing herself in their depths.

She'd said so much, but she hadn't told Dr Raf everything. She couldn't bear to. And that guilty knowledge made her blush and look down at the table again.

'How are you doing, Amber?' he asked gently. 'You've been very brave, but I don't want to tire you out.'

'I'm OK,' Amber said quickly. She might not be able to bare her soul to Dr Raf completely, but she didn't want to leave his presence either. Here, in his office, just a coffee-table's distance away from him, she could have reached out and touched him if she'd been brave enough. She could hear him breathe, smell that faint green-fern aftershave, sneak glances at him as he crossed one lean thigh over the other, or steepled his fingers together as he listened to her. The hairs on his forearms, his strong wrists, the way the folds of the rolled-up sleeves of his shirt caught on the swell of the muscles just below his elbows; she could sit happily here for ever, absorbing every detail of how he smelled, how he moved, how he talked.

Not that he had done much talking in the last hour. He had simply listened, seeming completely engrossed by everything she had to tell him.

'You're still pretty weak,' he observed, smiling at her. 'You haven't been able to keep much down for the last forty-eight hours.'

Amber writhed in embarrassment as he continued: 'That's completely normal in opiate withdrawal. We have to make sure you're hydrated, of course, and we're giving you meds to smooth over the transition.'

He looked at her compassionately.

'From what you've just told me, your opiate use started when you were fourteen, and continued ever since, correct? When your mother gave you pills to calm you down on modelling shoots.'

Amber nodded, her hair falling into her face. For the last two days, she'd been in the medical facility at Cascabel, racked with vomiting spasms. All she'd managed to do before this session with Dr Raf was brush her hair and apply some tinted Carmex lip balm.

Catching sight of herself in the mirror, she'd winced at how awful she looked. And yet as soon as she'd sat down in the armchair opposite Dr Raf, and met his steady dark gaze, she'd forgotten all about her appearance. Nothing really mattered, as long as she was in the same room as him.

'And your mother's in LA as well,' Dr Raf said, not making it a question. 'Well.' He looked down at his notes. 'It's early days, of course. But we'll have to strategize for your recovery. Make sure you don't slip back into old habits.'

He's being so tactful, Amber thought, her heart filling with gratitude at how carefully he was protecting her feelings, but I know exactly what he means.

'She did it for the best,' she blurted out, raising her head. '*Matka* only thought she was helping me. Because I was so frightened on those magazine shoots.' She remembered the fashion editors, poking and prodding her, digging pins into her, fixing clothes around her with bulldog clips, commenting loudly on her shortcomings as she stood there, shaking like a leaf. 'If *Matka* hadn't given me the pills, I couldn't have done it. And I *had* to do it! We couldn't go back to Margate!'

She swallowed. '*Matka* had put all her money into getting us to London, going round the model agencies. I had to be a success. I was booking all these jobs, and I had to make them work.'

Memories of the last night in Mayfair flooded into her mind, and her throat clenched, but she pushed on.

'She'd been working as a prostitute,' Amber mumbled, forcing herself to keep looking at Dr Raf, seeing nothing but sympathy in his eyes as she continued: 'For years and years. All that time, I thought she was out cleaning offices, but she was . . .' She swallowed. 'That's why she was so desperate for me to make it as a model. Anything was better than that.'

She was twisting her fingers in her lap now, noticing that the nail polish was chipped beyond repair.

'Everything she did – *everything* – it was all for me,' she insisted. 'I've always known that. She wanted to give me a better life. And maybe I was a bit young, but lots of girls start young nowadays.'

Dr Raf nodded neutrally. 'When did you find out how your mother had been earning her living?' he asked gently.

In a tiny voice, Amber admitted, 'The night I . . .' She hesitated, but Dr Raf didn't rush her into anything; he sat there as quietly as ever. 'The night I took too many pills.'

'Your accidental overdose,' he prompted.

'It was. An accident, I mean.' She reached up and pushed back her hair, all vanity forgotten, utterly earnest with the need to convince Dr Raf that she hadn't meant to kill herself. 'I've been thinking about it, and I'm *sure* it was an accident! I just wanted everything to stop for a while. Not for ever.'

Her green eyes looked straight into his for a long, dizzying moment. And it was Dr Raf who blinked first, who lowered his head, breaking the contact. He looked down at his notes again, making a procedure of flipping through the pages, recrossing his legs.

'Tell me,' he said, 'is your boyfriend aware of the extent to which you were dependent on prescription drugs?'

'My . . .' Amber flushed. 'Tony?'

He's not my boyfriend! she wanted to blurt out, like a teenager with a desperate crush, determined to let the object of her affection know she was single. *But if I tell Dr Raf that Tony's not my boyfriend, then his next question will be why someone would pay all this money, fly me and* Matka *over the Atlantic, and put her up in a nice house and cover all my expenses here, if I'm not dating him . . .*

That was the truth she couldn't confess to Dr Raf. It had been hard enough telling him about her mother's past; there was no way Amber could admit that she, too, had done the same as Slava to make money. Slava might have been at the lowest end of the scale, standing on street corners, getting into cars or going down alleyways with strange men, while Amber was helicoptered to five-star hotels by multimillionaires who gifted her with Vuitton luggage, jewellery and lavish tips, but in the end, when you came down to it, Slava and Amber were exactly the same. They'd both had sex for money. That made them both prostitutes.

Like mother, like daughter, Amber thought, tears pricking at her eyes. He'll never look at me the same way again, if he knows the truth. I'll never see that sympathy in his eyes.

I can never tell him.

Without realizing it, she had pushed the chair back and stood up. This time she was steady enough on her feet so that Dr Raf didn't need to catch her.

'I'm really tired,' she said swiftly. 'I need to go and lie down.'

'Of course.' He jumped up, a frown on his handsome face. 'I'm sorry. I shouldn't have let our session run so long. It's my fault. Get some rest, and I'll see you at group tomorrow, OK?'

They were face to face, the coffee table no longer between them. Without knowing what she intended, Amber put out her hand, reaching towards him, and his own hand rose to meet hers in response. Their fingers brushed against each other for a split second, a feather-light touch; definitely not the brisk handshake that might have been expected between doctor and patient at the end of a consultation.

Dr Raf dragged his hand away as if it had been scorched, shoving it into his pocket as he stepped back from Amber, bumping into his chair. He cleared his throat loudly.

Amber turned, bolting for the door. I'm such an idiot! she scolded herself. What was I thinking?

And then she admitted as she fumbled with the door handle: I wasn't thinking anything. I just wanted to touch him.

She was frantic to get out, to escape from her own humiliation. But right on the other side of the door was the girl from the therapy session a few days ago, the sulky one with the bright yellow bob. Petal, she was called.

'God! Finally! I've been waiting, like, *hours*,' Petal spat at her crossly. 'My appointment was *ages* ago!'

Petal's eyes were outlined heavily with black pencil; combined with the daffodil-tinted hair and her dead-white skin, it made her look like a Gothic doll. The resemblance was heightened by her ripped black leggings and stripy T-shirt.

'I'm sorry,' Amber said.

'You just hogged Dr Raf for *ages*! That's totally unfair! And selfish!' Petal complained angrily.

'Petal!' Dr Raf came up behind Amber. 'I'm so sorry to keep you waiting . . .'

Petal gazed up at him with big, adoring eyes.

'It's OK,' she said, her voice breathy now. 'I know it's not *your* fault.'

And, pushing past Amber, Petal swanned into Dr Raf's office, slamming the door shut behind her so sharply that Amber had to jump out of the way to avoid being hit by it.

Back in their shared room, Skye was curled up on her bed. She was wearing a dressing gown, her hair was pulled up into a high ponytail and her face was bare of makeup; she looked fresh from the shower. Headphones were plugged into her ears, and a notebook was open on her lap. Amber had to stand in front of her, waving, before Skye realized that there was someone else in the room.

'Oh, hey,' she said, pulling out the earbuds, R&B flooding through them before she found her MP3 player and turned it off. 'Feeling better?'

'They say I'm over the worst of it,' Amber said, sitting down on her own bed. 'I hope so, anyway.'

Skye grimaced. 'Can't have been much fun,' she said sympathetically. 'So, they moving you back into our room now?'

'Yes – I just saw Dr Raf,' Amber said, so infatuated that she got a little thrill each time she pronounced his name. 'He said I was doing better.'

'Ooh, Dr Raf!' Skye grinned. 'It was awesome when he carried you out of group. Dr Lucy was shooting daggers at you. And Petal was drooling in jealousy. I'm amazed she hasn't pulled a faint herself.'

'Oh God, Petal . . .' Amber pulled a face. 'She just yelled at me because my session with Dr Raf ran over. She *really* doesn't like me.'

'Well, what do you expect?' Skye said, laughing. 'First you do a romance-cover faint, and then you postpone her Dr Raf fix! It's the only thing she lives for at the moment! She follows him around like a little puppy! Have you *seen* the way she looks at him?'

Amber nodded.

'*Major* daddy issues,' Skye said gnomically. 'Believe me. I mean, her dad's *Gold*. Everyone in the world's got a crush on him, and from what she says, she's barely ever been alone with him. That's got to fuck you up.'

Amber pulled a pillow off her bed and curled up with it in her lap, hugging it. Skye was already making her feel a lot better about the Petal confrontation.

'Just stay out of her way,' Skye advised. 'She's like an open wound right now.'

'OK,' Amber said. 'Thanks.'

'Any time.' Skye sighed, looking down at her notebook. 'Dr Lucy told me to try some free association, but I'm totally sucking at it.

You know? You write down whatever comes into your head? I'm so bored I actually gave it a shot, and all I've done for, like, an *hour*, is write, "La la la Get me out of here" over and over again. Look.' She held up her open notebook so Amber could see.

Amber couldn't help cracking a smile. 'You seem – I don't know – *normal*,' she said before she could think it over. 'I mean, you seem like a – a happy person. Not like me and Petal.' She reflected. 'Or those other guys in group. Not Joe. You're like Joe – you both seem . . . happy.' She felt very inarticulate. 'I suppose I'm saying that I'm really fucked up. And I can see that most of the other people here are. But you don't seem fucked up. At all.'

'Interesting,' Skye said, looking at Amber hard. 'Dr Lucy thinks what she calls my "cheerful façade" is just a cover-up for all kinds of deep-buried crap.'

'But it isn't, is it?' Amber said, without knowing why.

'Ha!' Skye burst out laughing. She leaned over, holding her palm out flat to Amber, who took a moment to realize she was supposed to high-five the other girl. 'No, it isn't! You're smarter than Dr Lucy! And you know what?' She snapped shut the notebook and dropped it onto the floor. 'You're right about Joe too.' She grinned saucily. 'There's nothing wrong with that man either.'

'So why are you here?'

Skye shrugged, looking away.

'I told everyone in group, remember? This sugar daddy of mine made me come here. I go through rehab for "sex addiction" –' she raised her acrylic-tipped fingers and made the quotation mark sign with them – 'and he sets me up in a nice little love nest.' She grimaced again. 'I'm not really that talented a dancer, you know? All the girls at the Lounge, they want to be Diamond. That's their dream.'

Seeing Amber's blank face, she elaborated: 'The burlesque dancer who wears real diamonds in her costume? She's got her own show in Vegas now? And she does those vodka ads on the TV? But she's really *good*. I mean, she's a *star*. No way am I that good a dancer. I get by with this and these.' She pointed to her pretty face, her high firm breasts. 'That's all I've got. Snagging a sugar daddy, having someone buy me an apartment, put it in my name . . . Look, I'm not saying I'm any kind of role model, but this is the hand I got dealt, and I'm playing it out.'

Skye's head was tilted now as she looked at Amber, a challenge in her eyes; she was daring Amber to judge her.

'I mean, you're, like, a *supermodel*,' she continued. 'There are tons of girls who look like me.'

'No.' Amber was shaking her head vehemently. 'I'm nothing like a supermodel. And I'm over the hill now, anyway. Twenty-seven's like *sixty* in model years, believe me. I'm only here because someone's paying for me, too,' Amber found herself confessing. 'A sort of sugar daddy.'

'Really?' Skye's eyebrows arched.

'I met him through modelling,' Amber said, trying to stick as close to the truth as she dared. 'For him it's all about how I look. He has no idea who I am.' She paused. 'Which isn't really his fault,' she added to her own surprise. 'Because I have no idea who I am either.'

'Oh, *honey* . . .' Skye slid off her bed and onto Amber's, sitting next to her, taking her hands and squeezing them. 'I've met a *lot* of girls, believe me,' Skye said drily. 'You don't do the job I do without getting real good at sizing girls up. And whoever you are, you seem pretty nice to me.'

Amber thought she was about to cry. And then, to her great surprise and even greater pleasure, she realized that she was smiling back at Skye instead.

'Come on,' Skye said, pulling Amber to her feet. 'Let's go out in the garden and catch some rays.'

Pulling on a T-shirt and cut-offs, Skye led the way to the garden. She paused just as the two girls crossed the threshold out onto the patio, taking in the scene: the air outside was rich and warm after the air-conditioned facility. Purple bougainvillaea trailed down the wall behind the fountain, and the palm trees on the patio area were a canopy of leaves, sunlight dappling through them onto the flagstones.

Brian was sitting by the fountain, trailing his hand in the water, looking glum. And, lying on his favourite lounger on the lawn, rich cigar smoke rising into the air above him, was Joe Jeffreys, all six foot two inches of him, his Hawaiian shirt unbuttoned to show off his rock-hard, golden-tanned, rippling abs. Sunlight glinted on the belt buckle that fastened his faded old blue jeans. He looked like the Marlboro Man; all he needed was a cowboy hat to complete the picture.

Glancing over, he caught sight of Amber and Skye, and a huge smile spread over his handsome face, his blue eyes sparkling with enthusiasm. He lifted the hand holding the cigar and gestured at the girls to come over and join him.

Skye hesitated for a moment.

Joe called: 'Hey, Amber! Nice to see you up and about!'

Skye said swiftly to Amber: 'We're friends, right? You and me?'

Amber looked at Skye, confused. Skye was staring up at Amber with something very close to entreaty in her big blue eyes.

I barely know her, Amber thought, taken aback. But she's been really nice to me. And I need friends. I *really* need girlfriends.

'Um, yes,' Amber answered cautiously.

'So would you do me a huge favour?' Skye entreated. 'Would you dial it down with Joe?'

'I don't understand . . .'

'He has this whole wounded-bird fantasy going on about you. And I don't want him to get distracted from me.' Skye's voice was lowered. 'This could be my ticket out of everything, you know? Plus,' she jerked her head over at Joe, 'honestly, I don't think you're up to sneaking around with one of the most famous guys on the planet, behind the back of one of the most famous women on the planet. You've got yourself to take care of, and that's a full-time job at the moment.'

Amber couldn't help smiling. Skye was smart enough to put her case very well, and she was absolutely right. *The last thing I need is to be splashed all over the tabloids, or have paparazzi after me. Skye was tactful enough not to say it, but I'd relapse in two seconds with all that stress.*

She nodded, acknowledging the truth of Skye's words. 'And you think you can handle it?' she asked, her green eyes serious.

'Just watch me!' Skye said immediately. She took a breath, fiddling with her ponytail. 'I don't want you to think I'm a *total* slut,' she added. 'Jennifer – his fiancée – she's gay. It's all for publicity. I mean, he's got to get it *somewhere*.' She fixed Amber with a firm stare. 'I've got your back here. Whatever you need, you can count on me. You get sick again, I'll take care of you. And you leave Joe to me, OK?'

'All right,' Amber agreed, as Joe called: 'Ladies! Aren't you gonna come keep me company?'

'Well, since you're asking so nicely . . .' Skye called back, flashing her very best smile as she and Amber crossed the lawn to join him.

Petal

*P*etal couldn't ever remember feeling so lonely in her life.

She was sitting in the lounge, by the only phone they were allowed at Cascabel, apart from two hours on Sunday night when they got their cellphones back if their doctors thought they could be trusted with them. The lounge phone was so old-fashioned it was actually on a cord; you couldn't pick it up and take it into your room for a private conversation. So Petal was having to wait there, sprawled on the sofa, looking like an idiot, waiting for her boyfriend to ring her, because the phone didn't make outgoing calls, and after lots of sobbing and begging and pleading with Dr Raf, she'd negotiated a precious, scheduled call from Dan.

Only she'd been waiting forty minutes, and the call still hadn't come. Petal was pretty much ready to tear her face off with her fingernails.

The worst part was that a tech was hovering round, doing something meaningless in the office next door, but really there to listen in on Petal's call and make sure she didn't do something that Cascabel would term 'inappropriate'. Like asking Dan to fly over here and score her an eight-ball of coke on the way.

Ohmigod!

The phone was actually ringing! Petal sat up straight, afraid that she was hallucinating the sound because she wanted to hear it so much. She snatched it out of its cradle almost before the first ring had finished. Petal had never been any good at delayed anticipation.

'Dan?' she gasped into the receiver.

'Pet! Hey, I can't believe we finally get to talk! How are you?'

'*Shit*,' she said fervently, wrapping the cord around her wrist. 'Total, utter, fucking *shit*. It's horrible here. I hate it.'

'Well, we never thought it was going to be fun, did we?' Dan said sensibly. 'You're nearly halfway through, though.'

'That's easy for you to say,' Petal grumbled. 'You're not here. Why're you so late ringing me, anyway? I've been waiting *hours*!'

'We're recording, pet,' he said proudly. 'Wrote a song for the *Breaking Down* soundtrack, can you believe it? And looks like they're going to do a video! Us and some sexy vampires! Amazing, eh? We're so made up about it I can't tell you!'

'Sounds brilliant,' Petal said, her words dripping with acid. 'I'm so glad you're having a fantastic time without me.'

'Aw, pet, don't be like this! I miss you – you're my girl! But I thought you'd be pleased! This is the big time for us, yeah?'

'I waited *hours* for you to ring me,' Petal complained, tears rising to her eyes. 'You don't know what it's *like* here, Dan. It's like *prison*. I can't do anything I want. Everyone's horrible to me. And you couldn't even *ring* me when you said you were going to . . .'

'Pet, be reasonable,' he pleaded. 'I can't just down tools and walk out halfway through a bloody song, can I, now? I shot out as soon as I could. You want me to put one of the lads on to tell you it's true?'

'You've probably got tons of groupies hanging out in front of the studio right now, don't you?' Petal was digging her own grave. 'Where are you – Air?'

'Yeah, as a matter of fact.'

Petal pictured the big studios, a sprawling, red-brick Victorian converted church on Haverstock Hill in Hampstead; she'd practically lived there when her father or his friends were recording albums. She and Tas had loved hanging out there, wandering around the other studios, being alternately petted and hit on by other musicians and producers, treated as mascots by the recording staff; the best part of all was waltzing in and out at will, past the school-girls and groupies and hardcore fans camped out in the parking lot, sitting forlornly on the walls, waiting patiently for their idols to emerge, casting spiteful, jealous stares at Petal and Tas with their access-all-areas passes.

'Lots of girls waiting outside for you, are there?' Petal continued. 'Making goo-goo eyes at you, trying to give you their phone numbers?'

'Pet, there's always girls, but—'

'I knew it! It's so *unfair*!' Petal was sobbing full out now. 'I'm bloody *trapped* in here, and you're shagging your way through half of London!'

Even gentle, mild-mannered Dan could take only so much.

'Now hang on, pet,' he said angrily. 'You've gone too far. I said I'd wait for you, and I am. I've had to nip out of a really fucking impor-tant recording session to ring you – everyone's waiting for me to get back in there, and taking the mick 'cause I've been fussing about ringing you – and now you're giving me grief!'

'I'm having a miserable time!' Petal wept. 'And you're having fun without me!'

'I'm working!' Dan protested.

'Well, sorry for disturbing you!' Petal snapped. 'How incredibly fucking selfish of me to make you ring me while you're working! I'll just fuck off and leave you to it!'

She slammed down the phone, plastic smashing against plastic, her heart racing with fury. And then she folded her arms and stared at it, fully expecting Dan to ring right back and apologize.

Only he didn't.

And when, five minutes later, it dawned on Petal that he wasn't going to, she picked the phone up and threw it against the wall.

'Hey!' Daniyel promptly emerged from her office. 'What's going on in here?'

Petal was in floods of tears. 'I hate it here!' she sobbed. 'You're all trying to ruin my life!'

'Now, honey, you know that's not true,' Daniyel said soothingly. 'But you can't throw things just 'cause you're not happy right now.'

'I don't even have a *photo* of him!' Petal wept. 'I didn't even have time to get a photo of him done!'

She looked so forlorn, curled up in a ball on the sofa, weeping her heart out, that Daniyel reflected for a moment, then turned on her heel and went back inside the office, emerging with Petal's black sparkle-encrusted mobile.

'Here,' she said, holding it out to Petal. 'I shouldn't be doing this. And if I see you acting out at all, *any* infraction of the rules, I'll have it back off you faster than you can spit. Now pick up that phone you threw and put it back on the table before I give you this one.'

Petal jumped to obey, replacing the phone and then grabbing her mobile. Eyes lighting up, she immediately flicked it on, dying to call Dan back.

'There's no signal!' she said, vastly disappointed.

Daniyel grinned. 'Oh, no, honey. I'm not *that* nice. We've got a blocking system here – we triangulate from different buildings, or some such. You can look at your boyfriend's photo all you want, but you can't ring him outside of the designated hours for cellphone use. There won't be another window till tomorrow. And I'll be keeping an eye on you till then, seeing if you're behaving, OK?'

'Oh, *shit*,' Petal said, vastly disappointed.

Turning on her heel, she slumped off down the corridor, heading for the garden. She wanted to throw herself on the grass, in the shade of a tree, and have a big private sulk; but as soon as she reached the patio, and took in the scene outside, she realized that wouldn't be possible. Joe Jeffreys was stretched out on a lounger in the sunshine; Amber was on another lounger; and Skye, attention-hogging as ever, was doing stretches in the middle of the lawn, showing off her splits and giggling as Joe watched her with great enthusiasm.

Petal glanced over at Brian, who was sitting by the fountain, listening to music on his headphones, staring over at the group on the lawn with undisguised wistfulness.

Great, she thought sourly. It's like being at school. The cool kids and the nerds.

Petal had hung out with Brian before, talking about music, bands they liked, listening to tracks on Brian's MP3 player. Right then, however, she was in a filthy mood, and she was damned if she was going to go and sit with Brian in the rejects' section. Maybe if Brian had looked up, seen her, waved her over . . . but he was so busy gawking at Skye and her antics that he didn't even notice Petal's arrival.

At least I get my room to myself during the day. Petal trudged back there, shut the door, turned off all the lights and curled up in bed. Feelings of rejection and abandonment were flooding through her, and not just because her longed-for conversation with Dan had been such a disaster. All her life, she'd watched other women be more important to her father than she was. When her useless mother was still around, she'd hogged all Gold's attention, at first by being sexy, and then, when Gold's eye started wandering, by throwing ever more extreme and crazy scenes. After that, the procession of girlfriends, mistresses and one-night stands had always taken priority with Gold. Petal had been more of a nuisance than anything else.

All of this was, reluctantly, coming up in therapy; in the group sessions, and in her talks with Dr Raf. It was hard and painful, and Petal wasn't enjoying it one bit. And somehow, seeing Joe with Skye and Amber was bringing it back even more powerfully. It was like reliving a bad experience all over again. There was Joe, the world-famous, incredibly sexy film star, with the model and the stripper all over him, as far as Petal could see. And next to those girls, no one gave Petal a glance.

Apart from Dr Raf. He was the only person here who looked at Petal and really saw her. When he focused his attention on her, she felt like the only person in the room. Back in London, Petal had deliberately surrounded herself with a posse as soon as she could; Tas, JC, and all her other party friends made sure that she was never alone unless she really wanted to be. From the moment she met

Dan, they'd lived in each other's pockets.

And now she was not only all alone, but being totally ignored by practically everyone.

Amber deliberately hogs Dr Raf whenever she can. She's such a cow. I hate her.

Skye's just throwing herself at Joe, like a complete slut. He's got a fiancée, and Skye doesn't even care. She's fucking him right here in rehab, when they're both here for sex addiction! How messed up is that!

Misery, loneliness and frustration turned slowly into resentment. Gradually, as Petal lay on her bed, all the problems she was inexpertly wrestling morphed into being the fault of Amber and Skye. They were both acting like all those women in Petal's past, who'd trampled right over her to get to her dad. Or the ones now, in London, who were throwing themselves at Dan.

Skye doesn't give a shit that Joe's engaged to Jennifer Downs. And Amber's totally throwing herself at Dr Raf.

I hate them both.

Skye

Skye hadn't expected to like Amber one little bit. Gorgeous, fragile, and so vulnerable that every man in a mile-wide radius was panting to look after her and cushion her from the cruel hard world, Amber was exactly the kind of rival every girl like Skye dreaded. No way could Skye compete with Amber. Because while every man alive might want to fuck Skye, Amber was the girl he'd want to marry.

And yet, Amber hadn't turned out to be the man's woman Skye had assumed she was. She seemed genuinely grateful for Skye's offer of friendship, genuinely eager to open up to her, and genuinely willing not to compete with Skye for Joe's attention.

The trouble, of course, was that Amber was competition just by existing. All she had to do was waft into a room, her delicate cardigans and shawls trailing behind her, chestnut hair tumbling down her back, her slanting green eyes focused on distant horizons, for Joe to sigh and stare at her wistfully.

And now that Amber was back in their bedroom again, Skye couldn't slip out at night, or sneak Joe in there, to fuck his brains out so thoroughly that all thoughts of Amber were blotted out by the raging hard-on he had for Skye.

Plus, I need to film him doing it! she reminded herself firmly. That's what I'm here for! That's what I'm being paid for!

It was surprisingly easy to forget that fact. Daily life at Cascabel was unexpectedly absorbing. In her near-daily sessions with Dr Lucy, Skye was having a lot of fun feeding Dr Lucy made-up stories and watching her spin around them like a kid with a new toy, not smart enough to figure out that Skye was lying through her teeth. In Skye's opinion, Dr Lucy shouldn't be here at Cascabel at all.

She totally doesn't care about people, Skye thought as she left her most recent session, watching Dr Lucy's cold dark-pencilled eyes snap down to her paperwork again with relief at not having a living breathing human being to talk to any more. She should be in research – cutting up animals, or something. I bet she's only here to be close to Dr Raf.

Walking past her in the corridor was Dave, the orderly. His eyes met hers, and he jerked his head briefly back to the patients' lounge in a clear signal.

Dave's in on this too, Skye reminded herself. He's pushing me to get the goods on Joe. And he'll get paid a ton when I do. As will I. So why aren't I getting on with it?

As she entered the patients' lounge and saw Joe, sunk into an armchair, reading a sports magazine, Skye realized the answer from the happiness that lit her up at the sight of him.

Oh shit. I actually like him. I don't want to catch him out for the National Investigator: *I want to date him.*

I'm the biggest freaking idiot in the whole damn world.

Joe snapped his head up, hearing Skye come in, and flashed her a huge smile. There was a reason that Joe's face was famous all over the world, and that smile was an essential element, full of sunshine, so infectious you couldn't help smiling back. He winked at her, putting his magazine down on the arm of the chair, stretching his legs out luxuriously in front of him.

'Baby, I'd give a grand just to be able to ask you to come sit in my lap right now,' he said.

'Oooh, it'd cost you *way* more than that,' Skye said flirtatiously, tilting her head to one side, cocking one hip, standing there in a way that had guaranteed to get the guys in the Lounge clamouring for her attention. 'I charge a ton for one of my special lap dances.'

Joe had a well-documented weakness for strippers; every time she referred to her career, his eyes sparkled with excitement, and right then was no exception. Skye let her eyes drift to the crotch of his jeans, and smiled smugly.

'Though I suppose I could give you a discount for – uh, *quantity*,' she added sexily.

'Hold that thought, OK?' Joe said, beckoning her over. 'You, me, the storage cupboard in an hour?' he muttered when she was closer. 'I squared it with Dave. Daniyel goes on break, there'll be no one around.'

Can I figure out a way to get the camera in there? Skye hesitated, wondering if that would work.

'Please, baby, say yes!' Joe pleaded. 'I've been thinking about nothing else since the other night in the bathroom . . .'

'You look just like a horny dog,' Skye said saucily. 'I'm surprised your tongue isn't hanging out.'

'I can do that,' Joe said, lolling his tongue out of the corner of his mouth and panting.

He looked so funny that Skye couldn't help giggling, loudly enough that it alerted Daniyel, who popped her head into the open doorway of the lounge to see what was going on.

'Hey,' she said reprovingly. 'The contract you both signed when you entered Cascabel said no flirting, remember?'

'Daniyel!' Joe spread his hands wide as Skye backed away from his chair. 'You know you're the only lady in my life!'

'Addiction is a serious business, Joe Jeffreys,' said Daniyel, wagging her finger at him, but even she couldn't control an upward quirk of her lips in response to his grin. 'Skye, honey, why don't you come join me and take yourself away from this situation?'

'*Situation*,' Joe said with comic sadness. 'I'm a *situation* now.'

Daniyel was already whisking out of the lounge, and Skye had a chance to wink agreement at Joe before she followed dutifully.

Shower, shave everywhere, perfume, and my best lingerie, she listed quickly to herself. *I've got just enough time to get myself perfect . . . and camera-ready . . .*

Hovering just outside her bedroom was Dave, making a play of emptying the trash can in the corridor. He shot a look behind him, making sure no one was approaching, and Skye, picking up his cue, darted a glance inside the room to check for Amber: she wasn't there.

'Gimme your bag,' Dave hissed at Skye. 'I'll plant it in the storage room. It'll be running. Just make sure you're facing it, OK?'

'Gotcha.'

Skye nipped inside and handed it to him; he tucked it under his arm, which was so big and brawny that the tote bag half-vanished immediately in the folds of his green uniform top.

'You know where it is, yeah? On the way to the garden. Just make sure no one sees you going in. It's Daniyel's afternoon off, so she won't be doing no snooping around.'

Dave lumbered off down the corridor in the direction of the storage room as Skye vanished into the bedroom to embark on her beautifying session.

Next door, Petal had been alerted by the whispering. Running to her door to listen, she had heard Dave's last words with perfect clarity.

The storage room had overhead lights, but Joe hadn't switched them on, not wanting to alert anyone that the room was occupied. Still, there was a high, wire-covered window in the back wall, that let in plenty of natural light; enough for Skye to see Joe immediately as she sneaked in. Enough for her, darting a glance around as she pushed a step stool against the door to wedge it shut, to spot where Dave had concealed the camera – halfway up one of the galvanized steel units that lined the walls, stocked with boxes of stationery and cleaning products.

Dave did a good job, Skye thought, turning to face Joe. *You'd never see the bag if you weren't looking for it.*

'Wow, you look good enough to eat,' Joe said happily, taking in her short skirt, her snug T-shirt, and her gleaming, freshly washed golden hair.

He was sitting on a metal folding chair he'd brought out and placed in the middle of the room, and as he beckoned Skye towards him, she heard a very faint whirr as she passed the camera. Nothing that would attract the attention of anyone who wasn't looking for it, but another reassurance that the scene was set perfectly for the *National Investigator*'s scheme to work just as they'd planned it.

And suddenly, she paused, getting cold feet.

I'm not sure if I want to do this after all.

She looked at Joe.

He hasn't looked down on me or treated me like trash, like he can buy me, even though I've said a lot in group about taking money from guys at the Lounge. He acts like him and me are the same, even though he's a movie star and I'm a stripper. Like we're just two people having fun, getting it on, doing what comes naturally.

He's been nothing but a good guy to everyone here. Look how sweet he is to that poor sap Brian. He doesn't deserve to be set up like this.

'Skye?' he said, seeing her hesitation. 'Anything wrong?'

But then again, isn't Joe just using me? Getting a quick fuck in here and then bye-bye, back to his five-star life? Probably boasting to his famous friends about how he got laid in rehab? He'll forget my name the moment he gets in his limo and goes back to Malibu.

And how can I stop now? There's no way I can turn off the camera without giving myself away.

Plus, wouldn't I be kicking myself for the rest of my life if I had the chance to record me and Joe Jeffreys having sex and I didn't do it? I don't have to pass on the camera to the Investigator *if I decide not to . . .*

Before she knew it, she was walking up to Joe. He reached out for her eagerly, pulling her down on his lap.

'So here's the thing,' he said, kissing her neck and making her moan. 'You ran things last time, OK? And it blew my fucking mind.'

'We aim to please,' she managed to get out, though Joe was now nibbling at her earlobe in a way that was turning her brain to mush.

'And believe me,' he continued, running his tongue slowly round her ear, 'I've been thinking about nothing else ever since. You can feel it, yeah? You can feel what you do to me, can't you?' He shifted her on his lap so his cock, poking up through his jeans, rubbed between her legs just where she wanted it.

'Yeah . . .' she moaned, just about remembering to keep her voice down, wet already with anticipation.

'But *this* time,' he said, biting down on the soft skin of her ear, 'I'm the one with a plan. What do you say, honey? You OK with going along with what I have in mind?'

'Oh God,' she said, as his hands closed over her breasts and started squeezing them, his thumbs running over her hardening nipples. 'Whatever you want, baby—'

And then she bit her lip hard in a huge effort not to squeal out loud as his hands slid down to her waist, closed around it and he lifted her into the air, standing her up in front of him. Taking hold of the hem of her skirt, he pulled it up to her waist, bunching it there, staring in open appreciation at the sight of her in her little lace thong.

'You're the girl of my dreams, you know that?' he said.

Coquettishly, Skye hooked her thumbs in the lace band of the thong. 'Does your plan involve me taking this off?' she asked.

'I don't mean to rush you,' Joe said, unzipping his jeans and pulling them down to his ankles, revealing his lack of any underwear, 'but I went commando specially . . .'

Skye eased the band past the curve of her hips, and with one smooth wriggle, sent it falling, light as a feather, to her feet; by the time the soft white scrap of lace had reached them, she had kicked off her kitten-heel flip-flops, and was standing there, bare from the waist down, watching Joe settle back in the chair, his jeans round his ankles and his cock standing up like a flagpole, rosy, swollen, full and ready for her.

'So what—' she started.

But then she really did squeal. She couldn't help it. Because, as easily as if she were a rag doll, he picked her up by the waist again and whirled her through the air. Joe spun her round as if she were on a wheel, rotating a hundred and eighty degrees, so that her feet were up in the air and her head hanging down, her hair briefly brushing the ground. Before she had a chance to catch her breath, she was being pulled towards him, his arms wrapping round her waist, her legs falling open to either side of his neck, one draped over each shoulder, and Joe was adjusting her with a couple of quick shifts, settling her exactly where he wanted her.

'Wow,' she managed from her upside-down position, 'you *did* have a plan . . .'

And then she couldn't say another word, because Joe's lips were diving onto her pussy with such gusto that the last part of her sentence dissolved into one long moan of pleasure.

He lifted her just a fraction more, so it felt like his mouth was completely covering her pussy, his tongue flicking around it in wide generous circles, tracing the entire area, with her spread out directly below him like a feast. Six feet two, an ex-quarterback, an action hero who did his own stunts and pumped iron like a demon to stay in perfect shape, he was strong enough to support Skye's entire weight so easily that his hands weren't even digging into her.

She felt ridiculously comfortable, considering the position. Her thighs rested on his wide shoulders, her forearms on his knees. And as the circles that Joe was tracing became smaller and more concentrated, she wriggled with excitement, her breasts pressing against his lower groin, writhing and undulating, immediately aware that Joe knew exactly what he was doing. He must love to eat pussy. She was in the hands of an expert. He was going to make her come, and all she had to do was hang here like an upside-down doll and let his wet, lithe tongue lick her till she exploded.

Skye was almost there: she could feel it building in her abdomen, that heat and tension in the very pit of her womb that stoked itself up to furnace heat before a burst of fire and then a blissful meltdown. Her thighs clamped around Joe's neck, her strong dancer's muscles pulling her up, up, even further into his mouth, greedily pumping herself against his tongue, and he groaned with appreciation as he sank his tongue deep inside her, making her scream with delight.

She was dripping wet already, she could feel it. Joe's hot mouth was licking up her moisture eagerly, but she was melting for him already, liquefying . . .

He shifted, wrapping one arm round her waist as his other hand came free, leaning down and grabbing something from the floor, thumbing it open with a pop.

That can't be what it sounds like, Skye thought, dazed, a split second before something trickled down her smooth, shaved mound, and she felt the cold rounded edge of a bottle against her pussy.

'You like champagne, baby?' Joe said thickly. 'I got Dave to bring us in a little treat . . .'

He lowered his mouth to her again, pouring the bubbles into her, lapping them up, making a special cocktail of Skye and champagne.

Skye started to laugh with sheer happiness, her body bucking in Joe's arms. And as the laughter took hold of her, so did the orgasms, one after another, a stream of coming and coming, her thighs bouncing on Joe's shoulders, his tongue licking deep inside her, flicking on her clitoris at the end of every stroke, lightly enough just to tip her over the edge and keep her spasming there, not too much, not so much that she overloaded with sensation and couldn't come any more. Once he'd found the rhythm, he kept at it, tipping the bottle to send a steady stream of champagne between her open lips, sucking and licking it up as fast as it poured out. She could feel the cooler liquid trickling into her, mixing with her juices, feel the bubbles popping on Joe's tongue.

The sensation was exquisite, unbelievable. She was moaning constantly, the sound reverberating around her skull, a steady hum magnified hugely by the fact that she was upside down; her eyes were closed, she was in her own world of surging orgasms, one stacked on top of the next, waves and waves of them. She had no idea how long it lasted. But Joe really was an expert, because not only did he know how to bring her and keep on bringing her, but he could sense when she was getting to that point when her nerve endings would be so sensitive that any more stimulation would be more pain than pleasure.

Skye didn't even realize that Joe had stopped working on her. She hung there, her body twitching with the aftermath of her orgasms, slowly coming down, her pussy throbbing, feeling a cooler air on it as Joe lifted his mouth and turned his head to wipe it on her thigh.

'Wow,' she said eventually, her eyes fluttering open.

She shook her head, coming back to full consciousness, and realized that she was directly above Joe's crotch. Nor did he show any signs of being in a hurry to let her go. She reached for his cock, engorged and full, standing up straight against the long muscles of his stomach; it had been bobbing against her the whole time she was coming, and now it was his turn. Skye ducked her head round so she could reach it. And then she gasped as Joe hauled her up further, swinging one of her legs to meet the other, so that her whole body was lying over his right shoulder, higher up, now at the perfect angle to lower her head, open her mouth, and take his cock inside.

His head tilted to the side, resting against her bare buttocks, moaning into them as she took almost all of his penis into her mouth. Skye had never sucked a man off upside down before, but it was an amazing way to deep throat. Joe's cock slid deep inside, its tip butting against the back of her throat, and his hips started to jerk gently upwards, finding his rhythm, groaning against her smooth upper thighs.

Skye's mouth was impossibly stretched, accommodating itself to Joe's swollen, hard cock. She managed to stretch her lips over her teeth, rounding out the surface, closing them over the velvety-soft skin of his moving penis, giving him extra sensation, extra friction as he pumped himself evenly, steadily, up inside her hot wet mouth. His groans grew louder, his hands on her waist dug in tighter, but his pace stayed even and steady. Joe was as careful with his own climax as he had been with Skye's: nice and easy does it every time. No frenzied jerks, no desperation. He knew he was going to come, and he wanted to build up to it, take his time, savour every last stroke of his cock in her eager warm mouth as he raised and lowered his hips with total control.

Skye only knew Joe was seconds away from his orgasm because, just as his head began to swell even further, butting even harder against the roof of her mouth, his hands tightened even more on her waist and he hauled her up. She hung in the air, suspended, Joe holding her above his cock as it burst out of her mouth and pumped out a stream of white come, which poured, hot and wet, onto the small peaks of her breasts. She reached her hands down and grasped his thighs, helping to support herself as his head lolled against her buttocks and he moaned: 'Yeah, *yeah* . . . Oh God, there it is, there it is,' giving himself over completely to his orgasm.

Skye watched his cock throb and pulse until, finally, it had shot all of its load. Joe's hold on her had slackened; she slithered down him, grateful for her experience pole dancing, which meant at least that she didn't look ridiculously clumsy making her descent. She managed to land in a curled-up ball in his lap, and stretched her legs out across him, leaning over to drop a quick kiss on the top of his detumescing cock. Joe was breathing as if he'd run a marathon, his chest thudding against her in a steady, throbbing rhythm.

Years of experience had taught Skye never to be the first to talk in this kind of situation. *You let the guy come back from wherever he's been, and you see what kind of mood he's in when he does.*

But what Joe did next wasn't anything she'd been expecting.

'Here,' he said eventually, his hands reaching up to pull up her T-shirt and unclip her bra, exposing her breasts. He started to rub them in long slow strokes, and, feeling how warm and moist his hands were, she realized what he was doing: he was scooping up his semen from his stomach and rubbing it into her breasts.

'It's the best thing for your skin,' he said lazily against the top of her head. 'Full of proteins. Keeps you soft and supple.'

'That right?' Skye said, glad he couldn't see her smile.

Men. They're all the same. How they love to talk about their come. Like it was holy water or something.

'This facialist told me that once,' Joe said, 'believe it or not. You want to hear what she told me to do? Knock one off, rub it on my face and leave it for half an hour.'

'*No*. You're *kidding*.' Skye tilted her head back to check out his expression. 'Some woman told you to . . .'

'Uh-huh!' He was grinning now. 'I couldn't make that shit up. I'm an actor, baby, not a writer.'

'Did you ever—'

'No way!' He was grinning ever wider. 'Can you see me doing that?'

'You know, I can't,' Skye admitted, tucking her head back under his chin.

'You want some?' He ran his finger over his abs, finding a drop left, and brought it close to her cheek. 'Hey, look at that,' he said smugly. 'I've got tons to spare today. Want a Joe Jeffreys facial?'

'Maybe another time,' Skye said demurely, pushing his finger back to her breast. 'But thanks for the offer.'

'Definitely another time.' He sounded very happy. 'You bring it out of me, baby, you really do. You make me come so hard.'

'Aww,' Skye purred equally smugly. 'You say the most romantic things. And –' she reached down for the bottle of champagne – 'you even buy me drinks!'

'I saw that in a movie,' Joe said into her hair. 'Always wanted to try it out.' He snuggled her closer in his lap. 'Guess I was just waiting for the right girl.'

'You're breaking my heart,' Skye said lightly.

Oh God, she thought, looking guiltily over at the tote bag wedged unobtrusively between two boxes of office supplies, the camera inside it doubtless whirring happily away. Maybe, just maybe, I'm going to end up breaking my own damn heart . . .

As soon as Joe had put his hands on her, as soon as he had started kissing her, Skye had completely forgotten about the camera. Not that we didn't put on a damn good show, she thought, dying to play it back. But he really does something to me. There's some chemistry between us that makes us just go crazy for each other as soon as we touch.

But then, both Skye and Joe had been so caught up in the phenomenal sex they'd been having that neither of them had been remotely conscious enough of their surroundings to notice something that might have even more serious consequences. Petal had followed Skye as she sneaked off to the storage room, hidden round the corridor as Skye slipped inside, and then, prising the door open just enough to spy inside, had stuck her phone to the crack and taken a video of Joe and Skye.

A video that Petal, back in her room, was staring at in total disbelief. The tiny phone camera had been further inside the room than she was; its images, even without a flash, were shockingly clear.

I can't believe this, Petal thought, amazed. She hadn't expected anything like this – who would? *I mean, in broad daylight, in a storage cupboard without a door that locks from the inside . . .* She'd assumed Joe and Skye would be fooling around, and that if she took a couple of pictures of them at it, she'd have evened the balance, somehow, between her and Skye. Skye might trip around the place, blonde ponytail bouncing, flirting madly, drawing all eyes to her, but Petal, secretly, would be in possession of a piece of evidence that could get Skye kicked out any time Petal chose. Unlikely as she was to go that far, it was a little bit of power that Petal had anticipated having with great relish.

But this was way more than she'd expected. In broad daylight – Joe Jeffreys and Skye, not only having full-on sex, but in the weirdest position she'd ever seen in her life. This was dynamite. Petal felt a bit dirty looking at the video too much, so she clicked off, put the phone on her chest and lay back on her bed, staring up at the ceiling, debating with herself what to do next.

Because this secret was just too good not to share with someone.

Amber

'Hey.' Joe loomed up in front of Amber, who started in surprise; she'd been so absorbed in her thoughts that it was as if she'd wrapped a duvet round her. She was curled up on one of the wooden armchairs on the patio, drinking water, smoking, and staring ahead of her at the fountain. It was well into the evening, and she could barely see the play of water; but she could hear its slow, gentle trickle down the bamboo posts to the granite below, and the sound was very calming.

'You look exhausted,' Joe said gently.

He propped himself on the edge of the table, close enough so that they could talk easily, but not so near that he might be crowding her.

'Tell me if I'm bugging you,' he continued, 'but you look really out of it. You wanna talk to someone or should I just leave you alone?' He grinned. 'Don't be polite. Tell me if you want me to buzz off.'

Amber looked up at Joe; the patio lights cast shadows over his face, dimming the bright gold of his hair, throwing his strong masculine bone structure into relief. He might have been a sculpture of a Greek god. And the fact that he was so handsome, so famous, made her strangely relaxed with him. It was like talking to a god come down to earth, not a real living, breathing human.

'I'm so confused,' she said simply. 'I don't know what to think about anything.'

Joe nodded. 'I can see that.'

'I don't even know what to think about myself,' Amber said, pulling up her legs and hugging them. She rested her chin on her knees, her hair spilling around her. 'I'm confused about *everything*. I don't know what I want from one minute to the next.'

Apart from Dr Raf, she thought. I know I want Dr Raf.

'That's no bad thing,' Joe commented.

'Really?' Amber's eyes widened.

'You gotta start from scratch some time,' Joe said. 'You were saying in group today that you never figured out who you are, right? What you like, what you want, what you don't want?'

It sounded awful, put like that. What kind of person didn't even know what they didn't want?

But he's right, she reflected. There's no point pretending. I do have to start from scratch.

'And that's bound to be freaky,' he continued. 'I mean, you're a grown woman, you've travelled all over the world, you've been on the cover of magazines, and right now it feels like you don't know the first thing about yourself.'

Amber nodded, her green eyes fixed on his face.

'I mean –' Joe smiled ruefully – 'look at me. I may not be the best example out there of how to run your life, OK? I've always put my career first. This whole engagement thing –' he pulled a face – 'it's all for the publicity. Jennifer needed to get married – to a guy – and my people were saying I needed to settle down. For my image.' He sighed, stretching his arms above his head. 'So I'm going along with it. I got no problem with that, it's how Hollywood works.' He looked seriously at Amber. 'You see what I'm saying? It's not pretty, but hey, it's my choice. I know who I am.'

'And I don't know who I am,' Amber said.

'Not right now.' He smiled at her. 'But I think that when you connect with who you are, you're going to find out that you like that person a hell of a lot.'

And then, a few seconds later, as he registered what an impact that statement had had upon Amber: 'Oh, *shit*.' He frantically rummaged in his jeans pockets. 'Hell, honey, I didn't mean to make you cry!'

'No, it's OK,' Amber managed through her tears. She fished in the pocket of her loose silk cardigan and brought out a crumpled tissue, waving it at him. 'It's a good sign. That's what Dr Raf says. I'm getting in touch with my real feelings.' She dabbed at her tears, which were catching entrancingly in her long lashes.

'Here,' Joe said, leaning forward and taking the tissue from her, drying her eyes expertly. 'You wouldn't believe how many times I've played this scene. I've dried more girls' eyes than you've been on magazine covers.'

Amber's laugh was watery, but genuine.

'Course,' he added jokingly, 'I usually kiss 'em afterwards.'

'Joe . . . I—' she stuttered.

'No, no, don't worry. It'd be like hitting on a twelve-year-old, the state you're in now.' He handed her the tissue. 'Now blow.'

Dutifully, Amber blew her nose.

'I gotta say, though,' Joe added, 'you look better with a noseful of snot than most actresses I know do with a faceful of makeup. You ever thought about acting? The camera must love the hell out of you.'

She shook her head.

'Well, who knows? When you get your shit together, the world'll be your oyster,' he said.

'I don't think I could pretend to be someone else till I know who I am,' Amber said doubtfully.

'Oh, honey!' Joe burst out laughing. 'If that were really the way it worked, there'd be a *lot* fewer actresses out there, believe me!'

'You two look really cosy,' Skye said coldly, coming out onto the patio. 'I hate to break this up, but it's curfew. They sent me to tell you guys.'

'Hey, babe,' Joe said easily, swinging round to greet her, not a whit perturbed by his proximity to Amber.

Amber, however, was much more embarrassed. The ice in Skye's voice was unmistakable. And Skye was standing in the middle of the patio, arms folded just below her breasts; normally she'd have come over and sat down with them, pulling up a chair or curling up on the arm of Amber's.

Jumping up, grabbing her water, Amber practically darted past Joe to Skye's side.

'Ah,' Joe sighed, swivelling to look at the two girls. 'If I didn't know already I was a sex addict, just looking at the two of you heading off to bed together would tell me in a heartbeat. See you in my dreams tonight, ladies.'

'You're full of shit,' Skye snapped, and whirled on her heel, stomping back inside with Amber on her heels.

'I don't want you to think—' Amber said breathlessly, as Skye marched back to their room.

'Think what?' Skye said angrily. 'You *said* you wouldn't flirt with Joe! We had a deal! I only had to look at how you two were sitting to see what was going on!'

'I really wasn't!' Amber insisted. 'Honestly, Skye, I *promise*. I wouldn't do that. I don't even know how to flirt!'

Skye swung round and fixed Amber with a cold stare. 'Joe knows enough for both of you,' she said.

Reflecting on Skye's words for a moment, Amber had to admit that there was some truth in them. Joe might not have been flirting, strictly; but he'd talked about kissing, he'd paid her compliments.

'OK,' she admitted. 'He was, a little . . .'

They'd reached their bedroom. Skye stomped in and threw herself on her bed, staring up at the ceiling.

'But it was more like he was trying to take care of me,' Amber said. 'Make me feel better.'

Skye swung round, facing Amber now. 'That's exactly what makes me nervous!' she said. 'He sees you as this wounded angel. He wants to take care of you – mend your broken wings.' She waved her hands around furiously. 'He doesn't want to take care of me! He just wants to have a good time with me! *You*, he wants to pick up off the ground and nurse back to health!'

'You make me sound like a puppy with a broken leg,' Amber said with a sort of bitter humour, sitting down on her bed, pulling her cardigan tightly around her.

'You *are* kind of like a puppy with a broken leg,' Skye said, sitting up to face Amber. 'Sorry.' She grimaced. 'That's harsh.'

Amber twisted her hands in her lap. 'You don't need to worry about me with Joe,' she said quietly. 'He's so nice, and I really like him. But –' she hesitated, trying to collect her thoughts together into a neat sentence – 'he's too like the other men I've known. Paying me compliments. Talking about how I look. I don't think I want that any more.'

Skye's pretty eyebrows shot up. 'That's going to make it really hard for you to date,' she commented drily.

'I wouldn't know,' Amber said simply. 'I've never been on a real date in my life.'

Skye sank down to her own bed, never taking her eyes off Amber, kicking off her flip-flops and wrapping her arms around her legs. 'This,' she said frankly, 'I *have* to hear.'

'*Matka* – my mother – was very protective of me when I started modelling,' Amber began.

As always when Amber talked openly about her life, it was almost like an out-of-body experience. Before, it had been completely taboo. So now the freedom and release were extraordinary. She felt as if she were floating.

'She didn't want me going out with men, and honestly, I didn't want to either,' she went on. 'I was only fourteen. But that ended up meaning that I didn't know what I was doing. I was sort of a babe-in-the-woods. And eventually, photographers or clients would ask me to do things. Or have meetings with them after the shoot. *Matka* couldn't always be there. And I thought it was what all the girls were doing. What you had to do to be a model.'

'It probably is,' Skye said sympathetically.

'I wish I knew,' Amber said sadly. 'I didn't have anyone to talk to. Lots of the other girls were staying in model flats – you know, rented by their agencies – so they all made friends. But I was always—'

'With your mom,' Skye completed.

'She just wanted to take care of me,' Amber insisted, wrapping her cardigan tighter around herself. 'She wanted the best for us both. She just . . .' it was the first time she'd said this, and the relief was like a physical rush, '. . . she just lost her way. She didn't mean us both to get addicted to pills.'

In one smooth movement, Skye uncurled her legs, stood up and shifted over from her bed to Amber's, sitting down next to her roommate and wrapping her arm around Amber's shoulders.

'Honey, of course she didn't,' she said, hugging Amber. 'I mean, what mom would? I'm sure she thought she was helping you.'

'The pills *did* help,' Amber said wistfully, reaching up to hold Skye's hand. 'In the beginning, anyway. I had this one shoot for *Glamour* when I started out – I was so scared my teeth were chattering. I couldn't even smile. *Matka* gave me a Valium, and after that I was OK.'

'People wouldn't get hooked if they didn't work,' Skye pointed out with a smile in her voice, her arm warm round Amber. 'Don't beat yourself up, OK? You're here now, and like Dr Raf says, you're doing the work. You'll get through this just fine.'

Amber squeezed Skye's hand wordlessly in gratitude.

'I've done really dumb stuff on coke,' Skye confessed. 'I haven't said this in group, but the night before I came in, me and my roommate, we ordered in some coke 'cause we'd run out, and our dealer sent this hot boy round – you know, in New York you can just ring up and you get a bike messenger over with whatever you want? Anyway, I ended up partying with the damn bike boy while my roommate screwed the bouncer from the club we work at, which she'd totally *sworn* to herself she was never going to do again. But that's coke for you, right? You end up doing all kinds of stupid shit. I tell you, I'm totally swearing off it from now on.'

'I didn't just . . . do things with people on shoots, to get jobs,' Amber said in such a small voice Skye had to lean in even closer to hear her. 'The work started drying up. I'm a bit old to model now.'

Skye snorted sympathetically. 'Tell me about it,' she said wryly. 'Dancers don't exactly have a long shelf life either. And I'm not even that much of a dancer.'

Amber managed a faint smile.

'But my agent said he could get me jobs still,' she continued. 'Which paid a lot. Only—'

'I'm way ahead of you, honey,' Skye said.

'It wasn't bad at all,' Amber said, turning to look directly at Skye, wanting her to believe it. 'They took me to five-star hotels, gave me presents – it was like they were pretending I was their girlfriend. They'd seen me on the covers of magazines, so I had a really high value for them.' She managed a smile. 'I've got nothing to complain about, really. If you're going to have sex with men for money, you couldn't be treated better than I was. They never made me do anything I didn't want to do. One of them's even paying for my treatment here. He flew us over, put *Matka* up in a house his company owns in LA, took care of everything. God knows what'll happen when I get out.'

'Worry about that later,' Skye said. 'One thing at a time.'

'That's what I've been telling myself,' Amber agreed.

'Look,' Skye said gently, 'we've all done stuff we're not proud of. Don't beat yourself up for what you did in the past, OK? I could tell you stories that'd curl your hair. And the place I worked was a fricking convent compared with some. I've heard of strip clubs that make you blow the manager just to get a job. So cut yourself some slack.'

Amber nodded gratefully. 'My agent wanted me to go to Dubai,' she confessed. 'With some other girls. For a week. To party with some men. He said it would be fun, but one of the girls told me things – made me scared – I couldn't do it. That's when I took all those pills.'

'Oh, jeez, no,' Skye said, her blue eyes hard. 'Going to a foreign country for a whole week – with a group of girls – are you kidding me? That's hardcore.' She whistled softly. 'You got out just in time.'

Amber stared at her. 'It feels like I could tell you anything,' she blurted out. 'I mean, you wouldn't look down on me, no matter what I've done.'

'Hah! You're kidding, right?' Skye said cheerfully. 'You know what my job is! Like the one-star version of yours. And see, now you've told me all your dirty secrets, it's not so bad, is it?' Skye gave Amber a last hug, and stood up. 'You should have made friends with a stripper years ago, honey. We're not exactly the judgemental type.'

Amber actually found herself giggling at this, and after a second, Skye joined in.

'You really don't have to worry about me and Joe,' Amber assured Skye in heartfelt tones.

'If you say so.' Skye was pulling her T-shirt over her head, taking her clothes off ready for bed.

'No, honestly.' Amber stood up, facing Skye, who was now unclipping her bra. 'It's not just that I don't care about Joe. It's because –' she swallowed hard – 'I never had a friend before. None of the girls at school were ever my friends. First because I looked weird, and then because I didn't. And I never made friends with any of the models I worked with, because I was always with *Matka*. I've had quite a few really rich guys. I've got one waiting for me when I get out of here. So I don't need Joe – and I definitely don't need all the attention that would come with him,' she added. 'What I do need is a friend. That's much more important to me. I wouldn't do anything to mess this up.'

Naked to the waist, her impossibly high, perfect breasts jutting out at right angles to her slender ribcage, Skye paused, her pyjamas in her hand.

'You know,' she said, 'I actually believe you. Which is crazy. I actually believe that being friends with some random stripper is more important to you than a shot at Joe Jeffreys.'

'It is,' Amber said sincerely. 'Honestly.'

'Well, OK then,' Skye said, laughing. 'Friends it is!'

She enfolded Amber in a hug, her head barely coming up to the taller girl's shoulder, as unselfconscious as only a stripper or model could be about her semi-nakedness.

'You know something funny?' she said, still laughing. 'Can you *imagine* what Joe would do if he saw us like this? In each other's arms, me topless? It's got to be what he fantasizes about every single night!'

'You're absolutely right,' Amber said, starting to laugh too.

'He'd come in his fucking *pants*!' Skye giggled, and the two girls cracked up, laughing so hard that Daniyel, doing a curfew patrol to check everyone was in their rooms, tapped on the door and called: 'Ladies! It's way past bedtime!' which, for some reason, just made them laugh harder.

This is what I need, Amber thought, hugging Skye back as their bodies rocked with laughter. Someone to giggle with about silly things. Someone to be a girl with. Someone I can confide in, who won't judge me.

I really hope Skye believes me. Because it's true: right now, what I need more than anything is a friend.

It was inconceivable for Amber – unless she was just out of detox – not to make sure that every aspect of her appearance was perfect before she left her room. But, before her daily session with Dr Raf, she was practically obsessive about checking herself out in the mirror. She was wearing a Reiss strapless silk dress, very simply cut, in dip-dyed shades of pale green that brought out the emerald of her eyes; wrapped over it was a big, butter-soft cloud-grey pashmina. Her hair was curled and pinned back from her face, her makeup so carefully applied it was almost invisible: mascara, gel to smooth her eyebrows, the most delicate glow of pale coral blusher, rose lip stain. She had sprayed her Arpège perfume into the air and stepped into it, so it wouldn't be too obvious, just a subtle veil of scent, and her flat sandals were slender bands of gold leather over her perfectly manicured feet.

So it was no wonder that Dr Lucy, exiting her office in a swirl of white coat and shiny dark ponytail, took in Amber, looking as if she'd just stepped off a catwalk, and jerked her head back in reaction.

'Hi, Amber!' she said brightly. 'Don't you look smart! Where are you off to?'

Dr Lucy was effectively blocking Amber's path down the corridor. Amber had no option but to stop.

'I have my session with Dr Raf,' Amber said cautiously.

'Oh!' Dr Lucy's voice had a coating of frost on it now. 'Your makeup is *lovely*,' she said, smiling, her teeth white and perfectly even. 'I can tell you used to be a model.'

That 'used to be' grated on Amber exactly as Dr Lucy had meant it to, but her reaction was probably different from what Dr Lucy had been expecting.

'Oh, thank you. Yours is very good too,' Amber said, giving Dr Lucy the same scrutiny. 'Very natural.'

Dr Lucy's eyes widened fractionally before she smiled and said: 'Do you know, talking about this has given me a very useful idea. I have this exercise that I do with the women in group. I ask them all to take off their makeup, so they can interact with each other with bare faces, really get to know their essential selves without hiding behind a mask. We must do that very soon.' She narrowed her gaze, looking at Amber's luxuriant curled auburn tresses. 'And I get them to brush out their hair too. Undo the styling. Really get back to basics. You and Skye could certainly benefit from that.'

Amber had been on the receiving end of plenty of bitchery from women over the years, and she'd never known how to respond. She didn't want to be bitchy back; that wasn't in her character, and she wouldn't know how.

But that doesn't mean I can't stand up to her. That doesn't mean I can't say she's gone too far.

'Do you come in without makeup,' Amber asked, 'or do you take yours off at the same time we do?'

'I – *what*?' Dr Lucy stammered.

'You do it too, don't you?' Amber said, terrified now, but pressing on bravely. 'Otherwise your essential self wouldn't be interacting with us, right?'

Dr Lucy's lipsticked mouth flapped open. 'Well, I – I'm not sure how appropriate that would be—'

'Oh, look at the time!' Amber said quickly. 'I'll be late!'

She shot past Dr Lucy and hurried quickly down the corridor, not daring to look back.

I can't believe I did that, she thought, her body racing with adrenalin at the confrontation and triumph at how well she'd managed. I really stood up to her! I actually managed to go head to head with Dr Lucy. Rehab is completely changing my life.

'Amber!' Dr Raf jumped up as she entered his office, staring at her in open appreciation for a moment. 'You look – well, you look . . .'

He cleared his throat.

'Sorry,' he said, taking his glasses off and then looking rather hopelessly round for something to clean them with before he put them back on his nose again. He blushed. 'I shouldn't really comment – it's just that you look very, um, positive. In very good spirits.'

'I am,' Amber said, giving him such a dazzling smile that he hurried forward to pull her chair out for her.

She settled into it, arranging her skirts around her, as Dr Raf took the other seat, a matching leather chair with a small coffee table between them, in the centre of which was placed the obligatory box of tissues. It was noon, and his dark stubble had not yet begun to show; his olive skin was still smooth. Amber could never decide whether she thought he was more handsome clean-shaven, or with the shadow of his stubble outlining his features, giving him a rougher edge. She stared at him, considering, and her scrutiny made him lift one hand to his cheek, rubbing it self-consciously.

'So!' Dr Raf said, crossing one chino-clad leg over the other. 'Amber! I've scheduled you double sessions from now on, since we overran yesterday and cut into Petal's time.' He flashed a quick, enchantingly boyish grin. 'And neither of us wants Petal getting cross with us again, do we?'

God, he's so gorgeous, Amber thought, smiling back at him. Look at his *dimples*. I could look at him for ever and never get bored.

'Um . . .' It was as if Dr Raf had read her thoughts, because his light tenor voice was louder than normal as he continued: 'Did anything come up for you in group this morning that you want to talk about?'

Something came up for me a minute ago I want to talk about, Amber thought, but she knew she couldn't acknowledge Dr Lucy's hostility to her, not with Dr Raf. She'd had this scenario a million times in her working life: men – the nicer men – wanted to think that women got along fine. There was no point bitching or complaining.

But I could use it – I could talk about it without mentioning Dr Lucy.

'I'm feeling so much stronger than I used to,' she said. 'I open my mouth and these words come out. Words I wanted to say before, but never could.'

She couldn't look at Dr Raf while she talked. She'd never been able to. His gaze was fixed on her, his dark eyes soft and so full of empathy that she lost herself in them and couldn't get back.

So Amber looked down at her hands, twisted in the folds of her pashmina, as she continued: 'I could never stand up for myself before. Anything anyone wanted, I did it. I honestly don't think I knew how to use the word "no".'

Dr Raf was nodding. 'And that included drugs, of course,' he said.

'Yes.' She managed a faint smile. 'I never said "no" to a pill. You know, I look back and realize that for the last ten years or so I was always in a haze. And I didn't like it.' She met Dr Raf's eyes for a moment. 'I really didn't like it. Some people do. They want to be knocked out all the time. But actually, I think I'd've been a better model if I'd been sober. I bet if I got out some of my old photos, I'd see it in my eyes. That I'm not completely there.'

'You never did any professional work while you were sober?' he asked.

She shook her head. 'I was on tranquillizers from when I was fourteen.'

Amber expected Dr Raf to say something in response, but he didn't. He just went on looking at her. And she knew what he was waiting for; she had known it almost since the first session with him.

'I don't blame *Matka* – my mum,' she said eventually. 'She was just trying to help me.'

'And she's an addict herself, from what you say,' Dr Raf prompted.

'Yes. She always says it's for pain relief. You know, her back hurts, or her arthritis is worse, or something like that . . .' Amber trailed off, because she'd suddenly had a revelation: *All these years, Matka said her back was bad from all the cleaning work she'd done. Bending over, mopping and scrubbing floors. But she was never cleaning at all. That was a lie.*

How many other lies have there been?

'Amber, are you OK?' Dr Raf asked. 'You've gone very pale.'

'No,' Amber said slowly. 'I'm not OK . . .'

And then, to her horror and dismay, it came pouring out. Slava's story about being out every night cleaning offices, locking Amber into the flat for safety, when she was really working as a prostitute. The desperation with which Slava had pushed Amber into modelling, her stone-cold insistence that Amber had to succeed at all costs, because they could never go back to their old life in Margate. And Amber's realization of exactly what Slava had meant by that.

'I can't imagine it,' Amber whispered, her pashmina clutched into a tight damp ball now, her fingers working on it. 'She never told me anything.'

'It sounds as if she was trying to protect you,' Dr Raf suggested sympathetically.

Amber's head shot up, her green eyes full of misery as she looked at him.

That would be true – if she hadn't been OK with me doing it as well. If she hadn't told me she knew what all my 'dates' really were.

If she hadn't pushed me to go to Dubai.

'I don't know about that,' she said, and her eyes filled up with tears so fast they came pouring down her cheeks before she'd even realized she was crying.

Dr Raf was pushing the tissue box towards her. She reached into it, her fingers scrabbling against the cardboard base: it was empty. Muttering apologies, Dr Raf got up and rummaged on the shelves behind his desk for a fresh box, ripping it open. As he came back with it, passing Amber's chair, he leaned over and handed the box to her.

Her face was wet with tears. She could hardly see. She fumbled for the box, but it fell through her fingers, dropping to the floor between them. Dr Raf bent to pick it up, but it had slipped partially under her chair; he went to his knees to retrieve it, and when he straightened up, still on his knees, the tissue box in his hand, his face was directly on a level with Amber's.

For a split second, they looked at each other, so close that even through the tears clinging to her lashes, Amber could make out every tiny detail of his features. It was one of those moments on which everything hangs: waiting for one of you to lean forward, just a fraction . . . for the other one to lean forward too, acknowledging the tension hanging in the air between you, thick and heady as a cloud of incense.

Or for the moment to pass. For one of you to pull back, fumbling with something like a tissue box, remembering that he's a doctor and you're the patient and that having his mouth so close to yours is completely unprofessional.

I won't let that happen. I want this more than I've wanted anything in my life.

It was the bravest thing Amber had ever done, and if she'd given herself any time to think it over she would have stalled.

But she didn't. She leaned forward and kissed Dr Raf, her mouth tender and wet with her own tears, and as soon as their lips touched, the electricity that had sparked before, when their hands met, short-circuited and burst into flames. If Dr Raf had any resistance in him, it melted the moment he tasted the salt of Amber's tears against the warmth of his mouth.

The kiss was better than any drug Amber had ever taken. They were wrapped in a cloud now; heavy and dark, enveloping them so closely that their movements were long and slow and languorous, as if in a dream. Dr Raf's hands slid up Amber's arms, lingering on her bare skin, wrapping round her back, tangling into her hair, pulling her close, their mouths never leaving each other's. His tongue slid past her lips, and her whole body trembled with incredulity at how wonderful it felt; Dr Raf inside her, wanting her, his scent all around her, his hands on her body. She closed her hands over his arms, tracing his muscles, hearing him groan deep in his throat at the feel of her fingers against him, and she couldn't believe this was happening, that the world had spun so out of kilter that she was able to touch Dr Raf as she had yearned to ever since she'd first seen him, press herself against him, slide her fingers against his scalp, feeling the tight curls of his dark hair springing against her palms, absorbing every sensation as slowly as she could, not wanting to rush a second.

It felt like they never stopped kissing. Dr Raf was pulling her pashima off her shoulders now, the feel of his hands on her bare skin so wonderful that Amber heard herself moaning as if from a long way away. He had found the zip in the back of her dress and was sliding it down. She pressed herself against his chest, making it easier for him, helpless to do anything but wrap herself closer against him, and tilt her mouth up to his, so that they could keep kissing as her dress fell to her waist. And as his mouth left hers for a moment, so he could look down and see her, she started to unbutton his shirt, sliding one button and then the next out of their holes with ease, taking it as slowly as she could, unwrapping the best present she would ever have in her life, making each moment last as long as she possibly could.

Slava's rules for Amber's appearance had always been strict. Not only was her makeup to be perfect, her nails shiny and polished, she was never to wear lingerie that didn't match. Amber had never been more grateful than now for that rule; her pale green lacy Chantelle bra and knicker set was exquisite, and she knew it. Dr Raf sighed in sheer delight at the sight of her breasts in the strapless bra, his palms caressing her nipples through the lace till they stood up hard and eager against him. Amber was sighing too as she dragged the cotton of his shirt off his shoulders, baring his smooth warm tawny skin, running her hands over his toned pectorals, making his nipples as hard as hers.

They looked up at the same time. Their lips met again at the same time. It was as if they were choreographed, every movement paralleling the other one's, never needing to ask, because they already knew what their lover wanted. Amber slid off her chair just as Dr Raf pulled her towards him, and they tumbled to the carpet, pushing the chair back till they were lying in each other's arms. Dr Raf unclipped her bra, and the sensation of her breasts pressing against his naked chest sent them both to a new height of sensation. She writhed against him, their tongues twining so neither of them could have said where one began and the other ended.

He was pulling up the silk folds of her skirt; she was unbuttoning his trousers, his hips already rotating against hers, his cock hard. It pressed against her through the soft cotton fabric of his boxers, grinding the lace of her French knickers into her, an exquisite, delicately scratching sensation that stimulated her so much that she realized she was gripping onto his shoulders now, pushing herself down on him, working the lace of her knickers against her clitoris, feeling the swollen tip of his cock exactly where she wanted it, taking her pleasure in a way she never had before, his tongue filling her mouth, and before she knew it, she was coming, sighing and moaning her pleasure into his mouth, spasming again and again in a long slow series of orgasms that left her as dizzy as if she were blissfully high on vodka and Vicodin.

Better, so much better . . . Oh God, I've never felt anything like this in my life . . .

The cloud was lifting her up now; she was lying on it, floating, her limbs sprawled out in release, so completely relaxed that when Dr Raf's body pulled away, his heat fading, she didn't protest. Even though she was naked from the waist up, her dress pulled up to her hips, the sandals still on her feet, Amber didn't feel vulnerable in the slightest. Somehow, she knew he was coming back to lie beside her.

And she couldn't have moved even if she'd wanted to. Every muscle in her body was limp, every nerve overloaded. So she simply lay there, the afterglow of her orgasms still washing gently through her, keeping her aloft on the cloud, until a drawer slammed and a few quick footsteps brought Dr Raf back to her, kicking off his shoes, dragging down his boxers, dropping to his knees beside her. Her eyes fluttered open, and she took in the sight of him with awe. His shirt was hanging open, off his muscled shoulders and bare chest; he was naked to his knees, where his trousers and boxers were caught, and his thighs were just as strong, his quads just as defined, as they had looked through the material of his trousers. And his penis, rosy and full and stretching out towards her . . .

Dr Raf paused, looking down at her. In one hand was a condom packet which he had been about to tear open; at the sight of it she moaned in excitement, knowing it meant he would soon be inside her. But the reality of what they were about to do had just hit him the moment he ripped at the foil. In his eyes she read doubt, hesitation, and the beginnings of guilt.

And then she reached her arms up to him imploringly, and the look in her eyes overrode everything else. He dragged the condom on as she grabbed the lacy knickers and pulled them off, wriggling her hips to get them as far down as she could before Dr Raf dropped to the carpet, his hand around his cock, guiding it up inside her as her mouth dropped open in a silent scream of ecstasy. She was so wet that his cock drove up inside her easily, filling her at the first thrust. Their arms wrapped around each other tightly as their bodies pressed together, Dr Raf finding her mouth and kissing her again.

It was perfect. It was like coming home. It was as if their bodies had been made to fit together. Dr Raf rocked against her slowly, his cock scarcely moving in and out of her, but pressing inexorably against her clitoris, rubbing her G-spot, with such exquisitely gradual stimulation that she sobbed and bucked against him, begging him to go faster.

His elbows propped on either side of her head, his hands cradling her face, he whispered against her mouth, shushing her, kissing her, refusing to speed up his pace, building the fire between them with every slow stroke of his hips. Amber tilted her hips to meet him, pushing down against him every time he drove fully into her, making him groan against her mouth with pleasure, sending herself into a trance of delight. Her eyes closed, her head fell back. Waves of stronger and stronger excitement were rushing up her body, taking it over. She had stopped trying to rush, to force Dr Raf to go faster; she had surrendered completely to the rhythm, and now it was all she could feel.

She was going to come. Nothing could stop it. She was going to come just from having sex, and she was going to come stone-cold sober, without any drink or drugs to blur her sensations.

My God, she thought. If everyone could get this rehab treatment there'd be no addicts left in the world . . .

That reflection was so funny, and she felt so lucky, so happy, that she realized she was laughing, a laugh that started deep in her belly and sent ripples up through her body, rocking her against Dr Raf even more; she reached up and dragged his mouth against hers, kissing him with the laughter still on her lips, grinding her hips up against him, taking him so deeply inside her that he couldn't hold out any longer and started to come.

The sight of his face in ecstasy as he came, the feel of his cock spasming inside her, tipped Amber over the knife-edge on which she'd been balancing, and her body surrendered completely as she felt herself coming with him. It was like nothing she'd ever felt before; it took her over, flooding over and through her, scalding hot, sweeping her up and holding her in its grip as she orgasmed over and over again, waves of electricity running from her fingertips to her toes.

Amber couldn't have said how long it lasted. She might have lost consciousness at some stage. Eventually, her body still throbbing with the aftershocks, she came back to awareness enough to realize that Dr Raf was lying on top of her, his head on her shoulder, his breath panting out against her bare skin. She honestly thought she might never be able to move again; every nerve in her body was limp. She was flung out like a starfish underneath him, left there by the tide.

Opening her eyes was like lifting a hundred-pound weight. Dragging her hand along the carpet, pulling it up enough to rest it in his hair, was titanic. But she had to be able to look at him, to touch him. His eyelashes were thick and dark on his cheeks; he had pulled off his glasses, and he looked touchingly vulnerable without them, very boyish.

He stirred, his lashes fluttering open, and looked back at her. Then she bit back a wail of protest, because he shifted, getting his hands under him, pushing back, coming out of her, one hand on his cock to catch the condom, rubbing briefly against her as he pulled out and sending a last little shockwave of pleasure through her body.

'We should . . .' he mumbled, stumbling awkwardly as he tried to get to his feet, hoicking up the trousers and boxers that had caught around his calves.

'Yes, I know,' Amber said, sitting up, pulling down her skirt, looking around for her bra. For some reason, she wasn't embarrassed in the slightest. She fastened her bra and pulled her knickers up from her ankle, where they had ended up, and pulled the bodice of her dress up from her waist, smoothing everything out, her expression as serene as Dr Raf's was agonized.

Though she couldn't help smiling as she noticed his efforts to get rid of the condom. He'd grabbed a whole handful of tissues from the new box and bundled it up in that; but then he'd gone over to his wastepaper basket and was standing there, looking down at it, clearly debating whether or not he could throw a tissue-wrapped condom away in there for the cleaners, possibly, to find.

Amber stood up, retrieved her pashmina, and wrapped it around her shoulders, rearranging her hair with the skill of long practice.

'I'll go now,' she said simply, putting the final curl into place.

'Amber . . .'

Still standing over the wastebasket, Dr Raf looked back at Amber with dark, haunted eyes. His lips remained open as he struggled to find any more words, and failed.

But Amber didn't need him to say anything at all. With a last, beautiful smile, she turned and went towards the door.

Today, I've actually managed to make *two* psychiatrists lost for words, she thought, the smile deepening. I'm discovering I have a good sense of humour, I'm standing up for myself, and I just had the most amazing sex with the man I love. Rehab really is the best thing that ever happened to me.

Coming down the corridor were Joe and Brian, talking to each other about baseball: at the sight of Amber emerging from Dr Raf's office, however, they stopped dead in their tracks.

'Amber,' Joe said eventually. 'Jesus, you look amazing.'

'Thank you,' Amber said sweetly, flashing him a smile that rocked his and Brian's heads back.

'What the hell kind of session did you just have?' Joe said, grinning. 'Dr Raf handing out happy pills now?'

'Oh, I'm just high on therapy,' Amber said, turning on her heel with a swish of her skirt and strolling off, her curls bouncing over her shoulders.

'*Love* to watch that girl walking away,' Joe sighed to Brian. 'God, I could look at her walking away all damn day.'

'Did she ever do any posters?' Brian said hopefully. 'I'd really like to get a poster of her. In a bikini. She ever do anything like that?'

'I tell you, there's something magic about her,' Joe said in heartfelt tones, ignoring Brian. 'She's a goddamn angel come down from heaven.'

Skye, who had been sneaking up behind them, meaning to surprise Joe with a surreptitious pinch on his tight ass, froze dead at hearing this.

Again with the angel stuff! she thought furiously. I could have mind-blowing sex with him all day and he'd still be obsessed with Amber! She bit her lip.

It doesn't matter what Amber says to me about not being interested in Joe. I honestly think she means it. But as long as Joe's hung up on her, there's no real chance for me with him.

Shit, I'm an idiot. I should just get out of here and take that recording to the Investigator.

But as Skye stood there, watching Joe and Brian stroll away, she knew she wasn't quite ready to do that yet.

The damn truth of it is, I really like him. And if I go to the Investigator, *I'll never see him again.*

She had fallen, utterly and completely, for Joe Jeffreys. Which was a really bad idea. Because he couldn't stop mooning after a girl who was obviously hooked on her psychiatrist.

Give it up, Skye, she told herself.

She knew it was the only thing that made sense. But she just couldn't bring herself to walk away from Joe Jeffreys for ever.

Skye

Skye wrestled with her dilemma for hours. Joe, the *National Investigator*, and Amber tumbled and danced through her head in an endless series of different permutations, like puzzle pieces she needed to slot together.

Only she was failing. As they all filed into their early evening group session and took their seats, she was on autopilot at first, barely concentrating on a word anyone was saying. It was only gradually that she became aware that the vibe in the room was weird. It was often intense as the clients divulged embarrassing facts about themselves, or broke down in tears, or snapped at each other; but you knew that Dr Raf and Dr Lucy had seen it all before. Their trained, poised expressions showed no surprise, no distress at any revelations that might pop out, and they knew just how to work with or defuse any tension between clients.

Oh, Skye realized, detached enough from the therapy proceedings to be able to work out why things felt so jagged this session, it must be Dr Raf and Dr Lucy making this session feel so gnarly. Did they have a fight?

She looked closely at Dr Lucy for the first time. Dr Lucy's lips were drawn tightly together, her legs crossed equally tightly. She was staring straight at Amber, and her gaze was distinctly unfriendly. Not

that Amber showed any signs of noticing. Amber looked as if someone had switched on a light bulb in her face, a rosy-tone, pearlized
one; her skin was pink-tinged, her green eyes glowing.

She's totally stunning, Skye had to admit. Skye wasn't normally
the jealous type. Live and let live was her motto; it was what had
kept her happy and balanced in the Midnight Lounge, an atmosphere full of backstabbing and rivalries. But none of the girls at the
Lounge was an international supermodel. And though Skye knew
exactly how pretty she was, she didn't much enjoy being compared
with Amber, cover girl and *Sports Illustrated* star.

*No wonder Dr Lucy doesn't like her. I mean, for a doctor, Dr Lucy's
a knockout. She must feel like a supermodel all the time. Until she
meets a real one.*

Oh. That's weird. Skye's glance had slid sideways to Dr Raf, and
she noticed immediately how subdued he looked. Usually, when
group was in full swing, he'd be leaning forward, his dark eyes alert
and engaged on what was being said: Brian, in this case, droning on
about his previous rehabs and what he'd learned from them about
resolving his trust issues with women. This session, however, Dr Raf
was almost slumped in his chair, staring at the floor in front of him.
He seemed to have completely tuned out of the proceedings; none
of his usual, helpful interjections to move the group along, prompt
them into making connections, keep them working hard.

*He looks like he really doesn't want to be here. He and Dr Lucy must
have had one hell of a fight – if that's why they're acting so strange . . .*

But then Skye looked over at Joe, and she forgot completely
about any speculations as to why Dr Raf and Dr Lucy were in such
odd moods this evening.

Joe was lounging back in his chair, ankle hooked over the opposite knee, his blue eyes bright and clear, focused entirely on Amber,
a smile of utter and complete appreciation curving his lips.

I might as well not be in the room, Skye thought bitterly, and
realized that Amber was talking now.

'I know what you mean about the trust issue with women,
Brian,' Amber was saying, 'though in an opposite way. I never had

any positive experiences with men, really.' She grimaced. 'It's funny, but it never occurred to me in group that I couldn't say something in front of a man, or that it'd be easier to talk if there were only women in the room.'

'We *do* have women-only sessions,' Dr Lucy said snappishly. 'I've mentioned that to you.'

Amber favoured her with a beatific smile, looking so stunning that Joe and Brian instinctively leaned forward.

The admiring look in Joe's eyes was the last straw for Skye. Without thinking of the consequences, without giving herself a moment to take a breath, she blurted out: 'Amber, if you're OK with talking about things in front of the men, I think you should share what you told me yesterday. You know, the going on dates with guys for money? And the guy who's paying for you to be here?'

Amber turned her head to look at Skye, her green eyes widening in utter shock. Dr Raf stirred in his chair, sitting up straight.

But it was Dr Lucy who said reprovingly: 'Skye! We have an absolute rule here not to reveal *anything* that's told to us by another patient, unless it's against the Cascabel code of conduct!'

Skye couldn't believe what she had done. Everyone was staring at her now, horrified, their mouths gaping open. Everyone, that is, apart from Dr Raf, whose gaze had lifted from the floor and was now fixed squarely on Amber.

Amber was sheet white. Carefully, as if her bones were brittle, she pulled the pashmina over her shoulders and stood up.

'Amber?' Dr Raf said in a husky voice, but she shook her head, not looking at him. In complete silence the group watched her cross the room, heading for the door.

'I'll go after her,' Dr Lucy said a few seconds after Amber had exited the room.

Oh God, poor Amber! Talk about adding insult to injury!

'No, I will,' she said swiftly, jumping up from her chair. 'It was me who upset her – I should go—'

As Skye turned to leave, she was taken aback by the realization that Petal was glaring at her, the black panda makeup turning her eyes, narrowed into slits of resentment, into a mask of hate. If Skye had betrayed a secret of Petal's, rather than Amber's, Petal could not have looked at Skye with more disgust.

Skye couldn't look at Joe. She just wasn't brave enough.

I totally fucked up. Skye hung her head as she followed Amber. *I should never, ever have opened my dumb mouth about what she told me. Never.*

Skye looked first in their room, but Amber wasn't there. It took a while to track her down to the garden, where she was sitting next to the fountain, her auburn hair and green dress blending into the bougainvillaea-covered wall behind it, her grey pashmina wrapped tightly around her, like a blanket. Some of the patients actually brought their blankets to the morning group session, like insulation from the painful emotional work they were about to do; but they bundled themselves up like bulky packages, while Amber, in the folds of her pashmina, was slender and exquisite. Trust Amber to be elegant even when she's totally upset, Skye thought with another flash of resentment, before she took a good hard pull at herself.

The steady fall of water from the bamboo poles of the fountain was loud enough that Skye couldn't make enough noise to signal her presence to Amber. She had to reach out and tap Amber's shoulder; Amber jumped, and, looking up and seeing Skye, she frowned, edging back along the low stone wall on which she was sitting.

'I don't want to talk to you,' Amber said, turning her head away.

'Amber, I'm so sorry.' Skye hovered behind her awkwardly. 'I know I shouldn't have said anything. It was just—'

'Joe,' Amber finished for her. 'You wanted me to look bad in front of Joe.'

Skye writhed in embarrassment; there was no room to hide when Amber spoke the truth so simply.

'The funny thing is, I don't think it'll have made any difference to him,' Amber observed in a small cold detached voice. 'If he thinks I need rescuing, the worse things I've done in the past, the happier he'll be. More for me to be rescued from.'

This hadn't occurred to Skye. She gaped at Amber, realizing that the other girl was completely right.

When did Amber get so smart? When did she get so good at figuring people out? This is not the girl who came in ten days ago, hooked on opiates, so quiet she wouldn't say boo to a goose.

'So you haven't helped yourself. And you've hurt me,' Amber continued, still staring into the cascading water.

'Amber – I'm so sorry.' Skye bit her lip. 'I was just so jealous,' she confessed helplessly.

'Please leave me alone,' Amber said. 'I thought I could trust you. But if I can't, I don't have anything to say to you.'

Amber might as well have been hitting her with a carefully placed series of blows, each one perfectly calculated to achieve maximum pain. And Skye deserved every one. She turned away; all she could do now was what Amber asked her.

Skye couldn't face going back into group, having to admit that Amber had told her she couldn't trust her any more and asked her to go away. Instead, she went back to their room, lay down on her bed and burst into tears. She had ruined everything. Her budding friendship with Amber, the possibility of something with Joe. And she only had herself to blame.

Petal

Petal sat cross-legged on her bed, looking, for the umpteenth time, at the video on her phone that featured Skye and Joe in the storage unit. At first, simply possessing it had given her enough of a rush; the hugely satisfying knowledge that she – Petal, the girl whom no one paid much attention to round here – held something so explosive that it could blow up their entire little world here at Cascabel.

But the rush hadn't lasted for long. Petal was used to being the centre of attention. Her dating Dan, plus JC's canny dyeing of her hair bright yellow, had caused a bigger sensation than ever before. The paps had been climbing over each other to snap pictures of her, and her bloody father had packed her off here before she could fully enjoy it. Texts from Tas and JC confirmed that Petal's stay in rehab was all over the papers, so at least that meant that people weren't forgetting about her. But it wasn't enough. Even more than drugs or drink, Petal was addicted to people looking at her.

Her regular one-on-one therapy sessions, plus the work she was doing in group, had made it very clear to her why: all those years of desperately trying to get Gold to notice her, practically jumping up and down and screaming his name, acting up at school, being a brat, since behaving well didn't seem to score her any points at all.

Dr Raf had explained that children were so hard-wired to want attention that any kind was better than being ignored, and that had been a revelation to Petal.

All these years, I thought I was just bad. A wild child. And now it turns out I was only trying to get Gold to notice me.

She couldn't even call him 'dad' in her thoughts; it was weird even talking about him as her father.

And I thought it was cool to call him by his name, she reflected bitterly. Maybe when I get back to London, I'll start calling him 'Daddy'. That'd really freak him out; make him feel his age.

She sighed, a long deep sigh, turning the phone over in her hands. She was dying to share this unbelievably juicy gossip with JC and Tas. They'd kill her if they found out she'd been keeping something like this from them. And it was 5 p.m., the time that Cascabel unblocked its call jamming for an hour so that patients allowed cellphone privileges could ring their friends and whinge about how miserable they were. She could send the video right now if she wanted.

Petal was really and truly torn. Part of her still violently resented having been packed off to Cascabel; but another part of her knew that it was doing her a ton of good. Part of her was furious at being separated from Dan; another part knew that Dan was working like a maniac in the recording studio and that if she were in London too, she'd probably be driving him crazy trying to drag him out partying with her rather than let him get on with his work. And that wouldn't exactly be good for their long-term prospects.

Part of her was gagging to share this insanely hot piece of gossip with her best friends. But, bizarrely, another part of her was thinking of the trust that had built up in the rehab group in the time they'd spent together.

Joe's a really nice guy, she admitted to herself. She'd thought in the beginning he was totally full of himself, uninterested in anything but leching after Amber and Skye. *But he's been really cool with Brian. I've seen how much he's put into looking out for Brian, spending time with him. He's really been there for Brian. And Joe's been great in group. You feel like you can say anything and he won't judge you.*

Plus, he's never leched after me. Which would have been totally creepy, 'cause he's practically old enough to be my father.

That fact hadn't stopped more friends and acquaintances of Gold's than Petal could count trying to flirt with her. Ever since she hit thirteen or so, started wearing some makeup and short skirts, she'd been fending off creepy older guys. With no help from Gold, who'd never even noticed.

So I've got to give Joe points for that too. Even with Skye and Amber, he's been cool. He hasn't, like, been playing them off against each other or anything like that.

Petal discounted Jennifer Downs, Joe's world-famous film star fiancée. Growing up in Gold's household had made Petal completely aware of all the fake Hollywood marriages and relationships that were arranged to conceal one or both star's homosexuality, weird sexual preferences, or simply to promote their latest project. And she'd heard on the grapevine for years that Jennifer was a lesbian. So when Joe and Skye had got it on in the storage closet, he hadn't been betraying anyone who remotely cared where he put his willy.

But Skye . . . Skye was another story.

What Skye did to Amber in group today was awful. Really nasty.

Petal had seen every kind of manoeuvre by women frantic to get close to Gold, ready to trample anyone else underfoot if that was what they had to do to achieve it. And she knew that Amber wasn't after Joe; the only man here Amber cared about was Dr Raf. He's given her double sessions now, Petal thought jealously. Lucky bitch.

But, like everyone else in their rehab group, Petal was genuinely touched by Amber: her beauty was hypnotizing, but beneath it was the really heroic struggle Amber was undergoing, to clean up after so many years of being hooked on pills, and to find out who she was underneath her addiction. Plus that awful mum waiting for her when she gets out of here, Petal thought, shuddering. That's totally got to be hanging over her head.

Skye's attempt to bring Amber down had triggered plenty of memories for Petal, none of them pretty. All those women – many of whom were supposed to be looking after her – squabbling and fighting over Gold.

Skye's just like them. My nannies, the mums of my friends, my teachers. I thought she was nicer than that, but she isn't. She's just another bitch out for what she can get.

Her fingers danced over her phone keypad, pulling up Tas and JC's names, attaching them to the video, her thumb hovering over the Send button. She hesitated for a moment, her brain racing. After all, the whole reason she was here was that Rudy had taken those photos of her and Dan and sold them to the papers! Wasn't she doing exactly the same thing?

Nah. I'm just sharing it with my best mates. No one's going to be flogging it to the tabloids.

She hit Send, and watched, hypnotized, as the process was set in motion; the tiny globe popping up at the top of the screen, little arrows spinning round it, signalling the transmission of the mini-film all the way across the Atlantic. After a minute or two, she dialled Tas's number, and waited impatiently for her to pick up.

'Petal?' Tas yelled over the sound of pumping dance music behind her, people shouting; she must be in a club.

'You sound like you're having fun!' Petal hissed enviously.

'It's, like, really late!' Tas slurred. 'We've been out for hours . . . I can't hear you – it's well noisy here.'

'I just sent you a video!' Petal went into the bathroom and shut the door, so she could raise her voice a little without being over-heard. 'You've got to watch it!'

'What the fuck – I'm pissed out of my skull, man – I'm going into the bog so I can hear you . . .'

The noise behind Tas abated a little, as she said: 'Oh, I just got a message from you – hang on . . .'

A long pause followed. Petal knew she hadn't been cut off; she could still hear the driving beat of the music.

And then, eventually, Tas said: 'No. No. You are fucking messing with me, man. Is that—'

'Yes!'

'But what are they – oh my *God*, he's – and she's – oh my *God*!'

'Yeah!'

'Out*rageous*!' Tas breathed deeply. 'I got to show this to JC!'

'Tas! Oh my fucking *God*!' came JC's voice. 'Wait till you *see* what Petal just sent me!'

'She's on the phone now.'

JC grabbed the phone from Tas.

'Babe,' he said devoutly, sounding slightly more sober than Tas, 'we miss you *so* much! You *know* how much we miss you! But *this* goss – oh my *God* – it's almost worth missing you for! You're super-cool!'

A big smile was spreading over Petal's face. 'I miss you too,' she said.

'You're the gossip *queen*!' JC crowed. 'Who's the girl with him?'

'Just a slutty stripper in here with us,' Petal said vindictively. 'Don't send it to anyone,' she added quickly. 'You can show it but don't send it.'

'No worries,' he said. 'Promise promise. But, oh my *God*! Talk about *juice*!'

'We miss you!' Tas slurred into the phone. 'Come home soon!'

Petal was beaming from ear to ear. 'I miss you too,' she said happily.

They loved her; they missed her; they wanted her back. *And* she had re-established her cool credentials, even from rehab.

Sending that video had definitely been the right thing to do.

Amber

After the shattering events of the previous day, Amber had no idea what to expect from her individual session with Dr Raf the next morning. But as soon as she walked into his office, it was obvious that he had been preparing for this moment. He was standing behind his chair as the door opened, restraining himself from crossing the room towards her by grasping onto the leather back of the chair.

'Amber,' he said, his voice husky, 'please sit down.' He nodded towards the client chair. 'Would you like –' he blushed deeply – 'would you like someone else to be present while we talk?'

Amber stared at him, her green eyes widening, and shook her head so vehemently that it hurt.

'OK, that's fine,' he said quickly. 'I just thought I ought to ask . . .'

She settled into the chair, looking up at him, as he continued: 'First, I have to apologize to you for what happened between us yesterday. Obviously, it was completely and utterly inappropriate. It should never, ever have happened. That kind of contact between a doctor and patient – *any* kind of contact between a doctor and patient – is *absolutely* forbidden, for very good reasons—'

He broke off, clearing his throat, his dark eyes utterly focused on her. Still keeping the chair between them like a shield, he asked: 'Amber, do you know what transference is?'

Amber shook her head again, this time more gently.

'It's when you – the patient – develop feelings for your psychiatrist or therapist,' he explained. 'But those feelings aren't real. Or rather, they aren't really about the therapist. In other words, your feelings are just projected onto me. And counter-transference –' he blushed again – 'is when the therapist begins to feel they have feelings for the patient. But those feelings aren't real either. If it's properly directed, transference and even counter-transference are essential to the therapeutic process, because it means the patient is truly working through their issues. But if they're mishandled . . .'

His hands were digging deep into the back of the chair now, his knuckles whitening with the strain.

'If they're mishandled – and yesterday was a textbook example of exactly how to mishandle them – then the entire treatment is in jeopardy. And I want to stress that it's entirely the therapist's fault in that case. You're in no way to blame for what happened between us.'

He was clearly in such agony that Amber was craving to get up, go over and put her arms around him. His handsome face was tortured, his mouth tight.

'Of course, it goes without saying that I've never done anything like that with a patient before,' he said, ducking his head in shame. 'Really, I ought to report myself to the American Medical Association. And you could do that if you chose to. I've totally breached the trust you placed in me.'

'I would never do that!' Amber said quickly.

'Well, you might change your mind, and if you did, you have the absolute right to report me,' he said nobly. 'I've been struggling with this all night – I've barely had any sleep – Amber, I feel so terrible about what I did to you! And obviously, there's no way I can treat you any more. I'm transferring you over as a patient to Dr Lucy immediately.'

'Oh, *no*!'

Amber was on her feet; she didn't even realize she'd jumped up. The prospect of not being able to be alone with Dr Raf every day was more than she could bear.

To think I was so worried about what Skye said yesterday in group! she thought frantically. I was so scared it would put him off me – make him think I'm just like my mother, just another woman who'll have sex for money. Just another prostitute. And instead, he's been up all night worrying what I'll think of him . . .

'Please don't make me leave you!' she blurted out. And then, because that sounded desperately clingy: 'I can't be treated by Dr Lucy! She hates me!'

Dr Raf looked even more guilty than he had before. She would have expected him to deny it, but instead he mumbled: 'Well, that's not impossible.'

Amber stared at him blankly.

'We've been seeing each other,' Dr Raf clarified, red to the tips of his ears by now. 'Dr Lucy and I.'

Amber froze. Her lips felt as paralysed as if she'd had a shot of Novocaine from a dentist. But she managed to get out: 'Is it serious?'

She held her breath as she waited for his response. Dizziness ran through her; she thought she might faint if the answer was yes. It seemed to take for ever for Dr Raf to answer. He was struggling with himself, and by the time he said: 'I thought it was,' all the blood had drained from his face. The skin over his cheekbones was drawn tight, his jaw set; he was pale as a sheet of paper.

Amber wasn't conscious of making any decision to move. But she must have done, because, slowly, she was crossing the carpet, walking towards him, around the chair onto which he was still gripping for dear life.

'You thought it was,' she echoed softly.

'Amber . . .'

Hopelessly, Dr Raf looked into her eyes. She was so close now she could have touched him just by raising her hand. She could smell his aftershave and the warm heady scent of his skin, see the stubble on his chin where he had missed a tiny patch shaving this morning. A dark curl of hair was hanging down over his forehead, and she yearned to twist her fingers around it.

'What we're feeling isn't real,' he said. 'You're looking for someone to take care of you – you're lost and alone – and I'm looking for someone to take care of.'

What's wrong with that? Amber thought, a little puzzled.

Dr Raf must have realized that his objection wasn't as powerful as he had thought, because he continued swiftly: 'You came here for therapy, and I've betrayed you. I've done the worst thing a doctor can do to a patient. I should lose my licence for what I've done to you.'

His voice was getting stronger; his own words were convincing him. She needed to give this everything she had, every ounce of conviction and confidence and certainty that she had built up over her time in therapy.

But it's too soon! she thought, panicking. I'm not ready! I'm not strong enough!

And then another voice, clear and firm, said simply: *You have to be*.

'You're the best doctor I could ever have had,' she heard herself say out loud. 'You've saved me. You've showed me how to feel my own feelings. To be honest with myself, and know what I want. We keep talking in group about being connected. Well, I *am* connected now. I'm connected to my feelings, and I know they're real. They *are*.'

She looked at him pleadingly, her heart in her eyes.

'I know what I want. I want you,' she said, so bravely she could hardly believe her own courage. 'And you know what? I want you even if it goes horribly wrong. I want you even if you go back to Dr Lucy. I want you even if it causes me huge amounts of pain and suffering. And isn't that what being an adult's all about? Isn't that what I'm learning how to be? Isn't that what I'm supposed to be learning with all this therapy – knowing what I want, and being prepared to pay a price for it?'

She smiled, a huge, beautiful smile.

I'm so proud of myself, she thought, radiant with triumph. I've never been more proud of myself in my life.

'I want you,' she repeated, and in a final act of bravery, she took one step closer to him, so their bodies were brushing against each other. He was only a little taller than her, so when she tilted her head up, her lips were almost on a level with his.

And then she waited.

He has to do it. He has to kiss me. He has to meet me halfway.

It was unbearable. She held her breath and closed her eyes.

If he doesn't kiss me, I'll never take another breath again – never, never, never . . .

Dr Raf made a sound deep in his throat, a rough, guttural sound full of frustration and lust and confusion.

Amber tensed. And then the breath was squeezed out of her as his arms came around her so tightly, his mouth came down on hers so hard, that she would have gasped if she had been able. Instead, she threw her arms up round his neck, dragging his head even closer to hers, grinding her body into his, pressing her breasts against his chest, her crotch against his, dizzy now with the thrill of knowing that he couldn't control himself when it came to her. That her words had had the power to convince him.

That he had thought he was serious about Dr Lucy – before he'd met Amber.

She felt like crying and laughing all at once. Their bodies strained together, Dr Raf's hands running up and down her back, trying to mould her as close as he could, his legs wide to pull her between them, so that she felt his cock springing up against her as his tongue drove deep into her mouth. Amber dragged his shirt out of his waistband, sliding her hands up his bare skin, hearing him moan as she ran her hands over him. He twined his fingers into her hair as she tilted her head back eagerly, wanting him to kiss her neck, and it was as if he knew exactly what she needed, his lips tracing a line down to her throat. His hands left her hair, following his mouth, his fingers hot on her skin, making her writhe with excitement as they wrapped round her breasts, lifting them up to his mouth, kissing them through the fine cotton of her top.

Amber was arching back over the chair, her hands on his bottom now, dragging him even closer, glorying in the feel of his tight-muscled buttocks, completely and utterly out of control. As Dr Raf pulled down her T-shirt, enough to expose her silk bra, she writhed against him, half-delirious, wanting him inside her that moment.

'Amber – oh God, we can't do this again . . .' Dr Raf groaned, though the fact that he couldn't stop kissing her breasts contradicted his words.

'Yes we can,' Amber said firmly, sliding her hands round to the front of his trousers, stroking him through them, feeling his cock bound with excitement against his zipper. She reached for his belt buckle, but his hands closed around hers, pulling her up to stand again, holding her tightly against him, his lips against her forehead, his breath coming in fast, desperate gasps as he struggled to regain some mastery of himself.

'Not here, not like this . . .' he said, his chest heaving. 'Not like you're some cheap little fling. You deserve better than this.' He raised their joined hands to his lips, kissing her fingers. 'I won't treat you like other men have done, Amber.'

But I want you to! Amber thought frantically, her whole body sparking with desire for him.

And then she heard her own words, and took in the truth of what he was saying.

'You need to be respected,' Dr Raf said. 'I have to respect you, not just throw you down on the carpet like we're animals in heat—'

'Oh God, that was *wonderful*,' Amber said dreamily.

'Amber, you're not helping!' Dr Raf said, so reprovingly that she started giggling, light-headed with relief and excitement and the knowledge that he didn't just want her, he respected her, even though she'd made love with him yesterday on this very carpet, and he knew now, thanks to Skye, that she'd had sex with men for money.

Dr Raf tucked his shirt back into his trousers, stepped back from her and stabbed his fingers into the tight curls of his black hair, taking a long deep breath.

'This is *not* how I saw this conversation going,' he said, sounding so baffled that he made Amber laugh even harder.

He reached forward and pulled her T-shirt up to cover her bra, stroking it back into place so tenderly that she had to swallow hard. Then he lifted a lock of her hair off her cheek, arranging it gently back in place behind her ear. And his hands had just slowly, reluctantly, left her again when there came a knock on the door, followed immediately by the turning of the door knob, and the door being pushed open.

Amber was sensible enough not to jump back, or make any sudden movements that might be suspicious. She turned her head to see who was breaking in on her session, but somehow she had a feeling that she knew already who it would be.

'Lucy, I'm in *session*,' Dr Raf said angrily, managing to summon up just the right degree of justified indignation. 'This is absolutely not protocol. I can't have you doing this repeatedly—'

'*Look!*'

Amber had never seen Dr Lucy so agitated. A strand of her long straight dark hair had come loose from her ponytail and was hanging over her face, the clearest sign possible that Dr Lucy was not in complete control of herself. She positively raced towards Dr Raf, a newspaper flapping in her hand, her eyes dilated with agitation.

'I've just seen this!' she cried. 'Did you have *any* idea of what was going on?'

Dr Raf, frowning deeply, took the paper from her, saying curtly: 'Lucy, it really does have to be a cast-iron rule that a session can't be interrupted, short of some kind of medical emergency— Oh my *God!*'

That's weird. Amber craned her head to look at the paper. *It looks like a UK tabloid – but it can't be! What's that doing in California?*

And then, as she got a closer look and realized that it was the *Daily Mirror*, she gasped aloud in shock, just as Dr Raf had done.

'MYSTERY BLONDE FLIPS FOR JOE!' screamed the headline, but that wasn't exactly the first thing Amber's eye was drawn to. It was the blurry colour picture of two people in a position that looked at first glance like something halfway through a Cirque du Soleil act, and then, on second glance, had Amber gulping in embarrassment for both of them.

Because she'd recognized Joe Jeffreys. And though, for obvious reasons, his partner's face was obscured, she could guess, from the context, exactly who it was.

'That,' Dr Lucy said in a high, squeaky voice, 'is the *inside of the main storage closet*!'

'Dear Christ,' Dr Raf muttered, staring closely at the photo, turning it from side to side. 'Are they – is she – is that even *possible*?'

'They're both in for *sex rehab*,' Dr Lucy wailed. 'This is a *disaster*!'

'We need to get on top of this straight away,' Dr Raf said.

'It looks like that's what *she* said,' Amber commented before she could stop herself, and to her secret delight she saw Dr Raf's beautifully curved mouth quirk into a reluctant smile.

'Amber,' he said formally, turning to her, 'I'm so sorry about this. And, Lucy, I really don't want sessions interrupted for any reason short of medical emergencies, OK?'

The dark, fulminating glare Dr Lucy shot at Amber on hearing this was more than enough evidence for Dr Raf to confirm that Amber was absolutely right in saying that Dr Lucy hated her.

'But now we've been disturbed . . .' Dr Raf said pleadingly to Amber, who nodded. 'Hopefully we can reschedule later,' he added. 'I'm very aware there were – um – *issues* that came up today that we need to resolve as soon as possible.'

'*Please* . . .' Amber said, not caring that this conversation might ping Dr Lucy's radar.

'As soon as possible. I promise,' Dr Raf said softly.

They exchanged a long, lingering look before Amber turned away.

Behind her, she heard Dr Raf ask: 'Have you discussed this with the administrator yet, Lucy? I think we need to call an emergency meeting – involve the directors, as many as we can at this short notice.'

'I've got Admin trying to sort that out right now,' Dr Lucy said. 'We've got a conference call in twenty minutes.'

'And we need to find out how the hell Joe and Skye got into the storage cupboard in the first place – and who took the photos.'

'Oh, I've got a *very* good guess about that,' Dr Lucy said grimly as Amber closed the door behind her.

Amber stepped out onto the patio, breathing in the fresh sunny air, her arms wrapped around herself as she stood there, replaying in her head what had just happened between her and Dr Raf. His mouth on hers, his words to her, his hands touching her, not just sexually, but tenderly – pulling up her T-shirt, rearranging her hair —

'Amber!'

Skye jumped up from the lawn, where she'd been lying in the sunshine. Joe was stretched out on his favourite lounger beside her.

'Can we talk?' Skye dashed over to Amber's side. 'I was waiting for you to come out of your session with Dr Raf – I really want to say sorry again for yesterday.' She paused, looking puzzled. 'Did you finish early?'

Amber nodded, snapping out of her trance. 'And I wouldn't worry too much about me,' she said drily. 'You've got much bigger problems about to come down on your head any minute . . .'

'Skye? Joe?' Daniyel called, appearing at the patio doors. 'I need both of you to come to the main office, *now*!'

Skye's big blue eyes widened into saucers. 'What's up?' she asked swiftly.

But Amber didn't answer her. She strolled over to the fountain and sat down there, away from the scene that was about to unfold, so that she could happily replay the entire time she had just spent with Dr Raf over and over again.

I don't owe Skye anything, she told herself firmly. Nothing at all.

Skye

'*I* think mine's *Pretty Woman*,' Skye said thoughtfully, sucking on a blade of grass.

Joe rolled his eyes. 'Really? That's all you got?'

'Uh, I like *Legally Blonde* too,' Skye offered. 'I've seen that tons of times.'

'Skye. Baby. You really need to expand your horizons a bit,' Joe said. 'Tune into Turner Classic Movies or something every now and then. Watch something in black and white.'

Skye pouted; she could tell he was serious by the way he was frowning at her. She knew she was ignorant about a lot of things, but it wasn't very nice of him to look down on her for that.

'Well, what about your favourite movies?' she asked. 'I bet you've got some classy ones.'

Oh God, that sounds like I'm kissing his ass. I just can't get things right with Joe today. He's been weird with me ever since I went off on Amber. Shit, I fucked up there.

But at least her question had brought a grin to Joe's face, a sparkle in his bright blue eyes.

'*Red River*,' he said immediately, lounging back in his chair. 'Hell of a good movie. *The Searchers*. Boy, would I love to remake that one. Been tossing it around for years. And you know what? I'm gonna say *Die Hard* as well. I never get bored of *Die Hard*.'

'Hey, you're cheating,' Skye said, taking a gamble. But Joe loved it when she teased him; it was talking to him like a normal person, not a movie star.

'Say what?' Joe stared at her. 'What d'you mean?'

'You're just picking movies you want to star in,' Skye said, flashing him her best naughty smile.

'So?' Joe winked at her. 'Same thing you did, isn't it? *Die Hard*. What a great script,' he said dreamily. 'You know something? Much as I hate to say it, I couldn't have done that better than Bruce. No one could.'

Again, Skye knew better than to contradict him. 'He was great,' she agreed. 'Really funny.'

She could tell Joe had registered that she'd turned down the opportunity to compliment him; his lips quirked in approval as he said: 'Comedy – that's what counts in the end.' He smiled ruefully. 'You don't get awards for it, but you can work for ever, and the paycheque's great. When you get too old for the action movies, that's where you head. Meryl, Bob De Niro – even the serious guys are at it.' He tapped a cigarette out of his packet. 'Just save me from working with cute kids. I wrapped a dog movie this year, and that was more than enough.'

'Is that the one from the book?'

Joe nodded. '*Him, Me and Mr Paws*. Shitty title, huh? But we were stuck with it. It's gonna make a ton of money.' He lit up his cigarette and blew out a big fat smoke ring. 'I got points in it. Nice. There's this remake of a Hong Kong action movie I wanna get greenlit – very dark. The dog movie's gonna make that happen.'

Skye sat up, wrapping her arms around her knees. Her fair hair was loose down her back, her pale blue T-shirt matched her eyes, and she was wearing very little makeup, just some mascara and lipgloss; she looked very fresh and pretty, and even though Joe was happily musing on his bright work prospects ahead, his eyes lingered on her appreciatively.

'Joe,' she said hesitantly. 'I wanted to explain a bit about yesterday, with Amber.'

'Catfight,' Joe drawled, shrugging. 'Believe me, it's not the first one I've seen. They should've known not to put two girls as pretty as you two in the same room. Bound to lead to trouble.'

'It wasn't a catfight,' Skye said honestly. 'Amber didn't do anything. It was all me. I shouldn't have said something she told me in confidence.'

Joe's fair eyebrows raised in acknowledgement. 'No, you shouldn't,' he agreed. 'You told her you were sorry, right?'

Skye nodded. 'She's still pissed, though.'

'She's got a right to be pissed,' Joe said.

'I know.' Skye sighed. 'I have to make it right with her. I just don't want you thinking I'm a total bitch.'

'Hey,' Joe raised his hands. 'Live and let live. It's none of my business.'

Skye swallowed hard at this rebuff. But she had to persist.

'I don't want you to think badly of me,' she insisted. 'I like you. A lot.'

'Well, I like you, baby,' Joe said easily. 'We have a lot of fun.'

'No, I meant more than that,' Skye said a little sadly, looking down at her bare smooth golden-tanned knees. She curled her toes into the grass. 'More than "we have a lot of fun".'

Joe paused, cigarette halfway to his lips. 'Baby,' he started slowly, 'you know I'm in a bit of a situation here. I've got a fiancée waiting for me on the outside – Christ, it sounds like we're in prison! – and the moment they bust me out of here, I'm supposed to get down on my knees in front of her so's it looks like I've learned my lesson, staged so every single pap in Hollywood can get a nice clean shot of it, you know? And then I've got to keep my nose clean for a hell of a long time.' He took a long pull at his Camel. 'Which is OK. I get what they're telling me. The playboy thing was getting old. It doesn't play so well with the mini-van crowd.'

'The mini-van crowd?'

'Soccer moms,' Joe explained. 'Like I said, I can't do action movies for ever. I got to think about how I'm positioning myself. So far, it's been OK that I have a playboy rep, 'cause the guys who see my movies at the multiplex don't mind about that one little bit. But the clock's ticking. I'm not getting any younger. And I can't keep my career at this level if the soccer moms think I'm—'

'A big fat slut,' Skye finished.

'Yeah!' Joe cracked a smile. 'A big fat slut. Which doesn't play so well in the Midwest. Look at Clooney. Even he gets a steady girl-friend at Oscar time.'

Skye was poised to respond – she had a suggestion on the tip of her tongue, one that she'd been dying to make for days now – but then, out of the corner of her eye, she saw Amber's tall figure step out onto the patio, the sleek masses of chestnut hair glinting in the sunlight, and she knew she couldn't continue this conversation with Amber floating ethereally across the grass, distracting Joe's atten-tion.

Besides, I need to really apologize to Amber. I fucked up. She wouldn't say a word to me last night, but she's usually in a good mood after she's had a Dr Raf session. If she's anything like the way she was yesterday, she'll be high as a kite, and much more likely to forgive me.

'Hold that thought, OK?' she said to Joe, jumping up lithely. 'Well, not exactly that thought, but one in the general area . . .'

But she'd barely said a word to Amber before Daniyel emerged behind her, looking angrier than Skye had ever seen her before. Even Joe realized, from the sharp way Daniyel called their names, that something was up; he pulled a comical face as he crossed the grass to where Daniyel, hands on hips, was waiting. She swivelled smartly as he approached, marching back inside the building, Skye and Joe following dutifully.

'We are so busted,' Joe muttered to Skye.

This can't be happening! Skye thought frantically. *Not when I'd actually got Joe into sort of having The Conversation with me!*

The main office was full of people: Dr Lucy and Dr Raf; Daniyel;

the director of Cascabel, and the supervising clinician, the famous Dr Solomon, who was too old and important to treat patients any more; he had established the treatment centre decades ago, before rehab became so fashionable, and was now reaping the immense profits. Plus three lawyers – *Three*! Skye thought. *That's how important Joe is!* – brandishing copies of the behavioural contracts Skye and Joe had signed on entering Cascabel.

And, on the conference table, a copy of some British paper with a screaming headline and a photo that made Skye first blush from the roots of her hair to the tips of her toes, and then think: At least I look really good in it. I mean, if I'm gonna be naked and upside down for everyone to see, thank God my body looks really tight . . . you can totally tell I work out . . .

The entire group of clinic staff fell silent, ominously so, waiting for Joe and Skye's reaction. Every eye was on her. She couldn't get a word out. She just stared at that photo, her brain racing.

Who took that? Did Dave steal my bag and sell the film? Is that a still shot from it?

She looked over at Joe, desperately hoping he wouldn't realize she'd been responsible for this mess-up. It was obvious that Skye was tongue-tied: all the accusing, furious glances turned to Joe, waiting for him to say something.

'Huh,' he said eventually, straightening up after a long, thorough examination of the photo. 'You can put that kind of thing on the cover of a paper nowadays? Go figure.'

A short, incredulous silence greeted this. Joe looked round the room.

'I mean, seriously, can you believe it?' he asked amiably. 'They didn't even put one of those black lines over her ass! Which looks great, by the way,' he said to Skye as a sidebar. 'But, you know, *kids* can see this stuff!' He sighed. 'This society truly is going to hell in a handbasket.'

'Joe,' Dr Raf said reproachfully, 'that's not exactly the response I was hoping for.'

'You've brought this clinic into utter disrepute,' said Dr Solomon angrily. 'All the years I've run Cascabel, and *never* a scandal of this magnitude! Just because you couldn't keep your hands off some blonde woopsie for two seconds!'

Dr Solomon, in true LA doctor style, was nipped and tucked to within an inch of his life, the skin on his face tight and shiny from peels and near-motionless from Botox, his hair plugged and artfully dyed. Still, though his physical appearance might disguise his real age, his vocabulary gave it away.

'Hey,' Joe said. 'Her name's Skye, OK? And this –' he stabbed the paper with one big finger – 'was completely my fault.'

'Right,' Dr Lucy said sarcastically. 'She looks like a *very* unwilling participant.'

The most junior of the lawyers stifled a snigger.

'Joe, Skye,' Dr Raf said sadly, 'I'm afraid we have no choice here.'

'The wording of the contract is very clear,' the lead lawyer said. 'You have both violated several clauses – both as pertaining to your general conduct, and, as Dr Solomon says, bringing the good reputation and standing of the clinic into disrepute.'

'We sure are sorry about that last one,' Joe said sincerely. 'Dr Raf does a hell of a good job here. Helps a lot of people. I wouldn't want to do anything to get in the way of that.'

Just as she began to bridle, Joe turned to Dr Lucy, flashing a megawatt smile, and added: 'You too, of course, Dr Lucy.'

'Thank you, Joe,' Dr Raf said seriously. 'You've been a very good and supportive member of our group.' He smiled, dimples showing on each side of his mouth.

God, Dr Raf really is a hottie, Skye thought. He has the sweetest smile I've ever seen on a grown man.

'I can't say you've been making much of an attempt to dig deep in our individual sessions,' Dr Raf was continuing, 'but I've very much enjoyed having you here.'

'Thanks, Doc,' Joe said, nodding at him. 'Likewise.'

'And, Skye –' Dr Raf looked over at her – 'though I didn't treat you individually, I would truly say the same for you in group. You've reached out and made an effort with your peers.'

'Thank you,' Skye said, surprised at how moved she was by Dr Raf's words.

'This is all very touching,' Dr Solomon snapped grumpily, 'but you're both getting kicked out all the same. We can't be seen to be condoning this sort of behaviour.'

Joe sighed deeply. 'I guess I'm incorrigible,' he said gloomily. 'You can call my people to come pick me up.'

'We'll obviously be launching an internal investigation as to how a scandal like this was allowed to reach the press,' the director said ominously.

'I can hazard a pretty good guess,' Dr Lucy muttered. 'But Joe, Skye we need you to tell us if you had any help with . . . *that*.' She nodded at the copy of the *Daily Mirror*.

'Well, I got the idea from a movie I saw once—' Joe began, before a reproving frown from Dr Raf drew him up short. 'Sorry, Doc. Uh, what I meant to say was nope. No one helped us. It was all my fault from start to finish. I saw that closet door ajar and I talked Skye into coming inside with me. God knows who took that photo, but believe me, neither of us had anything to do with it. I sure as hell didn't, and Skye didn't either.'

He glanced reassuringly at Skye, who felt so guilty she couldn't even meet his eyes.

He's being so nice – he's protecting everyone. And the only reason I'm here is to set him up. God, I feel terrible.

'And because you are in breach of your behavioural contract, I should specify that your prepayment of the fee for your thirty-day stay will *not* be refunded on a pro-rated basis,' added the lead lawyer.

'Sure, whatever,' Joe said easily, dismissing this with a wave of his big hand. He heaved another deep sigh, his chest rising and falling majestically. 'Time to face the music. This'll be all over the news by now.'

'We'll need to plan your exit carefully,' Daniyel chimed in. 'There's a huge pack of paparazzi outside the main doors.'

'Oh, I just bet there is,' Joe said. 'I'll call my publicist, Carmen;

let her work out how she wants to handle this.' He pulled a face. 'Can I get a Valium from anyone? Carmen's gonna be yelling at me for the rest of the day, non-stop. I could do with a little something to take the edge off.'

'*Joe*,' Dr Raf said, but even he couldn't help smiling.

'Oh, give the man a Valium if he wants,' Dr Solomon said impatiently. 'He wasn't here for drug dependency, was he?'

'No, just blonde woopsies,' Skye said.

Dr Solomon actually had the grace to look embarrassed at this.

'Well, we're done here,' he said bluffly. 'Daniyel, would you arrange for these two to leave in whatever manner you think best to manage the crowd outside? Dr Raf, would you please draft a statement for me to make to the assembled ladies and gentlemen of the press, and then have the lawyers look at it? And I believe, Dr Lucy, you have a theory about who is responsible for this appalling situation?'

'*Oh*, yes,' Dr Lucy said grimly, as Skye and Joe, shepherded by Daniyel, turned to leave. 'An immature narcissist with highly developed attention-seeking tendencies and strong connections to the British press? I wouldn't say we have far to look. Raf, I can't *believe* we let her have her cell back!'

'She was doing very well in group, and really opening up and doing the work in our one-on-one sessions,' Dr Raf said unhappily. 'The phone was a reward for good behaviour. And we still don't have definite confirmation that it was Petal—'

'Oh my God, this is *Petal Gold* we're talking about?' Dr Solomon interrupted. 'Damn it! What the hell's been going on here? I leave you in charge so I can finally have some much-needed down time, and look what happens!'

Daniyel closed the door behind Skye and Joe, cutting off Dr Solomon's tirade. But they had both heard more than enough.

'*Petal?*' Joe said reflectively. 'Well, well, well. Didn't see that one coming.'

'I'm going to kill that little bitch when I get my hands on her!' Skye said between gritted teeth.

Petal

*P*etal was slumped next to a pile of her suitcases, tears trickling down her face. She'd tried everything she could to persuade them to let her stay; she'd begged, pleaded, cried, entreated, and eventually retreated to her room, sobbing, lying on the bed and refusing to pack her bags, so that Daniyel, together with another tech, had had to do it for her.

The one thing she hadn't been able to do was deny her crime. Because when they'd called her in, and Dr Lucy had told her to hand over her mobile, what could she have done? How could she have refused?

And then, when they'd found the clip of Joe and Skye, it was all over.

Bar the shouting. Because there had been a lot of shouting.

'Dr Raf!'

Seeing him emerge into the reception area, Petal jumped to her feet, and unfortunately caught sight of herself in one of the mirrored panels that decorated the pale green entrance walls of Cascabel's lobby. She looked like shit. Her white skin never did well when she cried; it went blotchy at once, bright patches of red on her nose and cheeks. And her eyes were red too, from rubbing them.

Great. Yellow hair, white skin and red nose. I look like a fucking clown.

'Dr Raf, have they changed their minds? Can I stay after all?'

She ran towards him eagerly, her voice thick with snot from all the tears she'd cried. But as soon as she got close, her heart sank again. She could tell from his expression that the answer was 'No'.

'I'm sorry, Petal,' he said sadly. 'You know I feel, on balance, that you should stay. You've made such strides since you've been here.'

'I *have*! I *have*!' she wailed.

And it was true: she had. Of course, she was desperate to stay because she knew very well that Gold would be as good as his word. If she didn't complete the thirty-day programme, her trust fund would be cut off.

But it isn't just that. This really is helping me. I'm talking about all this stuff I've never really acknowledged before. And when I do, I feel better afterwards. A lot better. And Dr Raf is so wonderful . . . he really understands me . . .

'The management won't be budged, I'm afraid,' he continued. 'And I can't blame them. You've caused incalculable harm to the reputation of this facility.'

Petal hung her head.

'We *help* people here, Petal,' he said gently. 'Vulnerable people who are in terrible trouble. Think of Amber, what she's going through. And Brian. And poor Mitch. Your actions have imperilled all of that. If people think rehab can't be taken seriously, that it's just somewhere to hook up or get laid—'

He broke off, going red. Petal looked behind her, to see if anything had happened that she didn't realize, but no. Something must have occurred to Dr Raf.

He cleared his throat, still blushing. 'Anyway – if rehab becomes a laughing stock, people won't try it, and that will deprive them of a resource that could literally save their lives,' he finished.

Petal could barely breathe for shame. 'I'm so sorry,' she whispered.

'We've decided you can continue as an out-patient,' he said kindly. 'I can continue to be your therapist with sessions on a daily basis.'

Oh, thank God. Petal's shoulders sagged in relief, but it was only momentary. 'That still won't count with Gold – with my *dad*!' she corrected herself. 'And where am I supposed to go? Where am I supposed to stay if I'm still having therapy here?'

Dr Raf's handsome face brightened into a smile. 'That's what I've been organizing,' he said more cheerfully. 'By California law, you're underage, so we wouldn't have admitted you if you didn't have a family member or responsible adult in the state.'

'Not my *mum*?' Petal exclaimed, her eyes widening in shock.

'I called her just now. She's on her way to pick you up,' Dr Raf said. 'She was near the Palisades, as it happens, so she should be here very soon. Traffic permitting,' he added wryly.

'*What?* What did she say? How did she sound?'

'Uh, she was a bit taken aback,' Dr Raf admitted. 'Clearly your dad hadn't told her that she'd been put down as an emergency contact for you, so it took a while to explain the situation . . . but I'm sure it'll be fine.' He looked down at her, his dark eyes serious. 'You know, Petal, I don't mean to play social worker, but this could be a great opportunity for you to reconnect with her.'

'Oh, *God*!' Petal collapsed onto the suitcases. 'You don't know what she's like now,' she wailed. 'She's had all this plastic surgery . . . she's doing a reality TV show, apparently . . . the last thing she's going to want is her daughter showing up on her doorstep.'

'Oh, I'm sure that's not true,' Dr Raf said, in an overbright encouraging voice. He fished in his pocket. 'And here's your phone. Dr Lucy's deleted the video, obviously.'

Petal took the phone. It felt like a huge anticlimax. Finally, she was free to use it whenever she wanted; but the price she'd paid for that freedom was much too high. Turning it over in her hands, staring gloomily at the shiny Swarovski crystals, she debated who to call first with her news.

But what can I tell them? Maybe my credit cards will work OK to get me a flight home, but what if Gold – Dad – cuts me off as soon as I'm there? At least if I stay in LA and finish therapy here with Dr Raf, Dad might agree to keep my cards funded . . .

'Hey! I'm looking for Petal Gold,' called a woman's voice from the doorway, her accent an odd blend of Cockney and American, her tone irritated. 'Some doctor called me from here and said I had to come get her. What's the parking situation here? Do I need to get something validated?'

'Mum?' Petal clambered to her feet, standing nervously in front of her cases.

'*Petal?* Look at the state of you! What have you done to your *hair?*' Linda exclaimed.

You're a fine one to talk, Petal thought crossly.

When Gold had met Linda, twenty years ago, Page Three girls were all-natural. The big boobs were what nature had given them, the equally voluminous hair might be teased up by a stylist, but was without benefit of hair extensions. And if their lips weren't full enough, they slicked on light-reflecting pale pink lip gloss, smiled their pretty faces off and stuck their bosoms out to distract the viewer.

So Linda had been, at twenty-one, an extremely attractive girl, albeit with a figure too generous for her to make it in mainstream modelling. It was no surprise that Gold had fallen for her, hard, enough to marry her and have a baby with her.

But if he met Mum now, I doubt he'd even recognize her, Petal reflected, staring at her mother. Linda had had work done on her face, clearly; her eyes had that wide, staring look that happened with over-enthusiastic eyelid lifts, and her lips were swollen beyond their natural contours.

And then there was the liposuction. Most actresses/models/whatever started off naturally thin, and bought their breasts as necessary; Linda had done the opposite. When she arrived in LA, after her divorce, and realized that the standard of beauty on the West Coast was pin-thin, she had promptly spent some of her very large divorce settlement on lipo and a personal trainer. She had had her boobs lifted a few years ago, but their size was all her own, and they were so disproportionate to her skinny frame that Linda looked as if she were about to topple over on her face.

Still, they were balanced to some degree by her hair, which was as pale as straw and as shiny as cheap gold-plated jewellery, the kind that tarnishes your skin. And it was piled up on the top of her head in a whole arrangement of curls that was so thick and heavy it must have been filled out with extensions.

'You look different,' Petal said frankly.

Linda, fortunately, took this as a compliment. She raised a manicured hand to pat at the back of her hair, smirking.

'I should say so!' she agreed happily. 'I've been filming a series for VH1 – I had a *lot* of work done.'

Linda looked her daughter up and down, taking in the suitcases. Then her gaze moved onto Dr Raf, and her eyes brightened visibly.

'Well, *hi*,' she said flirtatiously. 'Are you Dr Green? You're *much* hotter than you sounded on the phone!' She giggled. 'God, I'm awful, aren't I?'

She wriggled across the lobby to him on her flip-flop kitten heels, which were the same hot pink as her Juicy Couture velour hoodie.

'It's very nice of you to come to pick up Petal,' Dr Raf said.

'Yeah, about that . . .' Linda flashed him a smile. 'Do I *have* to take her with me? It's *really* inconvenient at the moment. I just wrapped a show, I have to do publicity for it . . . Couldn't she stay on here? Pretty, pretty please?' She fingered the lapel of Dr Raf's jacket, stroking it seductively.

Petal writhed with embarrassment. *As if that girlie stuff would ever have worked on Dr Raf – even when you were young and pretty enough to pull it off.*

Gently, Dr Raf removed Linda's hand.

'I'm sorry, Mrs Gold,' he said, his tone genuinely apologetic. 'I would have liked to keep Petal on as an inpatient, but it's not my decision. She can see me on a daily basis for therapy.'

'God! Do I have to drive her here every day?' Linda exclaimed, trying to frown and failing because of the Botox in her forehead. She turned to Petal, hands on her hips. 'What kind of stunt have you pulled that they're kicking you out?' she fumed. 'I should put you on a plane and send you straight back to your dad!'

'No, Mum, please . . .' Petal pleaded. 'I need to finish my treatment!'

Dr Raf smiled at her approvingly.

'Ugh! So I'm stuck with you!' Linda said crossly. 'This is lousy timing!' Then she brightened as a fresh thought occurred to her. 'Though, mind you, I suppose it might help with publicity for the show . . . I'll ring VH1 and see what they say . . . Maybe they'll give us a show together! Mother and daughter! Like *The Gastineau Girls*!'

Petal glanced at Dr Raf. He was too well-versed in the ways of Hollywood to be surprised at Linda's reaction, but he did give Petal a sympathetic glance.

'Well, come on then, if you're coming!' Linda said to Petal. She wiggled her fingers in farewell at Dr Raf. '*Lovely* to meet you,' she said. 'And you've got my number now . . . feel free to use it!'

Grabbing the handles of her Samsonites, Petal followed her mother out of the lobby, bumping the cases over the slate path. She loaded them into Linda's lime-green Beetle, Linda speculating loudly as she did so about the possibility of a new VH1 reality series.

'They have this whole strand called Celebreality,' she babbled happily, 'and they're always looking for new ideas . . . we could go in together and do a pitch . . .'

'I've had enough publicity for a while, Mum,' Petal said. She stopped for a moment, amazed. 'God! I can't believe I just said that!'

'You'll have to sleep in the pool house,' Linda said, starting up the car. 'It's a studio – it's got its own bathroom. Give us both some privacy that way.' She giggled. 'And I have to tell you about Bobby! Ooh, this show's been so much fun!'

'Who's Bobby?'

Petal closed her eyes as her mother pulled out into traffic without checking her mirrors or indicating; a car behind them beeped angrily.

'Bobby's my boytoy!' Linda said happily. 'I picked him out! This show, right, it's called *Cougar Hunt*. I had fifteen twenty-somethings to choose from – we all moved into this big house in the Hills to film it – apparently they usually hire it out for porn shoots, isn't that a blast? One of the kids recognized it from a porno he watched. *So* funny. Anyway, fifteen hot boys jumping through hoops to be with me! Can you imagine! Each episode I can one of them by saying: "Sorry, but you're not cougar bait!" Hilarious, right?'

'Hilarious, Mum,' Petal echoed drily.

'Oh –' Linda turned her head to look at Petal, taking her eyes completely off the road – 'about that? Could you call me Linda? Anything else makes me sound really old. I had you *so* young . . . I mean, really, I could be your older sister . . .'

Oh God, Petal thought hopelessly. Cascabel, with all its restrictions, was looking more and more like paradise on earth.

Skye

'Joe's publicists sure are doing a good job getting ahead of the story,' Kevin said, leaning back in his chair and watching the TV. It was showing *E! News*, and an excited presenter was saying breathlessly: 'And now, the biggest story in celebrity news, breaking live from Hollywood! Joe Jeffreys leaves sex rehab in disgrace after being caught with a stripper – and dashes straight to his fiancée, Jennifer Downs, to plead for forgiveness! Check out our footage!'

'Oh my *God*,' said another *National Investigator* journalist, coming into Kevin's office and staring at the screen. 'This is better than Hugh Grant and Elizabeth Hurley after he got caught with that tranny . . .'

'Check out what she's *wearing*,' said Kevin gleefully.

Carmen might have pushed the envelope just a little too far with Jennifer's styling this time. Jennifer's short crop had been dyed to a pale blonde, which gave her an even more ethereal appearance than usual; her huge, wide-set hazel eyes were heavily mascaraed, and she was wearing a white crepe slip dress, which fell to below the knee. Round her neck was—

'It's a freaking *cross*,' the other journalist breathed in awe, as the camera panned in on it.

The scene had been staged in the garden of a friend of Jennifer's, specifically chosen so that the news cameras (summoned by a tip-off from Carmen) could get a perfect view of Jennifer and Joe over the low stone wall. Jennifer was seated on a garden swing, its pale pink canopy casting a rosy glow over her. It was, indeed, a silver crucifix, large enough to be clearly visible, hanging round her slender neck.

And before her, in supplication, kneeled Joe.

'Too much,' Kevin said. 'Way too much.'

'He's been a bad, bad boy!' the *E! News* presenter continued, almost salivating in pleasure. 'And now the burning question is: will Jennifer forgive him? *Should* she forgive him? They were America's sweethearts – is it all over now for this golden couple?'

The focus was a little blurry, and the angle meant that all that could be seen of Joe was his back. Skye stared at his strong, muscular shoulders, his thick fair hair, with real yearning.

I'll never touch him again, she thought. I'll probably never even see him again, apart from up on a big screen, pretending to be in love with his gay fiancée. She heaved a deep sigh. I'm such an idiot. Falling for a movie star who was just killing time with me. Talk about your basic stripper mistake.

'Keep tuned for the latest on this breaking news with *E!*' said the presenter, as they went to a commercial. Kevin reached for the remote and clicked off the sound.

'We've gone through the footage you recorded, Skye,' he said, swivelling his chair to face hers, nodding at the other *Investigator* journalist to leave his office. 'Nice work! Though I don't understand why you didn't just leave when you had it and bring it straight to us.' He steepled his fingers together, propping his chin on top of them. 'That way we wouldn't have been pipped at the post by that damn British paper.'

'Joe was very into me,' Skye said. She'd known this question would be asked, and had already worked out an answer. 'I thought we'd definitely do it again, and I could record that too.'

'I can't believe anything else could be as hot as that!' he said cheerfully. 'But hey, what's done is done.' He pulled a face. 'Look, the bonus was dependent on your bringing the story to us first, so we could break it. Now that British tabloid's got there before us, the bonus is off the table. You get that, right?'

Skye couldn't argue. It was her own fault for not getting out of Cascabel as soon as she had that explosive piece of video safely recorded.

'*But*,' Kevin said cheerfully, throwing her a bone, 'we're gonna run a big tell-all piece by you. Well, "as told to" me. And you'll get a fee for that.'

'Great,' Skye said dully.

'And of course, there's the whole rights issue for a DVD,' he went on. 'We'd love to release it. You'd get a cut, naturally. Our lawyers are working on it right now – there are big issues with the hidden camera, plus being actually filmed at a medical facility like Cascabel. The pics are one thing, but putting out a sex DVD's bound to drive Joe's people crazy. We might not be able to pull that one off.'

'Oh, that's a shame,' Skye lied.

She hadn't even thought about their wanting to market the DVD, and crossed her fingers tightly now, praying they weren't able to do it. The thought of everyone, till the end of time, being able to watch her and Joe doing it turned her stomach.

What would Joe think?

God, what an idiot you are. As if Joe gives a shit about you.

'So, good news for you, Skye!' Kevin beamed, his eyes glinting behind the lenses of his preppie gold-framed glasses. 'We definitely want you to stay on in LA for a while – we'll need you for follow-ups. See how far we take this story. God knows if Jennifer will take Joe back – this one will run and run. *So*, we don't want you talking to anyone but us. We'll get you to sign an exclusive-access contract, give you a nice extra fee for that, and put you up at a hotel here, all expenses paid. My assistant's booked you into the Grafton, on the Sunset Strip. We'll get you checked in there just as soon as you've told me every single detail you can remember about your wild times with Joe Jeffreys.'

Beaming, he pulled out a mini digital recorder from his desk drawer, and slid it halfway across the desk, positioning it between them.

'I'm going to record this and take notes, OK?' he said. 'You want a coffee? Soda? Water?'

Skye shook her head.

'OK, let's get started!' he said happily. 'What was the first thing Joe said to you?'

I don't want to do this, Skye thought miserably. I really don't. But I'm not getting my bonus now – I need this money. If I don't tell him the story, they'll pack me back to New York. And then I'll be at square one again. I can't go back to the Lounge with my tail between my legs. I can't go back to that life.

'I don't remember exactly,' she heard herself say. 'Something like "Welcome to Cascabel".'

'Huh. I think we'll go with "Hi, gorgeous!",' Kevin said, starting to type. 'Or maybe "Hi, blondie!" Sounds sexier, doesn't it?'

Amber

'Amber! Honey!'

Even by Californian standards, Tony seemed impossibly tall and bronzed. His teeth flashed white against his tanned skin as he strode towards Amber; his outstretched hands – one glinting golden with a signet ring – looked huge.

'Let's get you out of here!' he said, reaching her and enveloping her in a big hug. 'Jeez, what a place I sent you to, baby! I'm so sorry!'

'Oh, no, it was fine,' Amber said into his shoulder.

'How're you doing?' He pulled back, looking down at her. 'Baby, you look *great*. Better than I've ever seen you.'

'I'm off the pills,' Amber said simply. 'Everything's in focus.'

'Wow, that's wonderful,' he said enthusiastically. 'I just hope you still like me now you're all cleaned up!'

You sound like we had a relationship; but I don't even know you, Amber thought, almost amused at Tony's level of self-delusion. I was paid to date you a few times. That's it.

'Thank you so much for sending me here,' she said sincerely, gazing up at Tony's handsome face. 'I really think you saved my life.'

'Oh, *baby* . . .' Tony shook his head. 'You were in a bad, bad way when I came round that day. Your mom was hysterical.'

He shrugged his impossibly wide shoulders. He was wearing a crisp white shirt, with a faint pink check, tucked into equally starched and ironed flat-fronted beige chinos. Both items of clothing smelled pleasantly of fabric conditioner, and both had definitely been bought from a shop that specialized in fitting men over six foot four. Amber remembered him telling her that his leather shoes were all custom-made.

'But that's what I'm for,' Tony continued seriously. 'Amber, I take care of things. That's what my job is. I'm a troubleshooter. They give me all these fancy titles, but that's the long and short of it. I fly round the world sorting out problems, making sure people can run pipelines from A to B. That's hardcore stuff, honey. So if I can take care of that kind of thing, no way I can't take care of you too.'

'I don't know what to say,' Amber said honestly. 'Tony, I need to pay you back for all the money you've spent on me. I have some savings – I can at least make a start. Can you tell me how much—'

'Shh now!' He raised a finger to his lips. 'Don't say anything! Tell you what. We're gonna take you to see your mom – she's dying to see you, I can tell you that. I got her settled in a nice house in the Hills my company rents for its people. We got places all over, so don't go thinking this is some sorta huge deal, OK? You and she can have a good old catch-up.' He grinned. 'I know how the ladies love to talk each other to death. These your cases?'

'Yes, but—'

'Later, baby. After we settle you in.'

Tony waved to someone outside the big glass doors of the Cascabel lobby; a driver in a dark suit entered, picking up Amber's suitcases and whisking them outside.

Daniyel, standing by the reception desk, said: 'Amber, sweetie, we're very sorry to see you leave before the end of your treatment month—'

'Well, what the hell do you expect?' Tony exclaimed. 'You got this huge scandal breaking over all your heads – Amber was room-mates with that stripper girl! I mean, I don't know much about this whole rehab setup, but I do know that you gotta trust everyone else is here for the right reasons, isn't that right?'

'Absolutely,' Daniyel said, nodding. 'We can't apologize enough for everything that's happened. And I know Amber's doctor has referred her to an outpatients programme.'

'I'm going to go for treatment every day,' Amber said to Daniyel. 'I just can't stay here any more.'

'Oh, I do understand,' Daniyel said sincerely, taking both Amber's hands in hers. 'You're a sweet, sweet girl, honey. We just all want the best for you, and it's really soon to be discharging yourself. I mean, you came here in a pretty bad state.'

Tony nodded.

'You talked all this over with Dr Raf, and you're still sure you want to go?' Daniyel asked, her brows drawn together in concern.

'Oh, yes,' Amber said quietly. 'I talked everything over with Dr Raf.'

'Amber!' Dr Raf wrung his hands together. 'I *can't* carry on treating you – you have to understand that! To put it simply, you wouldn't be able to confide in me – to tell me things that perhaps you're ashamed of, or don't want to –' he winced – 'don't want to tell to a man with whom you've been sexually intimate.'

'But I can't be treated by Dr Lucy!' Amber protested. 'You know I can't!'

Dr Raf looked even more agonized. 'No, I suppose you can't,' he said helplessly.

'So what am I supposed to do if you can't treat me, and I can't see Dr Lucy?' Amber insisted.

'I couldn't bring in another therapist,' he said, his dark eyes haunted. 'Not at this stage of treatment. It would look so strange, and you would have no continuity.' He hung his head. 'I've thought about nothing else, Amber. You have no idea how much you've been on my mind. Even this awful situation with Joe and Skye – normally that would be obsessing me. But all I can focus on is how I've let you down.'

Oh no! Amber's heart sank. *I was hoping he meant he was thinking about me so much because he really has feelings for me . . . not because of letting me down . . .*

'You haven't let me down!' she said desperately. 'You haven't!'

'What I've done has broken every rule of good practice,' Dr Raf said sadly.

'But wasn't it –' Amber leaned forward in her chair and touched Dr Raf's knee. He jumped as if she had scalded him – 'wasn't it wonderful?' she persisted. 'How can something that feels that good be a mistake?'

'That's probably just what Joe and Skye thought,' he said bitterly.

'Oh, that's not fair!' Amber protested. 'You can't say that's the same thing!'

Dr Raf took off his glasses, rubbing his eyes with his palms so hard that when he looked at Amber again, the whites of his eyes were streaked with red.

'No, it's not the same thing,' he said. 'What they did only involved a betrayal of the celibacy pledge they made when they came to Cascabel. What I did – having sex with a patient – is much, much worse than that.'

Amber wanted to scream with frustration.

'Amber,' he continued, 'you think you have feelings for me because of your transference. I assure you, those feelings simply aren't real.'

'They *are*,' Amber said defiantly. 'I *know* they are. Believe me, I've been with men before when I didn't feel anything for them. I know the difference. What I feel for you is real.' She shook back her hair from her face, confronting him with all her beauty, daring him to look at her and deny what he felt. 'And what you feel for me is real, too. I know it is.'

'Amber,' he said bleakly, 'this is the last time that you and I can ever be in a room together, alone, again.'

Amber had never felt pain like this. It was as if he had stabbed her in the chest.

'But then I can't stay here,' she said in a tiny voice, willing him, with everything she had, to contradict her; to realize that he couldn't bear to have her gone from Cascabel.

'No, you can't,' he agreed instead, and it was as if the knife was turning in the wound. 'I can arrange for you to enter another residential programme—'

'No,' she said instantly, her green eyes flashing with anger and the wish to hurt him as badly as he'd hurt her. 'No more residential places. After all, what if a doctor there takes advantage of me like you did?'

His handsome face went white, the skin seeming to draw tighter over his strong bones.

'I deserve that,' he said quietly.

'I'm going to ring my mother,' Amber said, standing up, 'and ask her to get in touch with Tony. He can sort everything out. It sounds like he's good at that.'

'I'm concerned about you going back to live with your mother,' Dr Raf said worriedly. 'After your past history of drug abuse together, is that wise?'

'What I do now is none of your business,' Amber said coldly. 'You've made that very clear.' She turned towards the door.

'And do you even know this Tony?' Dr Raf was on his feet too.

'More than I know you,' she snapped. 'At least he's not going to tell me he doesn't want to be alone in a room with me! Quite the opposite, I imagine!'

'*Amber* . . .' He looked devastated. His hands rose to reach out for her, before he realized what he was doing and dropped them again, shoving them in his pockets to keep him from making the same mistake again.

Great, she thought. I've hurt him as badly as he's hurt me. I've slid the knife in just as deep. Funny, though – I thought it would help me feel better to see him suffering this badly. And instead, it only makes me feel worse.

'Here we are!' Tony gloated, as the Lexus, after winding its way up a series of narrow little streets, houses clinging to their sides precariously, pulled in at a short driveway that led into a small walled courtyard. He jumped out, striding round the car to open Amber's door, nodding to the driver to bring her suitcases. 'You like it?'

Amber looked up at the pretty white two-storey stucco house, trellised with jasmine. 'It looks lovely,' she said truthfully.

Tony beamed. 'Your mom seems really happy here,' he said, as the front door opened and Slava appeared on the doorstep.

'Amber!' she cried, holding out her arms. '*Láska!* I miss you so much!'

Slava had adapted her style for LA's warmer weather effortlessly. She was wearing beige linen trousers and a cream silk short-sleeved blouse, her necklace of big cultured pearls fastened choker-style around her neck to conceal the wrinkles. Her ash-blonde hair was freshly styled, and her fingernails were painted coral, the same colour as her toenails, which were peeking through the pewter leather sandals on her feet.

She looks great, Amber thought. And, despite everything that had happened, she found herself running towards her mother, arms outstretched, a gulp catching in her throat. Slava was the only constant in her life, the only person who had always been there for Amber.

'*Matka!*' she cried, hugging her mother tightly. 'Oh, *Matka*, I missed you too!'

Without Matka, I'd be completely alone, Amber thought, breathing in her mother's familiar Rive Gauche perfume. She could scarcely count Tony; sweet as he was, he didn't know her at all.

'You're happy here, *láska*?' Slava pulled back, looking up at her tall, beautiful daughter. 'The sunshine, it's lovely! And Tony is so kind, so nice!' She smiled widely at Tony, who was hanging back politely to give mother and daughter a chance to reunite.

'I've made a lot of changes, *Matka*,' Amber said quietly. 'I need to sit and let everything settle for a while. And we need to talk about everything that went on. We need to make some changes together.'

Slava's eyes flickered away from her daughter's serious, direct gaze. 'You're all better,' she said brightly. 'And we are happy – we have no money worries – you have a nice boyfriend – what needs changing here?'

She waved at Tony, the heavy rings on her fingers catching the sunlight. Duly summoned, Tony loped up to them.

'I'll leave you two ladies for the moment,' he said. 'Let you show Amber round the house, Mrs Peters.'

'It's a *lovely* house,' Slava cooed.

'Amber –' Tony looked at her – 'I have to fly back to Houston tomorrow, first thing. Can I take you out to dinner tonight?'

How can I say no?

'Sure,' Amber said, as Slava pinched her encouragingly with the hand still wrapped around her arm.

'Great! I'll pick you up at eight!'

Tony bounded down the courtyard and into the Lexus.

'He's like Tigger,' Amber observed.

Slava wrapped her arm through Amber's and led her inside.

'Look!' she said, gesturing around them. 'Look! Beautiful!'

The house was built around a Tuscan-tiled central atrium, with a cluster of ferns in the centre to catch the sunlight that poured in from the skylight overhead. A staircase wrapped around the atrium in a dramatic sweep, and as Slava led Amber under its curve, they entered a glass-walled sitting room, beyond which water glittered against the bright blue tiles of a small oval swimming pool.

'I see you've made yourself comfy, *Matka*,' Amber said affectionately, squeezing her mother's waist.

Slava had re-created the cosy nest she had made for herself in the Mayfair flat: an upholstered loveseat was drawn up close to the flat-screen TV, with a stool in front of it for Slava's legs to rest on. A tangle of knitting wool and needles was coiled up on one arm of the loveseat, and on a small side table next to it was Slava's embroidery box and wooden petit-point frame.

The TV was tuned, naturally, to a daytime talk show, an earnest group of women sitting on a curving couch, leaning into each other as across the bottom of the screen ran the caption: 'Should Jennifer take Joe back after these latest shocking revelations? Go online to let us know what YOU think!'

'I am very happy here,' Slava said complacently, sinking into her favourite seat. 'The sunshine, it's good for my bones.'

'It's lovely,' Amber said, walking over to the garden door, surveying the garden beyond, with its swimming pool, twin loungers, and landscaped patio. They were high up in the Hollywood hills, and beyond the low stone wall, the ground dropped away, providing a stunning view of the canyons below.

'I want to stay here,' Slava announced, picking up her knitting.

'I'm not surprised,' Amber said wryly, turning to look at her mother. 'I would too. But, *Matka* –' Amber hesitated, trying to work out how to word what she needed to say – 'everything's up in the air for me right now. I have to work out what I want, where I'm going.' She took a breath. 'I'm off the pills, you know that. And they say I shouldn't drink any more, either. I have to go to Narcotics Anonymous meetings, and to my therapy.'

'Good!' Slava said, working away with her needles, half her attention already on the TV screen. 'That's good, yes?' She winked at her daughter. 'It costs less, too. Doctors are very expensive.'

'Yes, it's good,' Amber said a little hopelessly. '*Matka* –' she dropped onto the arm of the loveseat, forcing her mother to look at her – 'they say when you've been addicted, everything needs to change. That means not just me, but us. You and me. We've been living in a really unhealthy way.'

'I need my Vicodin,' Slava said sharply. 'For my back, I need it.'

She never had back problems, Amber thought unhappily. She made them up to justify popping the pills. But there's no point arguing. Dr Raf always said in group that people can't hear anything till they're ready to take it in. And *Matka* is definitely not ready.

Sighing, she stood up. 'I'm going to have to do a lot of thinking,' she said quietly.

'*Láska?*' Slava said, her voice wavering. 'I do some thinking too. I am wrong to tell you to go to Dubai. I see that now. It is too much. I tell you things I should not tell you.' Tears began to form in her eyes. 'I put too much on you, on your shoulders. When you get sick, I understand that, and I feel really bad.'

She held her hand out to Amber. 'You forgive me?' she said, dabbing at her cheeks with the other hand. 'All I want is for you, *láska*. All I do is for you. I am so sorry that I make you so upset.'

'Oh, *Matka* . . .' Amber dropped to her knees beside her mother, taking Slava's hand, holding it to her cheek. 'Of course I forgive you! When I think of what you've been through to look after me, how could I ever blame you for anything?'

'I love you, *láska*,' Slava said through her tears. 'I just want you to be happy. I want you to be happy. And maybe marry Tony. He's a good man.' Slava wiped her eyes. 'He likes to look after people. That will be good husband. Believe me, I know. I had bad husband. I see the difference.'

'*What!*' Amber exclaimed, dropping Slava's hand. 'We hardly know him! Besides, I met him when he paid to have sex with me!'

Slava shrugged. 'Lots of men pay to have sex,' she said matter-of-factly. 'It means nothing.'

'Oh God . . .' Amber took a deep breath. 'I'm going to unpack and have a bath,' she said firmly. 'And then I might have a rest.'

'You could swim,' Slava said, waving at the pool. 'They clean it yesterday. Very nice pool.'

'I'll see,' Amber said, her fingers to her temples, massaging away an incipient headache as she left the living room.

I need to stop living with *Matka*, she thought. She's going to drive me insane in a week. No wonder I popped all those pills – I'd have been in a mental ward otherwise. But how would *Matka* ever cope without me?

And what on earth am I going to do about Tony?

'You like it here?' Tony asked anxiously as he seated Amber. 'It's kind of simple, but my PA says it's where all the movie stars come to be romantic.'

'It looks lovely,' Amber said, glancing around her at the brick walls, the wooden tables, and the low-hanging, golden globe lights that gleamed off the stained-glass panels in the patio windows of the restaurant on Laurel Canyon Boulevard, just ten minutes from what, for now, she supposed she should call her home in the Hills.

'Welcome to Pace,' said the waitress, putting down the menus on the table. 'Everything's organic here, and our vegan soup today is carrot and coriander. Can I get you anything to drink?'

Amber ordered fizzy water, and Tony, following suit, a Coke.

'You're not drinking,' he said as the waitress left, 'so I won't either.'

'That's really thoughtful,' Amber said, smiling at him.

'You look beautiful,' he said, reaching for her hand across the table, enveloping it in his much larger one. 'I like your hair that way.'

Much to Slava's disapproval, Amber hadn't made her usual perfectionist effort in getting ready this evening, just pulled her hair back into a high ponytail and slipped on a simple strappy cotton sheath.

I think I must have wanted to see if Tony still liked me if I wasn't all done up, she reflected. And guess what? He does. *Matka* might be right about him being a good guy.

'I want to get things straight between us, Amber,' he said simply. 'I know we started off – uh – in a weird kind of way.' His square jaw tightened. 'I know I don't come out of it too well. I'm just on the road so much, I don't get a chance to meet quality girls like you, and I was lonely. I took the easy way, I guess. Cut some corners.'

'I don't come out of it any better than you,' Amber pointed out.

'Amber,' he said frankly, 'my folks didn't raise a fool. I can tell you're a good girl. You got yourself in a bind, and you won't ever hear any judgement from me about how we met. But I want to put all that behind us and start again. Can we try to do that?'

Amber stared at him. It was hard to see Tony as a real person; he was so much the larger-than-life Texan, with his easy grin and his cookie-cutter handsomeness. But his words sounded genuine, and she could read nothing but sincerity in his expression.

'I don't want you to worry about anything for a while,' he continued. 'You just take the time you need to get back on your feet.

I've got you a driver, and I've set up a credit card for you – it'll get dropped round tomorrow. I'm gonna give you my contact details and the PA in our LA office can help with any day-to-day stuff you need. I'm gonna be travelling big time for the next two weeks at least – Kazakhstan, Moscow, all over the Middle East – so I wanna make sure you're OK before I head out of town.'

'I've got money of my own for daily expenses,' Amber said quickly. 'I don't need a credit card from you. I feel bad enough about how much you've spent on me so far. I'm going to need to pay you back for that – you'll have to tell me how much it's been—'

'Please! Let's not ruin dinner by talking about money!'

Tony waved his hand in vehement negation, the big Patek Philippe watch sliding down his wide, tanned wrist and nearly knocking out the waitress, who had just arrived with their drinks.

'But I—' Amber insisted.

'Later, OK?' Tony said. 'Here's to starting over.' He held out his Coke to Amber, waiting till she gave in, picking up her Pellegrino glass to clink against it. 'So!' He grinned. 'You seen any good movies lately?'

'Not recently,' Amber said demurely, sipping her water. 'But my roommate at Cascabel was a big fan of *Pretty Woman* . . .'

Tony choked on his Coke.

'Funny!' he said when he could speak again. Amber reached out and dabbed his pale blue shirtfront with some fizzy water, in case it stained.

'Thanks, baby,' he said. 'Hey, who knew you had a great sense of humour too?'

'Not me!' Amber said happily.

They had just finished their dinner – beet and walnut salad for weight-conscious Amber, pepperoni and sausage pizza for Tony – when a rustle of excitement, blowing through the restaurant like a warm sirocco, alerted the more experienced diners to the fact that there was a major celebrity sighting in the offing. The waiting staff were sucked to the door as if its opening were a vacuum; a minute later, they flowed backwards, like a movie being shown in reverse; then the *maître d'* appeared, ushering a man who was instantly recognizable to everyone at Pace.

'Ohmigod, it's Joe Jeffreys!' hissed a woman at the next table to her date. 'And is that – *ohmigod*, it *is*! It's *her*!'

Joe towered over his companion, who was as small and fragile as he was tall and imposing. Jennifer Downs, angel-faced A-list movie star, was barely over five foot three and couldn't have weighed more than a hundred pounds soaking wet. Her huge, thickly lashed eyes were as big as Bambi's, her lips a pale pink Cupid's bow, her cropped pale blonde hair a halo of light that perfectly completed her waif-look. She wore the same white slip dress that she had had on earlier that day, but she had, thankfully, removed the theatrical crucifix that had been added for the hovering news cameras.

'So I guess they're back together?' Tony muttered to Amber.

At that moment, Joe's gaze, which had been roaming idly over the crowded dining room, lighted on Amber. His blue eyes widened as they met hers; obviously she was the last person he expected to see, having, as far as he knew, left her still in treatment at Cascabel when he was thrown out.

'*What the hell?*' he mouthed at her without breaking stride.

'He just stared right at you!' Tony exclaimed.

Amber shrugged. 'He didn't know I left this morning,' she pointed out. 'It must have been a shock to see me out and about.'

'Why would he care?' Tony asked possessively.

'Oh, we were together in rehab for weeks,' she explained, as Joe and Jennifer's entourage passed by, heading for a corner table, a stunning Latina woman in a red silk dress bringing up the rear. 'You see the same faces every day from eight in the morning till curfew. And you get to care about how everyone's doing. It's like a really intense instant friendship.'

Amber stifled a yawn. 'Actually,' she said, 'I'm used to going to bed early, and this is getting way past my bedtime. Do you mind if . . .?'

'No, of course not! I've got an early start tomorrow myself.'

Tony swivelled in his chair, looking for a waiter, but everyone was still distracted by the presence of Joe and Jennifer. Stars of so huge a wattage would have been mesmerizing in normal circumstances, but considering the size of the scandal that had broken that very day, it was near-impossible for anyone to look anywhere but over at their table.

'I'll go find someone,' Tony said, pushing back his chair and standing up. 'I'm not waiting around for 'em all to stop crawling up Joe Jeffreys' ass.'

I suppose I can't blame him for being a little jealous, Amber thought. Joe is pretty impressive.

'Amber?' A man in a tight-fitting black shirt and equally snug black trousers materialized beside her. 'My name's Kai, and I work for Joe Jeffreys. He's asked me for your contact details. Do you have a current phone number I can give him?'

Amber's lips parted in surprise. 'Seriously?' she said.

'I'm sorry?' The man leaned in closer.

Oh, why not? Amber shrugged.

'OK,' she said, giving him her mobile phone number. 'It's a UK number, but it works over here.'

'Great!' he said, noting it down quickly on his personal organizer and vanishing discreetly just as Tony returned to the table.

Never a dull moment, Amber thought, wondering what on earth she was getting into now . . .

Petal

'You should come outta the shade,' Bobby said to Petal. 'Soak up some rays. You're white as a ghost.' He guffawed at his own wit.

'I can't tan,' Petal said coldly, rubbing Factor 30 into her long pale legs. 'I just burn.'

'Go get sprayed then,' Bobby suggested. 'There's a Mystic Tan at the strip mall.'

'I like being white,' Petal said even more frigidly. 'It's my look. And if I were tanned, my hair wouldn't work.'

'Hey, you're in LA now, baby,' Bobby said complacently. 'You gotta fit in.'

He stretched out, flexing his big pumped arms behind his head, making the Lilo he was lying on bounce on the bright water of the pool.

'Me, I tan every day,' he said. 'And I do different positions. You can't just lie there in the booth, or you don't get even colour all over.'

'Fascinating,' Petal muttered.

He's such a moron! she thought vindictively. I don't know how Mum can bear him. He looks like a big slab of meat.

She looked over at Bobby, who was rocking on the Lilo, his skin orange, shiny with oil and stretched tightly over his large, juiced-up muscles.

'You don't need to keep your distance, if that's what you're getting your panties in a twist about,' he said to Petal. 'I don't go for little girls.' He scratched his balls through the Lycra fabric. 'Older ladies – sorry, *cougars* – know stuff you little girls would not *imagine*.'

'That's my mum you're talking about,' Petal said, outraged.

'Hey, you should be glad that she's happy,' Bobby said. 'You know. Getting some.' He leered again. 'And when I say "some", I mean "a lot".'

God, I'm so glad I'm not in the main house with them, Petal thought gratefully. The grandly named 'pool house' was basically a big garden shed, with a pull-out sofa bed, peeling paint, and narrow shower cubicle and toilet only concealed from the rest of the space by a wonky corrugated plastic sliding door. Still, it had a sink, and a fridge whose loud, steady hum was white noise to Petal, helping her to sleep. Its windows were large and the thin curtains didn't keep the sunlight out very well, but Petal still had her eyemask from the airline flight over.

And the crucial part was that she had her privacy from her mum and Bobby, who were hellish to be with. Linda acted kittenish around Bobby, which was very embarrassing for her daughter, and Bobby responded by smacking Linda playfully on her bottom and calling her 'doll', which, somehow, was even worse . . .

Petal's phone buzzed, and she grabbed for it eagerly, over the moon to hear Dan's voice.

'Ohmigod!' she exclaimed, jumping up to take the call inside the pool house. 'Baby! What's going on? Did you find out when you can come over?'

She'd rung Dan as soon as she got to Linda's, two days ago; it was the first time they'd talked since she hung up on him at the recording studio, but the news of her expulsion from Cascabel had overridden any lingering resentment from the fight they'd had. Now she was desperate for him to visit her here; if she'd been chucked out of rehab, she might as well have the benefit of being able to see her boyfriend.

'Pet—' Dan started hesitantly.

'Oh, *no!*' Petal's heart sank. 'You can't, can you?'

'Things are really blowing up here,' Dan said, the crack in his voice conveying how torn he was. 'The single's shooting up the charts – we're flat out, doing photoshoots and interviews and all sorts when we're not recording.'

'That's great,' Petal said a little flatly, 'but—'

'I really miss you, pet!' Dan said helplessly. 'I wish you were here! But I'd hardly see you anyway, you know? I mean, we sink a couple of pints down Camden way when we're done, but we're knackered, you know what I mean? Fig –' he named the singer – 'isn't even coming out with the lads any more. He's getting all freaked out about his voice. Goes home early to drink honey and lemon! Never thought I'd see the day!' Oh –' he cleared his throat – 'and I bumped into Tas and JC in the Hawley Arms.'

'*Really,*' Petal said ominously.

'Pet, you should ring 'em. They feel awful. Tas cried all over me shoulder. You know they didn't make a penny off selling that video to the *Mirror.* Someone nicked her phone at the club after she'd shown it around a bit. She doesn't even know who it was.'

'I believe that,' Petal admitted. 'I mean, I know she and JC would never go behind my back like that. But she should have been more careful with her phone . . .'

'Pet, you sent her that clip at three in the morning, she was pissed off her head . . . what did you think was gunna happen? Of course she was gunna show it around, and then someone was bound to have it off her!' he pointed out. 'I mean, a sex tape of *Joe Jeffreys* – you never should have sent it to anyone!'

Petal sighed, acknowledging her own responsibility for the first time.

'Tas and JC've been ringing and ringing,' she said. 'And texting non-stop. My phone's full of messages.'

'So ring back and let 'em know they're forgiven,' Dan advised.

'They're your mates. They didn't mean any harm and they're gutted that they got you chucked out of rehab. Tas looked bloody awful.'

'OK.' She sighed again. 'I will. I really miss them. And you.' Saying the words dropped her into a pit of misery. 'I'm all alone here,' she said sadly. 'It's *shit*, Dan. I never thought I'd say this, but I miss Cascabel.'

'You're having me on!' Dan sounded amazed. 'You hated it there!'

'Yeah, but at least I had people to talk to . . . there was this guy Brian, he was OK . . .'

'Oh yeah?' Dan said jealously. 'Brian, eh?'

'Oh, for fuck's sake, Dan, he was this whingy little wimp who followed Joe around like a dog. It was just that we liked the same music.'

'I still can't believe you were in there with *Joe Jeffreys*,' Dan said in awe.

'Well, yeah . . .' Petal sighed. 'If I hadn't been, I wouldn't have videoed them, and then I wouldn't be living in my mum's fucking *garden shed*, with her idiot boytoy telling me I'm as white as a ghost and I should go get a spray tan.'

'Don't you dare!' Dan said immediately. 'I like you white! You're my proper little Goth girl!'

Petal giggled.

'You'd better not come back all brown and tarty with fake tits and bleached hair,' he said. 'Or I'll scarper as soon as I see you at the airport.'

'Oh, *Dan* . . .' Petal was equally torn: happy that he was talking like a steady boyfriend, gutted that he was making it clear he couldn't come and visit. 'It's so shitty here! I've got nothing to do, no one to hang out with – I'm trying to be good, you know, not do anything I shouldn't—'

'You staying off the white stuff?' Dan asked.

'Yeah.'

'Good,' he said, breathing out a sigh of relief. 'We were caning it there. I was getting a bit carried away meself. I've knocked that on the head too. Just a pint or six for me in future. And you get to spend time with your mum, pet! That's got to be a good thing!'

Dan came from a nice, secure, mum-and-dad-still-together-in-their-council-house family; his sister was in her early twenties and already married with kids, to a solid bloke (in Dan's description) who worked as a welder.

He's got no idea what parents are like in my world, Petal thought sadly.

'She's not exactly—' she began.

'Ooops! They're calling me, yeah? Coming!' he yelled. 'Pet, sorry, it's the *NME* journo. I got to go, babe. Call you tomorrow if I can.'

'No, Dan, I—'

But Dan was gone. Tears sprung to Petal's eyes: tears of self-pity. She threw the phone onto her unmade bed, staring miserably out into the back garden. It was as shabby and dilapidated as the pool house. The pool tiles were chipped, the loungers showing signs of rust, the grass straggly and brown from lack of regular watering. The main house was a low red-roofed ranch-type bungalow, Spanish-style, and would have been lovely with a new coat of paint and fresh roof tiles.

Bobby had got out of the pool and was towelling himself down now. As Petal watched, he struck some body-building poses, dropping the towel and flexing his arms in front of his chest, popping out his pecs, veins straining in his arms; he curved out and pointed one leg, looking down to appreciate the big lumps of muscle on his quad and calf.

'Oooh! Sexy!'

Petal's mother tripped through the patio doors in her kitten-heel flip-flops, a white tank top and towelling Juicy shorts cut so high they were almost hot pants. From a distance, she looked very girlish; her blonde hair hung down her back like a teenager's. It was only as she ran towards Bobby, jumping into his arms and twining her legs around his waist, yelping as he spun her around, that Petal could see the artificially shiny skin on Linda's face and the cellulite on her upper thighs.

'Petal!' her mother screeched, as Bobby jerked her up and down, making lewd pumping gestures with his hips. 'You getting ready for tonight? You want to go get your nails and hair done?'

Reluctantly, Petal pushed open the screen door and emerged onto the porch.

'I don't do the whole mani-pedi thing, Mum,' she said, glancing down at her short stubby nails, off which the black polish was chipping. 'It's not street.'

'Men don't go for chicks that don't take care of themselves,' Bobby offered. 'Look at your mom!' He twirled Linda round by the waist as she giggled appreciatively. 'Nails all nice, hair all done – and I don't just mean on her head, you know what I'm saying? You gotta work at it, babe. You're in LA now.'

If he says that one more time—

'Maybe you should get your tits done too,' he suggested, head tilted to one side as he looked Petal up and down. 'You're like a board there. Guys like two nice handfuls. I bet your mom knows a good tit doctor.'

'Bobby!' Linda screamed in reproach, grabbing her own 34DDs. 'These are all real!'

'I just meant, a lot of your friends,' Bobby said. 'They're all siliconed.' He reached out for Linda's breasts. 'Not like these big babies . . .'

'Ugh, I'm going to puke,' Petal said. 'Can you not do that in front of me? It's *beyond* disgusting. And totally inappropriate.'

She pivoted on her heel, going back inside the pool house, slamming the screen door behind her as best she could.

'Just make sure you're ready by six!' Linda yelled at her daughter's retreating back. 'We've got a premiere to go to!'

'Ohmigod, this is the biggest pile of shit I've ever seen in my life,' Petal muttered to herself a few hours later, sneaking out of the back exit of the Lizard Room to have a smoke and escape from the first episode of *Cougar Hunt*. She had only been able to bear fifteen minutes' worth of her mother posing and preening in a minuscule bikini, in front of a testosterone-crazed group of baying twenty-something steroid-heads, before she made a break for it.

No one should have to watch their mum sleazing around like that, Petal thought, diving into her bag for her packet of Virginia Slims. It's like fucking child abuse. I mean, between my dad and my mum, I don't know who's worse. He ignores me, and she makes me watch this embarrassing bollocks.

Gold hadn't even deigned to communicate with her directly; his disapproval had been communicated through Jinhee, who had emailed Petal on hearing the news that Petal had been expelled from Cascabel. Petal was to stay at Linda's and attend therapy every day with Dr Raf. After a few weeks, Dr Raf would assess Petal and report back. Petal could use her credit card up to a pre-set limit, and Linda would be helped with Petal's expenses. One false step and Petal would be cut off completely.

I have to do something, Petal thought miserably as she leaned back against a dumpster, lighting a second cigarette from the butt of the first. I can't go on like this, with Gold – *Dad* – just pulling the strings and telling me what to do. I've got to get some more independence.

'Jesus Christ!' exclaimed a high-pitched, whiny male voice as the back door of the Lizard Room banged open. 'What the *hell* was that?'

'Zak—' a woman protested.

'No, Michelle, come *on*. You *know* what a steaming pile of shit that was!' said the man. 'You can't put lipstick on a pig, girl. No one wants to see that ageing whore rubbing her lipoed flesh over a bunch of young man-meat.'

Petal realized with dawning horror that she knew who these two people were, had been introduced to them by Linda: Michelle Lee-Glazer was the executive producer of *Cougar Hunt*, the person Linda was hoping would commission a reality series featuring her and Petal. And Zak No Last Name was the main TV writer for – *fuck* – *Entertainment Weekly*, one of the biggest and most influential magazines in the US.

Petal slid back around the dumpster so they wouldn't spot her.

'We think the show'll find its audience,' Michelle said weakly.

'Not on VH1 it won't! *What* were you thinking?' Zak said dismissively. 'Maybe on Lifetime – but now they're looking for the gays, and believe me, we do *not* want to see old lady snatch.'

'Zak!' Michelle started giggling.

'That woman just isn't interesting,' Zak sniffed. 'She comes across as some over-the-hill slut living off her past glories. This show is going to tank. I'd get out from under as soon as I could, if I were you. Find some flunky to pin the blame on, and make the rest of the episodes web-only.'

There was a hiss as Michelle sucked the breath in through her teeth. Petal could hear someone rubbing their heel into the concrete of the parking lot, crushing out their cigarette.

'I should get back there,' Michelle said, sounding deflated.

'Girl, I haven't told you anything you didn't already know,' Zak said as they re-entered the club.

Oh shit, Petal thought. *Mum's been pinning her entire hopes on this.*

With a sinking heart, she walked back inside, through the darkened club to the big main room where *Cougar Hunt* was being projected on a backdrop in front of the stage. It was in its last minutes, as Linda rejected the first candidate, known only by his nickname Jackass. Jackass raged, threw a stool at another contestant and then mooned the camera before storming out of the mansion in which the show was set.

But many of the invitees weren't even watching the show; they were hitting the bar, knocking back the free drinks, mocking it to their friends. Linda, at the front, was surrounded by a small group of cougar friends who'd made appearances on the show, D-list ageing celebrity women with leathery skin, fake boobs and faker smiles. As the lights came up, they all whooped and applauded.

'Go, Linda!' yelled one of them, who had her hair in bunches and breasts so high they were practically on a level with her chin. 'Go, cougars!'

'Whee!' Linda chorused, on her third margarita already. 'Baby, we're gonna be stars!'

Linda looked round for Bobby, but he was standing with a group of his co-stars, all of them oiled up in tight tank tops from which their arms burst like gigantic swollen fruit. He saw Linda calling for him, and raised his hand, but didn't go over to embrace her.

He knows the show's in the toilet, Petal thought. Bobby's smarter than Mum. Fuck, everyone's smarter than Mum. She and her friends are the only people here who don't know that *Cougar Hunt*'s a disaster.

'*Cougar Hunt*!' screeched Linda and her fellow cougars, clinking glasses above their heads in a toast. '*Cougar Hunt*!'

Petal glanced over at Michelle Lee-Glazer, who was staring at the credits as they rolled up against a black background. A round of tepid applause rang out, stopping almost as soon as it had started. And as Michelle's name came up at the end, alone on the screen as Executive Producer, Petal clearly saw her wince.

Oh God, Petal thought. This is really, really bad.

Skye

*T*he Grafton was a dream come true. Skye loved the hotel with total passion. Set on a busy stretch of Sunset Boulevard, it dropped away steeply down the hill behind it to the salt-water swimming pool three storeys below. The pool was surrounded by white-upholstered loungers, a lime-green towel rolled up on each one, awaiting an occupant. Behind it was a tall orange-painted water feature, flowing into a small fountain around which the staff arranged decorative candles every evening. It was flanked by tall cypresses and palm trees; by day it was a suntrap, and by night it was dreamy with blue and fuchsia uplighters, turning the pool area into the sexiest of bars, trip-hop and trance playing enticingly on hidden speakers, the clink of cocktail glasses and the play of water in the fountain a lullaby that rocked Skye to sleep every night, because her room had a garden door that opened directly onto a sitting area by the pool.

She had spent the last week sunbathing, eating lunch on the little terrace overlooking the pool – they did a chopped salad to which she had become addicted – working out in the gym, dining in the restaurant, drinking in the hotel bar, relishing the luxury of putting everything on the *National Investigator*'s bill. Margaritas by the pool, endless gossip magazines to read: for the first few days, Skye had been in such heaven that the days and night slid into each other as easily as she floated in the salt water of the pool.

In the last twenty-four hours, however, she had been getting restless. The *Investigator* had run the story of her encounters with Joe in Cascabel, complete with a couple of glamour photographs of her that they had shot by the Grafton's pool; it had come out the day before, and she had been hoping – stupidly, she supposed – that Joe would see it, miss her, and track her down.

I'm an idiot, she thought sadly, stretching out on her bed and admiring her freshly painted toenails. I'm the last person he'd call. He knows now I betrayed him.

Her cellphone rang, and – *again, like an idiot* – she snatched it up. Joe had tons of people working for him, people who could easily track down someone's cellphone number.

But, of course, it wasn't Joe. It was Jada, who had just seen the *Investigator* and was bubbling with excitement.

'You look *fantastic*, too,' she said excitedly. 'Your body's *sick* in those photos. You should totally get a publicist.'

'With what money?' Skye sighed. 'I never got that big bonus from the *Investigator* because they didn't break the story.'

'They still paid you, didn't they?' Jada said.

'Yeah, but most of it went to paying off my credit card,' Skye admitted. 'And the rent I sent you.'

'Hell, girl,' Jada said. 'You gotta get your ass out there and start working!'

'Why don't you come visit?' Skye suggested. 'You could stay in my room, we could eat here and charge it all to the *Investigator*.'

As soon as Skye said it, she was charged up with excitement. *Having Jada here – why didn't I think of that straight away? It would be so cool – we could hang out, hit some clubs together—*

'Girl! Stop!' Jada wailed. 'You're killing me! I just can't swing it – my cards are maxed out. I gotta work like a demon the rest of the month just to make the minimum payment . . .'

'How do we *spend* so much?' Skye asked hopelessly. 'When we think of how much we make in a night . . .'

'Blow and shopping, baby. Blow and shopping,' Jada said.

'I'm outta that loop now,' Skye said firmly. 'That's one thing rehab was good for.'

'Ooh, I Googled your hotel,' Jada said. 'You got one of those rooms with the orange walls and the zebra-print bedspread? They're *gorge*.'

'Yeah,' Skye said, looking round her complacently at the afternoon sunshine pouring through the white-louvred blinds, the blue of the pool beyond. 'And the free toiletries are amazing. Blood-orange scented.'

'Hey, I just had an idea,' Jada said. 'Go on some auditions while you're there!'

'I never took an acting class in my life . . .'

'So what? I bet Pamela Anderson never took a class either!' Jada said encouragingly.

'You're right,' Skye said slowly. 'You're absolutely right. I'm calling Kevin right now.'

Well, I really didn't need an acting class for this, Skye thought ruefully a couple of days later, staring down at the two-page script on her lap.

Kevin had been more than happy to fix Skye up with an agent, and the agent had been more than happy to send Skye on a series of auditions. Skye was currently sitting in the waiting room of her fourth appointment of that day, reading over the brief lines that the character she was auditioning for – Girl In Bar – would be called upon to say.

GIRL IN BAR (blonde, spilling out of a too-tight top, halfway
    to drunk): Hey, cutie! My name's Princess.
NICK: Princess, huh?
GIRL IN BAR: Yeah! What's yours?
NICK: King, baby. I'm the king.

GIRL IN BAR: (giggles) Wow! Cool!

STRIDER's men start firing into the bar. NICK pushes GIRL to
the ground while returning fire.

NICK: It's bedtime, Princess.

Skye sighed. Today she'd read for Girl on Beach, Cheerleader #3,
and Lindsay (ironically, the character with the actual name had
had the least to do). It wasn't that the parts were small; she could-
n't exactly expect to walk into leading-lady status with no past
credits to her name. It was that every single casting agent had
made it very clear exactly why they had agreed to see her – and
spent more time discussing her and Joe's sex scene, which had
gone viral on the net by now, than they had auditioning her. Two
had leered; the third one had told her she'd get the part if she gave
him a blow job.

It's nothing I didn't get in the Midnight Lounge every damn
night, Skye thought. But I wanted to leave that behind me. This is
just more of the same. And the money's worse.

Skye had already spent tons on cabs getting to all these appointments. With nothing to show for it. She might have paid off her
cards, but she was starting to rack up their balances again.

A girl came out of the office Skye was waiting to enter, an
opaque glass door with 'Julie Tanaka' etched across it. The girl was
ridiculously stunning, with a sleek dark ponytail and exotic features.

'Skye Simmons?' she said. 'Julie will see you now.'

'Thanks,' Skye said, rising from her seat.

Julie Tanaka had a mass of orange curls pulled back behind her
head, a cheerful smile, and a curvy figure clad in a grey business suit
that didn't do much for it. She came out from behind her desk to
greet Skye, taking Skye's hands in both of hers.

'Skye! Sit!' she said, gesturing to a couple of suede armchairs in
the corner of the office, a glass cube between them. 'How nice to
meet you! You're even prettier in the flesh. So! Tell me about yourself!'

There's no point bullshitting. After that sex tape, and all the press, everyone knows who I am and what I've done.

Skye launched into a brief summary of her life to date, trying to be as entertaining as possible. She sensed quickly that Julie Tanaka wasn't really listening to her words, but that was OK; why should she be interested in what Skye had to say? The words weren't important. She was checking out Skye's voice, how expressive her face was as she talked, her body language.

'And then you got to Hollywood and met Joe,' Julie said, when Skye paused for breath. 'And it looked like you had a lot of fun together!'

Skye nodded awkwardly. Everyone's seen the damn video clip by now, she thought wearily. They know it's there, I know it's there – why do they have to keep mentioning it?

'So, Skye,' Julie continued, 'I think you'd be perfect for this role. I'd love to send you to meet the director and get his OK.'

Skye sat bolt upright with surprise. After her previous encounters that day, she had given up any idea that she might be taken remotely seriously as an actress.

'That's great!' she stammered, feeling light as a feather with elation. 'But, uh, don't you want to hear me read the lines?'

'We'll put you in front of a camera when you meet the director,' Julie said, smiling. 'I'll be there too.'

'Shall I take them away and work on them?' Skye asked, flapping the two meagre sheets of paper.

'Sure! That'd be great!' Julie leaned forward. 'And tell me, do you like Japanese food?'

'I love sushi,' Skye said promptly, not sure where this was going, but happy to follow someone who'd just given her a callback.

'Great! Maybe you'd like to join me for an early dinner, and we can talk more? I'm booked solid with appointments today, but I've got a really good instinct about you and I'd love to grab some dinner.'

'Thank you,' Skye said.

'And I'll see if my husband can make it too,' Julie added.

She nodded over at a large framed photograph on the desk,

presumably of Mr Tanaka. He was standing on a beach, wearing a black wetsuit, holding a surfboard, smiling at the camera, the sun in his eyes.

Julie smiled proudly. 'He works out a lot. He's in really good shape.' She looked meaningfully at Skye. 'He's seen your video too, and he can't wait to meet you.'

Skye's stomach began to sink.

'We're very open as a couple,' Julie continued, leaning forward and touching Skye's knee. 'Seeing him happy makes me happy, if you know what I mean.'

'Um, I just remembered I'm busy this evening,' Skye said, pushing her chair back a little, and standing up. 'I have to see someone from the *Investigator*. Sorry about that.'

'Oh, no problem!' Julie's smile didn't fade, her voice remained just as cheerful. 'We'll take a raincheck.'

She stood up too, ushering Skye to the door.

'I tell you what,' she said, as she opened it. 'You get in touch when you're free for dinner, and then we'll talk about more casting opportunities, OK?'

'Sure,' Skye said, trying to handle this as smoothly as Julie was.

At least I can show this bitch I'm a good actress, Skye thought wryly as she left the room. The receptionist glanced over at her, and Skye read something in her expression; it was too fleeting a moment for Skye to decode all of it, but she sensed that the receptionist was perfectly aware of how Julie ran her particular brand of casting couch, and was assessing Skye to see if she'd taken up Julie's dinner invitation.

I wonder what she had to do to get her job? Skye wondered, as she slung her knockoff Louis Vuitton bag over her shoulder and headed out of the office. Did she have to make Mr Tanaka happy while Mrs Tanaka watched?

Waiting for the lift, she sighed, a long deep sigh that seemed to be pulled up right out of the soles of her feet. *This is how it's going to be, isn't it? Now everyone's seen that damn video clip, they're going to want a piece of me in return for any opportunity I get.*

Skye couldn't blame anyone for making assumptions about her. Plenty of actresses got their breaks just this way, by making nice with some producer or director or casting agent. But one thing the therapy sessions in rehab had done for her, much to her own surprise, was give her a sense of self-worth she hadn't even realized she was lacking.

Just because I had sex with Joe doesn't mean that I'll screw a casting agent's husband just to get a damn callback so the director can make a pass at me. Whatever anyone else thinks, I had sex with Joe because I wanted to. Because I really, really wanted to. And it was wonderful.

God. Joe.

Skye heaved another deep sigh.

I can't stop thinking about him. I can't stop missing him. And I bet, since he left rehab, he hasn't given me a thought.

I'm the biggest fucking idiot in the world.

Amber

'Joe Jeffreys! *Bože môj* – my God!'

Slava pressed her hands together, the freshly painted red nails gleaming.

'Joe Jeffreys, ringing you!' she chanted like an incantation. '*Bože môj*, we did well to come to Hollywood!'

'We didn't exactly choose to come, *Matka*,' Amber pointed out drily, picking up the jar of Lancôme Bienfait sunscreen and patting some more on her face. They were sitting outside by the pool, and though they were sheltered by a big white canvas umbrella, Amber was, like most models, very careful about sun damage to her skin.

Slava waved this objection away with a flick of her fingers. 'We should come to Hollywood many years before,' she said. '*Joe Jeffreys!* Forget Tony! Joe Jeffreys is much better!'

'Poor Tony,' Amber commented, putting on her sunglasses and lying back in her chair. 'After all he's done for you.'

Slava ignored this, as she ignored everything she didn't want to respond to.

'You say Joe Jeffreys will marry this woman who goes with other women?' she asked. 'So he will need sex. Men need sex.'

Women need it too, just as much, Amber thought wistfully, an instant image of herself and Dr Raf twined together flashing into her

brain, flooding her body with a warmth much stronger than the LA
sun.

'He sees you at the restaurant, and he rings you!' Slava went on.

'His assistant rang me,' Amber corrected.

Slava made a loud tutting noise.

'You make things difficult,' she said crossly. 'After you go to that
place, that hospital—'

'Rehab.'

'You come out of there and you are different. Difficult,' Slava
complained. 'You talk back to me. I don't like this. This is not how
good Slovakian daughter behaves.'

Before her overdose, before rehab, this would have wounded
Amber to the quick. But now, it was strangely easy to resist. Amber
didn't argue; she simply didn't respond. Instead, she slid a cigarette
out of the packet on the table and lit it. Slava darted a look sideways
at her, assessing the situation, and wisely decided not to push her
complaints any further.

'So! His assistant rings you!' she said, reaching for the pack of
cigarettes herself. 'And what does the assistant say?'

'Joe wants to see me,' Amber said, knowing how excited this
would make her mother. 'And he set up an audition for me.
Tomorrow morning.'

Slava's eyes nearly popped out of her head in shock.

'An audition?' She gripped the arms of her chair, using them to
turn to face her daughter fully. 'Like, for a film?'

Amber nodded. 'He thinks I'm a natural.'

With trembling hands, Slava reached out to the table, grabbed
the yellow plastic vial of Vicodin, shook out a pill with the ease of
long practice, and tossed it to the back of her throat, following it
down with a swig of the clear liquid in her glass, which Amber had
deliberately not sniffed, for fear of what it might contain.

'For a *film!*' she practically sang in delight. 'Joe Jeffreys will put
you in a film!' She clapped her hands, her heavy rings clinking
together. '*Láska!* This is better than anything!'

'*Matka,*' Amber said so firmly that her mother looked at her warily. 'I am *not* going to have sex with Joe Jeffreys. I'm not even going to *date* him.'

'But—' Slava's face froze.

'He's a really nice guy,' Amber said, 'and I like him a lot. And if he wants to help me get a part in a film, that's fine. I have to make some money somehow, and I don't mind trying to act. But I'm sure that Joe won't expect me to have sex with him in return for helping me. He's not that kind of man.'

'They're all that kind of man,' Slava muttered.

'No, *Matka*, they're not!' Amber stood up angrily. 'There *are* nice men out there – I'm just sorry you never met any!' She shook her head, as if getting rid of a cloud of flies around her. 'I've got my therapy in a couple of hours. I should go and get ready. And on the way back, I'm going to stop at that deli on Laurel Canyon and buy some food, and try to cook us dinner.'

Slava's eyebrows shot up to the white roots of her hair as Amber turned to go inside the house.

When *Matka* realizes I'm not going to have sex with Tony either, she's going to throw a fit, she thought, going upstairs to her bedroom to change out of her swimsuit. But I won't. I won't do anything any more that I genuinely don't want to do. That's the rule I made for myself in rehab, and I'm sticking to it.

And I can't imagine having sex with anyone but Dr Raf. Ever again.

The audition Joe Jeffreys – or, to be more realistic, one of his swarm of managers or assistants – had set up for Amber was on a studio lot. Despite the amount of shoots she'd done for the most prestigious clients in the world, she couldn't help but be excited as the car turned into the main entrance to Paramount, the security guards leaning down to check her ID against a list, then waving her through. Low, white-painted buildings stretched away as far as the eye could see, flanked with palm trees. Crawling along, the car passed what looked like the New York street set for *Friends*, recognizably Manhattan but much cleaner and newer-looking than the real thing. Beyond it Amber could see the soundstages; one had its main doors open, and, craning her neck to look, she saw it was as big as an aircraft hangar, bright floodlights trained on a stage inside, the rest of the interior pitch-black by comparison.

People are shooting a film, or a TV series, or a sitcom there right now, she thought. And I might be part of that soon.

It was a natural route, model to actress, though not many succeeded: for every Charlize Theron and Cameron Diaz, there were many more who had never jumped the first hurdle, or – like Cindy Crawford or Elle Macpherson – had tried and then conceded defeat. Amber had never considered it herself. But then, she'd been focusing all her energies on just making it through the day, ensuring she had enough drugs to keep her medicated. Now that she was clean, she could feel energies rising up in her, longing to find an outlet.

The driver had located their destination, the offices of Clearwater Productions, a little cluster of white bungalows with louvered window shutters, surrounded by carefully landscaped banks of flowering cactuses and palms. It looked pretty enough to be a home, rather than one of the many offices of the production companies that had development deals with Paramount and worked out of their enormous studio space.

Amber alighted from the car and was nearly run down by two golf carts buzzing past. This was the way high-ranking people who worked in the studios covered the distances between soundstages and offices, zipping past the peons who had to walk. Amber did a double take when she realized that the driver of the second one was Matthew McConaughey, looking even more gorgeous in real life than he did on screen, tanned and golden. Even with his sunglasses on, he was instantly recognizable. And, clocking Amber's beauty, he whistled as he went past, tipping the bill of his baseball cap to her in appreciation.

And that looked like the guy from *Twilight* next to him, in the check shirt, Amber thought as she crossed the street, looking out warily for more fast-moving golf carts driven by screen gods.

She couldn't help smiling. It was lovely to be a pretty girl in the Hollywood sunshine, walking across the Paramount studio lot, movie stars whistling at you as they buzzed by. It was great to be in the moment, to appreciate life's pleasures as they came along, without being so fuzzy and distracted by tranquillizers that it was all you could do just to put one foot in front of the other. And it was downright wonderful to be free of the endless worry all addicts had: *is it time for my next fix? Have I had enough, or do I need one more pill to get me through? And am I running out – do I need to ring the doctor now for a new prescription or can it wait till tomorrow?*

She pushed open the door of Clearwater Productions, the clammy chill of air-conditioning hitting her as soon as she stepped inside.

I hope I look OK, she thought, but she could tell by the receptionist's reaction to her that she looked more than OK. There was a shift in manner as the young man caught sight of her, a deferential homage to her appearance in his instant offer of green tea or mineral water while she waited. Amber wasn't vain; but she knew that her beauty was her main currency, and she needed to assess constantly how its value was holding up.

Wrapping her feather-light Armani silk cardigan around her to ward off the cold blast of air-conditioning, she stepped through into the waiting room he had indicated. And then she stopped dead, amazed at how happy she was to see the girl sitting on the white leather sofa, leafing through a copy of *W*, wearing a tight white T-shirt and khaki miniskirt that showed off every curve of her body.

'Skye!' she exclaimed.

Skye looked up, her blue eyes widening at the sight of Amber.

'Hey!' she said, her reaction not as instantly positive as the other girl's; there was pleasure in it, but also wariness. Skye was clearly remembering the terms they had parted on at Cascabel.

Amber took a deep breath, processing her own feelings. Skye was really nice to me, she remembered. She looked after me when I first came into Cascabel, when I was in withdrawal and feeling awful.

And she lashed out because was jealous – Joe was mooning after me while he was having sex with her. I can't blame her for that.

'Let's start again,' Amber heard herself say, crossing the room to Skye. 'Friends?'

Skye dropped the magazine, jumped up and hugged Amber, her head barely coming up to the taller girl's shoulder.

'I'm so sorry!' she said, pulling back to look up at Amber. 'I should never, ever have said it – it was in confidence – there's no excuse—'

'Forgiven and forgotten,' Amber said, as the receptionist came in with her green tea. 'Thanks,' she said, flashing him a smile that clearly dazzled him.

'Honestly,' Skye said, rolling her eyes. 'I thought *I* was good at getting guys to wait on me until I met you.'

She plopped back down on the sofa, curling her slender brown legs underneath her.

'So! What's up?' she asked, leaning forward as Amber took a seat in the armchair across from her. 'What's been happening with you? Wait!' Her pretty pink mouth opened in a perfect O. 'What the hell am I *saying* – what are you doing here? Did they, like, let you out for the day or something?'

'I left Cascabel early,' Amber admitted. 'I'm doing day therapy now.'

'You're kidding!' Skye's blonde curls tumbled over her face as she leaned even further forward, her blue eyes focused on Amber's face. 'What happened? Ohmigod, it wasn't anything to do with me and Joe, was it?'

I can't tell her anything about me and Dr Raf, Amber decided in a split second. I so wish I could – she's the closest thing I have to a friend. But she let me down before when I told her a secret. And it's not just my secret to share. Dr Raf could lose his licence.

'I had some clashes with Dr Lucy,' she said, amazed at her own capacity for lying – *well, not exactly lying, just taking the truth and twisting it a bit.* 'And there was an awful lot of fuss after those stories in the press about you and Joe. Dr Raf had a lot of emergency meetings, and he asked Dr Lucy to take private sessions with me, and we really didn't get on,' she continued, inspired now by her powers of invention. 'So I thought I'd leave and do day therapy instead. It's all working out well. My new therapist is great, she really is.'

'Jeez, it *is* all my fault, sort of!' Skye said, her hands rising to her face. 'I'm so sorry, Amber! The *idea* that you got stuck with that bitch because of me! She always hated you!'

Amber couldn't help smiling. 'She wasn't my biggest fan.'

'Are you *kidding*? She couldn't bear the way Dr Raf looked at you! She was always gunning for you!'

Amber couldn't help blushing at this.

'I'm amazed Dr Raf put you with her,' Skye said, shaking her head. 'Men are such idiots. Oh!' Another question occurred to her. 'What about Petal? They didn't let her stay, did they? That would really piss me off.'

'No,' Amber said. 'They kicked her out the day you two left.'

'Good.' Skye sagged back on the sofa. 'If that little bitch got to stay, I'd've been furious.'

'She needed help,' Amber pointed out, sipping some tea. 'She was really messed up. All that dad stuff.'

'OK,' Skye said militantly, 'but being messed up didn't stop her spying on me when I was having sex, did it? And recording it! Who *does* that?'

'You,' Amber said promptly.

Skye froze in shock, momentarily stunned. Oh no, Amber thought in panic: did I just go too far?

And then Skye's face cracked up and she burst out laughing. 'You got me!' she admitted through her giggles. 'Oh God, I can't smudge my makeup—' She patted gingerly round her eyes.

'But you know something?' she went on, calming down. 'Sure, I recorded the damn thing. But I was never, ever going to sell it. I mean, not after I got to know Joe.'

'Really?' Amber was taken aback.

'Nuh-uh.' Skye shook her head vehemently, her blonde curls dancing. 'Crazy, right? I should've just got out of there the day after we did it – when I had it on tape – and taken it straight to the *Investigator*. They promised me this huge bonus if I did. There was a contract and everything.' She sighed. 'Only I had to go and fall for Joe. What a moron. As if a huge movie star like him would give a shit about me when we got out of Cascabel.'

'You mean,' Amber said, her brow creasing, 'that if Petal hadn't videoed you on her phone—'

'I'd have stayed put and hoped Joe would want to go on seeing me after rehab,' Skye sighed. 'We had such an amazing connection. You know when that happens?' Her blue eyes went dreamy. 'When you just touch someone and all these sparks go off? But not just sex – even though you totally don't get that feeling with many people. It's when you just want to be near them all the time. When you feel you can say anything, and they'll get you. When you're just so relaxed with each other, straight away. It's like magic. And I know it sounds totally lame to say I thought I had that with *Joe Jeffreys* – like I've got a stupid crush on a movie star – but I really did. And I thought he felt something too.'

She swallowed hard. 'So of course,' she said sadly, 'I blew it. I'd never have taken that tape to the *Investigator* if Joe had tried to give me his number, or take mine, while we were getting kicked out. If he'd shown me the slightest sign that he wanted to keep in touch, I'd've hung on and waited and waited for him to call.' She sighed again. 'But he didn't.'

'I'm really sorry,' Amber said hopelessly.

'And now here I am, doing the rounds of auditions,' Skye said, 'and because everyone's seen the video – which the *Investigator* didn't even pay me that much for – the casting directors and producers I'm seeing are making it very clear that unless I play nice with them, they won't even give me a callback.'

'Oh, *Skye* . . .' Amber knew very well what it was like to have people expect sexual favours in return for jobs. She reached out and squeezed Skye's hand in sympathy.

'And I won't,' Skye said, squeezing Amber's hand back. 'I just won't do that any more.'

She smiled feebly at Amber. 'I suppose rehab did help me after all. Who'd've thought it?'

'You're doing the right thing,' Amber said quietly.

'Yeah? I hope so. But guess what? My agent rang me this morning. I got offered a *Hustler* shoot. A hundred grand. Full-frontal.'

'You can't do it,' Amber said immediately.

Skye ducked her head. 'I did ask if I could only do topless,' she said, 'but they said full-frontal or nothing.'

'Skye, you *can't*,' Amber said very seriously. 'Once those photos are out there, you can never take them back.'

'I know,' Skye mumbled. 'But it's a ton of money . . .'

'*Skye—*'

'Skye Simmons? Jeff can see you now,' announced the receptionist, appearing in the doorway of the waiting room.

'Wish me luck!' Skye said brightly, jumping up.

'Good luck,' Amber said so sincerely that Skye could hear it in her voice. Skye whisked out of the waiting room, holding a hand behind her back so that Amber could see her fingers, tightly crossed.

Amber picked up the copy of *W* and started flicking through it, but she barely saw the images in front of her.

I don't want Skye to do a *Hustler* shoot, she was thinking. And I had no idea that Skye was serious about Joe. Not like that. She talked about him the way I'd talk about Dr Raf. So I know she really means it.

Amber was still absorbed in her thoughts fifteen minutes later, when Skye bounced back through the door, eyes sparkling, curls bouncing on her shoulders; even her breasts looked perkier with her excitement.

'He liked me!' she announced ecstatically. 'He wants me to wait! And he saw two girls before me – before you got here – and he didn't ask either one of them to wait, so I know that's good!' She sank onto the leather sofa. 'And I read really well! It's, you know, the gorgeous girlfriend part. She's called Maia. I think I nailed it.' She was beaming, her enthusiasm infectious.

'I'm really happy for you,' Amber said.

'God, I shouldn't be saying this – you're going up for it too – sorry, I didn't mean to boast!' Skye said, pulling a repentant face. 'It's just the first time someone's given me a chance without asking to stick their hand up my skirt in return . . .'

'Amber Peters?' the receptionist said from the doorway.

Amber stood up, but before she could follow him, another man appeared behind him.

'Amber!' he said jovially. He was big and wide, with a suspiciously even hairline for a fifty-year-old man – hairplugs, Amber thought – wearing a baggy Lakers T-shirt over jeans. Though his voice was cheerful, and he was smiling, Amber could tell immediately from the sharpness of his gaze that he was sizing her up in an instant. 'I'm Jeff Ringquist. You're Joe's friend, right?'

Oh, no.

Amber didn't need to glance to the side to know that Skye's entire body had stiffened in shock.

'Well, I see why he sent you along!' Jeff Ringquist said, even more jovial; she had passed the first assessment. 'What's that you got there, honey?'

'My modelling portfolio,' Amber said, looking down at the big leather binder under her arm. Even in her rush to get to LA, Slava could never have forgotten to pack this, the most visible symbol of her daughter's success. 'I didn't know if I should bring it along . . .'

'Sure! Hey, give it here!' Jeff said enthusiastically, holding out a hand the size of a plate, watching Amber's walk as she crossed the waiting room, nodding approvingly at the grace with which she moved. He flicked through the pages, each a huge plastic window into which Slava had slid a blowup of one of Amber's ads or editorials.

'*Nice*,' he said, nodding as he turned the pages. '*Very* nice. You still in the same shape as this?' He stabbed a bikini picture with his sausage-like index finger. 'You look it,' he added, glancing at her.

'My weight's very stable,' Amber said, more and more uncomfortable now at Skye's presence, feeling as if she'd betrayed Skye with this whole setup.

'Perfect!' Jeff Ringquist closed the portfolio with a loud snap. 'You got the look, you got a nice voice, let's see where this takes us, OK? Come in my office. I got a DVD set up. Let's run some lines.' He cast a glance over at Skye, still sitting on the sofa. 'Honey, you don't need to wait around any more,' he said. 'I think I got my Maia right here. But leave your details with Jonathan, OK? Nice meeting you.'

He was already moving out of the room, not bothering to look back, and Amber started to follow him; there was nothing else to do. She turned her head and met Skye's gaze. If Skye could have killed her with that look, she would have done. Her blue eyes were cold as ice, narrowed into slits of hate.

'I can't believe you,' she mouthed at Amber.

'I'm sorry!' Amber mouthed back helplessly.

Skye jumped off the sofa, grabbing her bag. On her high wedge heels, she stalked to the door, shoving past Amber in the corridor.

'Backstabber!' she hissed at Amber as their paths crossed, just loud enough for Amber to hear.

Amber stared miserably after her.

Every time the two of us make friends, we mess it up, she thought sadly. And I don't blame Skye at all. I'd be furious if I were in her shoes. Maybe we're just destined to be enemies . . .

Petal

Linda was sobbing so loudly that Petal could hear her well before she walked into her bedroom. Petal paused in the doorway, wincing at the sight of her mother. Most of Linda's makeup had smeared onto the pillowcases, and what was left on her face was a disaster; her mascara had worked its way into the bags beneath her eyes, and her eyeliner was halfway down her cheeks.

'Oh, it's just you,' she said disconsolately, flopping back down again on seeing Petal.

'That's nice, Mum,' Petal said drily. 'Who were you expecting? Robert Pattinson, dropping in to say hi and would you like a bite on the neck?'

'*Bobby!*' wailed Linda into the pillows, thumping the mattress with both her fists. 'I want Bobby to come back!'

'Mum . . .' Petal sat down on the side of the bed. 'Bobby isn't coming back,' she said, as gently as she could. 'He packed up everything when he went.'

Bobby hadn't walked out the night the *Cougar Hunt* pilot had been shown at the Lizard Room. He'd hedged his bets, waiting a few days, until the pilot aired on VH1; when the reviews, the next day, were universally hostile, the ratings disastrous, he'd cut his losses and left.

It had been an awful scene. Petal had hidden in the pool house, but she hadn't been able to avoid seeing parts of it. Linda had beseeched Bobby not to go, grabbed his stuff so he couldn't take it, then started to throw things in the pool when it was clear she couldn't change his mind.

'I thought he loved me!' she wept pathetically now.

'Mum, you met on a *reality show*,' Petal said, beginning to lose patience.

'It could happen!' Linda raised her head again, staring at her daughter, her face so grotesquely smeared with makeup now that it was all Petal could do not to flinch back. 'Two of the couples who met on *The Bachelor* got married! At least two! And some on *The Bachelorette* as well!'

'Yeah, but aren't those programmes people go on to find a serious relationship?' Petal said. 'I mean, your show was called *Cougar Hunt*.'

Linda scrabbled her way to the headboard, pulling herself up and sitting against it, an armful of pillows clutched in her lap for comfort, staring with hostility at her daughter.

'This is *your* fault,' she said accusingly.

'What?' Petal was genuinely amazed.

'This is all your fault! You brought me bad luck! Everything was going fine before you came along! *Better* than fine! I had a TV show, a hunky boyfriend – and look at me now!'

'I'd rather not,' Petal muttered.

'*What* did you say?' Linda yelled.

'Mum –' Petal swallowed – 'you look a total mess. Can we get you into the bathroom, wash your face, at least—'

'I'm never getting out of bed again! You can't make me!' Linda wept, switching with terrifying speed from Outraged Parent to Sobbing Child.

'Mum,' Petal said with increasing desperation, 'we've got an appointment with that Michelle woman from VH1 this afternoon, about doing a reality show together. You know, a mother and daughter show? Going out in LA, getting to know each other?'

Ugh, it turns my stomach just to say that rubbish, let alone imagine actually doing it. But I have to get Mum out of bed somehow, and God knows, we could do with the money . . .

'Fuck VH1!' Linda screamed, hurling one of the pillows at the closest mirrored wardrobe door, which rattled ominously on impact. 'Fuck VH1, fuck Michelle, and fuck you! I'm not going *anywhere*!'

She collapsed in a heap again, wailing so loudly that Petal began to get a tension headache.

Before rehab I'd have gone into the bathroom to see if she had any pills I could give her to calm down, Petal reflected as she stood up. *But after seeing the state Amber was in, I'm shit-scared of anti-depressants now . . .*

'I'll make you a cup of tea,' she said rather hopelessly, leaving the bedroom. Even shutting the door behind her didn't do much to block out the sound of Linda's moans of grief.

Tea, however, was not on the agenda, or not in the form Petal had meant – a proper cup of British tea, strong enough, hopefully, to help Linda pull herself together. They were out of milk, and since Petal couldn't drive, there was no way for her to get more; the shops were literally miles away, and there was no public transport anywhere close by. She'd heard that LA cops arrested you if they saw you out walking, and while she didn't quite believe that, she wasn't up for a long sweaty trek in the blazing sunshine, especially as she had only the roughest idea where the closest strip mall was.

The kitchen was pretty much a disaster area. Linda seemed to live off cornflakes – eaten straight out of the packet – Pirate's Booty Veggie Puffs, and frozen edamame. In the glory days with Bobby, there had been fruit shakes and fat-free Frappuccinos, which at least balanced the frozen margaritas they'd whizzed up in the blender every afternoon; but now the food had pretty much run out, together with Linda's José Cuervo Margarita Mix, and Petal was getting desperate.

Sitting down on one of the kitchen stools, Petal pulled her mobile out of her pocket and rang her father's private line.

I can't believe I'm doing this, she thought as the phone began to ring. I can't believe I'm actually ringing Gold – my dad – for help.

But it's about time he started acting like a proper father. She cracked a small, wry smile. *Hey, thank you for the insight, Dr Raf.*

'Yes?' snapped a woman's voice, picking up the phone. 'Who is this?'

Lovely manners.

'Hi, Jinhee,' she said politely. 'It's Petal. How are you? Can I speak to my dad, please?'

There was a moment of silence as Jinhee absorbed Petal's words.

'*Gold,*' she said pointedly, 'is getting dressed to go out for the evening.'

'Well, I need to speak to him,' Petal said. 'It's an emergency.'

'*Really?*' Jinhee sneered. 'Have you been arrested? Or sold some more photos to the tabloids?'

Petal took a deep breath. 'Actually, no,' she said, managing to keep her voice reasonably level. 'It's a problem with my mum. I need to talk to my dad about it.'

Jinhee was one of those women who preferred to think that her man's life had begun the moment she met him; she disliked Petal on principle, as a living reminder that Gold had been married before, and made a policy of pretending that Linda did not exist. So there was a longer pause as Jinhee registered Petal's reference to her mother.

What can I do? Petal thought crossly. If you didn't want me ever to talk about my mum, you shouldn't have sent me out to LA and put her down as my emergency contact, should you? I mean, it wasn't my dad who organized all that, was it?

'I really don't want to disturb him for something trivial,' Jinhee finally said icily.

'This isn't trivial!' Petal's voice rose, despite her best efforts. 'It's an *emergency*, my mum's having a *meltdown*, and I need to talk to *my dad!*'

The line went dead. For a moment, Petal thought that Jinhee had cut her off, and her blood started to boil; then she realized that there was no loud beeping that would mean that Jinhee had hung up on her.

Eventually, Gold's unmistakable tenor drawl said: 'Petal? What's all this about your mother? I have an awards ceremony to go to.'

'She's having a total meltdown,' Petal blurted out. 'Yelling and crying and throwing a fit. It's been going on for days now. I can't get her out of bed, and we need to go out – we need to go shopping—'

'Surely you have enough clothes, Petal,' Gold said wearily.

'No, Dad! For food! We need to get, you know, milk and stuff! There's nothing in the house!'

Petal held her breath, not quite believing that she'd called Gold 'Dad', totally unsure whether she'd get away with it.

Gold sighed heavily. 'Petal, I really can't be bothered with this kind of petty detail—'

'It's not petty!' Petal tried to calm down, but without much success. 'I'm starting to get really worried about her! Her show's doing really badly, but the producers still want us to go in to see them this afternoon, which is pretty much a miracle, considering, and she won't get out of bed, not even to wash! She's beginning to *pong*!'

'Petal . . .' Gold drew a long, deep breath. 'I've been studying kabbala recently, and there's a great deal of wisdom in those ancient texts, you know? There's a kabbala centre in Los Angeles, obviously. I think you might derive a lot of benefit from taking some of its courses.'

'Have you been hanging out with Madonna again? I thought she was dead to you after she took your solo on that charity single.'

'Kabbala says that there are no coincidences in life,' Gold continued as smoothly as if she hadn't interrupted him. 'And especially not when it comes to the family. They have this fascinating concept called *tikun*. I don't remember what the exact translation is, but it's basically about the fact that you're born into your family for a really good reason. Your soul chooses your parents specifically because they present a series of obstacles that you have to overcome in order to achieve your divine purpose in life.'

Petal was clutching the phone so hard her fingers were hurting. 'OK, whatever, but I don't get—'

'Petal, in simple language,' he said patronizingly, 'you chose Linda as your mother. Your soul chose her before you were born, because working through your relationship with her is exactly what you need to do in order to fully experience the change that you need to reach your full potential.'

'Oh, really?' Petal said sarcastically. 'My soul must have been on drugs that day.'

'*Petal,*' Gold sighed patiently, 'you have to *embrace* Linda. *Accept* her. Work through her problems with her. And then you'll look back and realize how crucial doing that work was to your future achievements.'

'You know what, *Dad*?' Petal snapped. 'That's total bollocks. I'm stranded out here in a town where I don't know anyone, with a mother who's losing her mind. Telling me to embrace her is bullshit. *I'm* not the one who chose her. *You* did. And you made a kid with her, which means that you have some sodding responsibility for this whole sodding mess!' She was panting with fury by now.

'It means "correction"!' Gold exclaimed, as if he hadn't just heard his daughter's last words. 'I just remembered – that's what *tikun* means! It's a necessary correction to steer you on the right course in life. And, Petal, I've always asked you to call me Gold – can you respect that, please?'

'If I *chose* you as my father, though fuck knows why I would have done,' Petal said through gritted teeth, 'I can call you Dad, or Pops, or anything the fuck I like. You're about as much help as a sieve in a rainstorm. *And*, let me tell you, that whole kabbala bullshit about choosing your parents is incredibly offensive to people whose parents, like, bullied them or abused them or something. You should think about that.'

She had actually managed to stem the flow of kabbala for a moment. That's told him, she thought triumphantly. And then the line clicked, and Jinhee came on.

'Petal? Your father's given me the phone. We have to leave the house in ten minutes. You'll just have to sort things out with Linda as best you can,' she said, every word dripping icy satisfaction.

'Fine!' Petal yelled. 'You can both fuck off! Good riddance to bad rubbish! I'll manage on my own from now on!'

It's really annoying that you can't slam down phones any more, she thought, furiously pressing the Off key. She had to wrestle the temptation to throw the phone across the room and watch it splinter into shiny Swarovski-studded plastic pieces. Instead, her chest heaving with anger, she dropped the phone on the counter, ducked her head and ran her hands through her hair.

I've got to handle this, she told herself. I told that cow I'd manage on my own. I can't go crawling back to her and Dad now.

Petal raised her head and caught sight of herself in the chipped mirror tiles behind the built-in bar. Her jaw was set, her eyes were determined, her lips were pressed together with resolve; with the primrose-yellow hair, the black-and-white striped Kate Moss from Top Shop dress she was wearing, and her signature black eyeliner standing out like a mask against her white skin, she looked like a killer punk from a Quentin Tarantino film.

Good. I definitely want to look scary right now.

She marched back down the corridor and threw open the door of Linda's room with such force that it bounced against the wall behind it.

'Mum?' she said, hands on hips. 'No more lying in bed feeling sorry for yourself. We've got a meeting in three hours, and you're driving us there. So you can either get out of bed and start getting ready by yourself, or I'm going to pull you out, drag you into the bathroom and hold you under the shower till you're clean.'

She glared so hard at her mother's recumbent body she was

amazed her eyes didn't burn through the duvet Linda had shrouded herself in.

'Your choice.'

'Petal! Linda!' Michelle Lee-Glazer waved at Petal and her mother from the patio of the Ivy just as enthusiastically as if Linda's show weren't tanking faster than the *Titanic*.

'Two-faced bitch,' Linda muttered. 'I heard they're thinking of dumping the show into a graveyard slot. Three a.m. on Saturday. Unbelievable.'

But Petal paid no attention to her mother. Growing up in Gold's household had accustomed her to the concept that executives might give you all the encouragement in the world on a project, big smiles wreathing their faces, then turn round and cut you off at the knees with a machete, still wearing the same huge smiles.

You don't bitch about it. That's how the music industry works, and that's how TV works too. You smile back and get what you can out of them while they're offering stuff.

So Petal waved back at Michelle cheerfully and nudged her mother hard in the ribs as they walked past the cameras from TMZ, waiting for a celebrity sighting, and up the short steps, weaving their way through the tables to the corner of the patio where Michelle was sitting. The Ivy was one of the classic star hangouts in LA; its cute raised patio, surrounded by a white ivy-covered picket fence, with its green-painted iron tables and matching chairs with red gingham cushions, looked country-style and laid-back, but in fact provided the perfect stage for movie actors and musicians to see and be seen. Couples who wanted their new relationship to be chronicled would meet at the Ivy, sit outside and play cosy-cuddle with each other, feeding each other food, giggling playfully for the benefit of the paparazzi.

Michelle was sitting with another woman, who she introduced as Jenny Bui. The two VH1 executives were very similar: both lean as whippets from daily crack-of-dawn spinning and boxercise classes, their hair pulled back from their faces, their makeup minimal, wearing tight-fitting black T-shirts and jeans, their teeth so perfect that Petal automatically ran her tongue over her own in embarrassment.

'So nice to meet you!' Jenny said, pumping hands with great enthusiasm. 'I met both of you at the launch party, of course, but there were so many people there, you probably don't remember. Petal! I love your hair! And your look! It's so *London*!'

'Oh, I *love* London,' Michelle sighed, as they all sat down. 'Swinging London! Those red buses, and ohmigod, the black cabs! Groovy, baby!'

Jenny nodded vigorously in agreement. 'It's a *total* trip,' she said.

Petal plastered a smile to her face and kept it there.

'Yeah, London's really cool,' she said. 'There's a brilliant music scene. In fact, my boyfriend's in this really great band. KillBuzz. Have you heard of it? They're about to go massive.'

'KillBuzz?' Jenny turned to Michelle. 'Have you . . .?'

Michelle shook her head and put the palms of her hands together, pantomiming a prayer for forgiveness. 'Sorry!' she said, tilting her head in apology. 'We're on the TV side. We're not, you know, the young hip gunslingers who are totally up with all the latest bands.'

'We're really a pair of old ladies,' Jenny chimed in, tilting her head to echo Michelle's and smiling to indicate that she was joking.

The thing is, they do look old to me, Petal thought. I mean, they must be nearly forty . . .

But she managed a merry laugh and an eye-roll that seemed successfully to convince Michelle and Jenny that the idea of them being considered old was laughable.

'And I *love* your accent,' Jenny added, leaning forward. 'America goes crazy for British accents.'

'Totally,' Michelle nodded. 'In fact, I think one of the mistakes we made on *Cougar Hunt* –' she looked at Linda for the first time – 'was not getting Linda to bring out her British accent more! And slang words – we *love* British slang over here!'

She looked at Linda expectantly, but Linda's tightly pulled face was blank.

'You mean like rhyming slang?' Linda asked finally. 'Apples and pears? Me old china?'

'Uh . . .' Jenny glanced quickly at Michelle, her face falling, 'not exactly . . .'

Petal had a sudden stroke of inspiration. 'I know just what you're talking about,' she said. 'Do you know what "snog" means? Or "shag"?'

Michelle and Jenny shook their heads in unison.

'Oh, no, wait!' Michelle said eagerly. 'Is "shag" like a haircut?'

'Or carpet?' Jenny said.

'Nope,' Petal said, sitting back, preparing to sell herself and her Englishness with everything she had to these bizarre Americans. 'It's sex. If you shag someone, you have sex with them. But, if you snog someone, you're just kissing them.'

'Ooh! You don't want to get those two muddled up!' Michelle crowed, clapping her hands.

'But then,' Petal said, on a roll now, 'there's a very rude word that sounds really like snog and shag. So you have to be *really* careful not to muddle that one up. It's slag.'

'Slag,' Michelle and Jenny chorused, their eyes sparkling.

'Yeah.' Petal was having a hard time not giggling now. 'It means someone who's really easy. You know, puts it about a lot.'

She could hear her accent becoming a parody of itself, like an actor auditioning to play a Cockney who was playing it up too much in an effort to convince the director that they could do the part; but Michelle and Jenny were eating it up with a spoon. The broader her accent got, the more they leaned towards her.

'Like a ho,' Jenny said, looking at Michelle.

'Yeah. It's like a ho over here. Which is a really funny word to us,' Petal said, deadpan, 'because in England, a hoe is, like, a tool you use for gardening.'

'Ohmigod! Hilarious!' Michelle clapped her hands again. 'You're, like, really funny!'

'And I *love* your look,' Jenny added. 'Did I say that already?'

'Ladies?' A ridiculously good-looking waiter hovered at Jenny's shoulder, proffering menus. 'I came over earlier, but you looked like you were having such a good time that I didn't want to interrupt – OK to give you the menus now?'

'Sure!' Jenny said enthusiastically. 'I could get a bite to eat – what about you, Michelle?'

'Totally,' Michelle agreed, smiling at Petal. 'Do you like Cajun food? They do nice Cajun here. Or pasta.'

Like you ever eat pasta, Petal thought, looking at Michelle's whip-thin figure. But hey, if they're buying us dinner, that means they're keen . . .

'Lovely!' she said. 'Isn't that nice, Mum?' She kicked Linda under the table. 'Mum and I are really strangers to each other,' she added. 'We're just getting to know each other again. It's pretty bloody weird, I can tell you.'

'Yeah, it is,' Linda said, duly prompted.

'*Pretty bloody weird*!' Michelle echoed happily. 'That's *so* funny!' She took the menu and put it down without looking at it. 'I'll just have the Caesar salad, low-fat dressing on the side,' she said automatically. 'And a Bellini.'

'I say, Michelle! A Bellini! That's *pretty bloody weird*!' Jenny said, in the worst British accent Petal had ever heard.

'Oh, go snog me!' Michelle said, giggling madly.

These people are insane, Petal thought, taking her floral-covered menu. But hey, if it gets me and Mum a TV show, I'll give them all the damn British slang they want.

'Hey,' she said to Michelle and Jenny. 'Do you know what the word "prat" means? Or "twat"?'

They shook their heads, eyes wide in anticipation.

'Well,' Petal said cheerfully, 'brace yourselves . . .'

Amber

'*O*h my God! *Bože môj!*' Slava was practically hyperventilating with excitement.

If I didn't know better by now, I'd tell her to take a pill and calm down, Amber thought drily.

'He's here! At our house! Joe Jeffreys is *at our house!*'

Rushing to the mirror with a surprising turn of speed, Slava patted her already perfectly coiffed hair, making sure there wasn't anything out of place. Then she turned to look at Amber.

'Smart,' she said distractedly, 'you look smart, that's good – like a girlfriend, someone he can take out to have dinner with—'

'*Matka!*' Amber rolled her eyes. 'I'm not dating Joe! This is not a date! We're going to Cascabel for Brian's leaving ceremony! We're all going to cry a lot and talk about really personal stuff. In fact, it's exactly the opposite of what you're supposed to do on a date,' she added. 'That's a joke. You can laugh now.' But she didn't really expect her mother to get it. 'And if I *were* going on a date with Joe,' she continued, 'it would be pretty bad of me, considering Tony's paying for the roof over our head.'

Slava waved Amber's moral concerns away with one swift downward flap of her hand. Adjusting her pearls, she scurried to the door.

'I come to meet him,' she said decidedly. 'This I must see with my own two eyes.'

Amber glanced at herself in the mirror. Slava had been right, she was very smartly dressed, in a Diane von Furstenberg silk crepe wrap dress in a dark green jungle print, which she'd cinched at the waist with a wide brown leather belt. Gold chandelier earrings dangled almost to her shoulders, and her hair was pulled back into a ponytail, smooth as silk, to show off her perfect bone structure. Her brown Prada kitten-heel peep-toe shoes matched her belt, and her lightly tanned legs were bare. She could have been going to lunch with royalty, or a celebrity wedding.

But her destination was much more important than either of those. She was going to see Dr Raf again, and she could barely breathe with excitement. Ever since Daniyel's phone call two days ago, setting up this reunion, Amber's anticipation had been building, and now it was at fever pitch.

Slava was already scampering down the steps to the courtyard, where Joe's black stretch Hummer was parked, the driver standing by the passenger door, ready to open it for Amber. He looked doubtfully at Slava, as if nervous that she would try to climb in too.

Oh, Matka. Amber felt a wave of fondness for Slava well up inside her. Seeing her usually composed mother as starstruck as a teenager touched her unexpectedly, making her want to give Slava the kind of gigantic hug that her mother – always careful of getting her hair crushed – would certainly not have appreciated. Amber followed Slava out to the courtyard; the driver's face brightened instantly at the sight of Amber, who could not have looked a more suitable companion for his extremely famous boss.

'Miss Peters? Please,' he said, pulling open the passenger door.

'Hey, honey!' Joe called from inside. 'Hop on in!'

'Joe . . .' Amber put her head in. 'Could you just say hi to my mother? I think she's dying to meet you.'

Joe Jeffreys was nothing if not a gentleman when it came to elderly ladies in general, and mothers in particular.

'Mrs Peters! Very nice to meet you!' Joe said, jumping out of the

Hummer and enveloping Slava's hands in his huge ones. 'I can see where Amber got her looks from!'

'Actually, no,' Slava corrected him, blinking up at the blinding sight of over six foot of blond, blue-eyed, strongly muscled Hollywood action star. 'Amber's father was very handsome. That is why Amber is so beautiful. She looks like a Slovak girl, yes. That is me. But the beauty, not.'

Joe's jaw dropped at Slava's paralysing frankness. 'Wow,' he said. 'You're a toughie, Mrs Peters.'

'Slovak people, they tell things like they are,' Slava said proudly.

'I can see that! Well, it was a pleasure to meet you,' Joe said, releasing her hands.

'You too.' Slava nodded at him approvingly, her narrow lips curving in a genuine smile. 'They say actors are not so handsome when you meet them. Not true for you. You are more handsome.'

'You'll have me blushing, Mrs Peters,' Joe said amiably, glancing for a moment in amusement at his driver, who was grinning openly now. 'See you again, I hope. Amber, honey, shall we get going?'

He handed Amber up into the Hummer and swung himself back in, taking a seat next to her as she looked around, assessing her surroundings: four huge black leather seats, facing each other in pairs, with sunken tables between each pair, and a bar running along the far side of the Hummer, blocking the door on that side. The seat was ridiculously comfortable, so deep that it was like sinking into the most luxurious beanbag in the world.

'They're recliners,' Joe said smugly. 'I had 'em installed. Here.'

He reached over and flipped up one of the arms of Amber's seat, revealing a control panel that might have come straight from NASA. Joe hit a button; Amber squealed as the back of her chair tipped back and a footrest shot up beneath her legs.

'You want a massage?' he asked, grinning at her reaction. 'Hell, who doesn't?'

He tapped two more buttons. Under the heavy leather of the seat upholstery, a series of wheels started to move, running up and down

Amber's spine, tapping at her shoulder blades, easing out her lower back.

'It's like those ones they have in the pedicure places,' he said cheerfully. 'Only much fancier.'

'Wow,' Amber said, closing her eyes in bliss as her vertebrae stretched out under the pressure of the chair mechanism. The Hummer pulled out of the courtyard, its nose dipping as it negotiated slowly down the steep slope of the hill to Laurel Canyon Boulevard. 'I'd just drive around all day if I had this.'

'You know, since this whole thing blew up in the papers, I've been doing just that,' Joe said. 'This is my sneaky secret transportation. I drive my Prius to the studio, jump in this baby and then I can go where I want without the paps catching me.' He tapped on the windows. 'Total blackout from the outside. They can't see in.' He grinned. 'Couple of days ago, I drove to Vegas. Got a private room, played some poker, kicked back. It was great.' He stretched back in his seat. 'Good system, eh? Means I can sneak back to Cascabel for Brian's last day. I wouldn't't've wanted to miss that. Brian's a good kid. I just needed to figure out a way that the papers can't get wind of it.'

'It's very nice of you to bother,' Amber said. 'I know it'll mean a lot to Brian. He really looked up to you.'

Joe winced. 'I feel shitty about being there under false pretences,' he admitted. 'And then, everything that happened – it's the least I could do, coming back for him.'

Most people as famous as Joe would walk away and never look back, Amber thought. Joe's a really good guy.

'And I kind of like the idea anyway,' Joe added. 'I mean, I didn't even get to say goodbye to anyone. That was a real shame. This way we get to do the thing right.' He grinned. 'Get some closure, as the shrinks say.'

'Daniyel said everyone from our group's coming,' Amber said. 'Even Petal. Brian asked for everyone to be there.'

'That's pretty brave of Petal,' Joe said, grinning. 'Considering there are plenty of people who'll be wanting to rip her a new one. I can't wait to see what Skye says to her.'

Amber glanced at him, trying to gauge his feelings about Skye. 'Are you looking forward to seeing her? Skye, I mean,' she prompted.

'Yeah! Cool! She's a great girl.' Joe smiled reminiscently. 'We had us a lot of fun.'

Amber waited to see if Joe would say anything more about Skye, but instead he cleared his throat and went on a little awkwardly: 'Honey, I need to ask you something. I've been kind of worried about your situation, and now I've seen you're still living with your mom . . .' He ran one hand through his thick hair. 'D'you think that's a great idea? How are you doing with what Dr Raf would call retaining your sobriety?'

Amber clicked off the massage programme and swung round in the chair to look at Joe properly. His handsome face was full of concern.

'I know it's not ideal that I'm still living with her,' she said simply. 'But I have a lot of stuff to work out. I've got an entire life to put together – I have to sort out some way to take care of her, for a start. I'm going to meetings every day, and to a therapist Dr Raf found for me. But if I try to do everything at once, I'm scared I'll freak myself out, and that *will* endanger my sobriety.'

Joe nodded slowly. 'I get it,' he said. 'I don't like it, but I get it. Your mom still popping pills like something out of *Valley of the Dolls*?'

'Oh, yes,' Amber said wryly. 'That'll never change.'

Joe sighed. 'That's why I wanted to set you up with Jeff Ringquist,' he said. 'Get you some paying work. Give you some income of your own, so you can move out.' He grinned. 'Jeff said you nailed the audition.'

'It wasn't that different to shooting a commercial,' Amber admitted. 'I tried not to think too much about what I was doing.'

Joe burst out laughing. 'You're a natural!' he said cheerfully. 'You know that's the hardest thing of all – not thinking too much about it. Just get out there and do it. Most people get stuck in their own heads. They over-think their line readings.'

'I suppose I'm lucky,' Amber said, giggling. 'I don't think I've ever had the problem of thinking too much.'

'Me neither, baby!' Joe said, roaring with laughter now. 'Secret of my success!'

He popped a button on his own control panel, tipping up the footrest and stretching out on it luxuriantly.

I want to talk to him about Skye and the audition, Amber thought, but before she could speak, Joe was saying: 'Amber, babe, you get that I'm locked into this whole situation with Jennifer, don't you?' He groaned. 'Y'know, I look back and ask myself what the hell I was thinking, agreeing to the setup. But Carmen – that's my publicist, and Jennifer's publicist – she and Jennifer are an item, you know. Long-term. Been together for years.' He grinned. 'Women, eh? You ladies are *much* better at settling down. Anyway, this is perfect for them. Jennifer gets me to cover up the rumours, she's got Carmen to boff, *and* the movie makes boatloads of money, which means she can finally make this little indie script she's been dying to do for years. Thinks it'll snag her an Oscar. She plays a blind girl with MS who dies, or something.'

He spread his hands wide as the Hummer turned onto the freeway.

'But me? What do I get out of it, apart from the boatloads of money? Not only am I not getting laid – if I even *try*, I get a ton of crap raining down on me!' He sighed again. 'Carmen suckered me in. I swear, that woman's really good at what she does.'

'Can you not call off the engagement?' Amber suggested.

Joe shook his head vehemently. 'Believe me, I suggested that after the whole rehab fuckup. But no way. It's not just Carmen and Jen pressuring me now – I had the whole studio come down on my head. They just took a huge hit on that gigantic alien movie that bombed big time, and they're pinning all their hopes on *Him, Me and Mr Paws*. If Jen and I don't walk off into the sunset together in "real life" –' he put the last two words in audible inverted commas – 'they're scared the movie will tank.'

'Do you actually have to get married?' Amber asked.

He grimaced. 'I'm hoping to slip out of that one,' he said. 'Keep postponing – you know, pressures of work, conflicting shooting schedules . . . and then Jen finally says that she loves me but she's not in love with me any more, she can't make her peace with the past, she can't get over the fact that I cheated. That plays well for her, 'cause she looks like a strong independent woman.' He rolled his eyes. 'So we go our separate ways. I'm heartbroken, of course. But finally I move on. Jen doesn't date for a while, because she's getting over me – which is perfect for her, natch, as really she's hooking up with Carmen.'

Amber nodded. 'That sounds plausible.'

'It does, doesn't it?' Joe leaned over to look at her. 'But you see where it leaves me in the meantime.'

He put his hand over hers. 'I like women, Amber,' he said frankly. 'I can't just go cold turkey on the ladies for six months to a year while Jen and I get this mess sorted out in the best PR way possible. And obviously, I can't let off steam in strip clubs any more.' He looked unexpectedly serious. 'Plus, I'm asking myself why I'm still doing that. Cascabel got to me, you know? All those sessions with Dr Raf, talking about stuff I never even thought about before. I really do like women. I don't want to be the dick that pays for a girl half my age to sit on my lap in a thong.' He grimaced. 'Well, I want it, but I don't want it, you know? I mean, what happens when I get older? I don't want to be a dirty old man. Even Warren Beatty settled down. It's time for me to start thinking about it. Dr Raf really got to me. He's a damn good guy.'

'Yes, he is,' Amber said so quietly Joe didn't even hear her.

'So, I need to date someone grown up enough to get what's going on,' he continued. 'Someone who I can see going forward with, after all the dust clears.'

Joe twined his fingers through hers. 'Someone like you, babe.'

And just as Amber was opening her mouth to tell him no, he leaned over and kissed her with an expertise that took her breath away.

*

It was a world-class kiss. Joe knew exactly what he was doing; by the time Amber had lifted her hand to push him away, she was already under his spell, and her hand dropped back to her side as he kissed her long and thoroughly. It was Joe who eventually ended it, sitting back with a smug expression on his face, saying: 'Well, we definitely have chemistry . . .'

'You'd have chemistry with a dead goat,' Amber said dazedly, making Joe smirk complacently. She sat for a moment, coming back to full consciousness; then she leaned forward and slapped Joe hard across his cheek.

'What the—' Joe looked totally stunned.

'You're a slut, Joe Jeffreys!' she said furiously. 'Even when we were in Cascabel, you were a slut! Flirting with me, and sneaking off to have sex with Skye!'

'I didn't mean to make you feel bad—' he started.

'Not me, you idiot! I couldn't care less about whether you flirt with me!' she snapped. 'I'm talking about *Skye*! How do you think that made *her* feel?'

Joe's jaw dropped. He stared at her blankly.

'You didn't even think about her, did you?' she said angrily. 'You were happy enough to get your rocks off with her, but the rest of the time you were mooning after me, because you've got this ridiculous fallen angel fantasy about me! Oh, yes, don't think I didn't know all about that! *Men!* You're *pathetic*!'

Amber narrowed her eyes in fury. 'What, you thought you were going to ride in on your white horse and save me?' she continued. 'You *moron*! Didn't it occur to you that I have to save *myself*?' She pounded at her chest with her fist, completely carried away by now. 'What good would it do if you, or anyone, did it *for* me?'

Joe was hanging his head in shame by now.

'And suggesting to me that I be your *secret girlfriend*?' she continued angrily. 'Do you really think *that* would be a good idea for me? I've been an addict for almost half of my life, and I've hidden it from almost everyone. And it nearly killed me! I can't do any more secrets!'

'Babe, I'm sorry—' Joe started, red in the face now.

'You barely know me!' she charged on. 'It's crazy to think we could jump into a relationship just like that! Especially when there's someone right under your nose who'd *die* to have you suggest something like that to her! Someone who has real feelings for you – someone you really get on with, who you laugh and joke with – someone you're *yourself* with! You were never really yourself with me, because you were all tangled up in your *immature, teenage* rescue fantasy!'

Joe was holding up both hands in surrender. 'Stop!' he pleaded. 'I get it! I'm an idiot! I'm a total fucking idiot! I've got everything completely wrong! Please, just don't shout at me any more!'

Amber stared at him, panting from her tirade; she didn't feel she'd got out half of what she wanted to say.

'You're talking about Skye, right?' Joe said. 'You're saying Skye has feelings for me?'

'Of course I'm talking about Skye!' she said, still loudly enough to make him cower. 'She really cares about you! I think she's fallen for you! And you didn't even bother to get in contact with her after you left Cascabel!'

'It was all such a mess,' Joe said apologetically. 'I meant to. I was just letting the dust settle. And then that story came out in the *Investigator*, and I realized she'd been a plant all along . . .'

'She'd never have talked to them if you'd got in touch with her!' Amber insisted. 'She told me that, and I believe her! She was waiting and hoping that you'd track her down and try to see her again!'

'Huh,' Joe said slowly, taking this in.

This isn't all about Joe, Amber realized suddenly. Part of this is about me being angry with Dr Raf. I wish he'd got in touch with me after I left – to see how I was doing. I'm upset he didn't, and I'm taking it out on Joe.

The Hummer had pulled to a halt a while ago, but Joe and Amber had been oblivious to the fact that they were no longer in motion. Finally, the driver tapped on the mike of his intercom to get their attention; they both jumped.

'So sorry, Mr Jeffreys, but we're at our destination, and I think that your, uh, event is just about to start,' he said, sounding embarrassed even through the speakers. 'May I—'

'Yeah, yeah. You can open the door,' Joe said, sitting back, grabbing a bottle of water and uncapping it.

The passenger side door swung open, and Amber jumped out without waiting for Joe. She looked back into the Hummer, where Joe was still sitting, drinking water and looking dazed.

'Give up the fantasies,' she said to him firmly. 'Focus on what's staring you in the face. You don't need a fallen angel. What you *really* need is a partner in crime.'

Turning on her heel, she walked up the slate path to Cascabel's main entrance. Behind her, Joe swung out of the Hummer, staring after Amber as the silk skirt of her dress swirled around her long legs. Slowly, he whistled through his teeth, a long, slow, thoughtful whistle, as he watched her disappear into the building.

Skye

Sitting in the lobby of Cascabel's reception, staring at the three huge vases ranged along the front desk, filled with masses of pale yellow orchids that looked like sunshine against the light green walls, Skye had been early for this meeting. She had been checking her appearance in the mirror panels between the vases, but when she saw Amber coming up the path, she jumped to her feet.

She walks like she's on a catwalk, Skye thought resentfully. Hair bouncing like a shampoo ad, legs stepping high as a pony, just like a runway model. Never looks down once, even though that path is like slate stepping stones. I hate her.

And then, beyond Amber, at the bottom of the winding path, Skye spotted a tall figure, wide-shouldered, long-legged, standing in the shade of the two high palm trees that framed the entrance to Cascabel. He was dressed uncharacteristically smartly in a white shirt and grey trousers, but even if he'd been wearing a floor-length kaftan, Skye – like millions of his fans – would have instantly recognized that handsome face, that distinctive shock of blond hair.

I don't believe it! Skye's hands curled into fists by her sides, her nails digging into her palms. *She got a ride here with Joe! I spilled my heart out to her in that producer's office, and she let me, and all the time she must have been dating Joe and laughing at me, letting me go on about how much I cared about him – God, I'd like to strangle both of them!*

'Skye!' Amber said nervously as she stepped through the glass sliding entrance door and spotted Skye, whose expression wasn't exactly welcoming. Skye caught sight of herself in one of the mirrors: her entire body looked like a coiled spring about to burst.

'I wanted to explain – about the audition—' Amber started, but Skye held up one hand, palm facing Amber, cutting her off.

'I don't want to hear it,' she said, as the glass door slid open again and Joe appeared, his big frame blotting out the sunlight as he entered.

'Hey, Skye,' he said awkwardly.

'Whatever,' Skye said coldly, turning away, doing her best not to cry.

'Am I late?' Petal tripped through the entrance, sounding out of breath. 'The traffic was terrible, it took me ages to get out of the Valley—'

In cut-offs, a strapless bright orange terry top, and flip-flops, she looked very LA; the only difference was that the long legs were dead white, the yellow of her hair glaringly artificial. LA girls tried to look as natural as possible: London girls didn't even eat natural for breakfast.

'I see you really made an effort to dress up for Brian's final day here,' Skye said snarkily.

Petal's face fell as she looked around the lobby, taking in everyone else's appearances. Joe, in his smart shirt and trousers; Amber, in her designer silk dress; even Skye was in a pretty, strappy sundress.

'I didn't think,' she confessed.

'Yeah, well, that wouldn't be the first time, would it?' Skye commented, dropping into one of the armchairs.

Petal bit her lip. 'I'm so sorry about the video,' she said, looking from Skye to Joe. 'I really didn't mean it all to blow up like that. I was just sharing it with a couple of mates – and then someone stole one of their phones—'

'*Right*,' Skye said sarcastically.

'Hey, she's just a kid. And they kicked her out too,' Joe said to Skye, as Petal's shoulders slumped.

'What, you're defending her now?' Skye said to him furiously. 'She ruined everything, and you're *defending* her?'

The double doors that led through to the treatment facility swung open, and Dr Lucy emerged into the middle of this scene, Dr Raf on her heels.

'Hello, everyone,' she said brightly. 'Well!' She surveyed the group gathered in the lobby. 'It's very nice of you all to show up on Brian's leaving day! Let me say a word here, before we go through to the meeting room.' She held up one hand in a gesture rather like a priest absolving a penitent. 'What's done is done. You were all invited here in a spirit of forgiveness, to celebrate Brian's treatment and recovery, and give him support.'

She tilted her head on one side, her smile fixed, not looking at anyone in particular as she continued: 'Actions against the Cascabel policy were committed, and consequences have been taken. But now we're moving on.'

God, she talks to us like we're a bunch of idiot kids, Skye thought, annoyed, as Dr Lucy glanced sideways at Dr Raf, clearly expecting him to chime in.

Dr Raf, however, didn't meet Dr Lucy's gaze, didn't even seem to realize she was looking at him. He was staring at Amber, and Amber was staring right back at him as if they were in some sort of trance.

Impatiently, Dr Lucy elbowed him, and he stammered something, turning to lead the way into the meeting room. Dr Lucy directed a stare at Amber that would have sliced right through her if it could, and raised her hand even higher, passing it across her already perfectly smooth black wing of hair.

Why's she doing that? Skye wondered. She'll just mess it up if she actually touches it – not that she needs to, she's got that pony-tail sprayed into place with half a can of Elnett . . .

And then she realized. It was Dr Lucy's left hand. And on the fourth finger was a large, shiny, square-cut diamond solitaire, which Dr Lucy was tilting back and forth to make sure it caught the light.

Oh.

A lot of things began to dawn on Skye, one after the other.

It's Amber she's staring at. It's Amber she wants to tell that she's engaged – and obviously, Dr Raf's the fiancé. Poor guy.

Having gesticulated enough with her hand to call plenty of attention to her diamond, Dr Lucy let it fall to her side again, her smile even brighter, positively victorious.

'Well, Brian will be waiting!' she said. 'This is one of the most important days in his life! Let's all go and make it special for him, shall we?'

The Cascabel meeting room was eerily familiar to Petal, as if she were coming back to a family home. It had barely been ten days since she'd been kicked out, and she was surprised at how nostalgic she felt to be back here, in a room where she'd spent so much time kicking the chair legs or crying, bundled up in a blanket. And she was amazed at how happy she was to see Brian too, skinny Brian with his piercings and his slumped shoulders.

'Dude!' he said, almost running towards her to give her a hug. 'How are you doing?' He slapped her back awkwardly, as if she were a guy friend. 'I missed having you here, you know?' he said. 'And Joe.' He grinned shyly over her shoulder at his idol. 'I mean, I missed everyone in group,' he said, still hugging Petal. 'But it was weird not having you round to talk music with.'

'Brian,' Joe said, striding up to him and executing the male hug and backslap so well that by the time he was released, Brian was pink with excitement at being greeted in such a friendly way by Joe. 'Good to see you again, man. And well done for finishing treatment.'

Brian ducked his head, red to the tips of his ears.

'Shall we get started?' Dr Lucy, who seemed to be running this session, asked pointedly.

But Joe, taking his seat, indicating for Brian to sit next to him, ignored her; and there was no way that even Dr Lucy's head-mistressy authority could prevail over a movie star who was used to having the eyes of the world on his smallest gesture.

'First things first,' Joe said in a leisurely drawl, stretching his long legs out in front of him, looking around the circle of chairs, his blue eyes passing over each participant in turn. He raised his hands in apology.

'I'd like to point out the elephant in the room,' he said. 'Me and Skye weren't taking this rehab as seriously as some of you, and I'm gonna apologize for that straight away. It wasn't respectful.' He grimaced. 'I mean, I never thought rehab was a walk in the park, but what some of you have gone through – well, I don't want you to think we were just pissing on it when we sneaked off and fooled around, OK? I'm real sorry about how everything went down.'

'Me too,' Skye chimed in, ridiculously happy that he'd named her. She wanted very badly for him to look at her: to smile, maybe. To remember what a great time they'd had together.

'I'm very glad you realize that, Joe. And Skye,' Dr Raf said, leaning forward, his handsome face concentrated. 'You could seriously have damaged the recovery of some vulnerable patients.'

Dr Raf's being very careful not to look at Amber now, Skye noticed. I wonder if Dr Lucy's picking that up too?

'I'm doing OK, Dr Raf,' Brian chirped up. 'I'm working the steps. I was just sorry that you guys left,' he said, looking shyly at Joe and Skye. 'It was cool having you around.'

'And they were good in group,' Mitch, the near-silent coke addict, chimed in, to everyone's surprise; all the heads in the room turned as one to look at Mitch, who, uncomfortable as always at having any attention directed his way, started scratching his stubbly beard furiously in an effort to cope.

'The last thing I wanted to do was to mess up anyone's recovery,' Skye said in a heartfelt tone. 'I don't mean to make this all about me, but I really do want to say that.' She smiled at Brian. 'This is about you getting clean. It's your day. And we're all really proud of you.'

'That's great, Skye,' Dr Raf said, nodding. 'We're here to celebrate Brian. Let's remember, the reason we do so much group work is for mutual support—'

'I got triggered,' Mitch blurted out, so loudly that Dr Raf broke off what he was saying. 'I got triggered when all of that went down.'

He was scratching his beard now even more frantically; Skye could hear the hairs rasping against his nails.

'Mitch?' Dr Raf began. 'I think—'

'I used to do *coke* with *strippers*,' Mitch announced at high volume. '*With* strippers, *off* strippers, you name it, I did it. And she shows up here –' he pointed at Skye – 'looking really hot, and talks about being a stripper and doing coke and all that, and I got really *triggered.*'

'This is great, Mitch,' Dr Lucy chipped in now, 'but let's put a pin in it till we can talk about it in a one-on-one session—'

But Mitch, having once started to talk in group, was now unstoppable. It was like a dammed-up fountain suddenly breaking its bonds and pouring itself out in an endlessly flowing gush of water.

'I thought about it *all the time*,' he continued, his eyes darting restlessly around the room. 'Coke and strippers! All the time! Shit, you wouldn't *believe* the amount of money I blew on that, back in the day! And then we heard they were actually doing it! Those two!'

His finger wobbled between Skye and Joe, as if anyone in the room needed precise indications about who he was referring to.

'And *then* I went off the deep end!' he said, snatching his hand back and using it to grate his cheek again. 'I mean, they were actually *doing* it! In here! I thought I was gonna go nuts! And then I thought, shit, I'm actually a sex addict as well! Because I just kept having all these *pictures* in my *head* – of *her*—'

'*Eew,*' Skye said, wriggling uncomfortably in her seat as Mitch stared at her beadily.

'Mitch—' Dr Lucy tried again.

'But I don't even *blame* you two!' Mitch went on, looking from Joe to Skye. 'I don't blame *you*, man!' he said to Joe, giggling in a way that made Skye even more uncomfortable. 'I'd *totally* hit that! Are you kidding me? You know who messed this all up? Who put all these thoughts in my head? *You!*' He pointed accusingly at Petal, who jumped in shock.

'What the hell were you *doing*,' he continued, 'sneaking around and taking *photos* of them? You put all these *ideas* in my head! All these *pictures*! I mean, before I was just *imagining* stuff, but after I knew they'd actually been *doing* it, I couldn't stop *picturing* it! It was like I was going *insane*!'

You *are* freaking insane, Skye thought, her eyes meeting Joe's for an agonized moment of embarrassment. Even Joe, who never lost his cool, had squinched up his face in an expression that said, louder than words, how much he wished to be somewhere else, anywhere but here.

'Mitch, do you need to take a break?' Dr Raf said.

'*She* needs to take a break!' Mitch said, narrowing his eyes at Petal, his finger never wavering from her. 'She shouldn't be here! I don't blame *them*.' His head wobbled again between Skye and Joe. 'They were just doing what comes naturally! But *her* – sneaking around, *spying* on them, taking *photos*, showing them to the *papers*—'

Skye realized suddenly what this was about: Mitch was dying of frustration that he hadn't been the one to spy on her and Joe. He couldn't bear it that Petal had seen them, and he hadn't.

'*You* – this is all *your* fault!' Mitch was almost sobbing now as he accused Petal. 'You ruined *everything*! You got them kicked out . . . we were such a nice group . . . you, sneaking around, spying on them . . . you spoiled little rich kid with nothing better to do! You and all your daddy issues!'

'Mitch, *please*,' Amber said. 'You're really picking on her—'

Petal's head was ducked, her cheeks flushed red with anger and embarrassment.

'What *are* you! Some sort of peeping Tom?' Mitch snapped at Petal. 'You should be *ashamed* of yourself!'

'*Mitch!*' Dr Lucy leaned forward and held up a hand right in

Mitch's face, which actually had the effect of silencing him. 'Please respect the rules of the session!'

Oh, thank God, Skye thought, relaxing slightly in her chair. Finally, things are calming down. I never thought I'd be grateful to Dr Lucy . . .

'Having said that,' Dr Lucy said, looking around the circle of chairs, 'I think Mitch is vocalizing an important outstanding issue for the group, which we do need to resolve to give everyone some closure. Particularly as it's Brian's final day. We want to send him out into the world with no unfinished business here.'

She smiled smugly at Petal.

'It's true that Skye and Joe went behind everyone's backs,' Dr Lucy went on, 'and they've apologized for that. But the real issue of betrayal is when someone takes private business in rehab to the outside world, and *that* is what Mitch is confronting Petal about.' Dr Lucy folded her arms across her chest. 'I think we all feel betrayed by you, Petal, don't we? This would be a really good opportunity for you to talk about what you did, and apologize to the group. I'm concerned that you may be underestimating the seriousness of your action. This is the worst betrayal of group trust we've ever had in Cascabel history.'

'Lucy, this is neither the time nor the place—' Dr Raf said urgently, twisting to try to look her in the face.

Good luck with that, Skye thought, staring wide-eyed at the scene developing in front of her. She's got the bit between her teeth now.

'This whole situation has been very difficult for all of us!' Dr Lucy was saying, her tone as bright and sharp as the diamond on her finger. 'Very difficult *indeed*! And *you*, Petal, are the one who's let us down the most!'

Petal raised her head. Tears were streaming down her cheeks, taking quantities of her eyeliner with them. Her swollen eyes were as red as her cheeks, and just as angry.

'I said sorry!' she said furiously. 'I *said* I was sorry, and I didn't mean those photos to be published, and you're *still* going on at me, which is *totally* unfair!' She narrowed her eyes at Dr Lucy. '*I'm* not the person betraying everyone round here! You've been flashing your ring at us like it's a sodding torch – well, you should look at your own fiancé!'

Across the circle, Skye saw Amber jump as Petal continued: 'I know he and Amber were doing something! I had my session with Dr Raf after Amber, and I *know* something was going on between them! You should have *seen* how they looked afterwards!'

Petal was panting now in anger. 'You think you're so above us all!' she said, jumping up, hands on hips, staring down at Dr Lucy. 'Well, you're not, you smug cow! You're not! How dare you lecture *me* about betrayal, like I was the worst person in this room – while your *fiancé*'s been cheating on you with a *patient*!'

Practically everyone gasped in shock. Skye heard her own near-yelp of surprise; she couldn't believe Petal had gone this far, had actually accused Dr Raf and Amber of getting it on.

'OK, I'm calling time out,' Joe said, standing up too. 'This is out of control. I'm sure no one actually believes what Petal just said. I sure as hell don't—'

'You *bitch*!' Dr Lucy shrieked, coming out of her seat as if she'd been ejected from a plane.

Petal squared up to her, but she wasn't Dr Lucy's target.

'I *knew* something was going on!' Dr Lucy screamed, launching herself at Amber.

Amber didn't have time to get out of the armchair: it was Brian, sitting next to her, who lunged forward and tackled Dr Lucy, dragging her back. Dr Lucy landed awkwardly on Brian's lap, his arms around her waist in a parody of an embrace.

'You bitch!' she yelled at Amber, kicking at Brian. 'I *saw* you making eyes at him! I saw you doing that whole poor-little-me routine!'

'I did *not*!' Amber yelled back, shoving back her chair and standing up. 'I did *not* do that! Believe me, if there's one man I've met in my life who *doesn't* think I'm some poor little thing who needs to be rescued, it's Dr Raf! He *respects* me! He taught me how to think of myself as a grown woman!'

'Oh, I bet he did!' Dr Lucy snarled, elbowing Brian in the stomach to make him let her go. With a desperate whooping sound, Brian slackened his grip, and Dr Lucy was on her feet again.

'Ladies!' Joe got between her and Amber, all six foot three of him, wide as a brick wall. 'Please! Let's all calm down here!'

Skye had pushed her chair back a little, to avoid getting trampled or fallen on. Glancing over, she caught Petal's eye.

'You really stirred up the shit this time!' she mouthed.

'She deserved it!' Petal muttered back.

Yeah, but did Amber and Dr Raf? Skye thought. She caught Mitch's eye again – he was staring at her very creepily, as if he were imagining her and Joe together. *Well, I guess not all the guys here fell for Amber. I got the weirdo freak crushing on me.*

'Hey, lady—' Dr Lucy flailed at Joe, who caught her shoulders and held her away from him. 'Calm down, OK? Petal was just running her mouth. You *were* pretty hard on her.'

'Lucy,' Dr Raf said, coming up next to Joe, 'this is totally inappropriate—'

'Don't you talk to me about *appropriate*, you *bastard*!'

Dr Lucy wrenched free of Joe and swung round on Dr Raf, her eyes glittering angrily.

'We need to stop this session,' Dr Raf said very calmly and quietly, raising his hands to waist level and making a pushing motion down. 'This is doing no good. Lucy, we need to stop this session right now, OK?'

Dr Lucy took a deep breath, getting herself back under control.

'We obviously need to talk,' Dr Raf said. 'But this isn't exactly the forum.' He even managed a wry smile. 'This was supposed to be all about Brian – Brian, I can't apologize to you enough—'

Everyone swivelled to look at Brian, who was still clutching his stomach and coughing from the blow Dr Lucy had landed with her elbow.

'Dude, no need,' Brian wheezed, holding up one hand. 'That was the best last day in rehab *ever*.'

'Lucy, let's take a moment,' Dr Raf said, reaching out and taking hold of his fiancée's upper arm.

Everyone caught their breath, but Dr Lucy didn't swing round and punch him in the face; instead, her shoulders sagged, as if in defeat, and she let him lead her away to the windows at the far side of the meeting room.

'Whooh,' Joe said, letting out his breath in a long rush. 'Intense.'

'I'm overloaded!' Mitch announced loudly to no one in particular, getting up from his chair. 'I'm overloaded!' He stumped across the room, head ducked, and slammed his way through the door, disappearing from sight.

'Damn, I'm glad I didn't have to share with him,' Joe said. 'What a nutcase.'

'Brian . . .' Petal went over to Brian's chair and ducked down beside him. 'I'm really sorry about all this. I didn't mean to mess up your leaving day—'

'You *do* like to be the centre of attention,' Brian said, grinning at her. 'Can you get me some water?'

As Petal went to find Brian a bottle of water, Skye was taken completely aback to realize that Joe had approached her.

'Come out into the garden with me, willya?' he asked.

She looked around quickly, but, for the first time that afternoon, no one was paying any attention to them. No one stopped them as they left the meeting room; there was no staff member in the corridor to ask them what they were doing.

A couple of people Skye didn't recognize were lying on the loungers, smoking, at the far end of the garden. Her heart beating fast with nerves and excitement, Skye went over to the fountain and sat down on the wide stone rim. Joe followed, propping his hips against it, pulling out a pack of cigarettes from the back pocket of his trousers.

'So,' he began, and then fell silent, staring past her.

What's going on? Skye thought frantically. He can't have asked me out here just to have someone to smoke with! She glanced up at him under her lashes. He looked . . . Confused, she realized. *This is the first time I've ever seen Joe looking less than sure of himself.*

'Why didn't you try to find me after we got kicked out of here?' she blurted out, her voice wistful. 'You didn't bother to track me down, but you got in touch with Amber . . .' She could have kicked herself for sounding needy as soon as the words were out. But she couldn't help it. She cared about him, a lot, and she'd thought she'd never see him again.

Joe looked down at her, seeing the naked imploring expression in her eyes. 'Babe,' he said gently, 'I bumped into Amber in a restaurant, OK? Yeah, I got my assistant to get her number, but it wasn't like I got some PI to find out where she was.'

'Really?' Skye's face brightened at once.

It's ridiculous how much this means to me, she thought. But I can't help it. When I'm around Joe, I'm like a sixteen-year-old with her first crush.

'Sure it is,' Joe said reassuringly. 'I was happy to see her. But I had enough shit of my own to be sorting out after everything that went down here, you know?' Joe shrugged his wide shoulders. 'You wouldn't believe the hell Carmen and Jen put me through. Carmen yells and Jen sort of shrills at you. It's like being attacked by an Alsatian and a Chihuahua.'

Skye couldn't help smiling.

'That's better,' Joe said approvingly, reaching down to trace her lips with his thumb. 'And hon,' he added ruefully, 'it's not like you just wanted me for my blue eyes, is it?' He tapped a cigarette out of the packet. 'You were filming me all the time. That hurt a bit, I have to tell you.'

Skye bit her lip. 'I wish I hadn't,' she said sadly. 'I really wish I hadn't. And I was just going to keep it for myself. If Petal hadn't gone to the papers, I'd never have shown that film to anyone.' She managed a little grin. 'Except you.'

'Well, it *was* hot,' Joe admitted, lighting up his cigarette. 'I watched it a few times on the net.' He grinned as he blew a smoke ring. 'We put on a damn good show, didn't we?'

Skye took a deep breath. 'Joe, I'm going to tell you everything,' she said.

'OK,' he said, twisting to look at her fully. 'Fire away.'

This is my last shot, Skye knew with cold clear certainty. If he walks out of here without feeling any connection between us, I'll never see him again.

'The *National Investigator* did hire me,' she said, putting her hand on his big thigh, as if to hold him there, make sure he couldn't leave till she'd finished. 'There was this journalist I knew from the club I worked at in New York. He picked me out and flew me to LA to set you up. They gave me the bag with the camera, everything. Paid Dave to get it past the intake search.'

'Huh,' Joe said, taken aback. 'So when I thought I was being so cute, bribing Dave to get us somewhere to be alone, he was already on the payroll?' He shook his head. 'I guess I'm not quite as sneaky as I thought.'

'But then,' Skye pressed on, 'then I realized I was really attracted to you. And I don't mean just sex.' She couldn't help smiling. 'I mean, everyone must want to have sex with you.'

'Back atcha, babe,' Joe said amiably.

'I *like* you,' Skye insisted. 'I really like you. I like talking to you. I like hanging out with you. I like just – being with you, even when we're not saying anything at all.'

Then she realized that she had Joe's full attention. He was looking down at her, a genuine smile sparking in his eyes.

'That's it?' he asked, taking another drag of his cigarette, his eyes never leaving her face. 'You like me?'

'What am I supposed to say?' Skye said crossly. 'That I'm madly in love with you? Well, I'm not! I don't know you that well! I'm not going to bullshit you!'

'I guess you're not,' Joe said, smiling. 'Well, hey. I can live with being liked.'

'Don't make fun of me!' Skye pulled away from him, really angry now. 'I know I should never have sold that video to the *Investigator*, and I'm really sorry I did! Not just for you, for me. I shouldn't have done it. But I was out in LA without any money, I didn't want to go back to stripping –' all her resentment burst out now – 'and it wasn't me you were helping with jobs! I got some auditions, and the only one I nailed without the director asking me to blow him, you'd fixed up with Amber to go in, and he picked her because she was a "friend" of yours! I lost that part because of you!'

'That sucks,' Joe said sincerely, covering her hand on his leg with his own, squeezing it gently. 'I'm really sorry about that.'

Skye refused to look at him.

'You took care of *Amber*,' she said resentfully, trailing her fingers in the water, sounding more than ever like a sixteen-year-old. 'You didn't even *think* about me. You didn't think about what I'd do, kicked out of here like that, all the way across the country from where I live . . .'

'You know what? You're right,' Joe admitted. 'I should've thought about that. We got busted together. I should've done something to make sure you were OK afterwards. Believe me, that point's already been made to me, loud and clear.' He grinned. 'But I did enjoy reading your tell-all about what it was like having sex with me in a store cupboard.'

Skye writhed with humiliation. 'They wrote most of that themselves,' she mumbled.

'As long as it was you that told 'em to put in that story I have a big dick,' Joe said. ''Cause I do, right? You weren't just making that up 'cause it sounded better for the *Investigator*?'

'Of course you have a big dick!' Skye snapped at him, swinging round to look at him. 'You're just trying to embarrass me now!' She made a face at him. 'Well, let me tell you something – you can't embarrass a stripper. We've seen everything there is to see.'

'You know, that shouldn't be a turn-on, but it is,' Joe drawled. 'Maybe I am a sex addict after all.'

'I hate you!' Skye snapped at him.

'Really, babe? I thought you *liked* me,' Joe said teasingly.

Skye raised her hand to slap the smirk off his face, but Joe batted it away as easily as swatting a fly; he leaned into her in countermotion, and the next thing she knew, he was kissing her.

I should push him away, she thought swiftly. I should make it harder for him – not just kiss him back straight away, make him work for it, at least a little bit longer—

Oh, who am I kidding?

Her arms wrapped round his neck, pulling him closer. His hands slid down to her waist, picking her up as if she weighed nothing, settling her on his lap. Skye could have burst out crying in sheer relief at being back in Joe's arms again, kissing him, his mouth hard and eager on hers. He was so confident, so sure of himself; it was one of the things she loved most about him.

'Ah, baby,' Joe said against her mouth, 'I forgot how good you feel – how come I forgot how damn good you feel?'

'Back atcha,' she said, curling even tighter into him, feeling the rumble of his laughter in his chest as she echoed his earlier words.

'*Joe!*' shrieked a woman's voice, high and squeaky with shock.

'Oh, *shit*,' Joe said, reluctantly lifting his mouth from Skye's. 'See what I mean? She sounds like a Chihuahua when she gets angry. Worked with a voice coach for years, and she still can't get rid of it.'

'What the hell are you *doing*?' the woman yelped. 'Why did you come here without telling us where you were going? You shouldn't be here at *all*!'

Skye's eyes widened at the sight of the frail-looking girl who was practically running across the patio towards them. In faded old jeans hanging off her hipbones, Dockers, and a butterfly beaded Temperley top that must have cost thousands of dollars, Jennifer Downs was instantly recognizable.

She's so tiny! Skye thought in shock. She doesn't look that tiny on-screen . . .

Jennifer's huge, thick-lashed eyes took in the scene before her, Skye still sitting on Joe's lap.

'Is that the girl from the video?' she asked, horrified.

'Hi,' Skye said weakly, sliding off Joe and onto the stone rim of the fountain.

'Jen? What's up?' A stunning woman appeared in the patio doorway.

Now *she* looks like a movie star, Skye thought appreciatively. Tall, imposing and slender without being scarily thin, the woman's blue-black hair was piled on top of her head, her thick eyebrows shaped into perfect commas above her long, slightly slanted dark eyes. Her crimson trouser suit fitted her perfectly.

'Ah, shit,' Joe sighed, standing up. 'The Alsatian.'

'What did you say?' Jennifer snapped.

'I said, Hi, Carmen,' Joe said, nodding at his publicist.

'What the hell are you doing here, Joe?' Carmen demanded.

'It's a reunion,' Joe said, shrugging. 'This kid I got to know wanted us all here the day he left.'

'Touching,' Carmen said bitingly. 'And you couldn't spare the time to let me know?'

'Hey, Carmen, I took a dump this morning,' Joe said. 'Sorry I didn't IM you about that too.'

Carmen sneered at him magnificently down her long, elegant nose.

'He was making out with her, Carmen,' Jennifer Downs said, gesturing at Skye.

Carmen and Jennifer both turned to look at Skye, who instinctively sat up straighter under their scrutiny. Being stared at by Carmen was like being skewered with a javelin.

'Pretty,' Carmen said, shrugging. 'But God, you're such a straight man, Joe! Blonde with big boobs – talk about conventional taste!'

'Hey,' Skye said angrily, 'I'm right here!'

But Carmen was already turning away.

'We can spin this,' she said over her shoulder. 'If anyone finds out, you came to meet Jen here, have some counselling, help her to forgive you. But I don't want *anything* more about you and this fucking rehab shit if I can avoid it. We need to get out of here, pronto.'

'And that's an order,' Joe said, swinging himself to his feet, holding out his arm for Jen to take. 'Come on, darling!' he said in a fake British accent. 'Let's get out of here and have a cup of tea!'

Is that it? Skye thought, unable to believe the speed with which everything had been ripped away from her.

Joe looked back at her for a moment, sitting by the fountain, her blonde curls hanging to her shoulders, the printed skirt of her sundress belling out to her knees, looking as pretty as a picture, the heroine in a fairy tale. Apart from the shock and anger in her big blue eyes.

Joe took in the sight, smiling at her. One eye closed in a long wink. And then he was ushering Jennifer through the door, into the Cascabel building, vanishing from sight.

Skye had to sink her nails into her palms to fight the urge to jump up, run after him, grab the world-famous movie star hanging on his arm and drag Jennifer off him.

I've already lost him. I'm not going to make a fool of myself as well.

But she had never felt so bleak as she did then, staring at the door through which Joe had disappeared. Knowing that she would never see him again; unless she turned on the TV and caught sight of him. Or bought a ticket to one of his movies.

Amber

*A*mber was still holding onto the back of her chair, unable to move. She couldn't take her eyes off Dr Lucy and Dr Raf, who were standing by the windows. Dr Lucy was hissing furiously into his face like an enraged cobra spitting venom; Dr Raf was barely speaking, but had a hand on her elbow like a gentle restraint, clearly to block her from lunging back into the room to launch another attack on Amber.

I should just go, Amber thought sadly. There's nothing here for me.

She glanced over at Petal, who was curled up on the arm of Brian's chair as Brian patted her arm rather awkwardly with one hand; in the other he was sipping from a bottle of water.

'I'm sorry,' Petal was muttering. 'I ruined everything.'

'Oh, come on, dude,' Brian said. 'You're not *that* important.'

Petal managed a stifled giggle. Neither of them looked over at Amber. Joe had slipped off with Skye – Good, Amber thought; she wants him, and I don't – but it left Amber with no one in the room to talk to. No one in the whole of Cascabel.

Practically no one in the world.

Slowly, she unclamped her fingers from the chair back, and walked across the room to the door, telling herself not to look back for one last glimpse of Dr Raf.

What would be the point? He's Dr Lucy's now. He put his ring on her finger. He's made his choice.

There was a lump in her throat the size of a golf ball. She wanted very badly to go home, grab one of Slava's many vials of pills, and sink as many as she needed to float away on a happy haze where Dr Raf was just another indistinct figure in the far distance.

But if I did that, I'd lose my memories of Dr Raf. And those are worth any amount of pain.

She was at the door, succeeding in her resolution not to look back, when Dr Lucy said vindictively: 'That's right! Get out of here and don't come back!'

'Lucy—' Dr Raf protested.

'She's a whore!' Dr Lucy insisted.

Amber's hand was on the door handle, but that insult made her swing round.

'Hey!' Brian said, shoving Petal aside so that he could stand up. 'That's, like, totally going too far.' His voice was cracking with the stress of confronting Dr Lucy, but he continued bravely: 'You shouldn't talk to anyone like that. It's, like, really sexist. Besides, no one believes what Petal said. She was just acting out because she felt like you were picking on her.'

'I bloody wasn't,' Petal muttered. 'And I bet the *National Investigator*'d like to hear about this as well.'

'Petal! Shut up!' Brian said crossly. 'Haven't you done enough?' He stared back at Dr Lucy. 'But you *were* picking on her. You shouldn't have done that either.'

'Brian,' Amber said to him, 'I'm really sorry your leaving day got so messed up. But I'll tell you something – as far as I can see, you're totally ready to leave here. I think you're more than capable of standing up to anything you come across on the outside.'

'Thanks,' Brian said, the tips of his ears going pink with pleasure.

Outside in the corridor, Amber stood for a moment, trying to catch her breath. Trying not to cry. Hearing Dr Raf call Dr Lucy by her first name had hurt like a knife twisting deep inside her. She was realizing, slowly, how much she had secretly been hoping that somehow she and Dr Raf would end up together, one day; she had been putting her life on hold, waiting for some sign that it might happen. Today, getting dressed, doing her makeup and hair, all she had been able to think about was that she would see him again, and that being in the same room with her, he would realize that he couldn't live without her.

Well, he's doing fine without me, she thought miserably. It didn't take him any time at all to forget about me and move on. So that's what I have to do too. Move on. But, oh God, it's going to be so hard. I don't know if I have the strength to do it without the pills . . .

'Where is he? Down here?'

A tiny girl, skinny as a fourteen-year-old Eastern European pre-pubescent model, came barrelling down the corridor, passing Amber as if she didn't exist. Amber blinked, convinced that they'd met before; and then she realized she'd made the classic mistake of recognizing a celebrity whose face was so familiar it convinced you that they were an acquaintance, rather than someone you'd seen on your TV so often you thought you knew them.

Jennifer Downs, Amber realized, remembering her from a TV series eight years ago, which had given the actress her big break. *Wow, she doesn't look like she's aged a day since then.* Amber smiled to herself bleakly; no one knew better than she how girls like Jennifer stayed looking so young. *She'll be starving herself so she doesn't grow any curves. Poor thing probably doesn't get her periods, either.*

Another woman came marching towards Amber, this one certainly not lacking in the curve department, a stunning Latina brunette in red, who gave Amber enough of a once-over in passing to leave Amber in no doubt as to which team the woman batted for.

OK, that'll be Jennifer's girlfriend, Amber thought, watching the red-clad hips swish sexily in Jennifer's wake. I just hope Skye and Joe aren't doing anything too compromising. That woman'll tear both of them to pieces if she catches them at it.

She walked slowly back to the lobby, leaving all the drama at her back, and asked the receptionist to call her a taxi. Then she sat down in the furthest chair from the door, and stared through the glass walls at the frothy pale pink oleander bushes moving gently in the breeze.

I'm so tired, she thought dully. I need to get home and sleep for a week.

A few minutes later, the trio of Joe, Jennifer and Carmen came bustling back through the lobby, Carmen talking nineteen to the dozen, a stream of instructions and invective that had the receptionist agog with excitement. Joe threw a swift, pity-me glance at Amber as they swept past, the star presence of him and Jennifer so potent that it was as if they were surrounded by a golden cloud; the receptionist breathed a sigh of pure delight as they exited the building, propping her arms on the desk and staring after them.

'They're such a gorgeous couple!' she breathed. 'I can't *wait* to see their new movie! The one with the dog! It looks awesome! And did you check out her top? Totally fabulous.'

The phone shrilled, and she picked it up. 'Your cab's waiting in the drive,' she said to Amber.

'Thanks,' Amber said, picking up her bag, getting to her feet. She was out of the lobby, walking down the path, when she heard her name called.

'Amber?'

She swung round, her heart pounding. Dr Raf was coming out of the building, walking swiftly towards her; when he saw her, he paused, taking in the sight of her. The sweet, spicy scent of oleander rose around them, heady and rich. Amber's lips parted; her breath caught in her throat.

'Amber,' he repeated, as if simply for the pleasure of saying her name. 'I wanted to . . .' He was looking at her as if he wanted to eat her up, his eyes dark and sad. 'You look wonderful,' he said quietly. 'How are you doing?'

Amber opened her mouth, about to say that she was doing fine, thanks; but she couldn't lie to him.

'Not so good,' she said simply.

'You're not—'

'No.'

She shook her head, never taking her eyes off his face. They were staring at each other so intently that the entire Cascabel complex could have exploded and they would barely have noticed.

'I'm not back on the pills,' she said. 'And I'm not drinking either.'

'Good. That's excellent,' he said in heartfelt tones. He lifted his hand as if to take hers, then let it fall back to his side.

'I think about you all the time,' she said softly.

He closed his eyes, his forehead creasing with strain. Amber longed to reach out and smooth out the lines, but it was as if there was a forcefield between them. If they touched, here in the Cascabel garden, neither of them could deal with the consequences.

'I know,' he whispered. 'I think about you all the time too.'

'Raf . . .' Amber was so overwhelmed by her daring in using his first name that she felt dizzy with it. 'You're *engaged* to her.'

Dr Raf raised his hands to his hair and tangled his fingers into the dark curls.

'It's the right thing to do,' he said hopelessly. 'You were a *patient* of mine, Amber—'

A series of honks sounded from further down the path.

'That's my taxi,' she said. 'I should go.'

Please don't let me, she prayed, turning away. Please grab my arm, beg me to stay, tell me that you were wrong just now when you said that marrying Dr Lucy was the right thing to do . . .

Every step she took, every time her heel came down on the slate paving stones, she was waiting to hear him call her name, run after her, saying that he had changed his mind. Even when the cab driver, catching sight of her, jumped out to hold the door open, smiling appreciatively, she was hoping that Dr Raf would come racing down the path, telling her not to go.

The driver shut the door behind her and got in. The cab was pulling away. And still nothing. She looked sideways, back at Cascabel, and saw that he was still standing there, on the path, where she had left him. Amber could see his white shirt and grey trousers through the palm trees, the thick oleander bushes, but she could barely make out his face.

That's the last glimpse I'll ever have of him, and I can't even see his face.

The cab had a soggy suspension from years of battling the freeway bumps and the Hollywood canyon roads; it bounced as if it were on springs. But Amber barely moved with it. She sat like a statue, every muscle frozen. Frightened to move, in case she broke into pieces.

'So?'

Slava came running out as soon as she had buzzed open the gates to the courtyard, her face falling when she saw that it was a standard LA cab and not Joe's Hummer bringing Amber home.

'What happens?' she demanded the moment Amber emerged. 'Oh God . . .' Slava clapped her hands to her cheeks. 'Something is bad! I see your face! What happens to you?'

Amber knew her expression must be set in stone.

'I can't talk right now, *Matka*,' she said quietly. 'I need to lie down.'

'Is it Joe Jeffreys?' Slava scurried after her, wringing her hands now in panic. 'There is a problem with Joe Jeffreys?'

Slava seemed incapable of calling Joe by anything but his full name.

'He likes you!' Slava wailed as she followed Amber into the house. 'I can see this! What *happens* to change his mind? What, my God, what do you do *wrong*?'

Amber swung round, pulling herself up to look down at her mother with every inch of height that she had.

'I didn't do anything wrong, *Matka*!' she said angrily. 'How dare you?'

Slava's eyes were squeezed tight with concern, her lips pursed.

'He likes you!' she repeated. 'I know when a man wants you!' She beat one small ringed fist on her chest in emphasis. 'When he wants you, he doesn't stop until—' She looked horrified. 'No! You didn't—'

'*No*, I did *not* just have sex with Joe, *Matka*! God!' Amber's face hardened even further. 'What's *wrong* with you? You knew I was going to the rehab centre for a reunion! What do you think I did, gave Joe a blow job in the limo?'

Slava flapped her hand at her daughter. 'You don't need to talk like that!' she snapped.

'Yes, I do!' Amber was on fire now. 'Because it's what you want me to do! You want me to be his mistress, because he's rich and famous and could look after us! You don't care what *I* want! Before Joe came along, you wanted me to marry Tony, and you didn't ask me what I thought about that either. You didn't care what I wanted, you just wanted me to open my legs for the richest guy who was in our lives at the time—'

There was a resounding slap as Slava hit her daughter across the face.

'You don't talk like that to me!' she shouted.

It was as if a switch had gone off inside Amber, releasing all the pent-up tears that had been building up since seeing Dr Raf. They poured down her face as she took a step back, one hand coming up to her cheek in shock.

'You shouldn't hit me for telling the truth, *Matka*,' she said more quietly. 'In London, you said you knew those men I was seeing were paying Jared. You knew I was selling myself. Now you want me to go on doing it. That's the truth, isn't it?'

Slava's face crumpled. 'I just want us to be happy!' she wailed. 'I want us to be happy and not have problems with money!'

'Maybe we'd be happier if we thought about money a bit less,' Amber said. 'We don't need all this.' She waved a hand round the marble atrium with its decorative skylight and sweeping staircase.

'I just told Joe that I wouldn't date him, because I wasn't in love with him,' she said. 'Tony comes back next week, and I'll have to tell him the same thing. I'll start looking for a small flat for us. I'll be making some money from the film part Joe got me. I'll find an agent and try to get some more work – pay Tony back for what he's spent on us. We'll have to live really simply for a while, but now that I'm sober I might be able to get some modelling jobs too. I'll waitress if I have to.'

'*Waitress . . .*' Slava said dully.

'We'll be OK, *Matka*,' Amber said, her tears gradually ceasing to flow. 'I'll take care of us. We'll manage somehow.'

'You won't see these men because you're not in love with them?' Slava repeated, shaking her head in disbelief. 'They're nice men! You're crazy!' She tapped her head with one long red-tipped finger. 'Crazy! You date them, then you see! Maybe you fall in love with one of these two nice men who like you? How do you know you don't fall in love?'

Her voice had been rising, and now she was shouting again, her eyes flashing with fury.

'How do you *know*? How do you *know* you don't fall in love? You're *crazy*!'

'I know I won't fall in love with them,' Amber yelled back, 'because I'm already in love with someone, *Matka*!'

Slava fell back, stunned. 'You're in *love*? Who is it?'

'It doesn't matter,' Amber said, beginning to feel a throbbing at her temples that indicated a massive headache was on its way. 'He's engaged to someone else.'

'He's going to marry *someone else*?' Slava screamed. 'And for this you turn down *Joe Jeffreys*, and Tony, who gives us this house to live in? For a man who's going to *marry another woman*? *Bože môj*!' She hit her chest with both fists now, her rings clinking against the heavy chains of her necklace. 'I kill myself! I kill myself! My daughter is crazy!'

Amber walked towards the staircase, her head pounding. 'I'm going to go and lie down,' she said, as calmly as she could. 'I have a terrible headache.'

'Good!' Slava yelled. 'You lie down! And when you wake up, you come back down here and you tell me you know you were crazy and you're not crazy any more, OK? You tell me you pick Joe or Tony and you let them take you out, you go to dinner, you see what happens! You tell me you stop thinking about this man who marries someone else!'

Every stair up to her bedroom felt three feet high. Amber leaned heavily on the banister, dragging herself upstairs, vividly aware of Slava standing in the atrium, staring up at her, watching her go.

I meant it, Matka. Every word. I know you don't believe it yet, but you will. I'll convince you, no matter what it takes.

Amber wasn't just bracing herself to climb the stairs. She knew she was in for the fight of her life.

Once and for all, she was going to have to stand up to her mother.

Petal

'*A*mber! What're you doing here?' Petal said, throwing the door open, dumbfounded to see who was standing on the doorstep of Linda's house.

'Can I come in?' Amber pushed up her sunglasses to the crown of her head so that she could look Petal directly in the eyes. Her expression was so serious that Petal got butterflies in her stomach.

Uh-oh.

'Okay,' Petal said nervously, stepping back to let Amber come in. 'Um, want to come out to the pool? My mum's in the living room and she's waiting for a phone call – she's in a bit of a state at the moment, you might want to steer clear of her.'

'All right,' Amber said, following Petal through the kitchen, outside into the scraggy garden, across the dry brownish grass verge of the pool.

'I hang out here a lot,' Petal said, stepping up onto the covered sitting area in front of the pool house. 'It's shady, and I can't take the sun.' She gestured at her white skin as she flopped into one of the lounge chairs.

'Sorry, it's all a bit shabby,' she said, looking around her at the sun-damaged wood, the peeling paint of the pool house, the fraying canvas pulling away from the aluminium frames of the lounge chairs. 'You want a drink or something? Water, I mean,' she added hurriedly. 'Or Coke.'

Amber shook her head.

'This is about yesterday,' Petal said, sighing. 'I really fucked up. I'm sorry. Brian read me the riot act, and he was totally right. Dr Lucy just pressed my buttons.' She grimaced. 'As Mitch would say, she triggers me like mad.'

Petal curled up like a ball in her chair, pulling up her legs. She looked frankly at Amber.

'I really resented you at Cascabel,' she confessed. 'You're so beautiful, and everyone was so sorry for you. They all wanted to take care of you.'

Amber rolled her eyes. 'I'm pretty sick of that,' she said. 'I need to start taking care of myself.'

'Yeah. Me too,' Petal said. 'I'm not sure I know how.'

'Let me know when you work it out,' Amber said, only half-joking. 'I could do with all the suggestions I can get.'

'Ditto.' Petal pulled a face. 'Well, this is weird,' she said, looking down at her knees as she wrapped her arms around them. 'I've, like, been resenting you for ages, and now we've sort of got this stuff in common. I feel a bit of an idiot.'

'Petal—' Amber leaned forward, fixing Petal with an intense stare.

She doesn't look like she did at Cascabel, Petal realized. She's usually all dressed up like she's going out somewhere posh – makeup, hair, jewellery, everything perfect.

Amber didn't look scruffy – she probably wouldn't know how, Petal reflected drily – but her hair was pulled off her face in a ponytail, her skin looked bare of makeup, and, though her clothes fit her like a glove, they were a simple pair of jeans and a grey marl T-shirt.

I get it, Petal thought. She's not messing around.

'Did you already talk to the *Investigator* about what you said yesterday?' Amber continued. 'About me and Dr Raf?'

Petal stared at her, taken aback. 'No,' she said. 'I—'

'You mustn't!' Amber's eyes were huge as they focused on

Petal. 'It's totally not true! But you could get Dr Raf in so much trouble . . .'

'Look, I—'

'Nothing happened,' Amber insisted, riding over her. 'At least, Dr Raf did nothing wrong. You have to believe that. I did have a crush on him –' she blushed – 'but then, who doesn't?'

Petal found herself nodding in agreement. *It's true. Everyone sort of had a crush on Dr Raf. Even Daniyel would go all soft and mushy-eyed when she talked to him, and Daniyel was hard as nails.*

'I pretty much threw myself at him,' Amber admitted. A blush rose again in her cheeks. 'You were right, there *was* something.'

'I knew it,' Petal said complacently. 'I'm not an idiot. I mean, I saw my dad with women going after him all the time. I *knew* there was that –' she searched briefly for the word, and then came up with it – '*atmosphere* at the end of your sessions.'

'Well,' Amber said, 'I had a huge crush on him and I did my best to get him to – you know. But he turned me down.'

'It probably happens all the time,' Petal said wisely. 'I mean, he's so gorgeous. And he really understands what you're going through.' She fiddled with a thread that was coming off the canvas of her chair, looking sad. 'I miss my sessions with him. I wish I hadn't fucked up like that and got kicked out.'

She looked at Amber. 'You shouldn't feel bad about it,' she advised kindly. 'I'm sure he's really used to women trying to get off with him.'

Amber's expression was unreadable. 'So you see,' she said insistently, 'you mustn't go to the *Investigator*. On top of what happened before, it would be a terrible scandal. Dr Raf would be in real trouble. Everyone would say "no smoke without fire".'

She reached out and pressed Petal's knee. 'He was so nice to you,' she said. 'I know Dr Lucy's a total bitch—'

Petal snorted. 'Understatement of the fucking *year*,' she said.

'But Dr Raf doesn't deserve you dragging him through the

mud, just to get back at Dr Lucy,' Amber finished, her voice passionate.

'Honestly,' Petal said, 'I never actually meant to go to the *Investigator*. I mean, I've done enough damage. I just threw it out to get back at Dr Lucy.'

Amber's shoulders sagged in relief. 'Oh, thank *God*,' she said fervently.

'You must think I'm a real bitch,' Petal said, rather sadly.

'No!' Amber looked embarrassed.

'Hey, I fucked up once,' Petal finished. 'Give a dog a bad name. It's OK.' She grimaced again. 'I know it's my own fault.'

'*Petal!*' came a scream from inside the main house.

'Oh God,' Petal said, hunching up.

Petal had got to know her mother's moods fairly well, even though she hadn't been staying with her that long: just from the way Linda had yelled her name, Petal had the sense that bad news was just about to be delivered. Sure enough, a second later, Linda burst out of the kitchen door, looking around her wildly.

'Petal!' she screeched. 'Where the hell are you?'

'I'm here, Mum! Where I always am!' Petal called, rolling her eyes.

'Don't talk to me like that!' Linda stormed around the pool. Her breasts bounced inside her skimpy white halter top so violently that Petal almost expected one of them to detach itself and come flying off.

'I wish she'd wear a bra,' Petal said *sotto voce* to Amber. 'It's really embarrassing when she doesn't.'

Linda caught the kitten heel of her diamanté-studded flip-flop on a loose tile, and stumbled.

'Fucking piece of crap!' she wailed furiously. 'Everything's just fucking falling *apart*! And all you do is sit around all day – I thought your father was going to send some money for your keep, but he's always been a tight bastard – all those millions and he's as tight as a bloody virgin's arsehole – bloody s—'

'Oh God, here we go,' Petal said wearily to Amber. 'Sorry about this.'

'VH1 called!' Linda had reached the pool house, and stopped, hands on hips, staring furiously at her daughter. 'They don't want the series! Can you *believe* it? I thought that meeting went so well!'

Petal stared at her, genuinely taken aback. 'So did I,' she said, biting her lip. 'God, I really thought they liked us.'

'Well, they didn't! They didn't fucking like us!' Linda wept. 'I was *counting* on that!'

Her breasts heaved terrifyingly as she said suddenly: 'Do you think if I told them your father would make a guest appearance—'

'Mum.' Petal shook her head. 'He won't. You know he won't do some shitty little show on VH1.'

'The Osbournes did!' Linda said angrily.

'Yeah, but Ozzy's the star and he was out of it the whole time,' Petal pointed out. 'One thing you can't say about Dad, he isn't exactly out of it. Unless he's meditating, I suppose.'

'Ugh!' Linda dragged on one of her bleached-blonde plaits.

I hate when she does her hair like that, Petal thought, writhing. It's like she's trying to pretend that she's my age. Which she totally isn't.

'I should just take my fucking clothes off!' Linda said, sighing and collapsing to the grass.

'*Mum!*' Petal said in shock. 'There's someone else here!' She gestured frantically at Amber, hoping her presence would prevent her mother from stripping off and running round the pool naked, or whatever she was planning to do.

'No, I mean for *Playboy!*' Linda said crossly. 'They used to ask me all the time!' She sighed. 'Offered me a ton of money too! But I was trying to act, and I thought I shouldn't do nude shots if people were going to take me seriously. God, the world's changed. Nowadays you do sex tapes if you want people to notice you.' She brightened. 'Maybe I should—'

'*No*, Mum!' Petal said in panic.

'Bobby and I made some,' Linda said. 'And he didn't take them when he left.'

'Oh *God*.' Petal got up. 'I can't listen to this, Mum.'

'I should probably be going,' Amber said, standing up too.

'Wow,' Linda said, her heavily made-up eyes widening as she took in Amber's appearance. 'You done *Playboy* yet, honey? You should.'

'Mum, *please*!' Petal said. 'Amber's, like, a *supermodel*. She's done *Vogue* and *Harper's* and everything.'

'She'd make a damn sight more posing for straight men than the gay guys who read *Vogue*,' Linda sniffed. 'Hey! I meant to tell you! That stripper girl, the one you caught at rehab fucking Joe Jeffreys?' She snorted. 'I watched that online. *Christ*. Did you see it? She's got some imagination.'

'She isn't even drunk,' Petal muttered miserably to Amber. 'She talks like this when she's sober. Can you believe it?'

'What?' Linda yelled. 'Don't whisper! It's rude!'

'What were you saying about Skye?' Amber asked her urgently. 'The stripper from rehab?'

'Oh, yeah! She's doing a shoot for *Hustler*, I heard. Smart girl. Get it while you can, I say.' Linda sighed. 'You think I'd be too old for *Playboy*?' She put her hands under her breasts and weighed them thoughtfully.

'*Hustler*?' Amber said in horror. 'That's much worse than *Playboy*!'

'Hey,' Linda said, shrugging. 'She's already got her coochie out on film for the world to see.'

'Yeah, but that's different from letting someone put a camera between your legs, Mum,' Petal said, wincing. 'That's just *disgusting*. It's like you're a bit of meat in a butcher's shop.'

'You wait till you get old and no one wants you any more, Little Miss Snob!' Linda said, hauling herself to her feet. 'You'll be *happy* for someone to offer you a nude shoot! You wait till your bastard ex-husband dumps your daughter on you without even giving you any money for her room and board!'

She stormed back to the house, slamming the door behind her.

'I've *got* to get out of here,' Petal said miserably, collapsing back into her chair. 'Can you believe, Dr Raf actually thought it would be good for me to get to know my mother? "Build some bridges", he said.' She sighed deeply. 'That's going *really* well, isn't it?'

But Amber was already heading for the door through which Linda had just disappeared.

Skye

I'm going to puke, Skye thought, putting her hands over her stomach as she felt a heaving in her guts.

'Hey!' The girl who was spray-tanning Skye knocked her hands away. 'I gotta get it even.' On her knees in front of Skye, she glanced up. 'You don't need to worry,' she added in a friendly voice. 'I'm contouring you a bit, but you don't need it. You're in great shape. Can you open your legs a bit more?'

Skye obeyed, taking a deep breath to make the nausea recede.

'Cool. They waxed you already, right?' the girl said, sticking her thumb into the inner crease of one of Skye's legs and opening her up to take a look. 'Oh yeah. Nice and smooth. Your backside should be dry by now. You wanna sit down on that chair and let me touch up your pussy?'

Well, this is classy, Skye thought, trying to cheer herself up as she duly sat down on the chair (an old wooden one that wouldn't show stains from the self-tanner) and splayed her legs wide so the girl could make sure the fake tan round her crotch was even.

I guess for them it's just like those women who do waxing. Or doctors. Seen one pussy, seen 'em all.

'Sometimes they like the natural look,' the girl observed as she sprayed and wiped Skye's most sensitive area. 'Well, not, like, *really* natural.' She giggled. ''Cause that would be *gross*. But, you know, a landing strip, or a little triangle or something. But for this one they want you all glossy, don't they? We'll oil you up once the tan's dry. You're on the plastic furniture, aren't you?'

'Yeah,' Skye said, as the girl seemed to expect a response.

'I saw that! Super-sexy! They might want us to pour some more oil on you too. You know, while you're posing.' She giggled again. 'I'll be standing by.'

The set for Skye's *Hustler* shoot was like a grown-up version of a kids' playroom. Blue plastic gym mats laid side by side and end to end on the floor of the studio, like gigantic tiles. A big yellow plastic chair, which the photographer was making his assistant bend over in various poses, to get the lighting right. A bright red Pilates ball, over which they wanted Skye to do a nude backbend. And a green vinyl sofa – fresh from a porn shoot, apparently.

Skye's blonde hair was fluffed into bunches, layers of fake lashes so thickly applied that it was hard to keep her eyes open. Her only costume would be a pair of clear plastic heels, five inches high.

Oh, wait, she thought sarcastically. Don't forget the litres of baby oil.

She looked down at the girl between her legs, who was nudging them still further apart, her head inches from Skye's naked crotch.

'They missed a couple of hairs,' she said, clucking her tongue. 'Lucky I spotted that – retouching costs a fucking fortune. Hang on, I'll just get the tweezers.'

It's just like stripping, Skye observed. In the end, everyone's paying way more attention to your pussy than to your face.

She took another deep breath. Thirty grand, she said to herself. Thirty grand after the agent's cut. Just for opening your legs. Thirty grand's a deposit on an apartment rental here in LA. A cheap car, so you can get to auditions. And enough to float you for a couple of months, while you try to snag some acting gigs.

'Hey! Looking great!' the photographer said, sticking his head round the corner of the scrim. 'They're gonna oil you up, right?'

Should I close my legs? Or is that totally dumb? It's not like I'm not going to be spreading them in a few minutes anyway . . .

In a split-second decision, Skye compromised by sliding her legs half shut – not completely closed, because that would look weirdly prudish, but enough so that her knees were pointed towards him.

'Yeah,' she said. 'When my tan's dry.'

'Cool! Can't wait to get bending you over some furniture!' He grinned at her lasciviously. 'Hey, those tits. They real?'

'They had a bit of help,' Skye admitted.

'Great! They'll stand up nicely when we get you over that ball. Wow.' He waggled his eyebrows. 'Take this as a *big* compliment, OK! I'm getting a boner. And believe me, that doesn't always happen.'

'Uh, thanks,' Skye said, trying as hard not to stare at his crotch area as he was ogling hers.

'I got the tweezers,' said the makeup girl, appearing with them.

'Great! And baby, *lots* of oil on her pussy, okay?' He licked his lips. 'I wanna see that thing shining like fucking glass.'

'You got it.'

Thirty grand, Skye said to herself, really loudly now. *THIRTY GRAND.*

Joe hadn't been in touch. Of course he hadn't. It had been three days since the reunion at Cascabel, and this time she'd really thought she had a shot at him. *The way he looked at me, the way he kissed me – the way he teased me – I know we had a real connection. But not enough of one, I guess.*

So I can't wait around for him any more. The Investigator*'s kicking me out of the Grafton. It's go back to New York, or try to make a new life for myself here. And to do that, I need money.*

'Ow!'

She winced as the makeup girl tweezed the rogue hairs from between her legs.

'All done! Stand up and let's get you nice and oily!'

Skye's bunches of hair stuck out enough so that they wouldn't get drenched as the makeup girl worked the oil into her body, dripping onto the black plastic sheet she was standing on, more and more oil pouring over her shoulders, saturating her pores till she was a shiny, slippery, oil slick, her nipples standing up in tight points.

'Here,' the makeup girl said, holding out her arm. 'You'd better let me help you to the set – we don't want you falling over and cracking your head open—'

Squelching, flat-footed, Skye picked her way gingerly over the floor and through into the main studio.

Well, hey. At least I'm used to being naked in front of a ton of guys.

Besides the photographer and his assistants, there was a whole group of *Hustler* people standing round the monitor that was going to film the shoot; the black-painted walls seemed to narrow in as she stepped onto the gym mats and grabbed the back of the green sofa for balance. Bright light picked out every inch of her body, the oil gleaming, reflecting it back. The costume girl tripped towards her, the Perspex shoes dangling from one hand.

'Skye! Love it!' The photographer clapped his hands in pleasure. 'Let's get you bending back over that ball! And hey, can you really crack your legs open when you do it? I know it's not, like, "gymnastic technique" –' he made inverted commas with his fingers on the last two words – 'but we want you to spread that pussy over the ball like butter, you know what I'm saying?'

He leered at her, his expression identical to that of every single other person present.

Oh God, Skye thought grimly. This is going to be bad.

'*Skye!*'

The woman's voice was such a shock that Skye spun round, lost her grip on the sofa, and fell flat on her ass.

Thank God for the gym mats, she thought, staring up, unable to believe what she was seeing.

Because marching towards her was Amber, hair pulled back, legs taking long strides, elbows out, looking like a captain in a new model army.

'What the *hell* are you doing?' Amber said furiously, reaching Skye's side. She reached down, grabbed Skye's arm, and hauled her to her feet. Skye skidded against her, getting oil all over Amber's clothes, but Amber didn't seem to care one bit. 'I'm taking you out of here right now!' Amber said, dragging Skye off the set.

The costume girl jumped out of the way of Skye's flailing arms, but not fast enough to stop one of them hitting the Perspex shoes, which went flying.

'Hey! Stop! What the fuck's going on?' yelled the photographer, looking up from the monitor.

'She's not doing the shoot,' Amber said between gritted teeth. 'Where are your clothes?' she snapped at Skye.

'Huh? What do you *mean*, she's not doing the shoot? She's our cover girl!' said a *Hustler* executive angrily.

'*You* take off your clothes and get over that ball!' Amber hissed back at her. 'If you want someone to do it that badly!'

'Look, lady,' the woman said, coming across the set to confront Amber, 'I don't know who the hell you think you are, but—'

'Oh, *I* know who she is,' said the photographer, grinning. 'She's Amber Peters. *Sports Illustrated*, pink swimsuit, a few years ago.'

'*Hell*, yeah,' breathed another *Hustler* exec in appreciation.

Skye was writhing, trying to get away from Amber, but she was amazed at how strong Amber was; her grip on Skye's arm, even despite the oil, was like grim death.

'Hey, Amber, what d'you say? Want to pose with your girlfriend?' the photographer suggested, his grin deepening to a leer. 'Tell you what – you take off your clothes too and throw that ball to her, and I'll leave off the whole bending-over thing if that bothers you. What about it?'

'Shut up, you pornographer,' Amber said so loudly that everyone actually gasped.

What the hell happened to Amber? Skye wondered in amazement.

'Come on, Skye,' Amber said firmly, tugging at Skye's arm so hard that Skye found herself obeying as Amber dragged her around the scrim to the changing area.

'Where the hell do you get off, coming in here and talking to us like that?' the *Hustler* woman demanded, following them, but Amber was already grabbing Skye's clothes.

'Are these yours? Put them on,' she ordered Skye. 'We're getting out of here.'

'Now, hold on . . .' said the *Hustler* woman.

But Amber, fixing Skye with a piercing green stare, yelled: '*Do* it!' with such authority that Skye found herself scrabbling for her denim mini and T-shirt, pulling them on over her oily body, grabbing for her flip-flops, her bag, her underwear forgotten as Amber frogmarched her to the door.

'Don't be stingy, honey!' yelled the photographer after them. 'Share the love!'

The bright LA sunlight of the concrete parking lot outside was dazzling after the comparative darkness of the studio; it was in a strip mall, no tall buildings nearby to block the sun. The concrete had heated up, making the parking lot steam with warmth.

Amber and Skye stopped in their tracks, blinking, reaching for their sunglasses. And that gave Skye time to recover from her shock, to round on Amber and say furiously: 'What the *fuck*? That was thirty grand you just dragged me away from!'

'I don't *believe* you,' Amber said, shaking her head. 'I just can't believe you were seriously going to do that.'

'Everyone does it nowadays!' Skye protested.

'No, Skye!' Amber's hands were on her hips, her head jutting forwards. 'They don't! Everyone *doesn't* open up their legs for everyone to see what they've got down there!' She remembered what Petal had said. 'It's like being a piece of meat in a butcher's shop!'

'How did you even *know* about this?' Skye couldn't help asking.

'Petal's mum.' Amber pulled a face. 'She isn't exactly Mother of the Year. But she turns out to know a lot of people in the porn industry.'

'This isn't—'

'Don't even *start*!' Amber said martially. 'I *know* you didn't want to do this! You told me you didn't want to do it!'

'That was before you came in and took that movie part from me!' Skye said equally furiously, her own hands on her hips now. Her palms were making oil prints on her skirt, her clothes were sticking to her revoltingly. She'd have to throw everything away. 'You cosied up to Joe and batted your eyes at him and got him to pull strings for you! Behind my back! You make me want to puke!'

'I got out of the way of you and Joe as soon as I realized—'

'Oh, yeah? Is that why you turned up at Cascabel in his limo?'

'He was giving me a lift!' Amber protested. 'We're just friends!'

'You can't tell me he didn't try it on with you!' Skye said accusingly.

Amber flushed. 'We're just friends,' she repeated, though a little less vigorously. 'Skye, the important thing here is, if you do this, you can never take it back. You need to—'

'Don't you *dare* tell me what I need to do!' Skye yelled at full volume. 'You've got *everything*, and you're lecturing *me*? When you pose sexily, it's for fucking *Sports Illustrated*, OK? Well, I don't have the height for that, and I don't have model looks! I don't have that little-lost-bird thing that has Joe and Dr Raf and the guy who's currently paying your rent duking it out to look after you! I've got nothing but my tits and my face, and I'm going back in there right now and earning some money with them, because I don't see any rich guys queuing up for the honour of paying *my* fucking rent!'

It was impossible to turn on her heel and storm off successfully while oiled up and wearing flip-flops, but Skye managed as best she could, the plastic soles squeaking against her slippery feet with every step she took.

The photographer, the makeup girl and a couple of the *Hustler* execs had come out of the studio and were standing by the door. Skye squelched back to them, her jaw set with determination.

'Right!' she said furiously, turning to give Amber the finger. '*That*'s told her where she can get off! Let's go back in there and pour some more oil on me!'

Amber

I can't believe I did that, Amber thought, watching Skye march back inside the studio, followed by the rest of the *Hustler* crew. What on earth is happening to me? All these impulses keep bubbling up inside me, and I just keep following them.

No wonder I was scared to be sober, she reflected, with the ghost of a smile. It's pretty frightening to have impulses like this. Let alone act on them.

The door of the studio banged shut. Skye was gone. Sadly, Amber turned back to the waiting car.

At least I did everything I could, she thought with deep regret. She was very worried about Skye. Agreeing to the *Hustler* shoot – presumably it had offered more than *Playboy* – was the first step on a very steep slope. Once Skye had done this, they'd be circling her like vultures, wanting her to make porn films, to capitalize on her brief notoriety.

Linda had described this all too well, when Amber had been getting her to track down the location of Skye's shoot. They'd offer a comparatively huge amount of money for the first one, cast an actor who looked as much like Joe as possible – Amber had winced at this – and persuade Skye to re-enact as many scenes from the rehab tape as she could.

'And no one ever stops at doing one porno,' Linda had said, shrugging. 'She's young, she's hot, the money's amazing. They're really good at talking you into stuff, as well. You wouldn't believe. And after that . . . well, you're talking yourself into it, you know? Because you want the cash. It's sort of like drugs,' she'd added, warming to her theme. 'They get you hooked, and then you're chasing them. You can do pretty well out of it too. Porno, I mean. Marry a singer, or a boxer, or something. Get knocked up, you got an income for the next eighteen years.'

Linda had cast a rueful look out of the window at Petal, sitting by the pool house, on the phone to one of her friends in London.

'But that only works if you get custody of the kids,' she'd said gloomily. 'You get shitloads of money when you have custody. I was too young, you know? I didn't think that through. I should've held on to her with both hands. It'd've been worth a fortune.'

Poor Petal, Amber thought now, as the car pulled away from the parking lot. I know she can be a terrible brat, but she didn't stand much of a chance, growing up. Her father may have done an awful job, but she'd have been even worse off with her mother.

And, inevitably, that snapped Amber back to thinking about one of her biggest problems: the Slava situation. Slava was dealing with Amber's declaration of independence from men by using the technique she had honed so well over the years. She was simply refusing to think about it. Her line was that Amber was too hysterical and confused at the moment by her therapy to have any idea what she really wanted. Every time Amber insisted that she had made up her mind, that Slava would have to get used to a lot of changes in their lives, Slava waved it away, smiling benignly and saying that it was much too early for Amber to make any big decisions.

She had even headed out to Rodeo Drive that morning, saying that maybe Amber was right, maybe they were living too much on top of each other. Slava had been watching reality shows set in LA ever since they had arrived here, seeing golden children of privilege stroll down its wide sidewalks, laden with shopping bags. Clutches from Judith Leiber, diamonds from Harry Winston, high heels from Stuart Weitzman; Slava had collected a list of shops she wanted to visit, dressed in her smartest clothes, and booked a car to take her to the corner of Wilshire and North Rodeo in great excitement.

I should be looking forward to having the house to myself, Amber thought, but somehow the prospect felt more lonely than she had expected. The scene with Skye had not only been upsetting, because she had completely failed in what she'd set out to do; it had drawn on reserves of courage and energy she hadn't even known she possessed.

Remembering something Joe had talked about at Cascabel, she leaned forward and tapped on the glass partition that separated her from the limo driver.

'Can you take me to Runyon Canyon?' she asked. 'I need to get some fresh air.'

God! Amber thought forty minutes later, collapsing onto a sun-warmed rock. I can't believe I'm so unfit!

Mind you, a fashionable LA canyon was not the ideal choice of place to try climbing a steep hill for the first time in your entire life. Every single person making the same ascent up the wide path had passed Amber; many had been running, leaping past her as easily as mountain goats, but even the walkers had sped past her, casting pitying glances back over their Lycra-clad shoulders as she wheezed and heaved herself grimly upwards in her tight jeans. Men bare to the waist in running shorts; women in snug-fitting capri pants and exercise bras they barely needed, their hair bouncing in ponytails. All of them with earbuds plugged in and iPod shuffles strapped to their waists or upper arms, light sweat on their smooth tanned bodies, looking in good enough shape to do triathlons every week-end. She'd envied the dog walkers, towed along by their leashes; a German shepherd or a Great Dane on each arm would have helped tremendously to propel her upwards.

I need to join a gym, Amber thought, her chest still heaving as she fought to get her breath back to anything resembling normal.

This is totally embarrassing. I don't want to have a heart attack at twenty-seven just from trying to walk up a hill.

She had never had to work out before, being lucky enough to be born with one of those bodies that had a naturally firm musculature. But never having used those muscles for any real physical activity meant that they were all screaming at once right now, shocked at what they'd been asked to do.

She pulled at the waistband of her jeans, which was cutting into her. They were tucked into boots, and the zip of the boots had been harder to pull up over her calves this morning than it had ever been.

Those pills Matka gave me did more than just stop me being anxious all the time. They made me forget about food. Now I'm eating more than I ever did when I was popping pills. I can feel it. My bras leave red marks on me when I take them off. I wore that Diane von Furstenberg dress to Cascabel because it wraps round me, so I wouldn't have to struggle with zipping up one that was too tight.

It should have been a gloomy thought, but Amber realized she was smiling instead.

I'm not going to do that part. The bikini girl, in Joe's friend's film. I probably won't even look good enough in a bikini by the time they start shooting. And I'm not going to starve myself back to my modelling weight. If I start that, I'll find it really hard not to reach for the pills again.

Skye can do it. I'll ring the producer and tell him I'm pulling out. He really liked her. If he thinks Joe wants him to, he'll be happy to give her the part instead.

I have to take a different road from now on. I've got to stop doing jobs where I'm judged by how good I look in a bloody bikini. If I have to put on an apron instead and clear tables, that's what I'll do.

She pulled her phone out of her jeans pocket, wincing at how tightly it was wedged in there, and dialled Tony's number. I should have done this days ago, she told herself. But it was with great relief that she heard his answerphone message, rather than his voice.

'Tony?' she said, tentatively at first, but gaining confidence as she went on. 'Tony, it's Amber. I'm sorry to do this by leaving you a message, but I need to tell you this now. I can't date you. I'm so sorry, but I can't. I'm looking for somewhere Mum and I can live, and I'll move us out as soon as we can. We're giving up the flat in London. I don't know where we'll end up, but we'll be fine. Don't worry about us. And thank you so much for all you've done, Tony. I wish I could date you, but I can't. I'm sorry.'

She clicked off and put the phone back in her pocket.

It's done, Matka. *You can't talk me out of it. No Joe, and no Tony. If I can't have Dr Raf, I don't want second best.*

Suddenly, she felt very weary. The sun, beating down on her, the thought of the scene with her mother when Slava got home that afternoon to Amber's announcement that she'd turned down the part and said a definitive 'no' to both Joe and Tony . . . she grimaced, overwhelmed by how excruciating the next few days were going to be.

Stuck with Matka, *trying to get my life together, trying to keep her as happy as I can, trying to cope with the fact that Dr Raf is going to marry Dr Lucy and I'll never see him again . . .*

Oh God . . .

Closing her eyes, Amber slid down the rock, resting her back against it, grass under her legs. A niche in the rock cradled her head, surprisingly comfortably, and she let herself slip off into a much-needed drowsy reverie. Sun bathed her face, and she didn't even care; *I'm not a model any more. I can get a suntan if I want.* Dr Raf's face floated into her dreams; his face, his hands, his body against hers.

I can't believe I'll never see him again, she thought, as she drifted away into a daytime sleep. I just can't believe it . . .

Amber was swimming in a sea of vodka with Vicodin islands floating in it. The islands were sharp-edged, and when she bumped into them, they cut her; dully at first, but then the pain started to blossom. Her left arm felt as if it had been sliced open. Something was trickling down it, something heavy that itched her, irritated her, made her want to rub it away. She lifted her hand, and gasped in pain; she must have caught her fingers between two of the islands, slammed them between them somehow, because they felt bruised to the bone—

No. Not islands. A door.

Someone slammed your fingers in a door when you tried to open it. The door of your bedroom.

You're not floating in a sea at all, you're lying on your bedroom carpet, bleeding.

And someone's trying to kill you.

Her eyes snapped open.

Someone was calling her name, from very, very far away, so distantly she couldn't tell if it was a man or a woman. It was so muffled it might have been coming through layers of padding wrapped around her head.

And she seemed to have gone blind.

She turned her head from side to side in panic, starting to thrash around, realizing that she couldn't breathe, because there was something pressing on her face. Stopping her from seeing anything. Stopping her from taking a breath—

The pain in her arm, in her hands, was blocked out now in her panic to stop herself suffocating to death. With everything she had, she reached up and hit at the heavy cloud enveloping her head. And through it, she felt something else.

A pair of hands, holding it down. Holding a pillow over her face, trying to suffocate her.

The rush of strength that Amber had summoned up earlier that day, dragging a naked Skye off the porn set, flooded back through her now. She twisted sharply to the side, using her hands pressed on the carpet, her shoulders rising up, to heave the weight off her face. Dragging a deep breath back into her lungs, she managed a yell for help.

It was a hoarse, rasping shout, more like a bark than a human sound. She couldn't believe it had come out of her mouth.

'Shut up!' the woman said violently.

And Amber realized for the first time what she was hearing.

She started to scream again, her vocal cords warmer now, more sure of producing something audible; but the next second the pillow came back over her face, and she writhed against it, fighting as hard as she could. She was on her knees, her hands coming up to the pillow, trying to push it away; she thought she heard her name being called again, but for all she knew, she was so desperate for rescue that she might be hallucinating.

They were wrestling now in a frantic struggle for control of the pillow. The woman was standing behind her, pressing the pillow violently into her face, jamming Amber's head back against her knees in a vicelike grip. And Amber was losing. Weakened by the drugs she had taken, the vodka that had been poured down her throat, her head was still swimming with a dizziness that she was terrified would prove fatal.

I can't, she thought, frenzied with fear as she clawed at the pillow. I can't get it off!

Her breath caught, the dizziness was growing. Every time she got some purchase on the pillow it was pushed more firmly against her face, blocking her nose, her mouth, her eyes. Darkness flooded around her; tiny lights danced in front of her vision. She was tripping on lack of oxygen. Her clasp on the pillow loosened, her knees wobbled, and as she toppled over, she knew she had lost.

The pillow came down on her face with a slam that rattled her body, forcing a groan from her lungs as the air was expelled from them; the woman was on top of her, kneeling on her chest, forcing the pillow down with savage fury.

Amber's body was limp, her outthrown hands open. Nothing was left in her at all. No air. No fight. No chance for life.

The darkness washed over her, and she let herself fall into it.

Amber

Everything hurt, but breathing was the worst. Her lungs ached with every rise and fall as painfully as if she'd inhaled smoke; her chest felt bruised. And when she opened her eyes, she realized she was hallucinating.

Because, bending over her, was Dr Raf, cradling her head in one hand as he pushed her hair back from her face with the other.

'Amber,' he was saying gently. 'Amber, can you hear me?'

She managed a nod, not trusting her voice yet. His face came fully into focus, and her eyes swam with tears.

Only today I was sure I'd never see him again. And here I am, lying in his lap . . .

With a huge effort, she reached up a hand to touch his face, resting it against his jawline. The touch of his skin, the afternoon stubble breaking through the smoothness of his cheek, was so exquisite that her breath caught for a moment in her throat.

'What?' Dr Raf bent even closer to her. 'Amber? Did you say something?'

His lips were so close to hers now. Her hand slid around his head, pulling it down that fraction further, till she could feel his warm breath on her face, smell his aftershave. And that gave her the strength to lift her head, even though it felt as heavy as lead, and bring her lips to his.

'Amber,' he whispered against her mouth.

And then the hand behind her skull tightened, taking its weight, and he kissed her.

It hurt even worse than before, because he was hugging her so tight. And she must have been a complete masochist, because she hugged him back just as tightly, pressing her bruised chest against his; her arms slid up round his neck, pulling him into her, rubbing her face against his stubble, relishing even that pain, because it meant that she wasn't hallucinating. He really was that close to her. No one ever hallucinated stubble.

His mouth was hard on hers; he was kissing her more deeply than he ever had before, more passionately. She wound herself around his neck, tangling her fingers into his curls, wanting to twist herself into him so tightly that he would never be able to let her go. His hand on her head held her locked against him, refusing to let her go, driving his tongue into her mouth, kissing her as if—

As if he thought I was dead, Amber thought, ecstatic at realizing how desperate he had been at the thought of losing her. Almost as if he loves me . . .

'For God's *sake*!' Skye's voice broke through her reverie. 'This is *not* the fucking time, you two!'

Reluctantly, Dr Raf and Amber pulled apart, as slowly as if they were glued together; it was like a physical effort for Amber to drag her eyes away from his. As he moved, helping her to sit up, she could see beyond him, the corner of her bedroom. Everything else came back into focus slowly and painfully.

The blood, coagulating now on her arm. The throbbing of her chest, every muscle aching, and the adrenalin flooding through her from the fight, her near-death experience, and the kiss with Dr Raf—

No, she thought firmly. No 'Dr'. Just Raf from now on.

And then, beyond Raf's broad shoulder, the strong bicep outlined by his snug pale pink shirt, she saw Skye.

Amber was still holding onto Raf for support. Her fingers must have sunk deep into him, but he didn't say a word. He wrapped his arms around her, making sure she was supported, turning his head to see what she saw.

Skye, sitting on the edge of the bed. In the oil-stained T-shirt and denim mini she had worn earlier that day, at her *Hustler* shoot. Her hair had been brushed out of the two kiddie-porn bunches and was pulled back into a fluffy knot at the back of her neck, but she was still wearing the heavy makeup and fake eyelashes that made her look like an inappropriate doll.

But there was nothing doll-like about her grim expression as she stared at the woman slumped in the corner of the bedroom.

Slava. Crumpled up over the pillow she had been trying to use to suffocate her daughter.

'I came to find you,' Skye said, answering the unspoken question in Amber's eyes. 'I walked out of the shoot after you left. Happy?' She puffed out a long slow breath. 'I just couldn't do it. So I tracked you down and came round to say thank you, tell you I didn't go through with it. And your mom –' she nodded bleakly at Slava – 'came to that entrance gate outside the house and told me you weren't in. She was *weird*. I mean, I never met her before, but she was really weird. And she reeked of vodka. I mean, vodka doesn't even have much of a smell, but she reeked of it, you know? It wasn't good.' She sighed. 'So when she closed the gate, I thought: shit. Amber's mom acting strange, not wanting me to see her . . . coming to the gate, not even letting me into the house . . . smelling of booze . . .'

She met Amber's eyes once more. 'I thought you were using again,' she confessed. 'That maybe you got psyched out and came home to see your mom, and started drinking with her, or taking pills. Or both. I'm sorry, Amber. But none of us at Cascabel thought it was a good idea for you to go back to live with your mom, you know? So I panicked. I rang Dr Raf to see what he thought I should do. We were both really worried. He said addicts who go back to it often overdose, 'cause they think they can take what they used to, and they can't any more, 'cause their tolerance drops right down.'

'I came over straight away,' Raf said into Amber's hair. 'And we came in through the gate and knocked at the door. But no one answered.'

'Which was even weirder,' Skye said, 'because I knew your mom was in, and she said you were too. So Dr Raf climbed over the gate—'

Amber's eyes widened. 'You climbed over the gate?' she said. 'It's ten feet high!'

'He was very cool,' Skye said. 'He jumped at it and caught the top and then pulled himself up.' She rolled her eyes as Amber stared adoringly up at Raf. 'He let me in, and then we went round the back and found the kitchen door open, and started looking for you—'

'I heard you calling,' Amber said. 'I tried to call back – and that's when she got the pillow—' Her voice cracked, and she started to cry.

'Oh, baby,' Raf said, stroking her hair, holding her against his chest. 'You're safe now. It's OK. You're safe now.'

'Oh, Raf . . .' she sobbed into his shirt.

'We saw the empty bottle and the pills,' Skye said grimly. 'Plus *that*.' She nodded over at the bedside table, where a small white plastic funnel lay on its side.

Amber struggled to remember what had happened. 'I came home,' she said slowly. 'After I went to Runyon Canyon. And *Matka* was here. I was surprised, because she'd said she would be on Rodeo Drive all day. She gave me a glass of Coke – she said I'd need it because I looked dehydrated.' Amber raised a hand to her throat, which burned as if it were bruised inside. 'There must have been something to knock me out in the Coke. And then she . . .' Amber swallowed, which hurt badly, '. . . she must have helped me up here, and put . . . and put . . .'

She couldn't say it.

'And put the funnel down your throat,' Skye said softly. 'Crushed up more pills, put them in a bottle of vodka and poured it down the funnel. And set up this whole scene.' She gestured to the coffee-table books and the magazines on the bed, the lipsticked words written on the bedroom wall. 'Then she'd have said she got back from Rodeo Drive much later, and found you when it was too late.'

'She didn't give you enough,' Raf said grimly, his arms tightening around her. 'Or you wouldn't have woken up at all without your stomach being pumped.'

'I do nothing,' Slava said, finally raising her head, staring at them with flat cold eyes. 'I do nothing. You don't understand. I was trying to make Amber better. Put this –' she tapped the pillow – 'under her head.'

'Yeah, right. I saw what I saw,' Skye said contemptuously. 'And I had to drag you off of her.'

'*Matka*,' Amber said quietly. 'I remember what you said. You were talking in Slovakian. I remember every word.'

Her mother looked at her for a long moment, her eyes narrowing dangerously.

'You were going to ruin everything,' she finally hissed at her daughter. 'No Tony, no Joe. Everything was going to go! No more nice house, no more car, no more nothing! All you think about is you! Not me!' She hit her chest with her hand. 'The child takes care of the mother! That's how it is!'

'But, *Matka* – why would you *kill* me?' Amber said hopelessly.

'I insure you,' Slava muttered. 'When we come here, after London. I insure you for a lot of money. In case it happens again.'

'Jesus,' Skye whispered, as the sound of rapidly approaching sirens tore up the steep hill below the house.

'The child takes care of the mother!' Slava said, her voice rising, cracking. 'The child takes care of the mother! If you don't take care of me, what use are you?' She was panting now, clutching the creased, vodka-stained pillow to her bosom. 'For years, I look after you! I do things for you! Bad things! And now you tell me you give me nothing for all those years!'

Slava's carefully arranged helmet of ash-blonde hair had been shaken out of shape in the struggle with her daughter and Skye. Locks of it were hanging over her face, teased and sprayed, and she shook them back angrily as she glared at Amber.

'I think we're even now, *Matka*,' Amber said quietly.

Vehicles were pulling into the courtyard of the house, their brakes squealing. Voices shouted to each other, doors slammed. Skye got up, giving Slava a hard glance, and walked out of the bedroom, leaning over the staircase balcony, calling: 'We're all up here.'

Heavy footsteps pounded over the marble of the hallway and up the stairs, the house rattling with the impact. Amber realized she was clinging even tighter to Raf.

'Don't let me go,' she whispered to him.

'I won't,' he said, cradling her in his arms.

Suddenly, she flashed on that scene at Cascabel, just a few days ago. Dr Lucy, so eager to show off her engagement ring, to warn Amber off . . .

'Wait,' she said, loosening her hold on Raf. 'I can't – not if you're still—'

Their closeness, the amount of time Amber and he had spent together in Cascabel, meant Raf could practically read her mind.

'I broke it off that day,' he said, drawing her close again. 'I was an idiot to do it in the first place. No, worse. I was mad. I couldn't think about anything but you – when I proposed to Lucy I knew it was a terrible idea, I regretted it immediately . . .' He sighed. 'She's left the clinic.'

It was with huge, guilty relief that Amber clung to him again as a pair of paramedics piled into the bedroom. On their heels were the cops Skye had called at the same time as the ambulance. Amber closed her eyes, overwhelmed.

'I'll be right here the whole time,' Raf said into her hair. 'Believe me. I'm never going to let you go again.'

Epilogue

Petal

'Coolest thing *ever*!' Tas sung out, hugging JC in delight. 'Coolest thing *ever*!'

'Red carpet, bitch!' JC squealed, hugging her back. '*Hollywood* red carpet!'

He looked back into the white stretch limo from which he and Tas had just emerged.

'Petal, put that boy down!' he said, giggling. 'Step away from the boy! Your public awaits!'

The interior of the limo was lit up with LED ceiling lights, twinkling like stars on Petal and Dan, entwined on the far curve of the leather seat, tangled in a complicated embrace.

'I missed you *so* much!' Petal mumbled into Dan's ear, running her tongue round it for good measure.

'Oh, pet, me too! I've had blue balls for a month!' Dan bit her neck so hard she squealed.

'You've got blue balls now,' Petal said naughtily, flicking his crotch, making him groan.

'How long is this bloody film anyway?' he grumbled. 'I can't believe we're going to a Hollywood premiere and it's a sodding *rom-com* . . .'

'There's a cute dog,' Petal said. 'And you get to meet Joe Jeffreys.'

'Cool!' Dan said, grinning. 'OK, let's get going . . .'

He hoisted her off his lap and pushed her towards the door, slapping her bottom. Bent nearly double to squeeze out of the limo, past the VH1 cameraman who had been recording the whole scene, Petal squealed happily.

'I'll get you for that!' she threatened, climbing out of the car, smoothing down her neon-pink Christopher Kane body-con dress. Tas adjusted the hem swiftly, checking Petal over, straightening her huge gold bib necklace, then backing off, nodding approval.

Dan's long skinny legs, clad in tight black jeans, emerged from the limo.

'It's loony how quickly you get used to it,' he commented to the group, nodding at the cameraman who was climbing out of the car too, joining the first one who had been there already to record Petal and her entourage exiting the limo.

'Oh, *darling*,' JC said, clapping his hands, 'I've been waiting to be followed around by cameras my whole *life*. This is like a dream come true.'

Tas held her hand up and he high-fived it.

'Flown over from London,' she sighed. 'Only economy, but *still*. Our own *rooms* in Petal's house.'

'Silverlake, not Malibu, but a whole *house* with a *pool* and a *hot tub*,' JC chanted.

'Pet's done good, hasn't she?' Dan hugged his girlfriend. 'Get packed off to rehab and come out of it with your own VH1 series!'

'OK, guys,' Michelle, the producer of *Petal Takes LA*, slipped out from behind one of the cameramen. 'I know you're all psyched up and everything, but you've got to stop talking about the show, OK? We can't use any of this.'

'Sorry, Michelle,' Petal said, casting a reproving glance around her posse. 'They just got here this morning, you know? They're still getting used to it.'

'Well, get used to it fast!' Michelle instructed, jaw set. 'Joe Jeffreys is due any second – we need to get this on tape—'

'*Joe! Joe! We love you!*' screamed a horde of girls cordoned off behind the red velvet rope on the other side of the street.

'Oh, *wow*,' Dan said in a devout voice, turning and craning his neck to see the tall blond figure of Joe Jeffreys walking along the rope, laughing, shaking hands with as many of the screaming fans as he could, taking their proffered mobile phones and holding them out, leaning back obligingly to pose for photos as they scrambled to put their heads beside his.

'Joe!' Petal called, jumping up and down to attract his attention.

Strolling across the pavement, looking ridiculously dashing in a dark blue suit and open-necked white shirt, which had clearly all been tailored to fit his large frame, Joe caught sight of Petal, raising his hand to her.

'Hey, baby,' he said, coming over, picking her up like a doll and planting a big smacking kiss on one cheek after the other. 'Couldn't miss that hair!'

Putting her down, he went to ruffle her bright yellow hair, which was piled up on top of her head, fixed with a huge black clip; JC, greatly daring, knocked Joe's hand away.

'*Naughty*,' he said flirtatiously. 'That took me *hours* to do this afternoon.'

'Sorry, fella,' Joe said, grinning. 'This your man, Petal?'

'Darling! As *if*!' JC winked at him. 'But I could be yours if you asked me nicely . . .'

'*This* is Dan,' Petal said, nudging him forward.

'Hey, Dan,' Joe said, giving Dan the classic American male greeting – a close handshake immediately followed by a quick hug, finished with a shoulder slap.

'Joe, Jen's limo is pulling up,' an assistant in a suit said to him urgently.

'Later,' Joe said, raising a hand, flashing a smile and turning away.

'God,' JC breathed. 'That man is *sex on a stick*.'

'And totally straight,' Tas said drily, though her eyes were as wide as the others' from the encounter with Joe Jeffreys and his extraordinary charisma.

'Oh, darling, I *know*,' JC sighed. 'But *still*. It was like being *bathed* in golden light. I wonder if it felt that good meeting Jesus?'

Michelle Lee-Glazer closed her eyes briefly in ecstasy: if the material kept being this juicy, *Petal Takes LA* was going to be a run-away hit.

Jennifer Downs' limo was pulling up, right at the foot of the red carpet, the place reserved only for A-listers. And no one right now was more A-list than Jennifer Downs. As she stepped out of the limo, all ninety pounds of her in a heavily ruched ankle-length Christian Siriano dress that probably weighed as much as she did, the screams of her fans were high-pitched enough to get every dog in a one-mile radius barking its head off in response.

Joe bent down, taking Jennifer's hand, helping her out. She stood there, winsomely smiling up at him, looking like a beautiful pixie, her bare shoulders gleaming against the frothy neckline of the dress. A diamond necklace was twined through her short pale blonde hair like a headband, and more diamonds glinted in her ears; as Joe raised her right hand to his lips to roars of approval from the crowd, she reached up with her other one, her left, touching his cheek, and not incidentally showing off the huge diamond engagement ring on her fourth finger.

'Damn, that's well-staged,' muttered Michelle Lee-Glazer, as Carmen, sliding elegantly out of the limo, smiled approvingly at Joe and Jennifer acting out the little scene she'd choreographed.

Joe and Jennifer turned, hand in hand, to walk up the red carpet; but then a positive outcry of oohs and aaahs greeted a new arrival. Straining at the end of her leash, bouncing with the excitement of a dog awaiting serious treats if she does exactly what her trainer says, the golden Labrador who had played the name part in *Him, Me and Mr Paws* bounded up to Joe with great enthusiasm, jumping up at him as Joe caught her front paws and bent over to let the dog lick his face.

The spectators went insane. Screams rent the air, so piercing that Petal clapped her hands over her ears. The dog, a seasoned profes-sional, was quite unfazed by her audience, dropping back to the ground and winding herself happily around Joe's legs as Joe took her leash from the trainer.

Jennifer on one side, the Lab on the other, a huge smile on his handsome face, Joe started up the red carpet, enough flashbulbs going off to cause an epileptic serious health problems. JC, Tas and Petal had been to plenty of premieres at Leicester Square, walking the red carpet there, Petal twirling and posing for the photographers, a British It girl. But this was a whole different level of star wattage. Joe and Jennifer, in that moment, golden-haired, instantly recognizable, ridiculously beautiful, were the reigning king and queen of Hollywood.

Plus they had a golden Lab walking the carpet with them who was just as photogenic as they were.

Petal and her entourage stared after them with dropped jaws, as dazzled as every single fan red-faced and shrieking behind the velvet ropes.

'Petal!' muttered Michelle Lee-Glazer furiously, nodding at Petal to line up with the rest of the celebrities scheduled to walk the carpet.

'Oh, right!' Petal snapped back to full awareness. 'Ready, Dan?'

She cocked her arm out for him to take it, and, still looking dazed, he wound his hand through it.

'Shut your mouth, sweetie!' she said, flicking his chin. 'You could catch flies in that!'

'*Joe Jeffreys hugged me,*' Dan muttered as they walked towards the photographers. 'And it was all on *film*! Everyone back in Newcastle's going to do their *nut* when they see that!'

Joe

*I*n common with many other actors, Joe had never been able to sit through his own movies. Jennifer couldn't get enough of herself onscreen: sometimes, in her huge living room in the guest house at Joe's, she and Carmen would curl up on the sofa and watch Jennifer's movies all day long. Joe seriously did not know how she could do it. The sight of himself, up there, acting away, looking – in his opinion – like a total jerk, pretty much brought him out in hives.

But he always gave it thirty minutes before sneaking out of a premiere. Long enough for the crowds to have dispersed, the photographers and TV cameras to have packed up their equipment, the gossip columnists to be back in their offices, filing their stories. By the time he emerged into the lobby, pulling his Marlboros out of his pocket, dragging off his suit jacket with relief, the theatre was mercifully empty.

His regular driver knew the drill; as Joe walked out into the warm evening air, the car was already waiting discreetly by the side the movie theatre.

'Home, James,' he said, sliding in, stretching his legs out in front of him, and lighting up.

'Mr Jeffreys? My name is Eduardo,' said the driver diffidently as he pulled away from the kerb.

'Yeah, Eduardo, I know,' Joe said, pouring himself a snifter of Glenfiddich, his favourite malt. He should really be smoking a cigar with it, but he drew the line at cigar smoke in a car. Maybe at home, later. A Cohiba Esplendido, smuggled in from Cuba. 'It's from an old movie,' he explained. 'Home, James, and don't spare the horses. I watched it the other night.'

'OK, Mr Jeffreys. Sorry,' Eduardo said. 'Home it is.'

The sight of his security gates swinging open always gave Joe a warm, relaxed feeling, anticipation rising in him of what was waiting for him at home. Hengist and Horsa, his Great Danes, had been waiting by the gates patiently; when they saw the familiar car coming through, they leaped around it in delight and then chased it along the drive, Joe winding down the windows and egging them on. He let them jump all over him as he got out, slapping their muzzles, wrestling with them for a while.

'Hey, you're picking up that Lab,' he said wryly, noticing that Horsa was sniffing his hand intently. 'It's the last time I come home from work smelling of another dog, OK, baby?' He patted her huge head hard, pulling her ears, as she groaned happily and butted against him with a push strong enough to have knocked over a weaker man.

My house, my dogs, he thought happily, taking a deep breath of the soft moist night air as Eduardo circled the car round the side of the compound. *Boy, life is good.* Tonight had been a job well done; the press coverage of his and Jennifer's romantic greeting on the red carpet would be totally positive, Carmen had assured him. He just had to keep one hundred per cent scandal-free for the next year: three months for the film to roll out around the world, three more months to release it on DVD, and then six more months to slowly plant stories that the strain of planning their wedding was telling on him and Jennifer, that their work commitments on different continents were pulling them apart; and finally, the sad announcement that Joe Jeffreys and Jennifer Downs were no longer a couple, with a plea for the press to respect their privacy and leave them alone at this difficult time.

My house, my dogs, Joe thought again, pushing open the main door of his mansion, sniffing, to his surprise and pleasure, the rich meat-and-cheese scent of a homecooked meal. And best of all, my woman, he added with amusement. Who'd have thought it? I was sitting in that movie theatre, counting down the minutes so I could sneak out and get back to her. No one's ever got under my skin like this before.

He made himself stroll, rather than run, across the huge foyer, across the living room and into the equally gigantic kitchen; he didn't want to look as eager as he felt. Skye, in an apron three sizes too big for her, and oven gloves that looked as if they'd never been used before, was pulling a pan of lasagne out of one of the Smeg ovens.

'Hey!' Joe said in amazement. 'I didn't know you could cook!'

Hengist bounded up to Skye, who deflected him with a jut of her hip.

'Greedy bastards,' she said crossly. 'I fed them already, but they're always hungry.'

'You should be careful,' Joe said cheerfully, leaning on the travertine L that projected round the kitchen, watching Skye struggle to close the oven and slide the heavy pan onto the counter. 'They weigh as much as you do. If they get too hungry, they could take one of your legs off.'

'As if they would,' Skye said, reaching down to stroke Horsa's head. 'They love me already. Ugh! She dribbles *bad*.'

'I don't blame her,' Joe said. 'I'm dribbling too. That lasagne smells damn good.'

'It needs to rest for a while,' Skye said, pulling off her oven gloves and wiping her forehead with them. She flashed him a smile. 'I could lie to you and tell you that I made this myself,' she said, walking across the kitchen towards him, 'but you'd figure out eventually that I didn't. I ordered it in. There are these places that sell real gourmet stuff you just put in the oven. They give you all the timings and everything.'

'Smart girl,' Joe said approvingly. Skye was leaning on the other side of the L, elbows propped on it, facing him. 'Save those pretty hands for more important work.'

'Oh, yeah?' Skye smiled at him enticingly. 'Like what, exactly?'

Joe took her wrists, pulled her towards him, and whispered a suggestion in her ear.

'*Joe Jeffreys!*' Skye pulled her hands away, feigning shock and horror. 'I would *never* have agreed to *any* kind of arrangement with you if I knew you had that kind of dirty mind!'

'Too late now,' Joe said, vaulting over the counter with the ease of a man who had been doing his own stunts for fifteen years. 'You're all signed up, babe. I got you locked down. You're not going anywhere.'

He bent down to plant a kiss on her lips, his arms wrapping round her waist.

'Don't remind me!' Skye said, laughing and slapping at him. 'Get off me – I can smell you've had a drink and I haven't had anything yet! That's *so* not fair!'

'All's fair in love and war, babe,' Joe said, enjoying the way her eyes sparkled and her cheeks went pink as he used the word 'love'.

Too early for that yet, he thought. But hell, I'm not that far off. Crazy, isn't it? She's only been here for a couple of weeks, and already I never want her to leave. She's got me. Got me good.

Happily, he watched her turn away to the Sub-Zero drinks fridge and pull out a bottle of Cristal, which had been chilling there.

'I'm sorry about making you sign that damn contract,' he said. 'Here, gimme that – you'll bust your nails.' He took the bottle from her, unpeeling the foil. 'It's just, that kind of paperwork is standard practice when you're, uh—'

'A world-famous movie star,' Skye finished, to save him having to say it. She went up on tiptoes to kiss him back. 'I get it, Joe. I really do. After the whole *Investigator* thing, I could see why Carmen insisted on the whole legal side of things.'

On moving in, Skye had had to sign a contract; she'd promised not to reveal a word about anything to do with Joe's private life, now and for ever, in return for a healthy bank account opened in her name and an endless series of perks that came with being Joe Jeffreys' secret girlfriend.

Joe popped the cork and filled the glass she was holding out to him.

'In one way, it wasn't the most romantic thing ever,' she added, 'but in another –' her cheeks went even pinker – 'it was.'

'Huh?' Joe poured himself a glass.

'A year,' Skye said, sipping her Cristal. 'The contract's for a year.' She ducked her head. 'I thought you must *really* like me, to be sure you wanted to spend a whole year with me . . .'

'Oh.' Joe felt the tips of his ears going red too. 'Uh. Yeah. You know, I never even thought about that. I mean, I just took it for granted. Funny, huh?'

He was grinning at her like a schoolboy with his first crush. He knew he was. And she was smiling down at the floor, looking so pretty and shy and sexy all at once that he couldn't keep his hands off her a second longer.

'You know what I love about you?' he said, which was as close to using that word as he dared to get, this soon into their relationship. 'You put a smile on my face whenever I see you.' He pulled her towards him, spun her round and bent to kiss her shoulder, his hands sliding down her arms. 'You never bore me. You get me hard as a tree and you fuck like a runaway train. That pretty much ticks all my boxes.'

'Wow,' Skye said, luxuriating in his use of the word 'love'. She ground her bottom sexily back against him. 'You *do* know how to make things sound romantic.'

Joe ran his hands down her back to her waist, finding the zipper of her skirt. 'Oh, yeah,' he said happily, as she wriggled her hips to help him push her skirt down. 'I'm about to romance you right off your pretty little feet.'

Her skirt fell to the ground, and Skye tilted her head round to look at him.

'I won't have to be a secret for ever, will I?' she said hopefully. 'I mean, I know I have to hide out here for now – hole up in hotels when you're filming – but if things work out between us –' she blushed again – 'I won't have to keep doing that . . . will I?'

'Hey, you're going to do that part for Jeff Ringquist over at Clearwater,' he pointed out. 'If it goes well, you can snag some more. In a year's time, you'll be an up-and-coming actress. No reason I can't date an up-and-coming actress, is there?'

He snagged his thumb into her thong and started pulling that down too.

'Might as well take everything off,' he mumbled into her hair. 'Since I seem to be going that way.'

'But I'll always be that stripper you screwed in rehab,' Skye said sadly. 'There's video of us all over the net. You could never date me for real. I mean, out in the open.'

'Are you kidding?' Joe took hold of the hem of her T-shirt and lifted it up to her armpits. His hands came round to her breasts, sliding over the lace of her bra, feeling for the clasp. 'Front-fastening,' he said appreciatively. 'My favourite. Mmm. *Anyway* –' he undid her bra, letting it fall open, and closed his hands snugly over her breasts – 'that's even better! You and I meet in rehab, we get up to stuff, we work through the programme, we clean up our act, realize we like each other and settle down – isn't that the cutest redemption story you ever heard?'

He pulled the bra straps off her shoulders, and Skye wriggled to make it easier for him, dragging her T-shirt over her head. When she turned to face him, she was completely naked.

'You've got *way* too many clothes on,' she said, her eyes sparkling with happiness at what he had just said. She reached for his belt, leaning up against him, pressing the full length of her naked body into him as she went up on her toes to whisper in his ear: 'You know what you wanted me to do with my hands? Get ready, baby.'

'Later,' Joe said happily. 'Right now, I'm thirsty.'

He picked her up by the waist, sat her on the marble counter, and said, picking up the bottle of champagne: 'Lie down, will you? I've got an idea.'

'Oh, *no*,' Skye fake-protested. 'You and your damn ideas.'

She leaned back on her elbows so her back arched up to the ceiling and her head tilted back, her hair spilling onto the marble. Joe moved between her legs, sliding one over each shoulder, then pouring champagne slowly and carefully into her navel, filling it up, letting it spill over; he leaned forward and lapped it up, his tongue so hot and sexy as he licked up the bubbles that she moaned, arching her pelvis up towards him. Joe filled her navel with more champagne, letting it flood down between her legs.

'Ooh! Too cold!' Skye said, wriggling happily.

'Really? You're complaining now?' Joe said, licking down her stomach, flicking her with his tongue, making her moan and buck beneath him, her hips pumping as he said, his voice mock-hurt: 'And there was me thinking you *liked* my ideas,' a second before he closed his mouth over her and made her scream so loudly that Hengist and Horsa, who had wandered off to slump onto the living-room floor, raised their heads, looked at each other in disgust and got up heavily to find a less noisy place to have a nap.

Amber

*I*n her career as a model, Amber had travelled all over the world. She had posed in fluttering silk on the Great Wall of China, emerged in a minuscule bikini from the Caribbean sea onto the pink sands of Eleuthera Island in the Bahamas, and done a shoot in Venice that required her to lie in a gondola wearing only lingerie as a photographer hung off the Accademia Bridge, pointing his lens down at her near-naked body while a bevy of excited tourists snapped her frantically on their phones and digital cameras.

But she remembered very little about her travels. She had been on a combination of pills the whole time, in a pleasant, half-tranced haze of medication that had given her a cushion of psychological padding, allowing her to do things like step into a rocking gondola in broad daylight, wearing only a transparent lace bra and knicker set, and a pair of Louboutins.

I could never do that now, she thought ruefully, looking down at the water below. She was standing on the little balcony of her hotel room, which faced onto the white dome and belltower of the church of Santa Maria della Salute; the church and the hotel were separated by a narrow canal, a little tributary that ran between the Grand Canal on one side and Giudecca on the other. Ca' Maria Adele, the hotel, had its own little pier, at which a motor taxi was pulling up to unload a lone passenger, an elegant silver-haired man in a white linen suit. He stepped onto the wooden pier, into the pool of golden light cast by the lamps above the hotel entrance, and took his leather overnight case from the taxi driver, entering the hotel without a glance up at Amber half-hidden in the twilight shadows above.

I hope he's meeting someone wonderful here, Amber thought. I hope the love of his life is waiting for him in a room almost as romantic as this one. I want everyone to be as happy as I am right now . . .

She might never have come to Venice before. Everything was new, everything perfect; it was as if she was seeing all this beauty for the first time. On the Grand Canal, a vaporetto passed, its wash causing the motor taxi below to rock as it backed slowly away from the hotel pier, its shiny wood and chrome trim glinting in the gentle light cast by the hotel lamps. The sun had set; the statues surrounding the basilica of Santa Maria della Salute, the detailed carving around the windows and belltowers, were fading against the sky, which glowed in a watercolour wash of deep blues and purples, tinged at the edges with gold.

The house next to Ca' Maria Adele, just over the little iron bridge, was covered with wisteria, thick green foliage heavily laden with clusters of mauve blossoms hanging down, reflected in the dark water below, filling the air with an intoxicating scent of honeyeyed vanilla. Amber breathed it in deeply, her head spinning with the perfume, and just then a different, equally rich scent came pouring out of the bathroom behind her, as its door opened: lemon and mandarin, the sweet fresh citrus smell of body wash and soap.

Turning round, she stretched her arms along the stone balcony, and a smile of pure happiness flooded over her face as she watched Raf emerge from the bathroom, wearing a white waffle robe, rubbing his hair with a white towel, his Mediterranean skin dark gold by contrast. He padded towards her across the tiled floor.

'I thought of running a bath,' he said. 'I figured, we have a room with a Jacuzzi, we should definitely use it. Can I persuade you to take a bubble bath with me? God.' He looked around briefly at the bedroom, its walls upholstered in the same white and blue brocade that covered the gilt chairs and the high bed, hung with gold-framed mirrors, white-painted statues of Moors holding lamps in the far corners of the room. 'This place is amazing. I never want to leave.'

He stepped out onto the balcony.

'But you know,' he said, looking at her, 'as far as I'm concerned, we didn't need to come to Venice. We could have stayed back in California. Because we might be in one of the most beautiful cities in the world, staying in a room like something out of a museum, but all I can really see is you.'

Amber reached up, winding her arms around his neck, pulling him down to kiss her.

'You're going to make me cry,' she said against his mouth.

'Oh, no,' he said. 'No more compliments, then. Not if they'll make you cry. No more tears.'

Their kiss was long and deep, and as drugging and heady as the scent of wisteria in the air. Amber wanted it to go on for ever. Still kissing him, she slid her hands down his body, finding the tie to his robe, undoing it and pulling the robe open, pressing herself against his naked body, inhaling the scent of his skin under the citrus of the body wash.

'Jesus, Amber,' he sighed, as her hands slipped down further, finding him already hard, 'you're going to use me up and wear me out.'

They had had sex already that day, waking up in a heavy daze of jet lag, weighed down by the brocade covers of the bed, reaching for each other still half-asleep; slow, drugged, it had been like making love underwater, lying side by side, his leg thrown over her hip, his fingers between her legs making her come over and over, like the water of the canal lapping at the pier below them as he rocked inside her, finally coming in a long, drawn-out shudder of pleasure against her back, falling back to sleep in the same position.

They'd woken up to bright Venetian afternoon sunshine, starving for a late lunch; gone out to a little local restaurant to eat a feast of sardines cooked in vinegar and raisins, tiny fried crabs, risotto, black and rich with squid ink, lemon sorbet and sweet polenta biscuits. They'd walked over the Rialto bridge, bought the obligatory souvenir of a Murano glass bowl, got lost in narrow back streets, and finally taken a water taxi back to the hotel to fall asleep again, overwhelmed by sunshine and jet lag and happiness.

'I've got a lot of lost time to make up for,' Amber pointed out, wrapping her fingers around him, twisting and stroking in a way that made him groan deep in his throat. 'All those years before I met you. All those years having sex with people I didn't choose.'

Twilight had come, night was falling; it was too dark on the balcony to see Raf's expression properly, but she could hear the laughter in his voice as he said: 'Well, you certainly chose me.'

'I did,' Amber said with great satisfaction. 'I chose you. I knew I wanted you as soon as I saw you. You were the first thing I ever truly wanted in my life.'

'And I chose you,' Raf said, cupping her face in his hands, kissing her lips softly.

'I've been thinking,' she said, her fingertips playing up and down the length of his cock, teasing him, drawing him slowly closer and closer to her. 'When we get back to LA, I want to train as a counsellor. To work with recovering addicts. I know it'll be a long process, but I want to try. Do you think I'd be any good at it?'

'I think you'll be amazing,' he said, letting her pull him towards her till his cock pushed up eagerly between her legs, 'but – *God* – can we please talk about this later?'

'Of course,' she said demurely, slipping up to sit on the stone edge of the balcony, widening her legs, adjusting herself so his cock could start to slide inside her. 'I just thought I'd ask if you thought it was a good idea—'

'Amber,' he said, gripping her hips, pushing further up, 'as long as I'm inside you, you could tell me you wanted to become an astronaut, and I'd say it was the best damn idea in the world—'

'Sssh!' She put her hand over his mouth. 'We're outside – people might hear us.'

He slid his hands under her bottom, lifting her fractionally, his cock driving right up inside her, filling her completely; she gasped and clung to his neck for balance, her eyes closing in ecstasy.

'Shall I carry you back in the room?' he whispered, looking over her shoulder at the Venetian night, the shadowed church beyond them. 'No one's going to see us in the dark, but—'

'No! Don't move!'

She wrapped her long legs around his waist, tilting back to get the exact angle she wanted, gasping again in sheer pleasure as she found it.

'*God*,' he whispered, starting to rock in and out of her, finding his rhythm.

'Sssh . . .'

Amber slid her fingers between her legs, as his hands were fully occupied in holding her on the balcony edge, and almost as soon as she touched herself, she started to come. A gondola poled into the canal below, the long slow strokes of its single oar in the deep water echoing what Raf was doing to her, driving back and forth, bringing her to an orgasm that seemed to last for ever, rising and falling with every stroke of his hips meeting hers.

'I'm going to come,' he whispered in her ear, his grip tightening on her hips, his cock swelling inside her. 'You're going to make me come . . .'

She pushed down against him, hearing him groan as he finally let go, feeling him surge up inside her, coming again herself as he did.

In my wildest dreams, I never thought I would have this. In my wildest imaginings, I never dared to hope that I would be in Venice, making love with Raf on a balcony. Feeling him come inside me.

His arms were tight around her, his biceps swelling as he held her. She pushed her face into his shoulder, and, despite what he'd said about her crying, she let the tears come, dampening his skin, feeling a total release of emotion wash over her, her body utterly relaxed, her eyes closing.

'Oh, Amber,' he said a little reproachfully, as he realized she was crying. 'Baby, I said no more tears, didn't I? I love you! We're so happy! Please don't cry!'

'I know,' she said, blinking them off her eyelashes, as he freed one hand to use his thumb to wipe the tears away. 'And I love you too, Raf.' She reached up to kiss him.

'I'm just crying because I'm so happy!' she said, sobbing. And then she started to giggle at what she'd just said, leaning her head into his shoulder, crying and laughing at the same time, as the water lapped against the pier below them, and the moon began to rise in the black velvet Venetian night sky.

POCKET
BOOKS

Rebecca Chance
DIVAS

Never get between a girl and her diamonds

Stunning good looks, a gorgeous fiancé, a limitless trust fund:
London's leading It Girl Lola Fitzsimmons leads a charmed life,
a pampered princess whose rich father funds her every whim.

Evie Lopez is just as beautiful, but she's had to work her
own way up life's greasy pole – literally. Now she's hooked
herself an indulgent sugar daddy, Evie has abandoned her
pole-dancing career, swapping New York's seedy strip bars
for a luxury Manhattan penthouse.

But Lola and Evie are on a collision course with their
nemesis. When Lola's father falls into a coma, her ruthless
stepmother Carin seizes control of the purse strings – and cuts
off her spoiled stepdaughter without a penny. Then Carin
evicts Evie, her husband's mistress, from her fabulous love-
nest and adds insult to injury by stealing her diamonds.

It's riches to rags overnight. Although they loathe one another
on sight, Lola and Evie must team up if they are to defeat their
common enemy: Carin, the Ice Queen. Let battle commence.

ISBN 978-1-84739-395-1
PRICE £6.99

**POCKET
BOOKS**

This book and other **Pocket Book** titles are available from your local bookshop or can be ordered direct from the publisher.

978 1 84739 395 1   Divas   £6.99

Free post and packing within the UK
Overseas customers please add £2 per paperback
Telephone Simon & Schuster Cash Sales at Bookpost
on 01624 677237 with your credit or debit card number
or send a cheque payable to Simon & Schuster Cash Sales to
PO Box 29, Douglas Isle of Man, IM99 1BQ
Fax: 01624 670923
Email: bookshop@enterprise.net
www.bookpost.co.uk

Please allow 14 days for delivery. Prices and availability
are subject to change without notice.